TA248981

DEADOUT

FORGE BOOKS BY JON MCGORAN

Drift
Deadout

DEADOUT

Jon McGoran

A Tom Doherty Associates Book
New York

DEADOUT

Copyright © 2014 by Jon McGoran

A Forge Book
Published by Tom Doherty Associates, LLC
175 Fifth Avenue
New York, NY 10010

www.tor-forge.com

Forge® is a registered trademark of Tom Doherty Associates, LLC.

The Library of Congress Cataloging-in-Publication Data is available upon request.

ISBN 978-0-7653-3471-8 (hardcover)
ISBN 978-1-4668-1525-4 (e-book)

Forge books may be purchased for educational, business, or promotional use. For information on bulk purchases, please contact Macmillan Corporate and Premium Sales Department at 1-800-221-7945, extension 5442, or write specialmarkets@macmillan.com.

First Edition: August 2014

Printed in the United States of America

0 9 8 7 6 5 4 3 2 1

For the bees

ACKNOWLEDGMENTS

When I first had the idea for *Deadout*, I knew I had a lot to learn about bees. Fortunately, I didn't know how much, otherwise I might have chosen to write about something else. More fortunate is the fact that so many of the people who are tireless in their efforts to understand honeybees and threats like colony collapse disorder are also generous with their knowledge, expertise, and time. I'd like to thank Dave Roubik, Mark Winston, Paul Goldstein, Deborah A. Delaney, and Amro Zayed for their eloquence and their patience in answering my many questions—my often slightly rephrased and occasionally repeated questions. I'd also like to thank Jerry Bromenshenk for his help in understanding LIDAR systems, and beekeepers like Don Schump and Susan Matlock, who were invaluable in helping me understand the life of honeybees. Very special thanks go to Annalise Paaby, who not only shared so much of her time and expertise, but who also shared my excitement about many of the ideas in this book. Thanks also to everyone else out there who is working to understand what is happening to the planet's bees, and to save them.

The issue of genetically engineered food is of great concern to me and of great relevance to this book, and I'd like to thank Katey Parker of Just Label It, Sam Bernahardt of Food and Water Watch, Zofia Hausman of Citizens for GMO Labeling, Karen Schumann-Stark of GMO Free PA, and Barbara Thomas of GMO Free NJ for all their support, and for the great work they do. And again, thanks to all the individuals and organizations who are fighting for our right to know what we are eating, and groups like the Center for Science in the Public Interest, the Center for Food Safety, and the Union of Concerned Scientists who are fighting to preserve the essence of the scientific method from those who seek to profit from its subversion.

My fondness and familiarity with the island of Martha's Vineyard goes back decades, but I would never have been able to write this book without the help of many of its residents. Special thanks go to Tisbury Police Chief Dan Hanavan and fellow author Cynthia Riggs, as well as Chrissy Kinsmen and Sue Murphy. (And my apologies to staff at various island businesses for the strange phone calls and bizarre questions.) Major thanks go to Terry and Tim Lowe and Josie Iadicicco, for more reasons than I can mention here, but most of all for their friendship, which I treasure.

Thanks to my editor, Kristin Sevick, and everyone else at Tor/Forge, for their enthusiasm and support and for being so good at what they do. As with everything I write, I owe a debt of gratitude to the amazing community of writers of which I am proud to be a part, especially the Philadelphia Liars Club and my friends in Team Decker. And as with everything I *publish*, I am eternally grateful for my amazing agent, Stacia Decker, and everyone at Donald Maass Literary Agency.

And as with everything else, more than anything else, I am grateful for the love and support of my wife, Elizabeth, and my son, Will, without which I would never have been able to write this book. Or do much of anything else.

DEADOUT

1

Danny and I paused at the bottom of the steps, holding our breath and listening as we looked up and down the dank, dark corridor. The only sound was the squeak of a not-too-distant rat. Danny shrugged and took off, running to the left. I watched him for half a second, listening to his shoes scraping against the gritty wet floor. Then I took off in the opposite direction, breathing through my mouth against the mildew that tickled my nose.

Simeon Jarrett had come down the same steps we had, no more than half a minute earlier. I wasn't entirely sure about coming down here after him, or about the idea of splitting up, but Danny was the cautious one, not me.

As I rounded a ninety-degree turn to the left, the sound of Danny's footsteps disappeared behind my own. The basement got darker the farther I ran, the spaces growing longer between the dim pools of light from grimy block windows set near the ceiling. The walls seemed to close in on me, and I wondered for a moment if I was having some sort of anxiety attack. Then I realized it wasn't the walls closing in on me, it was two very large men, and while neither of them was Simeon Jarrett, I was pretty sure they were on the same side of the good guy/bad guy divide.

A situation like that can make you want to start shooting, but that makes a lot of assumptions about your fellow man. And while it might make life simpler in the short run, it can make it a lot more complicated in the long run.

I didn't have the time or distance to slow down, so instead I slid feet-first between them.

The guy on my left apparently didn't share my reluctance to make assumptions because he opened fire on the area where I had just been running. It's possible he was gunning down a giant rat that had been poised to attack, but more likely he was shooting at me.

The sound of the gun was deafening, bouncing around in the corridor. In the muzzle flash, I recognized the two faces above me as Blink Taylor and Derrell Sims, two of Jarrett's close associates.

Sliding on the floor between them, I brought the butt of my Glock down as hard as I could, mashing the shooter's foot with a reassuring crunch. He howled and twisted as he fell, squeezing off another shot. This one passed over my head and apparently struck his partner in the hip, because suddenly the howling was in stereo. By the time I was back on my feet and turned around, they were both on the floor behind me. Twenty feet beyond them a cascade of sparks fell from the remnants of an old fluorescent light fixture, apparently struck by an errant bullet. I was shocked the dump had electricity, but grateful for the illumination, just enough to see the two of them grabbing their injuries and rolling around in the same muck that now soaked the left side of my body.

They had both dropped their weapons to grab their wounds, and I kicked the guns out of the way. I cuffed them both, hands and feet, advised them of their rights, and wished them luck with the rats. Then I took off after Simeon Jarrett.

The light from the sparks helped me see where I was going, but the strobe effect was unsettling. Ahead of me, the corridor ended in a perpendicular hallway.

As I approached it, I could see my silhouette against the far wall. The sight of it stopped me cold.

The last time I'd seen that image, it had been in the middle of an afternoon of carnage that left five people dead—nearly six, including me—and was followed a millisecond later by an explosion that threw me against the wall like overcooked pasta. I knew that wasn't happening now, but I felt trapped in that moment, waiting for that impact. Standing there, frozen, I heard footsteps approaching down the hallway to my left, but still I couldn't move. Then there he was, Simeon Jarrett, right in front of me.

It happened in an instant: him running up from the side, skidding to a stop, alarm and surprise on his face, followed by an evil smile as he raised his gun.

I think I was snapping out of it, but before I could move, I heard a thunderous, "Freeze!" coming from down the hallway to my left.

Jarrett pivoted and squeezed off two shots in the direction of the voice, and received several shots back in response.

Then he was gone, pounding down the hallway to my right. Danny Tennison ran up, staring at me with a mixture of confusion and concern. "You okay?" he said.

"Yeah, I'm good."

He stared at me for a moment longer. Then he turned and resumed his chase. I fell in behind him, then passed him. The hallway ended at a metal door outlined in silver light, and I burst through it, out into blinding sunshine and onto a deserted street.

Simeon Jarrett was gone.

Lieutenant Suarez stared blankly at me from across his desk. I could tell he wasn't buying it. Neither was Danny, sitting in the chair next to me, his eyes boring into the side of my head.

"Nothing," I'd said repeatedly when they'd repeatedly asked what had happened out there.

"Nothing?" Suarez said dubiously, almost mimicking me.

I knew Danny was concerned about me, but I was annoyed with him for diming me out. I loved him like a brother, and like a brother, sometimes I wanted to kick his ass. Yes, he deserved an explanation, and as soon as I had one, he'd be welcome to it.

Until then, fuck him.

"Whatever," Suarez said, closing the file in front of him and rubbing his eyes. "Look, you sure you don't want to take some time off?"

"I am taking some time off."

His eyes narrowed, as if he didn't believe me.

"Weekend with Nola. Visiting a friend on Martha's Vineyard."

"Martha's Vineyard? What's that?"

"Little island off Cape Cod."

"Sounds nice. Good for you. But that's not what I meant, and you know it. You've declined counseling, and apparently I can't force you to go. Okay. We're all grateful for what you did in Dunston," he said, waving his hand as though he was quoting a line he didn't believe. "Until I'm comfortable that you're one hundred percent—and frankly, the way I see it, you're not even close—you're on low-impact duty."

Six months earlier, while on suspension and out of jurisdiction, I'd stepped into a big case and got banged up. A lot. It had taken a while for things to get back to normal. Guess they weren't normal yet.

"So, I want you to think about it seriously: are you sure you don't want to take some leave time? You've already been approved for it. Just a few weeks on us, take your time and come back right."

I snuck a glance at Danny and got the look I expected: a little bit worried, a lot pissed off.

"No," I said, my eyes firmly back on Suarez. "I'm good."

2

The sun had been up since six, but you couldn't tell from the blue-gray light seeping through the window. I'd been awake since four, lying there looking at Nola, waiting for the moment when that first golden ray would play across her face. Wasn't going to happen today.

She looked beautiful as always, but the gray light brought out the sadness in her face. My insomnia had been going on for months, but this part I didn't mind. I loved watching as she slept, and not just because these days that was the time we got along best. Her face was endlessly fascinating, and I loved to study its lines. Lately, her brow would furrow as she slept, but in the suffused, early morning light, you almost couldn't see the crease between her eyes.

She sighed deeply, stretched, and rolled away from me. Soon, she'd be awake, and things would get tricky.

I got up and made coffee.

The place was tiny and a bit of a mess, not that I minded. When Nola first moved in, she'd enjoyed keeping it spotless. Now it was almost as bad as when I lived on my own. A few months earlier, we'd talked about buying a place. We even found one, at the edge of the city but right on the woods. We ran the numbers, figured out how much we'd need to make it happen. But then things started getting weird, and we both let it go. We hadn't mentioned it in weeks, like a silent agreement that we weren't ready and maybe never would be.

By the time the coffee was done, Nola was in the shower. I put hers on the sink, then pulled on my jeans and a shirt, grabbed my shoes, and got out of the way.

Twenty minutes later she came out of the bedroom wearing jeans and a T-shirt, boots in one hand, mug in the other. "Thanks for the coffee," she said as she drained it.

"You look great," I told her. "And Greensgrow would be crazy not to hire you."

She did look great, but not great for her. The stress was pulled tight across her face. She'd been looking for a job for months, but there wasn't a lot of work for an organic farmer in the middle of Philadelphia. And not too much else Nola felt comfortable doing. She had a history of chemical sensitivity; she'd ended up in the hospital a couple of times when she was younger because of lawn spray or new carpets. Greensgrow was an urban farm less than a mile from our apartment. I'd told Nola about it but had never been there, because before I met her it never would have crossed my mind. Now it seemed like the ideal job for her.

"Yeah, right," she said, her smile nervous but giddy with excitement. "I'll see you afterward for lunch, right?"

"Green Eggs Café," I said. "Two o'clock."

"This sucks," Danny muttered, breaking the silence between us.

"Tell me about it," I replied, immediately realizing my mistake.

I'd been watching the tension build in his jaw all morning, and I knew something was coming, but after standing in that hallway for four hours, I guess I'd gotten careless.

"Of course, it could be worse," he said. "You could be on paid leave. But then again, that would mean I could be out tracking down Simeon Jarrett instead of making sure the deputy assistant undersecretary of useless bullshit doesn't get ambushed by a Mexican drug cartel in the middle of Philadelphia's City Hall."

We were babysitting some low-level federal bureaucrat who was too big a deal for a regular uniform escort but too small for Federal Protective Services. Suarez had snickered when he assigned us. Danny's eyes hadn't stopped smoldering since.

"Come on, Danny," I said. "That's not fair."

"Life's not fair, Doyle. Besides, it's true and you know it. And while we're standing here with our dicks in our hands so you can try to prove whatever you're trying to prove, Jarrett's out there doing whatever he came to do and going on his merry way."

Danny had been closing in on Jarrett three years earlier, and the guy had vanished. Now he was back, and we didn't want him to get away again.

I kept quiet, hoping he was done.

He wasn't.

"I know you went through some crazy shit out there, and a lesser man might have crumbled completely, but you're delusional if you don't think you got a little dinged up." He pointed to his head, in case I missed the point. "You got to heal, buddy. You might have saved the day up there, proved you're a certifiable badass, but I'll tell you what—right now you're not. You walk into that same situation right now, and you're toast."

I don't know if I was more pissed off because what he was saying wasn't true or because it was. I didn't have an argument to make, but that had never stopped me before. I opened my mouth. Luckily, before I could say something stupid, the door behind us opened as well, and the deputy assistant undersecretary of useless bullshit walked out.

We escorted our guest back onto I-95 South under a light rain.

It was one-thirty and I wasn't supposed to meet Nola until two, but I had Danny drop me off near the restaurant anyway. I figured a walk in the rain would be more pleasant than hanging around with Danny. Besides, unencumbered by me, maybe he could go out and do some real police work.

I was walking north on Second Street, approaching Spring Garden, when the guy walking toward me stopped abruptly and turned down Green. Medium height and broad shoulders, face obscured by a blue hoodie. Something about him seemed suspicious, and familiar. I turned and followed. At the end of the block was a sheer concrete retaining wall with I-95 on top of it. Squeezed right up against it was a narrow block of Hancock Street. Not a typical pedestrian route. I kept back but kept up, and at the end of the block, he turned to look at me.

Simeon fucking Jarrett.

He took off like a shot. I paused long enough for a heavy sigh, because I really wasn't up for a chase. Then I took off after him.

"Police," I yelled, holding up my badge. "Simeon Jarrett, you are under arrest."

Jarrett cut down an alley next to a house being gutted and rebuilt. I followed, pushing as hard as I could and closing the distance between us. He was at least ten years younger than me, and if the chase dragged on I knew stamina would become an issue.

Halfway down the alley, he jumped onto a row of Dumpsters, running along the lids. I followed suit, maybe not quite so gracefully. As I was bounding across the third Dumpster, my foot hit the gap between the two sections of the lid, and my leg went in up to the thigh. The lid scraped the length of my leg, something pulled in my groin, and my foot hit something squishy, suddenly soaking wet. Jarrett was extending himself to reach for the bottom rung of a fire escape hanging over the last Dumpster. I knew if he pulled himself up, he was gone.

I launched myself at him, but my arms closed on air. I looked up to see him swinging around the ladder, using his momentum and his upper-body strength to propel himself back the way he had come.

He planted one foot between my neck and my right shoulder and landed his other foot on my left triceps, squashing me back into the Dumpster and using me as a springboard to vault back onto the pavement. By the time I pulled myself up, he was turning up another alley and out of sight.

I punched the lid of the Dumpster and growled, my face burning with a mixture of humiliation and fury as I climbed out. No way I was going to catch up with him, but there was a good chance he was going to double back up Second Street.

I sprinted, hoping to head him off. The sounds of my own heavy breathing and the rhythmic squelch of my wet left foot were soon drowned out by a pounding noise in my ears. My lungs were aching almost as much as my leg and my neck and my shoulder and my arm. I knew Jarrett was probably gone, halfway across the city, laughing once again at some dumbass cop who couldn't keep up. The heat from my face spread throughout my entire body with exertion and shame and anger. And hatred.

I threw myself around the corner, and was almost startled to see Simeon Jarrett coming straight at me.

I swung a left into the middle of his face. At the speed he was going, I could have just held up my fist and the effect would have been the same. His face seemed to split: the lower half trying to keep going until he flipped up into the air, ass over elbows. Somehow, he managed to land on his toes and his fingertips, ready to take off again, but I planted another left into his face, knocking him back onto his heels. As I closed on him, his right arm came around with a knife, sweeping toward my midsection in an arc that would have disemboweled me if I hadn't pulled back at the last second. I kicked him hard under the elbow, and I might have heard a crack, but I definitely heard the knife go spinning off across the concrete. I looked down and saw an eight-inch slit in my shirt, and that's when I set on him. Two more in the face with enough in them to push him back onto his ass. He still had a little fight left in him, landing a vigorous kick, so I used the last bit of mine to beat it out of him.

By the time we were both done, his face was a bloody mess, but only marginally worse than mine. I read him his rights and tumbled back onto the sidewalk.

That's when I saw Nola standing fifteen feet away, her face twisted in horror and disgust.

I went to her and she stepped back, away from me. "Are you okay?"

"I'm okay."

She wouldn't look at me. "Then I'll see you at home."

3

"I'm not saying he didn't resist, I'm not saying he didn't try to stab you, and I'm not saying he didn't hit you. I'm not denying he's an asshole who deserved everything he got and more, but Jesus, Carrick, you broke his wrist, fractured his jaw, and bruised his spleen for Chrissake." Suarez sat back and rubbed his face with both hands. "I mean, what did you do, run him over with a truck?"

"Hey, I got a little nicked up, too, you know. It's not like he's some boy scout."

"I know, Doyle. And I'm sure maybe you used appropriate force. But you busted up this asshole pretty good, and you're supposedly on light duty."

I didn't say anything.

"You sure you don't want to take some time off?"

"I'm leaving tonight."

"For how long?"

"The weekend."

"A long weekend?"

"Back on Monday."

He shook his head with a weary laugh. "That wouldn't be what I'm talking about anyway, Carrick. You need to take some time off."

"I'll take the weekend off, and I'll come back good as new."

"You'll take the weekend off, and you'll come back to admin duty."

"Bullshit, admin duty. You can't do that. I just brought in Simeon Jarrett."

"You think I want you on admin duty, Carrick? You think the folks in admin want you in admin? You don't think they die a little bit inside, knowing they're going to be working with you? Watching you move your fucking lips as you fill out forms, taking five times as long as them and they know they're going to have to redo it because you always fuck something up?"

"Fuck you, I'm not that bad."

"Worse, Carrick. Seriously, you suck. But that's what I'm going to have to do. You leave me no choice."

"But—"

He put up a hand to silence me. "Have a nice weekend."

When I got home that night, there were suitcases by the door, and my stomach lurched before I remembered we were going on a trip. Nola was putting dinner on the table. She smiled awkwardly and returned to the kitchen without looking at me.

"Sorry about today," I said when she came back with salad and bread.

"I know. You were just working." She sat down, still not looking at me. "It's just . . . I have a hard time thinking that's what you do when you're out there."

"Not usually, baby. But he resisted, he went after me." Even in my ears it sounded lame: *He started it.*

She closed her eyes, almost in time to hide them rolling. "A lot of them resist, don't they, Doyle? And that doesn't make it easier, knowing these criminals and drug dealers are attacking you." Her eyes went moist, and her voice thickened. "I worry about you out there. I worry about you getting hurt. And I worry about you hurting people. What does that do to you?"

"It's scrapes and bruises, Nola. It's just part of the job. Speaking of which," I said, grateful to change the subject, "how was your interview?"

She looked down, away from me. "They offered me the job," she said quietly.

"That's great—" I started to say, but when she looked up I stopped.

"I didn't take it." Her cheeks were wet.

"You didn't . . ."

"It's on a brownfield, Doyle. An industrial waste site. The ground is . . . tainted."

"I thought it was organic."

"It's all up on platforms, off the ground." She shook her head sadly.

"It sounds kind of cool."

"It is cool," she snapped. "And good for them, but it doesn't help me any. I can't work at a place like that."

"Well . . . are you sure?"

"Doyle, don't start that again."

"Well, it's just, you've been exposed to a lot of chemicals, and you haven't had a reaction, not even to the decontamination in Dunston. The whole reason you went to the biodetox center with Cheryl was because there was a chance it could cure you. Don't you think it's possible maybe it worked?"

"It didn't work for Cheryl."

"Yeah, but you're not Cheryl."

"Doyle, you just . . . you just don't understand." And then she started crying for real.

Part of me was annoyed at her, but seeing her like this was breaking my heart, too. I moved my chair next to hers, put my arm around her, and kissed her head. She leaned into me for a moment, then pulled back.

She turned to me and said, "I need a break from this city. I hate it."

Now, I hate this city, too, but I also love it. "Come on," I said softly. "You don't mean that."

She gave me a look that said yes, she did.

We were quiet after that. Finally, halfway through dinner, Nola said, "I spoke to Moose today," as if she had just remembered it. Moose was a friend of Nola's, and mine, too. We were driving up to Martha's Vineyard to visit him. It seemed crazy to me, spending most of a night driving up and another day driving back, for a little more than a day in between, but I had offered to do the driving and maybe getting away from the city would do us both some good.

"He's really looking forward to seeing us," she said, "but he says he's really busy with work. They're having trouble with the bees up there, so he might not be as available as he had hoped."

"What kind of trouble?"

She didn't know exactly, but I wasn't listening anyway, preoccupied with my own troubles at work. And at home.

"Don't you think?" Nola asked, bringing me back to the moment.

"Absolutely," I said, refilling her glass from the wine bottle.

"I shouldn't," she said, raising a hand next to her glass. I poured for another second before stopping.

"It's okay," I told her. "I'm driving."

Her brow furrowed. "Are you sure you want to drive the whole way?"

"Absolutely." I don't mind driving at night, but I don't like riding shotgun, and I wasn't looking forward to six hours of forced conversation. I poured her a little more wine.

* * *

I took a quick nap after dinner and we left around midnight so we'd be there for the first ferry of the day. Nola fell asleep as soon as we left, and I made good time. Would have been better in my own car, I thought sadly, but it was gone forever, demolished back in Dunston. I was driving a brand-new Chevy Impala on loan from a grateful nation until it could figure out how to replace the vastly superior Nissan Z that had been destroyed in its defense. I felt a wave of sadness thinking about the car, and a wave of something like vertigo as I tried not to think about how it had been destroyed.

Nola woke up when we got to the parking lot for the shuttle bus to the ferry.

"Are we there?" she asked, squinty-eyed and groggy. I don't think she quite knew which "there" she meant, but I said yes anyway.

I took our luggage out of the trunk, and as I was putting my Glock in the gun safe built into the trunk, she appeared at my side. She had asked me earlier not to bring it, saying it was like bringing work on vacation. Work that shoots bullets. I was ambivalent on the issue, but she smiled when I did it, so that was something.

The morning was gray and cold, with a stiff breeze. On the ferry, the breeze was even stronger. We sat inside, Nola leaning her head against my shoulder and drifting back into a semi-sleep as we watched the mainland receding. I felt somehow liberated, as if I had escaped the continent where all my troubles lay. I watched it slowly shrink, until the island in front of me was bigger than the continent behind me. Forty minutes later, the ferry shuddered as its engines thrust into reverse, and minutes after that, the entire vessel gently rocked as it came to rest against the dock.

4

Moose was waiting for us at the end of the gangway. I didn't see him at first, hidden as he was behind a woman and her children there to meet their dad. Moose stood up on his toes, and his face split wide with a smile that should have hurt so early in the morning.

Nola let out a squeal that sounded as perky as Moose looked, and she ran the last bit, wrapping him in a hug and swinging him around with a level of energy that made me think I should have gotten more sleep.

When she put him down, he turned to me. I put out my hand but he came past it for a hug, a quick squeeze and a pat on the shoulder. He stepped back and winced up at my face.

"You look tired," he said. Then he turned to Nola. "How was the trip?"

She gave an awkward shrug and looked at me. Moose followed her gaze.

I put my arm around her shoulder and pulled her in. "She took a shortcut through la-la land."

"Crafty," he said, giving her a sly wink. "So it was the red eye for the big guy, huh? You want coffee or sleep?"

Hotel check-in wasn't for a few hours yet, so sleep wasn't an option. We stopped in Oak Bluffs for coffee, a place called Mocha Mott's, then Moose took us on a quick tour of the island. Nola had known Moose longer than I had, so I sprawled across his pickup truck's narrow backseat.

Starting in Oak Bluffs, Moose pointed out the Flying Horses carousel, then Back Door Donuts, which apparently sells the best apple fritters in the world every night from the back door of a bakery.

Next we drove around the Campgrounds, an almost cloyingly cute community of miniature Victorian homes, many done up with ornate gingerbread wood trim and painted in vivid pastels. In the center of it was a big, open-air church with a cross on the top. At one point, we drove past a garish pink confection with a big tulip flag, but the effect was ruined by a massive brown puddle in the front lawn. As we got closer, we could tell from the smell that it was what it looked like.

Moose hit the power windows a moment too late, and the odor of it filled the truck.

"Septic systems," he said. "Something goes wrong, and it becomes a poop swamp." He sped up, and a few turns later we were driving along the ocean.

The island was larger than I had expected, and stunningly beautiful, speckled with ponds and inlets providing water views seemingly every few hundred yards. Inland, the rolling landscape was crisscrossed with walls made from smooth, round fieldstones.

Moose kept up a running monologue on the island's topography, geology, and agriculture that counteracted the effects of the caffeine. Nola peppered him with questions about what crops they were growing, and how: low-spray, no-spray, no-till, Integrated Pest Management, all the agricultural esoterica that had become vaguely familiar since I met Nola.

Once again the car filled with a noxious odor, but before I could ask, Moose said, "Skunks. Island's full of them. Some knuckle-head brought them over in the fifties, and they just went nuts, like the rabbits in Australia, no natural predator."

Moose was in the middle of a long stretch about something called Island Grown and the local agricultural and beekeeping groups when he snorted and said, "Speaking of exotic invasives."

On our left was a huge, brightly colored sign with incongruous palm trees and large gold script that said, "Johnny Blue's Berry Farm," and under it, "Home of Johnny Blue's Berry Jamz."

"What is that?" Nola asked with obvious distaste. I don't usually have strong opinions about signs, but it did seem out of place.

Moose shook his head. "You know Johnny Blue?" He named some reality talent show I'd never heard of.

"Well, I wouldn't know him either if he wasn't such a big story around here," Moose rushed to explain. "He's awful—I think he was like third runner-up or something—but he had a song that was big last summer, catchy in a fast-food-commercial kind of way. As far as I can tell, his entire interest in farming stems from the fact that his last name is Blue, and he thought Johnny Blue's Berry Farm would be a hoot. He's promoting some kind of berry-flavored snacks called Blueberry Jamz. Apparently, you can make a lot of money from one awful song, because it's a pretty big operation."

The sign loomed in front of the trees. Someone had nailed it with an egg.

Down the road was another farm, Squibnocket Biodynamic. Nola and Moose launched into a detailed discussion of the merits of biodynamic farming. I sat in the back, snickering at the name.

I was drifting off to sleep when Moose said something about how the situation with the bees had gotten really scary. I knew he had taken a job with a group called BeeWatch after Nola lost her farm. They sent him to Martha's Vineyard, which was so far pretty nice. I had no idea what he was actually doing, but I decided that if the whole police thing went down the tubes the way it was constantly threatening to, I could get a gig watching bees.

"What's scary?" I asked.

Moose turned around, surprised, like maybe he thought I'd fallen asleep. "The bees disappearing."

"Doesn't sound so scary," I said. I like honey, as far as it goes, but my relations with bees have generally involved swatting and flailing, the occasional smacking and squashing, and every now and then wincing and swelling.

Nola rolled her eyes. "It is if you're a farmer. Bees pollinate crops. No bees, no food. It's already affecting production."

"Well, yeah, that's the worst part," Moose said, "but the way the bees are disappearing is even creepier."

I sat forward. "What do you mean?"

"Well, bees have been in trouble for a while. There's mites that have been killing them for years, but more recently there's colony collapse disorder, or CCD. With CCD, when people talk about bees disappearing, they're not just dying, they're literally disappearing. They fly out of their hive like they do every morning, but then one day they just don't come back."

"Where do they go?"

"No one knows. First time it happened this big-time beekeeper has all these tractor trailers filled with bees. It's a big business. They drive around the country, down south for pecan season and peach season, come up north for blueberries and cranberries. Anyway, between seasons this guy parks his bees in this huge field in Florida. So there's all these trailers parked there, sixteen million bees. One day his workers come out to check on the bees, like they do every day, and three quarters of them are gone. Millions of bees. The hives are intact, but the bees are gone. And no one ever finds them, either. Millions of bees, vanished without a trace. And now it's happening everywhere. In England, they call it Mary Celeste Syndrome, after the famous ghost ship."

I actually felt a chill. "That is creepy. So what's causing it?"

"We don't know. Maybe pollen from the genetically modified crops, maybe parasites like mites, some people think it may have to do with cell-phone towers, or those big industrial-scaled bee pollinating operations. Pesticides are almost certainly involved. Most scientists think it's a combination of factors. The whole reason BeeWatch is here on the Vineyard is because the island has been untouched by CCD. We're part of an effort to find out why."

"Because they rely on their native pollinators," Nola cut in, "instead of bringing in trucks of bees from Georgia or Tennessee."

"Right," Moose said, his voice flat. Then he turned to look at her. "Only now we're starting to see the same thing on the island."

Nola whipped her head around. "Are you serious?"

He shrugged. "There's something going on. We have these monitoring stations set up—part of what we've been doing is a bee census. We were seeing plenty of bees, just like normal. Then, in the last two weeks, it's dropping off big time, especially up island, Aquinnah and Chilmark. Still early in the season, but there's definitely something going on."

As he said it, his phone issued the opening chord from "A Hard Day's Night."

"Speaking of which," he said, thumbing the phone and raising it to his ear. "Hey, Benjy. What's up?"

He listened for a second, his shoulders slumping as he did. "Right," he said. "Okay, I'll meet you over there." He put down his phone and turned to look at each of us. "I won't be able to take you to see the cliffs at Gay Head. It's a shame, they're really something."

"Trouble?" Nola asked.

He pulled over and started the first point of what would eventually be a nine-point U-turn. "Looks like we found our first deadout."

5

I had only seen Moose drive a handful of times, but this was by far the most urgency he had shown, exceeding the posted speed limit by numbers approaching double digits. I wondered if we were in the midst of some sort of bee emergency.

We made a left into a gap in one of the ubiquitous stone walls and drove down a dirt road between two fields. After a hundred yards the road widened and we parked alongside a handful of cars and trucks, including one immaculately restored fifties-era custard-colored Chevy pickup.

Off to the side was a row of nondescript wooden boxes up on cinder blocks. One of them was open, surrounded by a small group of people, all wearing the same expression of sad concern, tinged with anger.

"These are my friends Nola and Doyle," Moose announced quietly as we walked up. The air smelled of honey and something else.

To our far left was a heavyset guy with a bushy beard, an open face, and messed-up hair. He held up his arm, and as Moose stepped up, the arm came down and gave Moose's shoulder a reassuring shake.

Next to him was an older guy, wiry and small with graying hair. His eyes looked red, like he'd been crying.

The guy next to him was young, lean, and unlikably handsome. He eyed us suspiciously at first. Then his eyes hit Nola, and suspicion was replaced with something else as his eyebrows raised about a millimeter. I knew that look. I'd made that look. I'd probably made it the first time I met Nola. I didn't like the guy anyway, but that look made me like him even less.

Next to him was a gorgeous brunette in what looked like a beekeeping suit, except that it fit her surprisingly well. She had the hood tucked under her arm. I felt my eyebrows notch up a millimeter, but I don't think anybody noticed.

"So what's going on, Benjy?" Moose asked the guy who'd patted his shoulder.

"These hives are deadouts," said the woman in the bee suit, gesturing toward the handful of boxes sitting to her left. A handful of bees bobbed around us in the air, coming in and out of the boxes to her right. My skin prickled, but no one else seemed bothered.

Moose stayed focused on the bearded guy, Benjy. "Is it colony collapse?"

"The bees aren't gone, but they're all dead," she said. "It could be mites."

The older guy shook his head and sniffled.

She gave him a sad smile. "Sorry, Pete."

Moose looked over at her, then back at Benjy. "What's she doing here?"

I was kind of surprised by that. Very un-Moose-like. Her face tightened, like she was controlling her reaction.

Benjy held up a hand. "Annalisa's here to take samples to help us figure this out, okay? I called her."

Moose looked away. "Whatever."

Annalisa stared at him for a second. Then she shook her head and looked at the others. "There definitely seems to be mites involved, but that could be a symptom as much as a cause." She opened one of the boxes and scraped the inside of it with what looked like a popsicle stick. The smell got stronger. It was like yeast. "I'll take these samples back to the lab and see if I can learn anything."

"Thanks," Benjy said, giving Moose a sidelong look to let him know he was annoyed.

There was an awkward silence, and I felt compelled to fill it. "What's that smell?" I asked, directing the question vaguely at Moose.

The handsome guy smirked. "That's the smell of bees," he said. "There's a lot going on in those hives. The worker bees bring the pollen and nectar back from the flowers and transform it, feeding the queen and the drones and the eggs, making royal jelly and beeswax, and making honey. Honey doesn't comes from supermarkets, you know, it comes from bees."

"Honey comes from bees?" I said, relieved that I didn't have to dislike the guy just because of his looks.

Nola pinched my arm. Moose looked down and smiled.

"But how do the little plastic bears fit in?" I said in a loud whisper.

The silence returned, slightly more awkward than before.

Benjy glanced at his watch. "All right, we've got work to do. Let's meet at BeeWatch in an hour."

A bee buzzed right past my ear and I jerked my head back and stepped away.

The handsome douchebag snickered. "Nothing to be afraid of, ace. They're just bees. If you don't freak out they won't hurt you."

I wasn't freaking out, and I wasn't afraid, not really. But it's not the kind of thing you can deny without making it sound true. I gave him a big smile and tried to hide my evil thoughts.

Before I could say anything that would earn me another pinch, Benjy said, "We need to check the LIDAR stations." He turned to the handsome douchebag. "Teddy, that okay with you?"

Teddy spread his hands in humble magnanimity. "Mi casa es su casa." A little heavy on the pretentious accent.

Benjy nodded. "Thanks."

Instantly, the group split up. As she was turning to leave, the brunette, Annalisa, looked in my direction. It might have been my imagination, but I'm pretty sure her eyebrows slid higher a millimeter or so. Then she stooped to pick up a small plastic toolkit and some plastic bottles. When I looked away from her, Nola and Moose were already walking back to the car.

I caught up with them and climbed into the backseat. Teddy drove by in the restored pickup, and I knew without a doubt he hadn't done the work himself. He turned to look back at Nola as he drove by.

"Is it bad?" Nola asked as we closed our doors.

"It could be," Moose replied. He looked worried. "It looks like I'm going to have to work a little bit today."

"That's okay," Nola told him. "We can keep ourselves entertained."

I thought about making some adolescent remark, but things were a little tense between us, and it didn't seem to be the time. Besides, sprawling in the backseat, what I really wanted to do was get a little sleep.

"A lot of places are still closed for the off-season," Moose said, "but there are plenty open, in case you get hungry. Oak Bluffs is very walkable if you get bored."

I looked out the window just as we pulled past the brunette standing next to a black Nissan Xterra. She was stepping out of her bee suit, and looked right at me as she did. Then we both looked away.

"So who were all those people?" Nola asked. "I think you've mentioned Benjy—he's your boss, right?"

Moose nodded. "Yeah, that's Benjy. He's pretty cool. He's been up here since last year, starting the census and collecting samples of bees and mites and stuff. He's a little freaked out these last few days. The guy next to him was Pete Westcamp, the beekeeper."

"And the girl? Who's she? Seems to be a little tension between you two."

I made a conscious effort not to sit forward to listen better.

"That's Annalisa," said Moose. "She's a private researcher with a company called Bee Futures. She's been here for the last several months, researching native bees and other pollinators. And now researching what's happening to the hives, I guess."

"Why don't you like her?"

"I don't trust her."

"Why not?"

He thought about it for a second. "Bee Futures seemed like a cool company, doing some interesting research into the causes of colony collapse disorder, including some that suggested guess what?" He turned to look at me, but kept going. "Pollen from genetically modified crops." The events back in Dunston had involved genetically engineered crops. "Something about the pesticides inserted into the crops' DNA—surprise, surprise. So what do you think happens next?"

Nola shrugged. "What?"

"A few months ago Bee Futures is bought up by Stoma Corporation, the fucking evil empire of the GMO set. The owner of Bee Futures sold it and split."

"What about Annalisa?"

"Well, that's just it. She stayed where she was, kept right on working."

"Researching CCD?"

"Well, theoretically. But she's working for Stoma now. Those guys are evil. They've hired Darkstar to do their private security."

"The private army?" Nola said. "I though they only did military stuff outside the country."

He gave her a dubious look. "I've heard they're involved all

over: corporate security, surveillance. Trying to infiltrate environmental groups."

Sounded kind of paranoid to me. "You think Annalisa's doing
bad science?" I asked.

"I don't know. She's written a few papers over the last few
months, mildly interesting, but she's totally working for the man."

"Don't you think you're being a little harsh on her?" Nola asked.

"I just don't trust her, that's all."

A couple of seconds later Nola spoke again. "Who was the
other guy?"

I sat forward.

"Teddy Renfrew. He's okay, I guess. His family's been up here
for a while, at least for summers. An activist, working with groups
like Friends of the Earth, plus some fringier ones, pretty hard-core,
maybe even a little extreme. He's been busted a few times, which
he rarely misses an opportunity to mention. He can be a little
douchey but he's doing some cool stuff and he lets us keep bait stations on his land. He's got this big organic farm, but he's doing
SPIN farming, small plot intensive, so he doesn't use tractors or
anything. It's all people-powered. I not sure if he knows what he's
doing, but the farm seems to be doing okay, which is cool." He
shook his head and laughed. "He can be a bit much though, I guess.
He's trying to grow beach plums."

"Beach plums?" Nola asked.

"Little sour cherry kind of fruit. They grow wild all over the
place, but they're notoriously hard to domesticate. People have
been trying and failing for years. It's just funny that he thinks
he'll be the one to succeed."

From what I knew about Martha's Vineyard, land would be
pretty expensive for a do-gooder to own a big farm, but I was too
tired to say anything. My eyes were drifting closed. As the gentle
motion of the car rocked me to sleep, I heard Moose add, "He's
actually looking for skilled help."

6

The ten minutes I'd slept in the car before Moose dropped us off cast the antique charm of the Wesley Hotel in a surreal light. The old guy behind the desk had the air of someone completely in charge, and I pegged him as the owner.

"Welcome to the Wesley," he said, giving me a friendly smile before resting his eyes on Nola. He never looked at me again, and didn't even try to be subtle about checking out Nola. Apparently he was one of those dirty old men who thought other people would consider it adorable that he was a dirty old man. Nola didn't seem to notice, and I was too tired to care. She gave him her credit card, reminded him that she had asked that they not use any chemicals in the room prior to our stay. He assured her they hadn't.

The room was historically authentic, meaning it was tiny. The bed might or might not have been comfortable; I was asleep before I actually hit it.

When I woke up, Nola was gone and the angle of the sun had changed considerably. There was a note on the dresser. "Get some good rest. Went with Moose to look at bees. See you soon."

I was still behind on sleep, but mentally I had already switched over to coffee mode. I freshened up and changed, then went down-stairs. The guy at the desk directed me to Mocha Mott's, a few blocks away.

The breeze coming off the water was cold enough that it watered my eyes. Mocha Mott's was a few steps below street level on Circuit Avenue, the main street in Oak Bluffs. The coffee was strong, hot, and fresh. I grabbed a copy of the local paper, an old-fashioned wide broadsheet called the *Vineyard Gazette*, and took a booth. Mixed in with the local politics, land deals, and obituaries, I was surprised to find an article about the bee situation. It repeated much of what Moose had said, but also mentioned a controversy among the local farmers about whether or not to bring in bees from off-island to replace the missing natives.

They interviewed Teddy Renfrew, who was against it, and Johnny Blue, who was for it. At the end of the article, urging both sides not to panic, was Doctor Annalisa Paar, described as an in-ternationally recognized authority on honeybees, mites, and col-ony collapse disorder. The reporter's tone was almost fawning, going on at length about the island's good fortune to have Dr. Paar here when the issue with the bees arose.

Toward the end of the article, I got the feeling I was being watched, and when I put the paper down, I found I was.

"You're Dr. Paar," I said. She had an espresso cup in front of her and a clipboard and some papers scattered across the table. But she was looking at me.

"Annalisa," she corrected. "And you're Moose's friend, Doyle."

I held up the paper. "I was just reading about you."

She actually blushed. "The reporter was very nice, but perhaps she exaggerated a bit." She slid her papers to the side. "Care to join me?"

I paused, but then grabbed my coffee and paper and moved to her table. Just an innocent cup of coffee.

"Moose was pretty hard on you back there."

She let out a soft sigh. "He's suspicious. I don't blame him. Sometimes I'm suspicious myself."

"Suspicious of what?"

"Did he tell you who I work for?"

I could see red Stoma Corporation logos on a couple of the papers in her stack. "He did."

"We'd been doing really good work at Bee Futures, and I continue to, but Stoma . . . They haven't put any pressure on me in any way, but people don't trust me anymore. I'm not used to that. Academia is not without treachery, but Stoma . . . I don't know what to make of them. They make me very nervous."

"They definitely make Moose nervous."

She started to laugh, but then something caught her eye and she stopped and looked down.

"What is it?" I said, but she just kept her head down and gave it a little shake.

I turned and immediately knew who she was hiding from. He was standing at the counter, thin, maybe sixty, with gaunt cheeks and a sneer on his lips that didn't quite go with the haunted look in his eyes.

While he waited for his drink, his thin fingers tapped on the counter and his eyes swept the place. I looked away, but I could feel his eyes lingering on me. I heard the door open and close, and when I looked back I caught a glimpse of him through the window as he ascended the steps.

"He's gone," I whispered loudly.

Annalisa looked up tentatively. "Sorry," she said.

"Who was that?"

"Jordan Sumner. Kind of my boss."

"Kind of?"

"It's complicated. He's the head of Bee-Plus, Stoma's genetically engineered bee program."

"Genetically engineered bees?"

She nodded. "It used to be his company, until Stoma bought it—just like they bought Bee Futures. They put my company under him and his Bee-Plus division. They have this elaborate research-slash-breeding operation in the Bahamas. Samana Cay, a tiny uninhabited island. I worked there briefly after the takeover. It's very lovely. I haven't had much to do with him since then. A few months ago they sent me here to study the local bees, same as Moose and Benjy, see if we could figure out why they've been unaffected by colony collapse disorder. I kind of hoped he'd forgotten about me, but last week he showed up on the island."

"So, did you ditch work or something?"

She laughed, the warmth seeping back into her face. "No, just . . . he kind of creeps me out."

I could understand that. I wondered if he would be worse than Lieutenant Suarez, but decided it was a tie.

My phone buzzed with a text from Moose, asking me where I was. I looked up at Annalisa. "We're at Mocha Mott's, right?"

She laughed and nodded.

I texted Moose back.

"How do you know Moose?" she asked.

I didn't say he was friends with my girlfriend, and I didn't say we bonded while thwarting a crazy evil plot involving genetically modified crops and a scheme to make billions in pharmaceuticals. "He used to work for my parents. He took care of their garden, before they died last summer."

"I'm sorry," she said. "He seems like a nice young man."

"He is. He's a good kid."

There was a pause in the conversation, and I was looking at her and she was looking at me and I was thinking, what am I doing here?

Then the door opened and Moose walked in, and I could see he was thinking the exact same thing.

"Doyle!" he said, looking at her and making my name sound like an accusation.

Annalisa and I shared a little smile before I turned in my seat to face him. "Hey, Moose. How's it going?"

"Okay." He looked back and forth between Annalisa and me about six times. "I was wondering if you could lend me a hand with something."

"Uh, sure. With what?"

"With the bee lining. We're shorthanded."

"Bee lining?" I said. "I'm not really crazy about bees." Annalisa raised an eyebrow. "Um, okay. Sure. Right now?"

He nodded and snuck another look at Annalisa. She smiled at him.

"All right," I said, grabbing my coffee and my newspaper. "Well, it was very nice running into you."

"You, too," she replied with a smile. "Be careful with the bees. But don't worry, they're harmless."

7

"So what was that about?" Moose said as soon as we got outside.

"What do you mean?"

"Her. Why were you talking to her?"

"What?" I laughed. "Nola was gone when I woke up, so I went in for a cup of coffee. I recognized Annalisa from this morning. Wait a second, where is Nola? I thought she was with you."

"She was," he said, looking down at his car keys.

"Where is she now?"

"She's at one of the farms, learning some of the newer techniques."

Newer techniques, I thought, as we got into his car, consciously fighting the urge to stiffen my entire body. "Teddy what's-his-name?"

"Teddy Renfrew," he said nonchalantly. "Yeah, why?"

"No reason." It wasn't that I didn't trust Nola, I just really didn't like Teddy what's-his-name.

"So, I'm not really crazy about bees," I told him.

He gave me a half smile, deciding whether or not to mess with me about it. My less than half smile convinced him not to.

"They're okay," he said. "You just need to stay cool, and they'll stay cool, right? You don't swat at them, don't make loud noises, don't mess with their hive, and they'll be cool." He let out a sad laugh. "Besides, the way things are going, we might not even see any."

I looked out the window as we drove. "So where are we going?"

"I need to check the bee-lining stations so we can analyze the data."

"What are the bee-lining stations?"

"You know what a 'beeline' is?"

"A straight line."

"Exactly. When bees are out getting nectar from flowers, they zigzag all over the place. But once they're full, once they can't take any more, they fly straight back to their hive. Wherever they are, they know exactly where the hive is. They make a 'beeline' for the hive. That's where the phrase comes from. When you're bee lining, you set up bait stations filled with sugar water. The bees find it, they fill up and fly straight back to the hive. You set up three bait stations and plot the beelines on a map, the point where they intersect is where the hive is."

"Huh. That's actually pretty cool."

"It can be pretty tedious. Up until last year, you'd have to lie there for hours, watching and then trying to track the directions the bees were flying in."

"So what happened last year?"

He looked at me with a smug smile as we slowly turned down a bumpy driveway. "Benjy got a grant," he said, raising his voice over the sound of his tires grinding the dirt and gravel. "And Bee-Watch went hi-tech."

Forty yards down the driveway, a generator was quietly humming. We pulled up next to it, and Moose pressed a switch on the generator, sending it quiet. A cord ran from the generator to a small cluster of hi-tech equipment another twenty yards away. There was a cluster of metal cases, a couple of feet on each side. At the center was a pair of short tripods, each topped by a sleek black box about six inches high, a foot and a half wide, and three feet long. A red plastic bucket was hanging under one of them.

"That's the feeding station at the bottom," Moose said as we walked up. I looked around for bees, but didn't see any. "The things on the tripods are LIDAR units, like radar, only using lasers. A motion detector kicks them on if anything bee-sized comes into the area. The lasers sweep the area, take a few three-dimensional images, and then calculate the trajectory of the bee through space. Add some super-sensitive GPS. Bingo: instant beeline.

"Are bees the only things that set it off?"

"Anything close to a honeybee will set it off, but we know the wing-beat signature of a honeybee as opposed to a beetle or a mosquito. So we filter for that. The mapping software even plots the locations for us."

He walked up to the station and disconnected a small gray box and replaced it with the one under his arm, which seemed to be identical. "Pretty simple, right?"

"So . . . what do you need me for?"

"These units are pretty heavy, and sometimes we have to move them. It's a lot easier with two people." He shrugged, and his face colored a bit. "Plus, I figured we could hang out."

It seemed like he had something else on his mind, and once we got back in the car, he said, "So, how are things going with you and Nola? You guys doing okay?"

"Why do you ask?"

"Just a vibe. Is something up?"

I sighed. "Relationships are tricky. Living together is tricky. Apparently living with a cop is tricky."

"Nola told me about that Jarrett guy. She was a little freaked out by it."

"I was a little freaked out myself. It's not like that kind of thing happens all the time, but it happens. I know she doesn't like it, but that's the way it is. It's like, she's not a vegetarian, but she doesn't like to think of where meat comes from. And I get that, I'm the same way. Sometimes law and order isn't pretty. She's been seeing a little more of that side of things since moving in with me. With Simeon Jarrett, she got to look at it right up close."

"How about you? How are you doing?"

I turned to look at him, and he looked back, holding my gaze. Moose and I had been through some stuff in the short time we'd known each other, but it was still a short time.

"I'm getting there," I told him. "Sometimes it's easier than others."

"Still having nightmares?"

"I'm not 'having nightmares.' Did Nola tell you that? I had a couple of nightmares. What, you haven't?"

He looked away. "A few. But I think you saw a few more things than I did."

I wanted to remind him that I was kind of a badass and he was kind of not, but he had a point.

At the next stop, we had to move the whole station, which was a bit of a production. Moose asked if I could move it myself, because if I could then he could monitor the GPS and that way we could do it more precisely.

I said sure, because that's what you say when your little friend asks if you are strong enough to do something. But I didn't realize until too late that meant moving the whole tripod, with the LIDAR unit on the top, all the cables, et cetera, and the feeding station hanging from the bottom.

I wrapped my arms around the whole thing and lifted, inching forward and to the right according to Moose's directions. We were about ten seconds into it and the unit was starting to get heavy when two bees emerged from the top of the feeding station. I guess they weren't finished, because they did not fly straight back to their hive. Instead, they flew straight up at me, one land-ing on my shirt and the other one getting close enough to my ear that it sounded like a goddamned buzz saw.

I did not freak out, or at least not totally, but I wanted to, hav-ing bees on me and not being able to do anything about it. I planted the whole unit right where it was, and I backed the hell away from it.

"Nope, not yet," Moose said, oblivious as I brushed at my shirt and my hair. The bee near my head must have flown away, but the one on my shirt tumbled onto the ground in a little ball.

"Actually, that's close enough," Moose said, then he looked up at me. "Are you okay?"

I nodded. "Cramp."

He nodded back. "Okay, well, why don't you relax while I reat-tach the power supply."

I nodded, watching as the bee on the ground got its legs under it, then took a few steps and flew off. My stomach felt squirrelly from the little surge of adrenaline and I leaned against the truck. It was a kind of unreasoned, little-kid fear that I hadn't felt since I was eight years old. It reminded me of then, of being so afraid of bees that I used to wish I was allergic so I'd have an excuse for the terror bees provoked in me.

That summer, I had decided I wasn't going to be scared of bees anymore. I went out of my way to confront them, stomping on them and swatting them, proving I wasn't afraid. By the time school started, I tried killing a few with my bare hands. I got stung a couple of times, and it hurt, but it wasn't the end of the world. As the nights got cooler, I realized the bees would soon be gone, but I felt like I hadn't quite made my point.

On a warm Saturday afternoon that October, I caught a bee in a jar and put it in the freezer, just long enough to knock it out. I tied a piece of thread around its middle and the other end around a stick. I guess I thought I was taming it or something. Then the bee woke up and started flying in circles. I sat there, mesmerized, watching it go round and round. At first I thought I was really something. I had tamed this thing, dominated it, made it more scared of me than I was of it. And each time it came toward me, a blur of black and yellow, I felt like it was looking at me, afraid and wondering why I had done this, why I had been killing bees all summer long. Like it knew who I was and what I'd been doing.

I ran inside to get the scissors, but by the time I got back the bee was faltering, flying a few feet and then landing, and resting. I waited until it landed and snipped the thread as close to the bee as I dared.

I could remember how hot my face felt as I started to cry, watching it flying away, trailing the thread, bobbing and swaying, under the weight of it, exhausted. It disappeared over some bushes, but I knew it never got home.

"You okay?" Moose asked when he came back to the truck.

I nodded. He looked concerned. "How about you?"

"Have you seen any bees?" he asked.

I looked right at him. "A couple."

"Good," he said. "I haven't seen any since Pete's place this morning."

"So how serious is it?" I asked as we drove off. "The whole bee situation."

"We'll know more once we get this data analyzed. People are noticing though. They sent a news crew out to interview Benjy today." Moose smiled when he said it, like, as troubled as he was by the big picture, it was still kind of cool to get on TV. "It's great that people are starting to pay attention, but scary that the problem has gotten bad enough that they would, you know?"

By the time we were done, there was plenty of shade and the tops of the trees were a fiery orange. I knew the island wasn't small, almost ten miles wide and more than twenty miles long, but I was still surprised by how much of it there seemed to be.

We drove past Edgartown on the way back, the uniform white houses and black shutters a contrast to the colorful jumble of Oak Bluffs. A thin ribbon of road took us north, the ocean on our right and salt ponds sparkling in the late-afternoon sun to our left. The air still had a chill, but the warmth of the sun held a reminder that summer was coming.

Moose got a text while we were driving back. "Dinner tonight," he said, his eyes shifting back and forth between his screen and the road. "A bunch of folks are meeting up at Offshore Alehouse. You up for it? You'll love the Alehouse."

"Sounds good to me," I said as we swung into Oak Bluffs. "I'll check with Nola."

It seemed strange that I'd barely spoken to her since we arrived, but when Moose pulled in across from the hotel, she was standing on the big front porch, smiling and waving. With the sunlight behind her she seemed to be glowing, and I pictured her back on her farm, in Dunston, in the late-summer sun, looking beautiful and smiling at me. I felt a warm rush at the sight of her, and a tiny, inexplicable pang of sadness.

Moose parked next to the harbor, and as we crossed the road, Nola came down the steps. When she stepped up next to me and slid her arm around my waist, I realized how much I'd been missing her.

"You boys been out playing with bees?" she asked, stepping up to give me a kiss.

"Yeah, Doyle helped me with the monitoring stations while you were out there playing in the dirt. How was it anyway?"

"It's an amazing place. Teddy's got quite an operation."

I fought the urge to stiffen. "You were at Teddy's the whole time?"

"Yes, I had no idea the place was so big. It's impressive."

"Totally is," Moose conceded.

I kept my cool and was glad I did as Nola slid her hand up to the back of my neck and worked her fingers up into my hair.

"So did you guys talk about tonight?" she asked. "Are we on?"

"Yeah, Benjy sent me a text," Moose replied. "Sounds good."

"Great," she replied, sliding in front of me and wrapping my arms around her so her back was pressing against me. "Teddy said it was a good place, with room for the whole crowd."

Moose smiled at our embrace; then he looked at his watch. "Okay, well, it's just a few blocks from here, but how about I come by at seven and we can walk over together? That way you two can get some quiet time first."

"Sounds good," Nola said, leaning back a little more.

8

Quiet time was great, although not particularly quiet, especially when I kicked over the bedside lamp. We made fast work of each other's clothes and fell onto the bed, trying not to laugh as we almost bounced off it and onto the floor.

It had been a week, and a lot longer since we had done it in the daytime. I felt sneaky and young, and we fought off a conspiratorial laugh, until I was inside her. Nothing funny about that. We were both worked up, and it was frantic at first, but then we slowed down, taking our time, kissing and running our fingers through each other's hair. Looking into each other's eyes and smiling. Then smiling time was over for a while.

We finished just before the sun did, dropping onto our backs, sweaty and heaving, as a final sliver of bronze light slid up the wall and narrowed to nothing. I felt the tiniest flicker of regret at having missed what looked to have been a spectacular sunset. Then I looked down at Nola and smiled, because it couldn't have been as spectacular as she was. She looked up at me and smiled, and I held out my arm, curling it around her as she scooted up close.

We lay like that for a while, holding on to each other, holding on to the moment, watching the room slowly go dark.

When Nola's phone lit up the room, the gentle acoustic guitar ringtone sent us scrambling like a blaring trumpet. I landed on my feet in a combat stance, still half asleep. By the time I was fully awake, Nola had turned on the bedside lamp, squinting at me as she held her phone to her ear.

"Hi, Moose," she said, looking at her watch. "No, of course not . . . Ten minutes, that's fine."

One of the many things I liked about Nola was that she could get ready in a hurry, and I especially liked the way she got ready in a hurry and still looked great. We shared a purely utilitarian shower that was over before the water had fully heated up, and Moose texted us that he was outside on the porch a leisurely fifteen minutes later. The stiff breeze coming off the harbor was bracing, especially with my hair still wet from the shower.

It was a five-minute walk to the Alehouse, and after the first minute, conversation was replaced with hunched shoulders and hurrying. By the time we got there I was grateful to be enveloped in the boozy swell of warmth and loud conversation that greeted us. The place had a vaulted wood ceiling, and walls decked with oars and boats and flags and stuffed fish. At the far end was a massive fireplace made of the ubiquitous fieldstone.

Moose waved toward the back, where Teddy was standing in a little nook by the bar, giving him a semi-friendly smile and cool-guy tilt of his head. I told myself that maybe I had misjudged the guy, but then his eyes moved from Moose to Nola and his smile moved from fifty percent friendly to one hundred percent wolfish.

As we filed between the tightly packed tables, our feet crunching peanut shells on the floor, an older couple made their way past us toward the door. Their strained smiles faltered as one of the larger tables erupted in laughter. They'd probably had the place to themselves when they got there for the early bird special, and stayed just a little too long.

The crowd was an odd mix: a big table of rowdy college kids, a couple of booths of older working men with lined faces, and a few middle-aged couples. I recognized a face at one of the other large tables, a thin guy in an oversized hoodie sitting with two oversized friends wearing regular-sized clothes.

In the back corner, two beefy guys sitting at a booth were taking turns drinking their beers without smiling or talking. The younger one had a buzz cut and the older one had hair just long enough that you could see he'd lost most of it. They were wearing cheap suits— not that I'm judging—and looked like they maybe weren't as solid as they used to be. They were still on top of it enough that they each gave me exactly two seconds of eye-work before looking away and never once looking back. If I wasn't a cop, I might have thought they were cops. But I am, and they weren't. Maybe at one point, but not for a while.

I couldn't help wondering if the ex-cops and the oversized friends were there to keep an eye on each other. But what did I care? I was on vacation.

As we reached the end of the bar, I saw Benjy and Pete sitting on stools, tucked away behind Teddy. We all shook hands and Teddy gave that phony smile, but between each handshake his eyes flickered back toward Nola.

He leaned his head close to mine and said something I couldn't hear.

I said, "Milk comes from cows."

He scrunched up his face like he couldn't hear me.

I gave him a wink. "I know. Crazy, right?"

He shook his head and said, "What?"

I was about to repeat it when the waitress came to lead us to our table, next to the rowdy college kids.

Being a gentleman, I stood back to let Nola go first. Being a douchebag, Teddy went first. To be fair, though, he didn't sit next to Nola but took the far seat, with his back to the rear of the dining room. Nola ended up between Moose and me, and I ended up between Nola and an empty chair.

She turned to me and smiled, said something about how great the place was. I looked up to admire the impressive collection of nautical tchotchkes on the wall and nodded my agreement. When I looked back, she was talking to Moose and Teddy.

As the waitress brought our beers and we ordered our pizzas, my eyes made another appreciative sweep of the décor. I noticed Annalisa, sitting alone in the front booth with her back to the door and a sweep of dark hair obscuring her face. Perhaps she felt my eyes, because she turned and met my gaze for a second. Then she looked away and her face disappeared once again behind that curtain of hair. I looked away, too, and found Nola looking up at me, waiting.

"Did you hear me?" she asked. I shook my head and pointed to my ears. She cupped her mouth. "Do you see the guy in the hoodie over there?" I nodded. "I think that's Johnny Blue."

"How do you know what he looks like?"

Her cheeks colored slightly. "Well, I don't, really," she stammered. "I mean, I've seen pictures. And I watch TV sometimes. I'm home a lot, you know?"

She patted my knee under the table, then took her hand away as she dove back into the conversation. But I kept staring at her. I would never have pegged her as the reality TV type.

Our pizzas arrived on metal trays. After the first piece, Moose and Teddy switched seats so Moose could talk to Benjy. As Teddy took Moose's place next to Nola, he gave me a look over her shoulder, almost like he was challenging me. Then he turned his attention to Nola, flashing a smile that dripped with charm. He tilted his head close and said something frightfully witty.

He had green eyes. I wanted to hit him just for that.

9

I ate three slices of pizza and concentrated on my beer. Then I concentrated on another. I was contemplating a trip to the restroom just to escape the table, when a flash of dark hair caught my attention. Annalisa was getting up to leave.

Moose said something to Benjy, who turned in his chair and called out to her. Moose shook his head and slid down in his seat while Benjy beckoned her over, insisting over her protests. Her shoulders slumped, and as she gathered her things, Benjy beckoned the waitress, pointed at Annalisa, and ordered another of whatever she had been drinking.

She came over and stood next to Benjy, waving to each of us and looking around the table, maybe smiling when she got to me. I smiled tightly back at her, not in the best mood at the way dinner had turned out.

Nola and Teddy looked up at her, then returned to their conversation. Benjy said something to Annalisa, and she bent over to speak to him. By the time she straightened back up, the waitress had returned with a half pint of stout. Annalisa rolled her eyes but took the glass, thanking Benjy but adding a good-natured scolding. Moose rolled his eyes in an entirely different way, but Benjy smiled and gestured toward the empty chair. The one next to me.

She looked over at me and smiled, then shrugged.

By the time she had made her way to my side of the table, everyone else had returned to their conversations. She slid into the chair next to me and put a stack of folders on the table, raising her glass in my direction.

I raised mine back. "Dining alone?"

She indicated the pile of folders on the table. "Working dinner."

"This a good place for that?"

"It was a lot quieter two hours ago." As she said it, the table next to us erupted in laughter and cheers.

"I hate loud restaurants," I said, because I had to say something.

She leaned closer, smelling sweet and unfamiliar. "I don't know," she said, her breath on my ear. "They can be surprisingly intimate." She blushed and laughed. Just as she did, the room went quiet. The guys at the next table were getting up to leave, their raucous laughter replaced by the sound of chairs scraping the wood floor and Annalisa's laughter dying out.

There was a slight hint of menace in the air, like that whole table's collective drunk had suddenly turned belligerent. I watched them leave, wondering if there was going to be trouble. Then I noticed the bodyguards watching the same way I was, and the two guys in suits from the booth in the back, too.

The hum of conversation was just returning when the bartender started flicking through the channels on the TV over the bar, and someone called out, "Hey, look! It's Benjy!" The bartender flicked back and turned up the volume. Sure enough, there he was.

"We don't really have any idea what's going on," televised Benjy said, scratching the back of his head in a good imitation of bewilderment. "We're just trying to figure it out." The place erupted in cheers and laughter, drowning out whatever he said next.

"There are plenty of guesses as to what's going on," said the reporter, "but nobody really knows for sure. With me now is Mr. Teddy Renfrew, with the Native Grown Coalition."

The camera cut to Teddy, looking like he was made for TV. "We know what's causing these problems—pesticides, herbicides, genetically modified crops—those are the problems, not the solutions. The farmers on this island have been using natural farming techniques, native pollinators, and until now we've been spared these problems that have been plaguing the mainland. That means we'll continue to rely on our native pollinators, and we will not bring in industrial-scale pollinators that will make our bees sick with whatever is making the other bees sick." A few people in the bar hooted and clapped. A couple of hands reached out and patted Teddy on the back.

"Thank you, Mr. Renfrew," the reporter said. Then the camera cut to an extreme close-up of a tiny flower. "While everyone agrees the situation is serious, not everyone agrees on what to do about it. With us now is Johnny Blue, reality TV star and, if I understand correctly, now a farmer on Martha's Vineyard?" The camera panned to Johnny Blue, dressed in the same clothes he was wearing now. Sitting at the table, he raised his fists and his bodyguards bumped him.

"That's right," he said on TV. "I'm the proud proprietor of Johnny Blue's Berry Farm." He held up a silver and blue foil packet and mugged for the camera. "Home of Johnny Blue's Berry Jamz."

"And what do you think of the bee situation?"

"Well, you're absolutely right, the situation *bees* serious," he said, emphasizing the pun. "And they tell me if my blueberries aren't pollinated in time, I'm going to get *stung* right in my wallet."

"So what are you going to do about it?" she asked, pushing the microphone back into his face.

"Well, I'm not too worried. If the local bees don't show up soon, I have a guy, Jack O'Callaghan, who can bring bees to the island that are, like, trained or whatever." He held up the package again, and shook it in front of the camera. "So never fear, all you Johnny Blue fans out there, your Berry Jamz are coming."

"There you have it, Jim. Back to you." The bartender turned off the TV, and for a moment, everyone was quiet except for Johnny Blue, who was repeating his lines, and his bodyguards, who were pretending to laugh at them again.

Teddy stood up and walked over to Blue's table. "You're an idiot, Blue."

Blue shot to his feet, sending his chair sliding out behind him. He looked down at his pals, who slowly got up as well. They were huge. Both had shiny bald heads, one with a goatee. Once they were standing, Blue walked around the table, standing in front of Teddy but making sure his pals were right behind him.

"Nobody asked you, hippie," he said, his head bent to the side, like maybe someone had told him that looked tough. The two suits in the back booth slid their beers off to the side, the younger one glancing at the older one, looking for a cue. I wondered how they figured into all this.

"Nobody had to ask me, idiot. It's a fact. You're an idiot, and if you bring O'Callahan and those factory bees of his to this island, you're going to ruin something you're too stupid to even understand."

Blue was shaking his head and laughing, waiting for Teddy to finish. "Well, there's something you don't understand, motherfucker. I'm sick of your shit and I ain't going to let some punk-ass hippie disrespect me or my boys Dawson and Tyrique, bitch."

He tilted his head to one side, then the other as he said their names. Tyrique had the goatee.

10

I got to my feet and started working my way around the table. "Let's calm down here," I said. But as Blue said "bitch," he swung his open hand at Teddy's face. It was probably intended to be a surprise, a cheap shot, but long before he pursed his lips on the "b," his body was twisting and his arm tensing. I don't think there was a person in the place who hadn't known it was coming. Hell, I think the old couple who left when we got there knew it was coming.

The bodyguards were huffing and rolling their eyes, probably having seen this show a few times too many. But when Teddy put up his hand to block Blue, they jumped into action. Unfortunately, so did I. If I'd stayed where I was, Teddy probably would have gotten his ass handed to him, and that would have been the end of it. I should have stayed where I was.

Instead, Tyrique cocked his arm for a punch that would have been lights out for Teddy, giving almost as much notice as his boss had done. I stepped up and gave him a jab in the armpit. He dropped hard, rolling in the peanut shells on the floor.

Benjy and Pete got to their feet and stepped forward, while

Teddy stepped back behind them, holding up his hands. Blessed are the peacemakers. The two suits in the back had come forward as well, but when Teddy stepped back, they did, too.

The second goon, Dawson, grabbed Benjy by the front of his shirt and lifted him with one hand, pulling back to flatten his face. I don't know where these guys had learned to fight. They seemed plenty strong but the extent of their finesse was "Hulk smash." If I'd been closer, I might have punched him in the armpit, too, since that seemed so effective with his friend. But the place was packed tight to start with, and there was a mountain of flesh on the floor between us. Benjy's eyes went wide, staring at the massive fist aimed at his face.

Without thinking, I grabbed the empty metal pizza pan from our table and flung it, Frisbee style, catching Dawson in the temple. The thing rang like a cheap gong and bounced up into the air. Dawson gave Benjy a shove that took out Pete and Moose as well and snatched the pan out of the air as it fell.

With a growl, he flung it back at me, but he overextended and forgot to flick his wrist. I could see it was headed right at Annalisa. I sprang across the table and snagged it, fully extended. I may have knocked over a few beers, but it was a very athletic move. When I looked up, I saw Annalisa smiling down at me. Clearly, she approved. Then I saw Nola. Clearly, she did not. Before I could ponder their different reactions, I felt a hand on my waistband, and then I was off, flying through the air.

My ribs clipped one of the chairs at the next table, an instant after its occupant dove for cover. Tyrique and Dawson were coming around the table after me, one on each side. I met Dawson halfway, rushing him with a flurry of punches to his big meaty face. I had definitely softened him up and slowed him down, but he was still moving forward when Tyrique came up behind me and clamped his hands on my upper arms.

Dawson pulled his arm back, winding up for a massive punch, and I was sheepishly apologizing to God for having been so bad about keeping in touch, when a booming voice from the front of the room said, "Freeze!"

It was a masterful rendition, and I froze, not that I'd been all that mobile to begin with. But everybody else froze, too, and that's not always the case.

From the sound of his voice, I expected to see some hard-ass two-handing his revolver in front of him. Instead, he was a little older than me, wearing a rumpled work jacket. Still, definitely a cop.

"What the hell's going on in here?"

Tyrique let me go and Dawson lowered his fist, flashing me a grin that was probably supposed to be menacing. The menacing grin can be trickier than it sounds, and if it goes wrong it can get all sorts of goofy. I almost suggested he practice it in the mirror, but he didn't seem the type to take the advice constructively.

The bartender came out from behind the bar, brought the cop a beer, and said, "Here you go, Jimmy." Then he spoke into his ear, his finger pointing at us one by one. The cop drank the beer while he listened. At one point the bartender did a little mime of a Frisbee throw, and they both snickered.

When he was done, the cop asked the bartender, "Do you want to press charges?"

The bartender shrugged and shook his head.

The cop drained his glass and put it on the bar as he walked toward us. He took out his notebook and a pen, using the pen to point at us. "I want to see some IDs, you, you, and you." The two goons and me. "I know who you are," he said, pointing at Johnny Blue.

"This ain't Vineyard Haven," Blue protested.

"Shut up, Blue," the cop said. "I'm covering for Chief Bonner."

He started with the goons, taking their driver's licenses and writing down their names. When he got to me, I opened my wallet and showed him my badge.

He looked at it and then looked at me, studying my face for a second. Then he nodded, like, yeah, that made sense. He wrote down my name, then looked back up at me. "Not very professional behavior, huh?"

I didn't know if he was referring to me getting involved in the fight or him sucking down a fine pilsner in the middle of an investigation. I figured it was safer to assume the former.

"They started it," I said.

He laughed. "Yeah, with those knuckleheads, I kinda figured. Still, be better if you tried to calm things down, rather than jumping into the fray. How long you here for?"

"Leaving tomorrow morning."

"You think you can stay out of trouble that long?"

"Yeah, I can manage that."

"Safe trip home, then."

We gathered outside the bar, huddling against the cold, and said our good-byes. There was some awkward laughter about the brawl. Benjy slapped me on the shoulder and thanked me for averting the flattening of his face. Teddy didn't. Instead he solemnly said how sorry he was that things had to deteriorate into violence, which is never the answer.

Nola looked at him as if he were a cross between Gandhi and Martin Luther King. And maybe a little Brad Pitt.

We both hugged Moose, and I found myself surprisingly caught up in the emotion of it. I missed the little guy more than I had realized, and I was sad to be leaving.

Teddy offered to give us a lift back to the hotel, and I was relieved when Nola cheerfully declined. Then we finally left, and I realized the reason was that she couldn't maintain her cheerful façade any longer.

As soon as we turned to go, the bright smile fell off her face, replaced by stone. We walked quickly against the cold, and as soon as we turned the corner, she said, "That was humiliating."

"What?"

"You! We're here for two days and you can't resist getting into a fight? Jesus, Doyle, it's an embarrassment."

"Are you kidding me? I didn't start that. Your friend Teddy did."

"There's a difference between words and fists, Doyle. Or maybe that's what you don't get."

"Are you kidding me? He was about to get flattened. I saved him, and I don't even like the guy."

She spun to face me. "You don't even like him? Why, because he believes in something other than himself? Because he sees something wrong with the world and is working to make it better?"

"No, because he's a douchebag."

She growled and stormed off ahead of me.

I took two fast steps, then slowed down, realizing the conversation wasn't likely to improve.

By the time I got to the hotel, she was inside. I walked up to the front door, but instead of opening it, I plopped down in one of the rocking chairs looking out over the harbor. It was beautiful, but it was cold. When I couldn't take it anymore, I went inside. Nola had the decency to pretend she was asleep, so I climbed into bed beside her and did the same.

Driving home the next day, we spoke about as much as we had on the drive up, only this time Nola was awake for the whole ride. Seven hours of awkward silence. By the time we got home and unpacked, it was close enough to bedtime to call it a night. I got a polite peck on the cheek before we went to sleep.

It was as if we'd never left.

11

The next day, I left for work before Nola woke up, a little earlier than I had to. I was dreading going in, dreading the bullshit that seemed to be waiting for me there every day. I'd probably taken two mental health days in my life, and it bugged me that the one time I really could have used one I had more stress waiting for me at home than at work.

"You're back," Danny said when I walked in. He seemed disappointed, closing the folders he'd been working on and sticking them in a drawer. "Kinda thought you'd come to your senses up on the island and take some time off."

"Whatcha working on?" I asked.

"Nothing, now that you're back," he said with a sigh, pawing through a small pile of paper on his desk. "'Our' assignment is to work the front table as part of the security detail for a conference of municipal planners. . . . In case there's trouble."

The conference was as uneventful as expected. I stopped on my way home from work to get Nola some flowers, organic, from a co-op in West Philly. Seemed like maybe I should. But when I got home, the apartment was empty. A note on the fridge said, "Had to go out. Be home later."

I ate dinner by myself, canned chili and toast, then caught up on some stupid TV I had been missing. Nola came home around ten, and it wasn't until she walked in that I realized I didn't know whether or not I was supposed to ask her where she'd been.

"Hey," I said.

"Hey," she replied, sighing. Then she looked over my shoulder and smiled. "You got me flowers."

She came over and put her arms around my neck and squeezed, burying her head against mine. I reached up and hugged her, awkwardly because of the angle. She held on for a few seconds, then a few seconds longer. Her breath sounded congested, and I wondered if she was hiding tears. I wondered if, without those flowers, we would have been breaking up.

12

The next day, when I got home from work, Nola was waiting for me with a sparkle in her eye.

"Hey," I said tentatively. "How's it going?"

"Great," she said, coming up and giving me a hug. The place smelled of garlicky greens and baked ziti. She came away from the hug, but held my arms, pulling me toward the dinner table. "I got a call from Moose today," she said, almost singing it.

"How's he doing?"

She came up close and put her hands against my chest, looking up into my eyes. "He got me a job."

"What? That's . . . great."

"It's only a few weeks, but it sounds perfect, working on a vegetable farm. And the money is actually pretty decent."

"That's excellent. Where is it?"

Her eye twitched when I said it. "It's up there. On Martha's Vineyard."

"Oh." I knew I was supposed to have some sort of reaction, but I didn't know what that reaction was supposed to be. She was leaving, but she wasn't breaking up with me. I didn't know if I was supposed to be angry or sad or happy for her.

"The bee thing is getting serious, so they need people to hand-pollinate the spring crops."

"Hmm," I said, because "Oh" didn't seem adequate. "When do you start?"

She winced. "This weekend."

Now I was stumped. "Oh," I said.

We ate dinner quietly, not talking about her new job or anything else. Several times, she reached across the table to squeeze my hand, and somehow it bothered me that she thought I needed reassurance.

After dinner we talked a bit about the logistics of getting her there. She was planning on taking the train Friday night, which would get her to the 7:00 A.M. ferry. She'd start work at nine.

"You don't need to take the train," I said. "I'll drive you."

She smiled and patted my hand. "That's sweet, but you don't need to do that, drive all the way up and turn around and come back. I'll be fine on the train."

"I don't mind. I loved it up there and the cycle I'm on, I have Monday off anyway. I wouldn't mind an actual weekend there."

"Doyle, don't be silly," she said. "You're probably still tired from last weekend. Besides, I'll be working all weekend, as soon as I get up there. And anyway, I already bought my train ticket."

I didn't know what to make of the fact that she had bought a train ticket before she'd even told me she was going. We weren't married, but it seemed like the kind of thing normal couples would discuss. Not that I knew much about normal couples.

When we were talked out, she sat next to me on the sofa and put her hand on my cheek.

"I'm coming back," she said, reassuring me.

This time, it did make me feel better. "Good."

Then she pulled me to my feet and led me into the bedroom, where she reassured me some more.

Friday I didn't have to be in until noon, which was just as well, because we had been doing a lot of reassuring. I had the next three days off, and I felt like I'd need them to recover. Nola saw me off with a big, reassuring kiss, and said she'd see me in a couple of weeks. I was supposed to be working until midnight, and had offered to get off early to drive her to the station, but she insisted on taking a cab. I got off early anyway, maybe hoping I'd see her before she left, but knowing she'd probably be gone by the time I got home.

I was almost home when she called me in a panic.

"Doyle!" she said, out of breath. "I can't get inside the apartment! They're spraying." She was breathing fast, almost hyperventilating.

"What? What are you talking about?"

"I don't know, this fat little bald guy is spraying bug killer or something in the hallway. I went out to the drugstore to pick up a few last-minute things, and when I got back, there he was."

It sounded like Roskov, my landlord. "Look, I'll be there in a second, okay? Just sit tight."

Two minutes later, I pulled up in front of the apartment. She was standing by the curb, looking at our home with fear in her eyes.

"I asked him to stop, but he wouldn't," she said, running up to me. "I can't get inside to get my stuff." She looked at her watch. "I have to catch my train. The cab wouldn't wait."

"It's all right," I told her. "I'll get your stuff, and we'll figure this all out."

She stared at me with eyes that churned with emotions: fear and anger, gratitude and resentment. Love, maybe, and maybe loathing.

"What do you need?" I asked, stepping away from her.

For an instant the question seemed too much for her. She shook, like she was going to explode, then she got herself under control.

"It's all by the door, my suitcase and a travel bag. My jacket should be lying across it." I turned to go, and she shouted after me. "But I still need my toothbrush and deodorant, from the bathroom, and my hair brush, and I need my boots from the hall closet." She added half a dozen other items.

I let myself in and ran up the stairs. Rozkov was down the hall. I'd only met him a handful of times in the years I'd been living here. He looked up at me suspiciously. I felt a wave of anger, but he was just a guy doing his job, probably his second job, at midnight on a Friday night.

"What are you doing?"

He shrugged. "You don't want roaches, right? I gotta spray every month. Been doing it for years." He went back to spraying the baseboards.

I paused with my key in the lock, watching him for a second, trying to reconcile the images of an old man making an honest living and an ecological terrorist wantonly spraying poison on my home. Nola's home.

I shook my head and went inside. The place was very clean and very quiet. The suitcase and travel bag were by the door. I found a plastic grocery bag and grabbed her toothbrush, deodorant, and hairbrush, put the boots in another bag. Her wallet and book were on the coffee table, with the train ticket. I grabbed them all and dashed back outside.

Nola was pacing, eyeing me as I came out and mentally inventorying to make sure I had everything she needed.

I put the suitcase and travel bag in the trunk, next to my duffel, still there from the previous weekend. I put the other stuff in her arms. When she saw the wallet and the train ticket, she seemed to deflate a little, both from the near crisis and relief from having avoided it.

"Thanks," she said, looking up at me.

* * *

"It's twelve-oh-three," she said as I turned the car around. "The train's at twelve-thirteen."

I drove fast. Not quite "professional driver on a closed course" fast, but "I'm a cop in my own city" fast. I was starting to think we might make it until we turned onto the Schuylkill Expressway. I knew it was the only way we'd make it in time, but I also knew it was a risk. The Schuylkill Expressway was always a risk.

This time, there was an accident. I drove up onto the shoulder, holding my badge out the window. Nola generally didn't approve of those types of fringe benefits, but she didn't say anything this time.

Once we were past the accident, the road opened up and so did I, shooting up the ramp to Thirtieth Street Station and looping around to the passenger area.

Nola was out of the car before it stopped. I met her at the trunk, and handed over her bags. She gave me a kiss that brushed my cheek, and then she was gone, swallowed into the massive station. It was 12:13.

The signs in the drop-off area said "Do not leave your car unattended." But again, the job has its privileges, and one of them is being able to ignore stuff like that, at least for a few minutes.

I pulled the heavy brass handle and stepped through the glass doors. Nola was halfway across the station, running toward the stairs, her suitcase clacking loudly back and forth from one wheel to the other as she dragged it across the cavernous station.

Then she slid to a halt. The porter was already fastening the rope across the top of the steps. Nola hung her head for a moment. Then she threw it back and let out a growl of frustration that echoed through the station.

When she was done, she turned and looked directly at me. I had done all I could, and more than I should have. I knew she didn't blame me. But it hadn't been enough, and as she stalked back across the concrete floor, the look on her face said I was at least partly responsible, if only for being part of a world that would let such a thing happen.

I stepped back and opened the door for her, and she stomped past me, not slowing down until she reached the car. She tossed her bags into the backseat and dropped into the front seat, arms folded, shoulders hunched, her face furrowed in on itself.

"Sorry," I said as I started up the car.

"Next train's in five hours," she said quietly.

"I could drive you."

It wasn't how I had expected to spend the next six to ten hours of my life, but I had three days off. What else was I going to do? I merged onto the expressway, waiting our turn to squeeze past the remnants of the accident scene.

Nola let out a long low sigh. "Thanks, Doyle, but you don't have to."

As we turned onto the Vine Street Expressway, I gave her a look to remind her that I knew I didn't have to.

We drove in silence. I eased off the gas as we approached our exit at Seventh Street, looking over at her.

"Okay." She said quietly, nodding her head. "Thanks."

I eased the car out of the exit lane and back onto the highway.

13

Moose met us once again at the ferry terminal, looking confused when he saw me. He gave Nola a hug as we walked up, looking at me over her shoulder. His face was pale and drawn.

"Couldn't stay away, huh, big guy?"

Nola hung her head as she released him. "I missed my train."

"Ouch," he said, grimacing as he took her bag from her shoulder. "That sucks . . ." He turned to me. "So wait, you just drove her up here?"

She put her hand against my midsection and gave it an affectionate pat.

Moose let out a whistle. "Damn, Doyle, you're a hell of a guy."

"I keep saying."

"Yes," Nola said, with a sidelong look I didn't quite know how to read. "He's great."

"So, how long are you staying?" Moose asked as he started up the truck.

I still didn't know. When I'd grabbed my duffel bag and locked my gun in the trunk safe before we got on the ferry, Nola's face had been unreadable. It still was. "I don't know," I said. "Sunday or Monday, I guess."

The farm was in Tisbury, at the end of a long dirt driveway flanked by a fieldstone wall. A hundred yards up was a large cedar shake farmhouse with a wraparound porch. The driveway continued on, jagging to the right and down into a shallow bowl holding a couple of tiny cabins.

"Oh, my God, they're so cute!" Nola exclaimed, bolting forward in her seat.

Moose smiled. "That's the farmer housing."

They were cute, all right, but they were tiny. I wondered if I was going to make it, even for just the weekend.

Past them was a small red plywood structure with a wire enclosure next to it and four chickens pecking around.

The door to one of the cabins opened and two women in their early twenties came out, one large and solid, the other small and wiry with a long braid. They both wore shorts, T-shirts, big heavy boots, and bright faces that were ready to go. Maybe it was lack of sleep, but I felt suddenly old.

"This is you," Moose said as we pulled up in front of the second cabin.

"That is seriously adorable," Nola said, hopping out of the car and running up to the combination porch/front step.

I got out, too, stretching out my back. The place seemed to defy perspective, looking smaller and smaller the closer I got.

The heavier woman walked up to us, tipped her head to Moose, and held out her hand to Nola. "You must be Nola," she said. "I'm Elaine."

"Yes," said Nola, "Good to meet you."

"You'll be working with me," Elaine told her, glancing at a leather-mounted wristwatch that looked like something out of a gladiator movie. "You're just in time."

I couldn't tell if she was saying, "Good for you, you're right on time," or "Hey, you're almost late." I think it was the latter.

"Okay, great," Nola said. "Let me just put my things inside and I'll be ready to go."

Elaine looked at her watch again. I wondered if she had short-term memory issues.

Nola grabbed her bags and darted inside the cabin for one second, then another. Elaine looked at her watch yet again.

"I'm Doyle," I said, and Elaine looked at me and nodded, like, "Yes, you sure are."

Before we could get to know each other any better, Nola came back outside. "Ready," she said brightly.

Elaine nodded again. "Gwen's planting lettuce on the lower field," she said, gesturing at the smaller girl disappearing down a narrow path through the tall grass to the left. "We're working on the beach plums, this way," she said, turning and walking toward a second path.

Nola gave me an uncertain smile. I gave her a wink and a thumbs-up, and then she was gone.

"What's down there?" I asked, pointing to a third trail.

Moose shook his head. "That just goes to the compost heap. Beyond those trees is a rental property. Some rich asshole who's never there. Big and fancy, but no water access, so maybe he's not that rich."

I gave him a look to let him know I thought it all very strange. He shrugged, not denying it. Then he looked at his watch as well. "All right, man," he said. "Good to see you. I imagine you'll be wanting to get some rest. I have to get to work as well."

I nodded, looking around me and then back at him.

"I need a car," I said.

"What?"

"A car. I need a car."

He laughed. "You don't need a car. It's an island, man. Besides, I'm sure Teddy's got plenty of bikes lying around you can borrow. Just go knock at the big house."

"Teddy?"

"Yeah, Teddy Renfrew."

"This is Teddy's place?"

His face froze as he tried to figure out an appropriate expression. "Yes."

14

I almost cracked a tooth clenching my jaw, trying not to show I was angry until I could figure out why I was. I've been known to miss a lot of details, but I wouldn't have missed that.

Nola was working for Teddy Renfrew, and she hadn't told me.

"Come on," Moose said. "Teddy's not so bad."

I glanced over at the big house, and gave Moose a dubious look that made him laugh. Then I laughed, too.

"If you say so," I told him. "But I still need a car."

He shook his head. "Okay, there's a place at the airport. But I have to make a couple of stops on the way."

I tossed my bag into the cabin. It looked even smaller on the inside. Coming out, I bumped my head on the doorway.

Moose looked away as he laughed.

"Yes," I said as we got back into Moose's truck. "It's hilarious."

Moose was still smiling as we drove off, but after a few minutes the smile fell away and the lines came back around his eyes and his mouth. He wasn't even twenty-five, but those lines looked way older than that.

"You doing all right up here?" I asked.

He looked at me and gave me a half smile. "What do you mean?"

"You look kind of haggard." I shrugged.

He reached up and turned the rearview mirror so I could see myself.

"Hey, I was up all night driving. I have an excuse."

He laughed, but shook his head. "Actually, I'm worried. About the bees."

I might have laughed, too, but the look on his face was nothing funny. "You mean the dead bees? What you were talking about last week?"

"Yeah, but it's worse. Even in just a week. The whole reason Teddy's bringing more people in is to do work the bees would be doing. Otherwise the crops won't come in."

"So the farmers on the island are going to be screwed this year?"

"Yeah, but it's not just that. Part of the reason we're doing this research project here is looking into why the island has been spared whatever it is that's killing all the bees. Part of me feels like, if colony collapse is happening here now, it's going to happen everywhere."

"I thought colony collapse was only when the bees disappeared from the hives. Didn't Annalisa say it was mites or something?"

He shrugged. "Mites are bad, too. They're tiny little things, some microscopic, but devastating. The worst is called *varroa destructor*, which should tell you something about the damage they can do. You don't hear about mites so much, but they've probably killed as many bees as the CCD. Whatever it is, it's some serious shit. People don't like to think about it, but we need the bees to grow food. Once the bees are gone, we're next." He took a deep breath and let it out as a sigh. "Plus there's been a vibe."

"A vibe?"

"Yeah, on the island. Like there's something going on. Sometimes I feel like I'm being watched."

I didn't know what to say about that, and Moose could tell. He followed it up with an awkward smile and a shrug.

Moose was just swapping out the hard drives on the monitoring stations, no heavy lifting, so he didn't need my help, but I went with him anyway. I was relieved at first not to encounter any bees, but then I noticed an eerie quiet, a distinct lack of buzzing, from bees or any other insects, that made me anxious.

I felt a vague sense of relief each time we got back into the truck and drove off. After the third stop, Moose turned on the radio. It was James Taylor, almost as ubiquitous on the island as the fieldstone walls. He left it on anyway.

At the last stop, Moose looked up at me as he was swapping out the hard drives and told me that the land we were on was part of Teddy's property.

"Really?" I said, surprised. "I didn't think we were that close to the farm."

"We're not." He looked up at me. "It's a big property."

The car rental place was in a tiny compound of low-slung buildings next to an airport with two small runways and a fence that seemed mostly decorative.

Moose offered to wait with me, but I could tell he was antsy to get back to work, so I sent him on his way with tentative plans to get together when Nola was done work. I still wasn't sure what I thought about the whole Teddy Renfrew thing. Depending on how that conversation went, we might not be much in the way of company.

Steve at the car rental place was a little too happy to see me, like a people person who wasn't seeing enough people. We had a longer-than-anticipated conversation about what type of car I was looking for, especially considering he only had eight cars on the lot. They had a convertible Mustang and a Mini Cooper, and Steve thought they were both a great idea, but they seemed a little ostentatious. I already stuck out among the young idealistic farmer types. The cars were also expensive. I decided a Jeep would have more street cred, or off-road cred, or whatever cred was relevant up here.

The Jeep was fun, especially compared to the Impala. I felt strangely not tired, and it was turning into a nice day so I took the scenic way home, State Road through Chilmark. A sign pointed to Aquinnah and the Gay Head Cliffs. I'd missed them the week before, so I figured that was as good a place to go as any. I had the roads pretty much to myself, and I thought maybe Steve was right about the Mustang.

Gay Head Lighthouse sat back from the cliffs. But up the steps from the parking area was a cluster of gift shops and a snack bar, then a path leading to a cliff-top lookout surrounded on three sides by expansive views of the water. The wind was stiff and steady, and the cliffs were high enough that the waves seemed to be rolling in slow motion, crashing over the boulders that dotted the surf. It was an impressive sight, but it seemed to me the cliffs were something to be looked up at, not down from.

I got back in the Jeep and tried to find my way to the beach below. The place seemed designed to keep you away from the beach, which made me that much more determined. Finally, I parked in a small lot a quarter mile down the hill. After a hundred yards of sandy scrub, the beach came into sight, a broad swath of deserted yellow sand dotted with boulders that looked even more impressive up close, especially with the red, gold, black, and brown cliffs behind them. I walked along the beach for a while, then plopped down on the sand, my back against one of the boulders, and watched the waves for a while, mesmerized, squinting against the sun, the tiredness creeping up on me. I knew that if I didn't get moving I was going to fall asleep on the beach, and I was just getting to my feet when I saw a flash of long dark hair and curves in a jogging suit.

"Doctor Paar," I called out.

She turned with a start and stumbled against her momentum. There was fear in her eyes and a can of mace in her hand.

I put up my hands. "Don't shoot!"

"Doyle!" she exclaimed with a laugh that was on the far side of nervous. "Oh God, I'm sorry." She slipped the mace into her pocket.

"I didn't mean to sneak up on you," I said. "Expecting trouble?"

She laughed dismissively, but her eyes flickered with the fear I had seen in them earlier.

"Sorry. My imagination gets away from me sometimes."

"What are you imagining?"

"It's nothing," she said, her composure returning.

I raised an eyebrow, waiting.

"Well, lately, sometimes I feel like I'm being watched."

Just what Moose said. "By whom?"

She laughed nervously and shook her head. "Who knows? The boogeyman, a crazy ex-boyfriend . . . Maybe a crazy eco-warrior, like your friend Moose, or some eco-terrorist, like Teddy, who thinks I'm working for Stoma." Then she turned serious. "Maybe Stoma. I've been feeling like that at work ever since they bought us."

"Really?"

"We were pretty hard on them before the acquisition. Maybe they're following up on me, spying to see if my research is going to implicate them in any of this. Or to intimidate me. I don't know."

She looked up at me, waiting for a reaction that would tell her if I thought she was crazy or if I thought she had something to worry about.

"Moose said something similar," I told her. "About the vibe on the island, and feeling like he's being watched. He thinks maybe it has something to do with the bees, but he's pretty freaked out by the whole bee situation."

She let out a deep sigh. "I'm a little freaked out about it, too."

"Huh." It shook me a little that a trained scientist was as concerned about the bee situation as an environmental activist with a tendency toward the melodramatic.

She looked up at me and nodded, as if that summed it up. "I

should get going," she said, pointing back down the beach, "finish my run."

"I'll see you around," I said.

She gave me a smile. "I hope so."

I couldn't tell if she was sending me signals, or if that was just the vibe she gave off. Some women are like that, and they don't even know it.

Before I could figure it out, she turned and started jogging, picking her way through the rocks that dotted the beach. I stood there watching until she was very small, part of me glad she didn't turn around and see me. Part of me disappointed.

When I got back to the Jeep, I realized I was still smiling. I told myself that flirtation from a beautiful woman was a legitimate justification for a smile, even if you were in a serious relationship. But thinking about that relationship made the smile go away. Serious. Was that its level or its condition, like serious but stable, only without the stable? Day to day the days were up and down, but they seemed to be trending rockier. Acknowledging it made me feel old inside.

As I drove off, I thought of Annalisa, and I smiled again, just for a second.

15

On the advice of an old lady speed-walking on the side of the road, I got a lobster roll at a place called Menemsha, a scenic little harbor not far from Gay Head. The sandwich was as overpriced and overrated as every lobster roll I'd ever had, but it was nice sitting on the edge of the dock, listening to the water.

The tiredness started to creep back in, and I decided to head back to the cabin, catch a couple hours of sleep before Nola got done work.

On the way back, I got turned around. I was trying to regain my bearings at a little rural intersection called Beetlebung Corner when Teddy Renfrew drove by in his truck. On a whim, I fell in behind him, telling myself he was probably headed back to the farm and I could just follow him there. I wasn't trying to be sneaky, but I didn't want to tailgate, either, so I gave him some space. Just to be civil.

Unfortunately, the jackass behind me wasn't showing me the same civility. When I looked in the rearview, I recognized the two ex-cops from the Alehouse, the two suits who had been sitting quietly in the corner watching everyone else.

They seemed exasperated, and as I watched, their Buick La-Crosse disappeared from the rearview, pulling out into the other lane and inserting itself snugly into the reasonable distance I had left between myself and Teddy's truck.

I took a deep breath. Nola would have suggested that maybe they were going to visit a friend in the hospital or a pregnant spouse, maybe they were trying to catch an important ferry. So I gave them the benefit of the doubt and I hung back even more, hoping some other jackass didn't pull the same maneuver.

They pulled up close behind Teddy, but even on a long straightaway, they didn't pass him. They seemed content to ride up his ass and stay there. For some reason I found it fascinating.

Some guys are artists at tailing people, and I'm not one of them. But there are basic moves that everybody knows, and these guys weren't even trying.

Teddy made a few halfhearted attempts to lose them—sudden moves, dicey left turns—but the Buick stayed on his bumper. I kept tailing them, using my Junior Investigator Handbook techniques.

After a while, on a long stretch of country road, Teddy slowed to a stop, and I wondered if he was going to get out and cause a scene, goad these idiots into making a move. Instead, he put on his turn signal, and I realized we were back at his farm. He slowly turned into the entrance and then drove up the driveway.

The suits stayed where they were, sitting in the middle of the road. I was intrigued as hell, but it got to the point where it would be weird if I didn't honk, so I gave them a little toot. They pulled over onto the grass, and I drove on. I didn't want them to get a good look at me so I pretended to be picking my nose, hiding half my face behind my hand and giving them a nice incentive to look somewhere else.

I turned up the first side street after the road curved out of sight. Then I waited, letting a few cars and a few minutes go by before I went back. The Buick was still sitting there, engine running, both occupants staring at the driveway. I'd hoped they'd be gone, but I didn't really care all that much, so I turned into the driveway, too, scratching the side of my head as I did.

Halfway up the driveway, I came to a place where I was no longer visible from the road but not yet visible from the big house, and I let the Jeep coast to a halt. After a few seconds, I took my foot off the brake and crept along the driveway. As I rounded the house, I put it down again. Teddy was trotting down the back steps and heading down toward the compost heap, looking around him as he did. Skulking, I thought. I coasted the Jeep up next to Nola's cabin and parked. Then I followed him on foot.

The compost piles were forty yards behind the cabins, and by the time I could see them, I could see Teddy hurrying past them, toward the woods. I hung back, watching from behind the compost pile as Teddy made his way through the trees. There were four piles, with fresh scraps and rotten vegetables at one end, rich, dark soil at the other end. I hovered near the middle piles, and discovered they were the smelliest.

It was early enough in the spring that the brush was thin, but I was still starting to lose sight of Teddy as he moved through the trees. Then he stopped.

I could see someone standing with him, talking, hands gesturing. I couldn't see what the two were doing, but I could see that they were suddenly doing something different. I was leaning forward and squinting when I recognized the pattern of movement: Teddy was headed back, and he was getting close.

I ducked down low and took off, back toward the cabins, not even knowing why I was running. Rounding the front of the cabin, I almost tripped on the small step up onto the porch. Darting inside, I pulled the door almost closed behind me. I stumbled over the bed, which practically filled the tiny cabin, and moved back as far as I could into the shadows.

A few seconds later, Teddy emerged from between the cabins, walking at a fast clip. He was crossing the commons when he stopped and his head whipped around. At first I thought he had seen me. Then I realized he wasn't looking into my cabin, he was looking next to it. He'd seen the Jeep. Even from inside the cabin, I could hear it ticking and cooling. He turned slightly, squinting at the window for a moment. Then he looked around once more and hurried off.

I didn't know who the suits were who had been following him, and I didn't know who he had gone to meet. But it seemed like he was up to something and somebody was onto him.

I realized I'd been holding my breath, and I exhaled as I sat on the bed. I also realized I was exhausted. I lay back onto the bed, and I closed my eyes.

16

I awoke to the sensation of a slight weight on the bed next to me. It was getting dark, a few blades of orange slicing through the blue shadows that darkened the trees. In the dim light from the window I could see Nola sitting beside me on the bed. She had a complex smile on her face, but at least it was a smile. I wasn't sure if I was going to give her one back yet.

Before I could say anything, or decide not to, she said, "Sorry I didn't tell you I was going to be working for Teddy."

She put her hand on my stomach, rubbing gently. I rested my hand gently on hers.

"I just . . . I know you don't like him, and I figured you wouldn't want me to come up here in the first place. I didn't want to make it any worse."

Before I could ask her when she had been planning on telling me, she said, "I was going to tell you once I got up here." She looked down. "So you'd be over it by the time I got home. But then you drove me up, and I couldn't tell you then, not while we were stuck in the car for six hours. Then Moose picked me up, and then we were here."

We looked into each other's eyes for a long moment, hers blue, almost luminous in the disappearing light. Out of the corner of my eye, I saw movement outside the window. Nola followed my gaze.

"They're getting ready for dinner," she said. "Apparently, when it's warm, they set up tables and have dinner outside. It's kind of nice."

I nodded.

She tilted her head. "Did you rent a car?"

I nodded again. "A Jeep."

She gave me an exaggerated frown. "There's plenty of bikes," she said, disapprovingly. Then she reached up to caress the side of my face. "You hungry?"

I closed my eyes for a moment, just feeling her hand. "Sure."

By the time I'd splashed some water on my face and made my way outside, dinner was well underway. A big folding table with a few lanterns, a couple of bottles of wine, salad and pasta, a platter full of rolls, and eight or ten people.

Everyone else was seated when Nola led me out. We took the last two empty seats, all the way at the end of the table. Nola was to my right. To my left, an under-deodorized kid with a mustache-less beard was putting the moves on the small woman with the braid we'd seen that morning. She seemed like she might be interested. Maybe it was the pheromones. At the other end of the table was Elaine, who had taken Nola out into the field.

Teddy was sitting at the center of the table, holding court, like maybe he was putting out some pheromones of his own.

"Hey, everyone," Nola said as we found our seats. "This is Doyle."

A few of them looked up or waved. A few mumbled some kind of greeting. I mumbled one back.

As we sat, Nola introduced me to the woman with the braid. "Doyle, this is Gwen."

"Nice to meet you," she said, giving my hand a firm shake.

"You, too."

"Gwen and I worked together this afternoon," Nola explained. "She showed me the ropes."

Gwen laughed. "I think I learned more from you," she protested.

Nola laughed, too. "Oh, please," she said. "Using two Q-Tips was brilliant. I'd never seen anyone—"

And they're off, I thought, my ears glazing over as they dove deeper and deeper into the minutiae.

Teddy was in the middle of a war story about some protest he'd been on, getting locked up for a cause. The women on either side of him were hanging on every word. I thought about the poor cops who'd had to deal with him.

He didn't turn his head as we sat, but a couple of seconds later, his eyes hit me and stayed on me. Nola was dishing up salad and chatting with Gwen.

As Teddy stared at me, I gave him the stupidest, friendliest smile I could muster. He looked away, but I don't think he was buying it, at least not the friendly part.

The meal was simple but tasty. I hadn't realized how hungry I was. As we ate, the farmers traded stories about their day. The main topics were adorable tales about Paula, Georgia, Ringo, and John—the chickens—and tips on different techniques learned during the first day of hand-pollinating the crops.

All the farming talk gave me plenty of time to partake of my newest hobby: trying to figure out what was up with Teddy Renfrew.

Toward the end of the meal, Teddy pushed himself from the table, drawing everyone's attention like he was going to make a speech, but he just said, "I'll be back in a moment."

A few minutes later, he appeared at my elbow, placing a bottle of wine on the table in front of me.

"This round's on me," he said to a smattering of cheers and clapping, placing a second bottle at the other end of the table.

Half an hour later, a few people had left, but the ones who remained were getting louder to make up for it.

Teddy seemed as caught up in the buzz as everyone else, but I noticed he kept checking his watch, and as the motion grew more frequent, it was followed by a glance at me. I'm a trained surveillance professional and I can be pretty sneaky, but I figured I'd better put his mind at ease. I yawned and stretched and put my hand on Nola's back as I got up. She turned and looked up at me.

"I'm going to head in," I said.

"Okay," she said, her eyes sweeping my face.

I smiled and then she did, too.

"I'm going to hang out for a while."

"Of course," I said. "I'm just beat."

As Gwen and I said our goodnights, I snuck a glance at Teddy sneaking a glance at me. He looked relieved to see me going, a reaction I am not unfamiliar with.

The cabin was less than twenty feet away, but I had to put my hands out in front of me to feel for the porch post in the darkness. I turned the light on when I got inside, and then immediately turned it off.

I took off my boots in the darkness, then sidled up to the window so I could see the tables in the commons. I had to get pretty close in order to see Teddy. Sure enough, a couple minutes later, he stood, stretching in that same fake way I had done, and said his goodnights. I backed away from the window, waiting for him to pass. Then I stepped up and watched him walking up toward the big house. When I lost the angle, I opened the front door a crack, watching through the gap.

I could just make him out. Halfway to the big house, he looked over his shoulder. Then he stopped and turned, and headed off to the right, toward the compost piles and the tree line.

I stepped silently out onto the porch; then I looked down at my bare feet, stark white in the darkness. I'm not a barefoot-in-the-park kind of guy, but I figured it would help keep the noise down.

The porch floor felt smooth and cool as I padded across it, but when I stepped off, the ground was cold and damp, a mixture of grass and dirt and dew. Probably some bugs, too.

I crept through the gap between the two cabins, and stopped at the rear, letting my eyes adjust to the darkness. The moonlight seemed brighter back here, and I could see Teddy's silvery outline making its way toward the trees. When he disappeared behind the compost pile at the end, I crept forward to the space between the two in the middle. At first, I couldn't find him, and I was concerned that maybe he was headed back already. But then I saw a red glint through the trees.

I moved my head and got a better angle on it. It was the taillight of a car. I could see Teddy's outline moving toward it, disappearing and reappearing as he made his way through the trees. By the time he stopped, he was mostly obscured by the trees, partially outlined in red as he stood behind the car. For a moment, there was another light, the dim yellow of a dome light. Then it winked out. A few seconds later, a another figure appeared in the shallow pool of red light.

They stood there for a few seconds. Then they both disappeared. The dome light winked on, as I heard the car door close, and it winked off. The red light drifted off to the right before disappearing completely.

I turned to head back, but the moon had slipped back behind the clouds and the ground was transformed into a pit of blackness. I stepped forward and my foot landed on something wet and squishy, probably half-rotted garbage that had tumbled off the pile. The next step was good, but then the third step landed on what felt like a punji stick. I was convinced that if there was any light, I would see it protruding from the top of my foot. As I took a moment to catch my breath and bite my lip so I didn't curse out loud, I was rewarded with a soft wash of yellow light illuminating my way back. I hopped as quickly as I could back to the cabin, stopping only when I realized the source of the light.

Lights on in the cabin meant Nola was back. Probably wondering what I was up to. Creeping around the front of the cabin, I noticed everyone was gone except the skinny guy and the object of his affection.

When I got inside, Nola was lying in bed, reading. She looked at me over the book, up and down, lingering on my feet, then on my face.

"I went for a walk," I said.

She looked back down at my feet to let me know she didn't believe me. "Nice night for it."

Then she closed the book and rolled far enough away from me that even in the tiny bed there would be plenty of space between us.

17

Nola was gone when I woke up, and so was everyone else. It was only eight, but the sun was up and the morning was warm. I went outside in jeans and a T-shirt. No shoes, just to prove a point, and maybe to toughen up my feet a bit, since apparently they needed it.

It was Sunday morning. If there had been a communal breakfast, I had missed it. What I really missed was coffee.

I walked down to one of the trails at the far end of the commons. The fields spread out below on a gentle slope, rows of scrubby bushes covered with white blossoms, a few young farmers hard at work, dabbing little brushes in each little blossom. It looked like they were dusting for fingerprints.

I spotted Nola at the far end of the field. She might have seen me, but she didn't look up, so I didn't wave. Besides, she was at work.

Back in the cabin, I put on my boots and grabbed the car keys. I needed a coffee.

I half expected the Buick to still be parked in front of the driveway, but it wasn't. It was a hundred yards down the road, facing back toward the driveway. I slowed as I passed it, sharing a look with the two suits inside.

They scowled, but it wasn't like they were trying to be discreet. I tapped my forehead in a salute; then I tapped the accelerator and sped off.

I was starting to get my bearings on the island, and I drove into Oak Bluffs without looking at the map. I ended up at Mocha Mott's and ran into Moose, sitting at a table with Benjy and Pete. They each had a bagel and a coffee. A map and a bunch of papers were spread out in front of them. Moose and Benjy looked like they'd been up for a while. Pete didn't look much better. Moose did a double take when I walked in.

"You're still here?" he said.

"For the moment. Why?"

"Are you busy?"

I shrugged. "I have plans to get a cup of coffee, but I'm open after that. Why?"

"I need you to help move some of the bee stations. Can you give us a couple of hours?"

Benjy and Pete looked up for the first time, as if they had both just noticed me.

"Um . . ." That wasn't how I had planned on spending my morning, but I hadn't planned anything else, either. "Sure, I guess."

I got a large coffee with a double shot of espresso. It seemed like that kind of morning.

"I thought you were leaving this morning," Moose said, driving at a decent clip. "When are you here until?"

"I don't know. I have the next couple of days off, but it might be good to have some home-alone time. Besides, I'm not sure Nola likes the idea of me being here."

He looked at me like I was crazy. "Seriously? I'm sure that's not the case."

"You think?"

"No, she's crazy about you. She told me so."

I didn't ask when, but I had a feeling it might not have been recently. "So what's going on with you? You looked like crap yesterday, you look worse today. And your friends have the same look."

He shook his head, gave me a look so scared it scared me, too. "You can't tell anyone, okay? Not yet."

"I don't know anyone up here, and I don't talk to anyone anyway."

He nodded and took a deep breath, his face going pale. "It's the bees, man. Something very messed up is going on."

"What's wrong with them?"

He turned and gave me a look like stone. "They're all dying."

"What do you mean?"

"For weeks we've been tracking them, how many there are and where they're going. Or we were. From the first day of spring, something was up. They emerged from the winter, and then their numbers started dropping, almost immediately. In the last few days, it's been dramatic, like ninety percent declines. It started up island, first the stations in Aquinnah and Menemsha, then Chilmark and West Tisbury, too. Now it's almost the whole island. We thought there was an equipment malfunction, but we're pretty sure the equipment is fine. That's why we're resetting it all, so we can check it one last time."

"So, shouldn't you be telling someone? Why are you keeping it secret?"

"Because this is huge. We have to be totally sure, and then . . . I don't know, I guess folks are going to have to figure out the right way to tell people, because they are going to freak the fuck out." He shook his head. "And I'm going to be right there with them."

We worked in silence for the next few hours, covering one half of the island while Benjy and Pete covered the other half. We moved each station, just a few feet, then Moose switched out the hard drives and we reset them: turn the server off, disconnect the power source, wait a full minute, hold down the power switch, then reconnect it, and power up. Each time he pulled out the hard drive, he'd stare at it, as if by looking at it he could figure out what was on it.

When we were done, he drove me back to the coffee shop to pick up the Jeep.

"All right," he said as he pulled over. "I've got to drop these off at the lab. Then we're going to meet up at the Black Dog in Vineyard Haven for brunch."

I looked at my watch. "It's three o'clock."

He smiled, first time all day. "Yeah, Black Dog brunch is until four. And it's awesome. Everybody goes there."

I wasn't sure if I was up for brunch, and I didn't know what would be waiting for me back at the cabin. The suits in the Buick were gone and the campground was deserted. Inside the cabin, there was a note on the bed: "Finished early. Gone to brunch. See you later."

18

I'd always suspected the Black Dog existed only as a trademarked logo, but there it was, right on the water in Vineyard Haven, next to where the ferry had let us off. An honest-to-God place.

The parking spaces out front were full, so I parked in the lot across the street. Apparently, late brunch was a big deal around here.

The place had a vaguely rustic feel, done up in exposed wood, like the Alehouse, but instead of some of the nautical tchotchkes, it had windows all the way around.

As soon as I walked in, I saw Nola sitting with her coworkers at a large row of tables pushed together. She had her back to the door, and was sitting across from Teddy, who was once again in the center, talking. He looked up when I walked in, and I gave him a little nod, but he just kept talking.

The room was loud, festive but with a frantic edge to it. Dawson and Tyrique, Johnny Blue's bodyguards, were sitting in the corner with proportionately massive piles of food in front of them. They seemed to be watching Teddy, then Tyrique saw me and said something to Dawson, who turned to look in my direction. I wondered if there was going to be trouble, but they went back to their food.

I hadn't seen the Buick out front, but the two suits were there, too. It felt like a reunion from the Alehouse. I hoped it wasn't going to turn into a reenactment.

Pete was at a table with four other guys. I nodded to him and he nodded back, but the whole table seemed to be watching me warily.

Moose was sitting with Benjy in the other dining room. He waved me over and pointed to the two empty seats next to him. I held up a finger and headed over to Nola's table.

As I approached, Teddy looked up again. This time Nola turned around.

"Doyle!" she said with a slight smile. She stood and gave me a peck on the cheek. "You remember everyone, right?"

I smiled at the table, but no one was looking at me except Teddy. He didn't smile back.

"I saved you a seat, but then Elaine's friend showed up. Let's see if we can get another chair." She beckoned the hostess. The table was strewn with empty plates, all smeared with egg yolks or syrup.

"It's okay," I said, stopping her. "You guys are almost finished. Moose and his friends are here. I'll eat with them and see you back at the cabin."

"Are you sure? There's plenty of room."

There was absolutely no room. I wasn't sure I wanted to leave her with Teddy and his self-righteous eco-warrior charms, but I was sure I didn't want to sit with him and I was sure I didn't want to be sitting there waiting for my food to come out when everyone else was finished and leaving.

"I'm sure." This time I gave her a peck on the cheek. "I'll see you in a bit, okay?"

"Okay," she said, relieved but concerned.

As I made my way to the other dining room, I could feel her

looking at me. But by the time I got to Moose's table, she had turned back around, engrossed in conversation with the woman sitting next to Teddy.

As I sat, Benjy stood and waved over my shoulder. I turned to look and saw Annalisa coming our way, weaving through the tables.

Instinctively, I looked at Nola, and saw her eyes narrow as she watched Annalisa. She glanced at me, then turned back around and resumed her conversation.

Moose leaned close to me. "Benjy asked her to double-check our data."

"I got here as soon as I could," Annalisa said to Benjy, her eyes darting to meet mine, then back to the others. Her face was as somber as Moose's and Benjy's. She looked around the room, and I followed her gaze. A lot of the eyes in the room were on her, and I sensed that it was not just aesthetic appreciation. They were staring at our table, reading us. Benjy and Moose seemed to notice it, too. As Annalisa took the seat next to me, the buzz in the room seemed to change pitch.

Benjy leaned forward over the table, and the rest of us leaned toward him.

"They know," he said quietly. "Pete and his beekeeper buddies have been staring daggers at me since I came in."

Moose looked around. "Somebody said something," he whispered, looking at me, then turning to Benjy. "What did you tell Pete?"

Benjy shook his head. "Nothing. I just said we needed a hand. But he already knew something was up."

The buzz in the room became a whisper, and we heard a chair scraping the floor. One of the guys sitting with Pete stood up and slowly made his way to our table.

Benjy looked at Annalisa. "I hope you've got good news."

She slowly shook her head.

"My bees are just about all gone," the man said, looking down at us. "If you know something more about this, you need to tell us right now. You owe us at least that much."

Benjy stood up, working his mouth like he was trying to find a little bit of moisture in there. I met Nola's eyes across the room, and we both looked up at Benjy.

"We're collecting data and analyzing it, Paul, just like I told you," Benjy said. "We'll release the results as soon as we're done."

"You already know," someone else called out. "Why don't you just tell us?"

Benjy shook his head, holding out his hands, trying to calm things down. "Now, that's not true, and just as soon—"

While Benjy was talking, a cell phone chimed. One of Pete's beekeeper friends covered one ear and put his phone to the other. Then he shot to his feet. "Those bastards are doing it!" he exclaimed. "They're bringing in bees from the mainland."

"Who is?" Teddy called out.

"Johnny goddamned Blue. They're bringing them over on the ferry."

Every eye in the place was looking at the beekeeper—then they turned to the windows overlooking the harbor. The ferry was sliding across the water toward the dock, sixty yards away.

Teddy exhaled, shaking his head. "Son of a bitch," he said quietly. There was a moment of absolute stillness, except for the silent progress of the ferry on the water. Then half the people in the restaurant surged toward the door.

The farmers looked up at Teddy, and when he followed, they did, too. Nola looked at me, wondering what to do, but suddenly there were a lot of people between us, and she followed them out the front door before I could tell her to stay put. Tyrique and Dawson shared a look, threw their napkins on the table in unison, and headed out, focused on Teddy. The two suits scrambled to follow them.

There was a bottleneck at the door, and by the time it started to clear, the rest of the room had gotten up to follow, probably just to watch whatever was going to happen.

I looked over at Moose.

Benjy shook his head. "This isn't good."

We got up to follow them, but the door was still jammed. Good thing there wasn't a fire, I thought. "Follow me," I said, leading them through the kitchen, toward the back door.

The dishwasher looked up at us, surprised. "Sorry, you can't come back here."

"Oops," I said as we filed past him and out the back door. "My mistake."

We got out in front of the crowd and got to the terminal next door just as the ferry was touching the dock. The crowd from the Black Dog was right behind us.

We ran along the rows of cars waiting in the staging area to get on the ferry. By the time we got to the ramp, it was already down and cars were driving off. The crowd surged forward, Teddy out in front. The car coming off slammed its brakes, almost rear-ended by the car behind it.

Teddy put his hands on the car's hood—a bit dramatically, I thought—and peered through the windshield as the driver honked his horn and gave him the finger. Teddy straightened, looking around him as the vehicles streamed off the ferry.

The guys directing traffic yelled a few words, but at the sight of the crowd they backed up and got on their walkie-talkies.

There were only a few cars left when a black, unmarked flatbed with a tarp-covered load pulled off. Teddy ran toward it, the rest of the crowd following right behind him. The driver tried to go around him, but Teddy stayed in front of the truck, slamming his hands onto the hood. The driver started honking and yelling, but as the crowd wrapped around the truck, he began to look scared. The rest of the cars pulled around him and sped away.

I spotted Nola in the crowd, hanging back. She looked scared, too. Off to one side, Tyrique and Dawson were scowling at Teddy. To the other side, the two suits were looking around nervously.

I pushed through the crowd, stepping up next to Teddy and

holding up my hands. "Calm down, everybody," I shouted over the din. "Let's not get out of hand."

"No!" Teddy shouted. "Don't calm down! If they're bringing these bees onto our island, things are already out of hand!"

The crowd circling the truck roared in agreement. Half a bagel bounced off the windshield, leaving a smudge of cream cheese.

The driver revved his engine, scared and angry and threatening to drive off regardless of who was in front of him. I knew the scene could easily turn violent.

Then a voice boomed out, "Stop it!" and everybody did. The crowd parted, making way for Jimmy Frank, the cop who had showed up at the Alehouse. "What the hell is going on here?" he asked, scolding and incredulous. "What's gotten into you people?"

Teddy stepped forward, the self-appointed leader.

Jimmy rolled his eyes.

"This," Teddy said, pointing at the truck. "They're bringing those goddamned industrial bees onto the island, with all their death and diseases."

Jimmy stepped back. "Bees?"

The driver of the truck opened the door and stood up on the edge. "What are you talking about?"

"We've got enough problems on the island," Teddy said. "We're trying to salvage what we can of this growing season. This is the last thing we need."

The driver looked confused. "I ain't got no bees."

People turned to look at him.

The driver shrugged. "I ain't got no bees. I'm delivering drywall. You can look if you want."

Jimmy shook his head and waved the guy back. "No, that won't be necessary. Now, you people get out of his way, and let the man go about his business." The crowd stepped aside, grumbling, and as the truck drove slowly past, Teddy jumped up on the back bumper and tore back the tarp. Drywall.

The crowd went quiet as the truck drove off, and as the sound of its engine receded, another sound took its place, a rhythmic thumping, *whump, whump, whump,* soft and low, but powerful enough that it was shaking my sternum. People started looking around, trying to find the source of it, but I knew the sound and I spotted it right away. Out over the water, two specks flying low, getting bigger and growing louder.

19

They seemed ominous, like angry insects. Death from above, I thought.

As they got closer, the others picked them out. Soon everyone had turned to stare at them.

The helicopters were massive, bright yellow with red markings, each dangling a white box almost as big as the helicopters themselves. The boxes looked like cargo containers, or RV trailers. One looked sleek, with rounded corners and windows, the other more boxy. It wasn't until they were almost on top of us that the red markings plastered across both helicopters and both trailers resolved into the Stoma Corporation logo.

A gasp worked its way through the crowd as people recognized the logo, but it was drowned out as the helicopters roared overhead, banking slightly to the south, the trailers swinging out as they did. Flying that low, they disappeared in seconds, nothing left but the receding *whump, whump, whump,* and the cluster of shocked faces.

"Jesus Christ," someone said. "That's Stoma Corporation. They're bringing in GMO bees!"

"She brought them here," one of the beekeepers said, pointing at Annalisa, and the noise ratcheted up again as the crowd constricted around her, yelling and cursing. "She works for Stoma!"

"I had nothing to do with it," she protested, putting up her hands. I stepped in front of her and so did Jimmy Frank, though it looked like he was wondering what the hell was going on.

I put my head next to his. "These people are losing it," I said. "You need to get her out of here."

His eyes lit up before he could hide it. Then he nodded seriously and spoke into her ear. With one arm around her shoulder, he held up his badge and led her through the crowd.

Maybe they thought he was arresting her, or maybe he just commanded that much respect, but no one followed for more than a few steps.

The crowd scattered, people rushing in all directions. I had the impression that some of them were going after the helicopters. I looked around for Nola, and spotted her sitting on a curb comforting an upset Gwen.

I went over to them. "You okay?" I asked Nola.

Gwen nodded, wiping her nose.

Nola got to her feet. "We're okay. Do you think those are really genetically engineered bees?"

I nodded.

"People are going to go nuts."

"Well, yeah, especially with your friend Teddy getting them all riled up."

"They should be riled up," she said indignantly. "Doyle, this is important."

"I know it is, but so is not inciting a mob to tear apart an innocent drywall delivery man." From the corner of my eye I saw Teddy speaking furtively on his cell phone, his eyes looking around nervously.

"Teddy was just trying to stop something terrible from happening," Nola said. "No one was hurt."

"Not yet," I replied.

Gwen put away her tissue and stood.

"Okay," Nola said, putting her arm around Gwen. "I have to get Gwen home. We can talk about this later."

As she said it, Teddy started fast-walking toward the low wall that separated the staging area from the sliver of beach that ran from the ferry terminal past the Black Dog. He looked like he was up to no good, but he always looked that way to me. Then I saw the two suits jogging after him and Blue's bodyguards following after them. It was like he was the Pied Piper of assholes, except he wasn't leading them off the island.

Teddy hopped over the railing and onto the sand. A couple of seconds later the two suits climbed after him and then Tyrique and Dawson did, too, with a little more difficulty.

When I caught up with them, Teddy was scurrying down the beach. The two suits had turned to face Dawson and Tyrique, looking like they were ready for action, but by the time I jumped down from the wall, they were pushing themselves up onto their hands and knees, their faces covered with a mixture of sand and blood. I stuck the landing, planting myself in the sand next to the two suits, between Blue's bodyguards and the rapidly receding Teddy Renfrew. I immediately asked myself why.

Tyrique snorted and Dawson shook his head, putting his hands together and cracking the knuckles in his fist. It was a cheesy move, but he did it well, producing a lot of sound.

"Listen up, Shorty," he said, looking down at me. "I ain't got a problem with you and I don't want to mess with no cop, but Richie Rich over there has been poking my man Blue for months, so why don't you let us teach him some manners and we'll be on our way."

I shook my head. "Can't do it. You know that."

I hoped he wasn't going to ask me why, because I didn't have a good answer. Instead he took a swing, surprisingly fast for a big guy. I mostly got out of the way, but let his fist graze the tip of my nose, so I could go down on my hands and knees and come back up with a fist full of sand.

Apparently, they didn't watch a lot of bad movies, because they totally didn't see it coming. I whipped my hand hard, right to left, and sprayed both their faces with sand. I think their eyes actually widened, getting as much of it in there as possible. Maybe they were surprised I'd pull such a dick move.

The two of them were rubbing their eyes, stomping in little circles and dropping a lot of F-bombs. I felt bad.

"Don't rub it," I told them. "You'll make it worse."

"Fuck you, motherfucker," Dawson said. "I'm going to make *you* worse in a second, little piece of shit motherfucker."

"Aw, what now?" said a voice from on high.

We all looked up to see Jimmy Frank standing up on the wall. Actually, just me and the suits looked up; Tyrique and Dawson were just tracking the sound of his voice.

"What are you doing now?" he asked me with a tone of disapproval.

I pointed at the suits. "I didn't do those two," I said. Then I pointed at Tyrique and Dawson. "These two did those two." They were staggering toward the sound of my voice, so I took a few steps to the side. "Then they came at me, so I threw sand in their faces." I stepped to the side again.

Jimmy shook his head. "Kind of a dick move," he said. "You boys fell for that?"

They were both still rubbing their eyes, despite what I told them.

"Who even does shit like that?" Tyrique said.

"You tried to hit me," I reminded him.

"Pussy!"

"All right, stop," Jimmy said. "You guys want to file charges?"

"Them?" I asked.

"No, I want to file my foot up his ass," Dawson replied.

"I'll take that as a 'no.' How about you two?" he asked the two suits, now climbing to their feet, wiping the bloody sand off their faces and flinging it into the water.

The one with the buzz cut looked at the older one, who shook his head. "No."

"All right," Jimmy said with a snort. "I'm going to get these knuckleheads some water for their eyes." He turned to me. "You should probably clear out."

I climbed up onto the wall. "Annalisa is okay?"

He nodded, lowering his voice. "Dr. Paar is waiting for you at the station. Right across the street."

As I cut across the parking areas, everything seemed back to normal. A few latecomers were hurrying onto the ferry, probably with no idea what had just been going on.

Inside the police station, Annalisa was sitting in a plastic chair in the waiting area. She jumped to her feet and threw her arms around my neck, burying her face against my chest. Her hair smelled like flowers.

I knew she just needed to be held, so I put my arms around her. I could feel the warmth from her, feel her breasts pressing against me. Before my body could respond, I pulled away from her.

"Are you okay?" I asked.

She looked up at me, her eyes pooling with tears. "Those people wanted to tear me apart."

"No, they didn't. They were just upset."

"No, if you and Jimmy hadn't been there, they would have hurt me."

She took a step back and smoothed out her clothes. "Is it okay out there?"

"Totally okay."

She nodded. "Moose and Benjy want us to meet them back at the BeeWatch lab."

20

The lab was more like a hut attached to a shed. The shed was actually pretty nice, temperature controlled, watertight, made of reinforced steel. That's where the monitoring equipment was kept. The lab consisted of a ten-by-ten wooden structure with a window and a door and the BeeWatch logo on the side.

The tops of the trees were still bathed in a rosy glow, but the afternoon warmth was gone and sitting on plastic patio chairs, drinking beers, Benjy and Moose looked cold and grim.

They stood up when they saw us, and led us inside. It was warmer inside, but tight. There was a workstation along one wall, with two chairs, a couple of servers on the floor, and two large screens.

Benjy moved the mouse and the screen came to life. As we waited for the progress bar to make its way across the screen, Annalisa asked quietly, "So was that the GMO bees? Is that what that was?"

"You tell us," Moose replied.

Benjy gave him a disapproving look, then nodded. "Apparently the USDA gave Stoma a provisional approval for the bee usage on the Island of Martha's Vineyard. They got an application from Johnny Blue."

Annalisa put her hand over her mouth.

"Farmers in some other states have applied for a special exemption," Moose added, deliberately speaking to me and not to Annalisa. "They want to accelerate what little approval process there is so they can use the bees on the mainland. Stoma is using this as a pilot program. They're hoping if they can make it here, they can take it anywhere."

Benjy sighed. "Farmers are scared they're going to lose their crops."

Moose rolled his eyes. "Well, sure. But GMO bees for God's sake? Untested mutants that can fly around and mix with other bees? That can displace other bees? Hybridize with them? Christ, that can sting people and inject genetically modified venom into them?"

Benjy put up his hands. "Hey, I hear you buddy. I'm on your side. I'm just saying, it's not easy being a farmer."

The screen blinked and displayed a series of graphs, most of them incomprehensible. But it was easy enough to read the trends: from left to right a bunch of wavy lines, one bold and a half dozen other ones, all showing a brief gentle incline, then a jagged and erratic decline ending in a precipitous drop off, down to nearly nothing.

Benjy turned to Annalisa. "See?"

She nodded grimly.

"You come up with the same thing?" he asked her.

She nodded slightly. "Preliminary results are pretty clear, yeah. But the program was still crunching the numbers when I left."

"So what does that mean?" I asked, pointing at the screen.

"It means we're fucked," Moose whispered.

"That's the honeybee activity we've been tracking," Benjy replied, pointing to the most prominent line. "You can see it's been suffering for a while. But just this week, it's been plummeting. That's scary enough, but these"—he moved his hand over the lesser lines—"these are the other native pollinators, mostly bumblebees. The honeybee line is devastating and tragic, but not altogether unexpected. But these mean that whatever is happening to the honeybees is also happening to the other pollinators. That's new. And it's scary as hell."

"But there's still a chance it could be equipment failure, right?" Moose said. "I mean, all this cutting-edge equipment is still in the experimental stage, right?"

Benjy shrugged. "It's possible. We'll know more when we check the analysis Annalisa's been running. And when we get the next round of data after the resets."

He looked at Annalisa. "You think your data is ready?"

She looked at her watch. "I think so, yeah. We can go right now, if you'd like."

Everyone turned to leave except Moose. "Even if the data's wrong, if the honeybees are limping along like they have been, we're still fucked. If those helicopters were bringing in Stoma's GMO bees, we're fucked. The battle's over. Once they get out, they're out." He shook his head slowly. "No offense, Annalisa, but Stoma is bad news. They don't fuck around. And if they've spent millions of dollars on a genetically modified superbee, it's going to make its way onto the market. Right now, looks like we're the market."

Moose rode with Annalisa and me, a sort of chaperone, I think. Benjy followed behind us. We passed Johnny Blue's big gate, already pelted with eggs, and we shared a snicker over that. As the road turned to the left, I tapped the brakes.

The road up ahead was almost blocked by a milling crowd. Hard to tell in the waning light, but it looked like a lot of the same people from the incident at the ferry.

"Oh no," Annalisa said, her voice quavery as she put her hand over her mouth.

"Is that your lab?"

She nodded. "On the right."

"They might not be here for you," I told her.

"That's part of Johnny Blue's property," she said.

The crowd was on the left-hand side of the street, and as we got nearer, I could see they were facing away from her lab.

A couple of faces in the crowd turned to watch as we approached, but most ignored us completely. Benjy was a couple of car lengths back. When we reached the crowd, Annalisa pointed to a driveway on the right and said, "It's here."

As we turned in, I looked in the rearview mirror and saw what all the commotion was about. Across the road, forty yards back, were the two white lab units the helicopters had been carrying, a big red Stoma logo on each of them. Moose and Annalisa turned in their seats to look out the back window, gasping when they saw it.

"Holy shit," Moose said.

"Oh, no," Annalisa whispered, a new edge to her voice.

Before I could ask what about it was bothering her, the driveway turned to the right, and there, in front of us, was a similar lab unit, but smaller than the other two and more like a regular trailer. Above the Stoma logo was BEE FUTURES—A DIVISION OF in much smaller letters. Luckily, it wasn't visible from the road.

"This is where you work?" Moose snorted. "No, they don't own you."

She gave him a dirty look as we got out of the car, the closest thing to a rise I'd seen him get out of her. Benjy pulled in behind us.

"Look, I know this looks bad," Annalisa said as we walked up to the lab. "But this is the deal I have with them: they supply the equipment, so they put their name all over it." She took out her key card. "They leave me alone and let me do my work. And it's really nice equipment."

She opened the door and we followed her inside. By the way

Benjy and Moose were eyeing the equipment, I could tell it was as nice as it looked. The chairs and the carpet were nice, too.

Annalisa flipped on a couple of switches and the screens came to life. Then she opened the door to the next room and screamed.

21

Almost before the scream died in her throat, she was apologizing. "I'm so sorry," she said. "You startled me."

"My apologies to you, Dr. Paar," said a thin voice. As he emerged from the shadows of the office, I recognized Jordan Sumner, her boss. "I certainly had no intention of frightening you. It seems as though we are going to be neighbors for a while, so I thought the neighborly thing would be to come and say hello."

As he looked from her to us, his smile drooped.

Annalisa cleared her throat. "Dr. Sumner, these are some of my colleagues from BeeWatch, the nonprofit entity I told you about. We are working together on a census of the local bee populations."

"I see," he said as he looked at Benjy and Moose. His smile faded further when he got to me, and his eyes lingered. I didn't think he was buying it.

"It's an honor, Dr. Sumner," I said.

His smile returned. "The honor is mine, Detective Carrick."

He looked away without watching my reaction, instead enjoying Annalisa's. Before she could try to explain, he clapped his hands together. "Well, I won't keep you any longer from your work. I just wanted to stop by and say hello. I'll let myself out."

As soon as he was gone, Annalisa slumped into one of the plush swivel chairs that lined the work space and the rest of us exhaled simultaneously.

"No," Moose said. "You don't work for the bad guys."

Benjy laughed. "Seriously, is that guy for real?"

"Yes," Annalisa said with a shudder. "He's for real."

It was almost dark when we left. Annalisa's numbers confirmed Benjy's, which meant that unless the monitoring equipment was malfunctioning, the situation was as bad as they'd feared. We filed outside and waited quietly while Annalisa locked up. She asked me for a ride, and I said yes.

Moose asked me when I was leaving the island.

"I don't know yet," I replied. "Tomorrow?" I wasn't working until Tuesday, and I realized I was dreading it. "Why?"

"We have to check all the data again tomorrow, see if the reset made any difference." He shrugged. "Could use the help. Even if just for the morning."

I nodded. "Yeah, I could do that."

He announced he was riding with Benjy, but he gave me a look as he said it, like, *I'm giving you some privacy, but I trust you to do the right thing with it.*

The crowd across the street had dwindled, but was still there. Benjy turned right out of the driveway, and I turned left, watching his truck dwindle in the rearview. I suddenly felt very alone with Annalisa.

When we pulled up next to her car, she turned to me. "If you want to follow me home, you could come in for coffee or a beer."

"You know I have a girlfriend, right?"

Her mouth twisted into a half smile. "I wondered about that.

Nola, right? Are you sure? You two don't seem like you are really together."

I shrugged. "We're going through a bit of a rough spot. That's all."

She opened the door. "You're a good man, Doyle Carrick."

I looked at her in mock horror. "I am many things, madam, but I am not a good man."

She laughed. "You deny it, but it's true."

I didn't point out that I hadn't said no, but the moment had passed and it was for the best.

"I hope Nola appreciates what she's got."

I watched her get into her car and waited as she drove off. Then I drove back to the farm.

I felt guilty when I pulled up next to the cabin, even if I was technically, a "good man."

Nola was standing with a group of young farmers in front of the other cabin. As I walked up, I saw that Teddy was in the middle, sitting on the step. Had I known, I wouldn't have gone over, but I'd already been spotted, so it was too late to turn back.

"Hey," Nola called out.

"Hey, you. What're you doing?"

"Strategizing," Teddy said. He had a stick in his hand and he was drawing in the dirt. In the darkness. "Figuring out the next steps with these damned GMO bees."

I nodded. "Say, who were those guys on the beach today?"

Nola did a quick back and forth between us.

"Johnny Blue's thugs."

"No, I meant the other two."

He laughed. "That's a long story."

"I'd love to hear it some day."

He laughed again. "So, Nola tells me you're leaving tomorrow."

That bothered me. "Probably."

Nola's head snapped around to look at me.

"Moose asked me to help him with the bee monitoring."

I couldn't read her reaction.

"You're a helpful guy. Anyway," Teddy said, looking back down at the ground, "like I was saying, we need a legal effort, a public relations effort—"

"Public relations?" said the guy with the Amish beard. "Are you kidding? We need to—"

Teddy silenced him with a look, then made enough of a show of looking at me that the bearded wonder followed his gaze and fell quiet.

Sure, my feelings were a little hurt, but to be fair, I am a narc.

I kissed Nola on the side of the head and retreated to the cabin.

When she came in a half hour later, I was already in bed, my feet sticking out the bottom. It had been a tiring couple of days, and Friday's all-nighter was sneaking back up on me. It wasn't even nine o'clock, and I was starting to think of sleep. I had been thinking of other things—things like Annalisa—and trying desperately not to.

When Nola came in, she pressed the door closed behind her with a soft but firm click. There was something almost seductive about it, something that stirred me.

That's right, I thought. Nola, not Annalisa.

"Hey," I said.

"Hey," she replied quietly as she pulled each of the blinds down.

I took a deep breath. "Look, sorry about today, if it seemed like I don't think this is important. I know it is. It's just, I've seen situations like that get out of control. Innocent people get hurt."

"I know," she said, pulling off her T-shirt. She reached behind her and undid her bra. Obviously, I'd seen them a hundred times. A hundred times each. But somehow the distance between us made it seem more provocative, a sexy and seductive gesture. She saw me looking, and she smiled. She wriggled out of her jeans and walked to the small sink in just her panties, her pert behind shaking as she brushed her teeth.

I reached for her as she got into bed and she gave me a friendly peck. When I reached for her again, she pulled away. "You know we can't, right? There's people all around. These walls are like paper. Teddy's right out front."

I would have been disappointed, but invoking Teddy's name while explaining why we couldn't have sex left me downright grumpy.

"Okay," I said, rolling over. "Well, goodnight."

"Are you all right?" she said. "We just can't, okay?"

"Okay," I said, closing my eyes. As I drifted off to sleep, thoughts of Annalisa returned. This time, I let them.

22

"I have to go to work." The voice filtered through a haze, penetrating my sleeping brain. Nola was smiling down on me, her hand on my forehead, caressing my cheek.

I smiled back at her.

"Let me know when you leave, okay? I'll take a break."

"Okay," I said, still half asleep.

She kissed me on my forehead. "You take care of yourself, Doyle Carrick."

I closed my eyes, and when I opened them I was alone. The room was a little brighter and the sun a little higher. Still only ten after seven.

I was supposed to meet Moose at eight, but I needed a coffee, so I left early and headed over to Vineyard Haven. Somewhere, I'd seen that Mocha Mott had a location there as well.

I was turning onto Edgartown Road when I saw them, a few car lengths back. It was the two suits, this time driving what looked like a Bentley. When I looked closer I saw that they had changed their suits as well.

I was impressed that they were at least trying to be discreet, but as soon as the thought crossed my mind, they swerved into the left lane and passed two cars, now coming up on me. For a moment I thought they were going to try to run me off the road, but you wouldn't use a Bentley for that. As they pulled up behind me, I noticed a third person sitting in the backseat.

I pulled over abruptly and stopped on the side of the road. The younger one was behind the wheel, and he seemed stymied by the move. He didn't have enough warning to pull in behind me, so he found himself stopped beside me, double-parked and blocking traffic. He tried to back into the space behind me, but the guy behind him had already pulled up too close. Finally, he swung into the space in front of me.

I got out and walked up to the driver's side window. It was open.

"License and registration please," I said, using the same tone I used when giving out tickets.

The driver looked flustered. "License and registration," I repeated, waving my hand like, "Come on."

The kid was reaching for his wallet when his partner placed a hand on his arm.

The kid looked out the window at me. "So what, are you a cop?"

"Yes," I said.

That was when the back window slowly rolled down. "Detective Carrick," said the older man sitting in the back.

"Look," I said. "I don't have any Grey Poupon in my car, if that's what this is about."

The guy in the back smiled. I didn't like it. "Detective Carrick, I apologize for sneaking up on you like that. But I was hoping I could have a word with you. Just a few minutes of your time."

"Who are you?"

"Darren Renfrew. I'm Teddy's father."

Interesting. "What do you want to talk about?"

"It's somewhat delicate. Could we go somewhere else?"

I looked at my watch. "I'm actually busy at the moment. I've got places to go and coffee to drink. I could meet you this afternoon."

"Why don't you come out to the compound? You can be my guest for lunch. The house is called Windshift. It's on Main Street in West Chop."

Part of me was screaming, *Get the hell away from here and have no part of it.* But I was curious about Teddy Renfrew. I liked the idea of finding out more about him.

"What time?"

It took four hours to switch out all the hard drives and reposition all the monitoring stations. Moose asked several times if I was okay. He said I seemed distracted.

I was distracted. Some of it was because of Annalisa. She had invaded my dreams the night before, and throughout the morning, little snippets came back to me. *No, Annalisa, I am not a good man.*

Mostly, however, it was because of my meeting with Darren Renfrew. The Bentley made total sense; Teddy Renfrew reeked of spoiled little punk who didn't think about money because he didn't have to worry about money. I couldn't help wondering where his father stood in all this.

When we were done, Moose offered to buy me lunch, but I told him I was busy. He looked like he was assuming I was going to see Annalisa, but he didn't ask so I didn't offer.

"So you headed back to Philly, then?" he asked.

"I don't even know." Part of me didn't like the idea of leaving things so unsettled with Nola. And while things with Annalisa were settled, to be honest, I didn't want to leave without seeing her again. And there was definitely a part that thought the other two parts were crazy, and that I needed to get as far away from here as possible, before I got myself into real trouble.

West Chop was at the top of the island, across Vineyard Haven

Harbor from East Chop. Together, they formed the point at the top of the triangle. I had assumed a "chop" was some archaic New Englander phrase for an obscure coastal land formation, like a bight or a cove. Turns out, the two chops together look like a top jaw and bottom jaw of something taking a bite.

Both of them were very scenic, with expensive houses and great views overlooking the water. Renfrew's house might not have been the nicest, but of the houses I could see, that weren't hidden behind acres of scrub or huge fieldstone walls, it was by far the biggest, the most ostentatious, and presumably the most expensive.

I drove up the long driveway and parked in the circle by the wide front steps.

The place was a bit of an architectural mash-up, part mansion, part McMansion, with turrets and terraces and balconies, all covered with cedar shingles—I guess to make it fit in. In the back was a complex of tennis courts and gardens. The place had everything except taste or any sense of proportion.

A young dark-haired woman came to the door, but before she could open it, the young guy with the buzz cut came up behind her and sent her away. He opened the door and gave me a squint, letting me know he was a badass. He seemed a little ticked off, maybe because I almost gave him a ticket, or because I hadn't had any mustard.

"This way," he said, stepping back from the door. I followed him through a cavernous living room, out onto a slate patio and down a few steps to the expansive front lawn.

It was an impressive view, looking out onto the harbor and, beyond that, the ocean. A line of dark clouds was assembled to the north.

It looked as though a ferry was coming in, a big fancy white one I hadn't seen before. But it wasn't moving, and I realized it wasn't a ferry, it was either a small cruise ship or a very, very big yacht.

In the middle of the lawn was a cluster of white Adirondack furniture. Darren Renfrew was sitting in one of the chairs, looking out onto the water. It seemed a little too Zen for the mental image I had of him, but as I approached, I noticed he was on the phone. And he wasn't happy.

"Look, you flea, I don't care about any of that. I don't care whose water that is. This is my view, and I paid thirty million dollars for it. Having those bees of his on my island is bad enough, but you tell that Aussie trash that he needs to move that god-awful shit can out of my view. . . . Bullshit you can't do anything about it. Yes, you goddamn can, and you better, or you can kiss your job good-bye and I'll find a harbormaster who's not such a chicken shit, you hear me?" He shot to his feet. "Don't tell me about the goddamned town council. I can replace them, too, goddamn it. . . . *Enough!*" He held the phone in front of his face, screaming into it. "I want that boat gone *now!*"

His thumbs frantically jabbed at the screen until the phone was disconnected. Then he lowered it, his arm waving it around, like the limb itself needed the release of slamming the phone down. Eventually he just kind of ran out of steam, and fell back, limp, into his chair.

After a moment, he looked around, his face drained.

The suit standing beside me cleared his throat. "Carrick's here."

23

Renfrew managed a weak smile. "Thank you, Percy. Please tell Marta."

Percy nodded, glanced at me, and then turned and walked back across the grass.

"He's a good man," Renfrew said, causing me to reconsider my denials with Annalisa. Maybe the standards were lower than I had realized.

He sat up a little straighter, his moment of exhaustion apparently passed. "Thank you for coming, Mr. Carrick." He stood up and shook my hand, firm and measured if a little damp. He led me to a table set with fine china, glassware, and flowers, a pitcher of ice water with lemon slices. "I can assure you, the lunch itself will be worth the trip, apart from anything else. I hope you like lobster. No shellfish allergies or anything of that nature?"

"No, that sounds fine."

"I can easily arrange something else, but Marta's bisque is legendary. A favorite of presidents and celebrities."

I almost wanted to ask for something else just for that, but I actually like lobster bisque. "So what did you want to discuss?"

"Would you like something to drink, Mr. Carrick? Some local beer or imported wine?" He smiled, as if that were funny.

I filled my glass from the pitcher. "Water's fine."

"I love this view," he said, turning to look out across the water. "When I'm here I watch the sunrise every single day." The line of clouds was closer now, a sheer wall of ominous gray chasing the sunlight across the water. "It's quite something, isn't it?"

"Certainly is," I replied, thinking if this was what he wanted to talk about, the bisque had better be phenomenal. And there had better be crackers.

"It's perfect, except for that monstrosity out there." He pointed the corner of his phone at the anchored ship. It didn't really bother me, but I thought it best to keep that thought to myself. "Garish and ostentatious. Tacky, really, don't you think?"

It reminded me a bit of his house, but I kept that quiet, too.

"Do you know who Archibald Pearce is?" he asked, apparently not really caring about my opinion of the boat. I knew the name, but before I could place it, he went on. "He's the head of Stoma Corporation . . . A bit of a rival of mine."

I willed my eyebrows not to rise at that. If this guy was a rival of Archie Pearce, he was richer than I thought. Stoma was massive, and Archie Pearce had made it that way.

Renfrew shook his head. "He's parked that thing in my front yard, just to get my goat." He smiled, looking out at the boat as if it wasn't bothering him. As if I hadn't just seen his little hissy fit. As he continued to stare, his face grew red.

I cleared my throat, wondering if I should let him know that marine demolition wasn't my specialty.

"Sorry," he said, snapping out of it, his face once again placid. A heavy-set, dark-haired woman of about sixty arrived with a tray: two bowls of faintly pink bisque and a heavy glass chalice of oyster crackers. Marta, I assumed.

Renfrew acknowledged her with a twitch of his eyebrow as he

placed his napkin on his lap. I gave her a nice smile, which she seemed to think was very strange.

"I wanted to thank you for your efforts on behalf of my son," Renfrew continued. I didn't reply, and he looked up at me. "Teddy. From what I hear, you've saved his bacon more than once these last few days."

Renfrew spooned into his bisque, so I dropped a few crackers in mine and did the same. I had to restrain myself from running into the house and asking Marta to marry me. It was good soup. Renfrew nodded, as if he had some idea of what I was thinking and he understood.

"Are you and Teddy friends?" he asked.

"Not really," I said. "No."

"Good." He nodded. "The boy's a bit of a hippie reprobate. He tends to attract trouble. Actually, he tends to seek it out. All well and good, I guess, if you have to get it out of your system in your teens. I did my share of cow-tipping in my day, but by now he should be over it." He looked at me. "And he's not."

I stopped eating and wiped my mouth. My soup was almost gone, and I needed Renfrew to catch up, because if I finished before he did, I'd be tempted to take his. Maybe I could ask for seconds, but that seemed somehow uncouth.

"He seems to be doing okay, running that farm and everything. That's not an easy business to make a living." I couldn't believe I was defending the guy.

Renfrew laughed derisively. "He's not making a living from that farm, I assure you. It's been losing money since the day he bought it."

"So, what do you want from me?" I asked. Then I went back to the soup. I couldn't help it.

"You've met Percy and McCarter?"

"If that's their names, yes."

"It's their job to keep Teddy out of trouble, to keep an eye on him, and let him know they are keeping an eye on him."

I smiled condescendingly before I could hide my face.

Renfrew shrugged. "So far, they've actually been quite successful. Maybe he hasn't put them to the test, but before they were on the scene, Teddy was involved in a series of scrapes, legal and otherwise. He pulled several stunts with some college friends, a half-assed band of would-be eco-warriors. Not terribly serious, mind you: a little spray-paint, defacing a sign, letting some lab rats go. But embarrassing, nonetheless." He looked up meaningfully. "To me."

"I'm glad you've got it under control." I took another break from the soup, wiped my mouth, ate a cracker. The storm was getting closer, the wind picking up and the clouds sliding in front of the sun.

"That's just it, Mr. Carrick. Recent events have shaken my confidence in Percy and McCarter. They are what they are, and they can't get close to Teddy, wouldn't know what to do if they could. Plus, Teddy seems . . . restless. And I am at a very sensitive stage of some very important negotiations. Very important, indeed. I cannot afford any distractions, or embarrassments."

"Can't you just threaten to cut him off?"

"I wish I could. His grandmother left him that land. The money he is losing is from a very healthy trust fund."

I finished my soup, and as I put the spoon down, a raindrop landed in the middle of the bowl, making a little crater in the last of the bisque.

Renfrew looked up at the sky, squinting. A raindrop landed on his forehead, and he blinked. Then he looked down at his bowl, still half full. A raindrop landed in the middle of it, then another. He looked sad. I was sad, too, and it wasn't even my soup. He smiled wistfully. "Perhaps we should go inside."

It started to rain in earnest as we walked across the lawn, but there was an unspoken agreement that we were men, and this was serious, and we weren't going to run. And we definitely weren't going to squeal or giggle.

Marta was waiting for us at the door with two towels. I wanted to tell her how good her bisque was, but she gave me a stony look that convinced me not to.

"Well," I said, wiping off my face, "thanks for the bisque. It was as good as you said, but I'm still not sure why I am here."

Renfrew stopped blotting his face and folded the towel, placing it on a mahogany sideboard behind him. "I have a proposition for you."

I waited.

"I would like you to keep an eye on Teddy. You don't have to do anything, mind you, just keep an eye on him. Let me know if he's up to anything that could hurt him. Or hurt me. Just for the next few weeks."

"You want me to spy on him?"

"I want you to look out for him, keep him out of trouble."

"What makes you think I'm the guy for that job?"

He shrugged. "You've been doing a pretty good job of it so far. And Percy and McCarter haven't."

"I already have a job. I'm a cop."

"Yes, I know. And I know you have plenty of vacation time accrued and a boss who wants you to take it—"

I opened my mouth to protest, but he held up a hand. "Please. I have many friends, and I was just doing my due diligence. If I didn't know a lot about you, I wouldn't be making you this offer."

When I closed my mouth, he lowered his hand. "You also have an employment contract that allows you to take jobs on the side."

"I don't think—"

"I'll pay you five thousand dollars a day if you can help me until Friday. After that, if you no longer want to do it, fine. If you want to stay, I'll give you a bonus, with another bonus each week for the next six weeks."

"That's a lot of money."

He smiled condescendingly. "To you it is. I'm not going to pay you any more than that, but believe me, there are many people I am paying a lot more than that, and they will not be doing anything remotely as valuable to me. And I'd hate to tell you how much I have been paying those two."

I laughed. I'm not crazy about people looking into my private matters, but apparently I mind it less when they offer me thirty grand. "Well, yes, I am allowed to do side jobs, but nothing illegal, and this sounds a little shady."

Renfrew threw back his head and had a big, loud, fake laugh. "Detective Carrick, I am a very successful, very legitimate businessman. Frankly, my main concern is in avoiding anything illegal or untoward. Here." He turned to the sideboard and opened a cabinet. He turned back holding four bundles of fifties and four bundles of hundreds. "Here is thirty thousand dollars, cash, in advance. I'll send you a 1099 form so you know everything is on the up and up. I'll even call this net, and I'll take care of your withholding, Social Security, all of that. All very up and up."

He sighed and held down the money. I didn't like seeing it go away. "Here's the thing," he said, lowering his voice. "I'm hosting an event here on Wednesday. It is extremely important. Senators, heads of state, you name it. Percy and McCarter are too obvious, too clumsy, and too stupid, and I simply cannot afford to have that little whelp causing me any embarrassment between now and then. Between now and the end of the week, really, but first things first. You're already traveling in the same circles as Teddy. So please . . ." He held up the money again. "You don't even have to be as involved as you've been. Just keep an eye on him, let me know if you notice anything suspicious. If you decide after Wednesday even that is too onerous, well, you can walk away, keep the money and I'll know I've misjudged you, even against your advice."

I wanted to keep an eye on Teddy Renfrew. I wanted to know what he was up to so it didn't blow back onto Nola. I thought about Nola and him, thought about his secret late-night meetings, and I thought about me being four hundred miles away, on the mainland.

I thought about Moose and Benjy and the bees. I thought about Annalisa, too, about people following her, threatening her. And even while I thought about her, I thought about Nola again, and the house we had looked at, the down payment we didn't have. I knew the money wasn't the main issue, but still, I pictured us again in that house and I felt my hands take the money.

"Excellent," Renfrew said. I half expected him to call me Smithers.

He handed me a card with his phone number on it. "You let me know if you find anything, anything suspicious or potentially embarrassing. Marta also makes a wonderful quahog chowder. Come for lunch next Saturday, and we can discuss the next phase of your employment."

24

By the time I left Renfrew, the sun was back out. I felt almost giddy. I had plenty of concerns about the whole turn of events, but for the moment, I was thinking happy thoughts.

I called Lieutenant Suarez and told him I was taking the time. He grunted. "You putting in for leave?"

"Vacation time, if that's okay with you."

"There's leave if you want it, but it's up to you. You got plenty of vacation, so suit yourself. When you coming back?"

"Probably next week. We'll see how it goes."

He grunted again. "Let me know." Then he was gone.

I texted Danny. "Hey partner. Taking another week."

He texted me back. "Good."

The interaction didn't fill me with warm fuzzies, but I did feel as though a weight had been lifted off of me. Maybe I'd been dreading going back to work more than I'd thought. Or maybe I'd been dreading leaving the island more than I'd thought. The question, then, was why? Maybe because of Nola, although she was a little hot and cold and tricky all over. Maybe it was Annalisa, although as much as she was haunting my thoughts, I knew she was probably never going to be anything more than something for Nola and me to fight about.

That left Teddy Renfrew and the crazy bee stuff going down on the island. It pained me to think that I might be more excited about a douchebag I detested and a case I wasn't involved in than the affections of two beautiful women.

The first stop was the rental place at the airport. Steve was very happy to see me, even happier that I was trading up into something sportier, and happier still that I went whole hog on the extra insurance.

After a quick lesson on how to lower the top, I was screaming across the island in a bright yellow convertible Mustang. I felt a little conspicuous, but I figured, if not now, when? I'd been driving these roads for a few days, and they were begging for something sporty.

The second stop was going to be the Wesley Hotel, to get the honeymoon suite and surprise Nola, so she could stay somewhere nice while she was working, somewhere my feet didn't stick out of the bed. But then I tapped the brakes. She might want a place closer to the farm. She might want to ask some questions, make sure the room was chemical-free. I smiled to myself—crisis averted—and turned the car around.

Instead, I bought a baguette and some cheese and a cold six-pack of Offshore Ale.

The Mustang hugged the road, surging through the curves and over the rolling hills. The afternoon was chilly, but I drove with the top down anyway.

When I arrived at the farm, Elaine and Gwen were just coming up from the fields. They stopped when they saw me. Elaine pointed at the car and laughed. Gwen turned and yelled back at the field. Then they went on their way, both of them shaking their heads.

I felt my cheeks redden a bit, but it was a fun car. I walked up to the path leading to the field and saw Nola coming up to greet me. We smiled and waved and came together in a long kiss. She held my hand as we walked back toward the cabin.

"How did it go with Moose?" she asked.

"Okay, I guess. I mean, we did all the work we had to do. They're pretty freaked out."

She sighed. "We all are."

"How's your day been going?"

"Farming," she said with a laugh and a shrug. "It's hard work, but I love it. I've never done all this hand-pollinating before. It's insanely labor-intensive, but it's giving me a much more intimate sense of how the whole thing works." She looked at me and smiled awkwardly. "So, I guess you're leaving, then," she said, sounding almost sad. Before I could answer, she said, "What's that?"

She was pointing at the Mustang.

"I have good news," I told her. Her face looked like it was not expecting good news. "I'm staying."

Her eye twitched. "What?"

"I'm staying." I added a little shrug, nonchalant. I was starting to wonder if I had somehow miscalculated. "For the week."

"What are you talking about? How? Why?"

It wasn't actually until that moment that I realized I needed a story. A story other than the truth.

I needed a lie.

"Um . . ."

"Doyle, what are you doing?"

Trying to think of a lie, I thought. Instead, I said, "What do you mean?"

"What do I mean?" She seemed like she was about to cry. "You can't stay."

"What?"

"Doyle, don't you get it? You can't stay." She wiped her eyes with the cuff of her shirt. "You know how much I care about you, but . . . but when I said I needed a break from the city, I wasn't just talking about the city. I meant you, too, Doyle. I need a break from you."

My brain knew that the best thing to do was to stay calm, tell her I understood. She needed some space. The last thing she needed was for me to overreact and cause a scene. My brain assured me her reaction was natural and healthy, and our relationship would be stronger for it. Unfortunately, by the time my brain had finished talking, I was fishtailing up the driveway in a cloud of dust.

Teddy Renfrew ran onto his back porch to see what was causing the commotion. He watched as I drove past, and just before I swung around the house, I saw him turn to look back at Nola, standing there crying into her hands.

I pushed the accelerator down to the floor.

25

Driving without direction, I ended up in Oak Bluffs, in the narrow winding streets and tiny cottages of the Campgrounds. I wanted to drive fast and angry and this was absolutely the wrong place for it. But once in, I couldn't seem to get out. No matter where I went, the big cross on top of the church loomed over me.

I was becoming increasingly frustrated when I pulled up next to the big pink house with the tulip flag and the bad smell. A rough-looking workman with an impressive belly and knee-high boots was standing ankle deep in the front lawn. The truck parked on the cross street said BILL'S SEPTIC SERVICE on the side.

"How do I get out of here?" I yelled.

He pointed at the next left, and I took it. Minutes later I was driving along the ocean.

West seemed to hold fewer people, and that's what I was in the mood for, so I drove toward the Gay Head Cliffs. Hell, if I could find my way there, maybe I'd drive right off them.

I smiled at the juvenile melodrama of it. Yeah, that'd show them, I thought, mocking myself. The speedometer was reading eighty-five, so I took my foot off the gas and coasted down to seventy. I'd calmed down a little, but figured maybe I should calm down a little more. I chucked the cheese and the bread into a trash can by the side of the road, then pried open one of the beers and drank half of it. I didn't want to risk getting caught with an open bottle in the car, so I drank the rest of it, too.

The Gay Head Lighthouse was rising up on the right. I knew that at the height of the summer, the road that looped in front of the lighthouse would be crawling with tourists, parked up with buses and cars. But as I rocketed toward it at seventy miles an hour, I could see it was completely deserted. I smiled and let my foot sink down again, shooting up the hill, then screeching around the first curve of the loop, my rear wheels drifting just enough to be fun. I laughed out loud on the straightaway, then held on, screeching around the second curve. As I straightened out to shoot back toward the entrance, though, I took my foot off the gas.

A police cruiser was stopped at the entrance to State Road, blocking both lanes. My foot came down on the brake, and I eased to a stop next to it.

It was Jimmy Frank. He shook his head as he got out of his car and walked over to mine.

I held up my license, making sure he saw my badge.

He waved it down. "I know who you are, Detective Doyle Carrick. I looked you up after the fight at the Alehouse. . . . Made some calls after the incident at the ferry, too. What I want to know is why you're driving like a maniac around one of our island treasures."

I nodded, like I understood. "Been a rough day, Sergeant Frank. Girl trouble. I was blowing off a little steam." I looked around us. "There wasn't anyone around, so I kind of hoped no one would mind."

He leaned toward the window, resting an arm across the top of the door. "Sorry to hear about your woes." He put his face closer to the window and sniffed. "Say, you been drinking?"

"I had a beer," I said, wondering which way this was going.

He nodded. "Take a walk with me," he said. "I'll buy you another."

"Okay." What was I going to say?

We parked our cars and walked down one of the side roads, in awkward manly silence until he said, "So, what's your story, Detective Doyle Carrick?"

I wondered myself what my story was. I decided to start with the basics.

"My girlfriend got a temporary job up here for a couple of weeks. I drove her up here, decided to take a little vacation time."

He looked at me. "That the girlfriend you're having problems with?"

I nodded. The road was secluded, lined with thick brush. I wondered where we were headed.

He nodded back. "What's the deal with you and Teddy Renfrew?"

"That's who she's working for. She's a farmer."

"A lot of people don't like that guy."

"I'm one of them."

He laughed at that, pointing to the left, down a side road that could have been a driveway. As we angled down it, he looked at me, serious. "What about that whole thing in Dunston? You want to tell me what that was about?"

"Most of it I can't talk about. My folks had a house there. When they died, I inherited it. I went up to take care of the house. That's where I met Nola."

"On suspension?" he asked as we turned from the narrow rutted road onto a narrow rutted driveway.

I sighed. "Yes, on suspension. Caught a lead, busted a drug ring. Turned into a whole lot of other stuff that I'm not allowed to talk about."

"I heard it was some crazy shit."

"You heard right about that." Crazy shit, indeed.

We walked a little farther without talking but I knew we weren't done.

"What's the deal with you and Dr. Paar?"

"Annalisa?" I laughed for no reason. "Why do you ask?"

He gave me a sidelong look. "That part of the problem with your girlfriend?"

"No. Why do you ask?"

He let out a deep sigh. "This whole bee thing has a lot of people worked up. People on the island, but people off the island, too." He looked at me. "People in high-up places. And they don't want any trouble however any of this goes." He shook his head, laughing. "It's like a goddamned mantra, 'smooth, smooth, smooth.' Even more than usual, you know?"

"From where?"

"Who knows? Upstairs somewhere."

At the end of the driveway was a modern house, mostly glass, but still tasteful. In the back, surrounded by tall sea grass, was a slate patio with a massive fieldstone fireplace. Beyond it was a hundred yards of brush, then the ocean.

"Nice place," I said.

We walked up the steps to the front door, and Jimmy turned to give me a serious stare. "You don't see this, okay?"

I nodded and he unscrewed the porch light and took out a key, opened the front door. "Most of the local cops have side work caretaking some of these properties. Some of them do a bunch, make a nice supplement from it. I have this and a couple of others."

As we walked through the house, he flicked a couple of light switches but that was about it.

"These people are loaded," he said, as if reading my mind.

We walked into the kitchen and he took two beers out of the fridge.

"So what's your deal?" I asked as we stood in some rich guy's kitchen, drinking some rich guy's beer.

"Me? I don't have a deal."

I gave him a look.

He opened the door from the kitchen to the garage and motioned me to follow.

The garage held a black Tesla Roadster, plugged into the wall. I made a sound in my throat.

Jimmy smiled and disconnected the plug. "Sweet, ain't it? I have to take it out every now and again so it don't get lonely."

"And that's electric."

"Crazy, ain't it?"

We got in and put our beers in the cup holders. He pressed a couple of buttons. The garage door opened, and we silently surged down the driveway.

"So you were telling me your deal," I reminded him.

He laughed, turning onto the road and rocketing forward. "Okay. Grew up in Tisbury, left the island to seek my fortune. Joined the Boston P.D., but didn't like it. Realized that just because my fortune wasn't on the island, didn't mean it was off it, either. Figured some folks don't get a fortune. Met an island girl. Married for six wonderful years, then another four after that. Been on my own a year and a half." He took another swig of beer, then looked at the bottle. "Had my eye on being chief, but things got a little bumpy when Diane left."

He raised his bottle, like a toast, and winked at it. "So, if Dr. Paar isn't the issue, what did you do to get yourself in the doghouse?"

"With Nola you mean?" I shrugged. "I think at this point me just being here is annoying her." I paused. I didn't really know the guy, but I felt like I could trust him. At least a little bit. "We've been living together eight months or so, and it isn't always easy. I found a little work up here, too. A side job. So I could stay up here while she's here. I thought she'd be happy I was staying." I took a drink. "She wasn't."

He smiled. "That work have anything to do with Renfrew senior?"

I'd like to think I didn't show any reaction.

He leaned toward me conspiratorially. "I saw you going over to his humble abode."

I nodded.

"Well, that whole family's a pain in the ass," he said, "but if you're working for senior, he's probably paying you well. Most likely you're going to earn it." He took a deep drink of his beer. "My instincts tell me you're a stand-up guy. You've been on the right side of two bad situations, and I feel I can trust you. Plus I have my sources, and not everyone's as tight-lipped as you are about what went on up in Dunston. Hero might be a little much, but from what I hear you're one righteous badass."

I laughed and started to protest, but he put up a hand to stop me.

"So I'm going to give you a little background on these Renfrews."

He waited to see if I had any objections.

I raised my beer: have at it.

"Renfrew family has roots here, and they've been coming up summers for generations. They're not real old money, not for up here—no whaling money. But they're plenty rich. You ever hear of Thompson Chemical Company? They sell lawn care and garden products?"

I nodded.

"That's Renfrew. Big, established, family-owned company. One of their first locations was up here, but worth millions now. Anyway, Renfrew senior is running the family business, selling fertilizers and weed killers and pesticides, and your friend Teddy, he's running around with these eco-warrior knuckleheads, pulling stunts like putting red dye in the chemical in the lawn trucks, so when the trucks spray the lawns, they're painting them red."

I laughed. I couldn't help it.

Jimmy did, too, shaking his head. "I know, almost makes you like him, right?"

I shook my head and said, "Not even close," earning me a clink of our beer bottles.

"Some of the stuff is not so harmless, either. He seems to love tweaking the old man. Him and some of his friends hung banners from one of Thompson's regional headquarters, embarrassed the hell out of them. But he's also been arrested for some other stuff that was more serious. They set off the sprinklers at a biotech lab in Atlanta, protesting pharmaceuticals in the water. Short-circuited a bunch of equipment and actually started a fire. Three people got pretty badly hurt, trampled by folks trying to get out of there. He was also involved in a group that was spiking trees. I don't know if he was directly involved, but someone lost an eye.

"Anyway, we got all sorts of rich assholes up here, even in the off-season, all different orders of magnitude. The Renfrews are among the richest and the assholiest."

"Do you think young Renfrew is one of the reasons your higher-ups are so nervous?"

"Probably. But I think they would be anyway. My sense is this thing is just big."

I nodded. "What about Johnny Blue? What's his story?"

Jimmy laughed and shook his head "You seen him on TV, you know his story. He ain't that rich, but he is for sure a big asshole."

"Not that rich? What's he doing with that big farm, then?"

Jimmy shrugged. "His investors are rich. I don't know what he's doing, and I doubt he does, either. But I wish he was doing it somewhere else."

He held up his bottle and looked at it again, maybe checking the level, maybe just admiring the bubbles. Then he put it to his mouth and tilted it back. We came to a stop, and I realized we were next to my car.

"Anyway," he said, "you be careful around these rich mother-fuckers. They don't call them that just because they're rich, you know what I mean? From what I hear, Renfrew's been on a bit of a tear, bringing in lots of VIPs, buying back shares in the company, and leveraging himself to the hilt to do it. He's up to something."

"Seems to be doing something right, living in that massive house."

"Yeah, it's big, ain't it? It actually belongs to the company."

"Really?"

"Yeah, but he owns most of the company. It's all the same in the end, I guess. They've got everything twisted this way and that, avoiding taxes over here and sheltering assets over there. It's crazy."

"I guess that's how they get to be so rich."

"Yeah, and a lot worse stuff than that. Like I said, you've been on the right side of two bad situations. I'd just as soon not see you on the wrong side of the next one."

26

Driving back down island at a reasonable speed, I realized I still didn't have a good excuse for staying. Part of me wanted to stop in and see Nola, try to patch things up. Part of me wanted to stop in and get my stuff, maybe fire off a few choice words, something stinging that would even us up a bit. A growing part of me just wanted to get off this damned island. I thought about telling Renfrew I'd changed my mind, giving him his money back and going home. Then I pictured my apartment.

For years it had been just right, and for months it had felt too small. Picturing it without Nola now, it seemed cavernous, empty, and lonely.

The part of me that was sitting on the gas pedal decided to just keep driving, but while my right foot was decisive on the matter of acceleration, it hadn't communicated anything to my hands regarding steering. Not only did I not know what I was doing, I didn't know where I was staying, either.

An image of Annalisa flared in my mind's eye, but I snuffed it out, smothering it with a damp cloth until it was gone.

It might have taken longer than I thought, though, because by the time I'd stopped thinking about her, the sky was dark and I was pulling up at the Wesley Hotel.

It was like a different place from the week before—bustling like it was the height of the season, people coming and going through the lobby, heading up and down the steps. Everyone was moving with a kind of crispness, a sense of purpose, but there was something else that stood out.

The guests were all men. All young, in their twenties and thirties. A tiny bit of salt sprinkled over one or two forty-year-olds. I stood in the middle of the lobby, looking around, but there were no women, no children. And no seniors except for the old guy at the desk, who observed the buzz of paying guests with a satisfied smile.

"You're back," he said, looking to my right, then my left, before settling back on me.

"I need a room."

He raised an eyebrow. "Just you?"

I nodded.

He nodded back, like he understood, a muted smile on his craggy face reflecting both commiseration and maybe a glint of excitement that Nola was now unencumbered.

I laughed despite myself.

He looked up at me and shrugged, like he knew why I was laughing and he didn't care. Maybe he liked his chances.

The room didn't feel quite so claustrophobic this time. Maybe because it was just me, or maybe compared to that tiny cabin nothing would feel claustrophobic. But in the dark, and without Nola brightening it up, it seemed a lot more depressing.

Within ten minutes I was headed back downstairs, struck once more by the strange homogeneity of the other guests. It wasn't just the demographic that they shared; they all had a certain hardness and efficiency, like ex-military. A few looked up at me as I walked through, but more striking than the eyes that were on me was the strange tension of the averted gazes, as though other eyes were intentionally not looking at me. Maybe I was being paranoid, but stepping out onto the porch, I could feel glances exchanged behind me.

Given my situation, the Mustang was only slightly less depressing than the room. It felt weird to be sharing an island with Nola against her will, and I found myself driving toward Teddy's farm. Maybe I'd slip in and apologize, grab my things and go. Maybe I'd get a peck on the cheek as a peace offering. Maybe she'd miss me when I was gone. Maybe, down the road, we could salvage things between us.

I slowed as I approached the entrance to the farm, but I didn't stop. Instead of turning in, I coasted past it, drifting onto the shoulder a hundred yards beyond.

It was a conversation I wasn't looking forward to, and I probably would have wussed out anyway, but I was rescued from that fate by a pair of headlights knifing across the road in my rearview. It was Teddy's vintage Chevy turning out of the driveway, its taillights receding into the darkness.

Technically, I was still on the clock, so I swung the car around and followed, back the way I had just come. Teddy sped up as we approached the Wesley, and turned a few blocks later, making a right onto Circuit Avenue. Traffic was light, and I knew the bright yellow Mustang would be easy to make, so I hung way back. Several blocks later, I saw Teddy's brake lights as he swung into a parking space on the side of the road.

I quickly did the same, keeping as much space between us as possible. I got out and caught a glimpse of him as he slipped between two storefronts, looking both ways as he did, like a schoolchild crossing the street.

As I hurried along behind him, I thought about how sure I was he was up to something. I had to ask myself how much of it was real and how much was the fact that I didn't like the way he looked at my girlfriend. Or more to the point, the way she looked at him.

I crept up to the gap where he had disappeared and looked around, the same guilty way he had. Then I followed after him.

The shadows between the stores were the kind of black that gives you vertigo. I emerged onto a narrow lane that was only marginally brighter. In the dim light, I sensed motion across the street and a few houses down: Teddy, doing the same guilty scan as he ducked between two darkened houses. I pulled back so he wouldn't see me, then I followed once more.

The houses were tiny but elaborately ornate. We were in the Campgrounds, the maze-like village of gingerbread houses. Even in the darkness, I could make out the multicolored paint on the scrolling wood trim.

The deeper we went into the Campgrounds, the narrower and darker it got. A couple of times I lost Teddy, but each time I found him again, a shadow among shadows, walking in a brisk tight gait, like what he really needed was a bathroom.

When I emerged onto the next street, the spire of the big open-air church, the Tabernacle, was looming in front of us, illuminated in the sky. Teddy was headed across the grassy area surrounding it, looking increasingly suspicious the farther we went. He knew the island and its layout better than I did, and it made no sense for him to have parked where he had unless he didn't want anyone to see where he was headed.

I wondered for a moment if he was checking in with God and he didn't want his ironic hipster farmer friends to know it. But he didn't go into the Tabernacle. He went around it.

Just past the Tabernacle was another building, an old white clapboard that looked like a church. Teddy walked toward the back door and stopped abruptly, looking around him yet again. I hugged a tree, peering around it as he checked his watch. He stayed there for five minutes that seemed to stretch on forever. I could feel the nervousness coming off him. I would have felt bad for him if I didn't dislike him so much.

Finally, he jumped like a startled cat as a dark figure appeared at the edge of the shadows under a clump of trees. Light fell across a pair of boots and lower legs, then hands, beckoning Teddy closer. Teddy hurried over, his legs looking wobbly beneath him.

The other guy stepped forward, but his face remained in the shadows. He said a few words, and Teddy blurted out a hundred, his hands jittery and nervous. They went back and forth a few times like that.

I heard a twig snap behind me, and simultaneously an open hand connected on the side of my head, smashing it against the tree.

It wasn't a knockout blow, but it dazed me enough that I couldn't evade the hand that grabbed me by my throat and slammed me back against the tree, cutting off my air.

He was big, with a flat face, like a pug, but angry. I hadn't done anything to him, and I wondered if maybe it wasn't about me. Maybe he was just an angry person.

He locked his elbow, holding me in place, and pulled his other arm back, like an archer about to send an arrow or a meathead about to flatten someone else's skull. I was thinking of my gun, safely locked away on the mainland, as I swung my forearm as hard as I could against his elbow. I was rewarded with a popping sound and a lungful of air.

His face was all pain now instead of anger. But I knew the anger would return, and I didn't want to be there when it did. I didn't want him coming right up behind me either, so I punched him in the throat. Not hard enough to crush his larynx, I hoped, but enough to get him off his feet. He went down hard, his left arm flapping, like maybe he was trying to break his fall with it and had forgotten his elbow was dislocated.

I rubbed my throat, coaxing the circulation back as I looked around the tree. Teddy and his friend were gone. I decided I should be, too. I could hear voices not too far away, and I knew it was only a matter of time before someone came upon us. The guy on the ground was gurgling and groaning, but he was also getting up.

And he looked angry again. It occurred to me that maybe I should have been a little less worried about his throat and a little more concerned about my own.

My natural inclination was to cuff him and read him his rights, start asking questions. But I didn't have cuffs and I wasn't acting in an official capacity, and the only answer I was likely to get out of him was to the question, "Could this guy kick my ass with only one arm?"

I suspected the answer was yes, but I didn't need to know for sure, so I kicked him in the stomach, hard, and I took off running.

I zigzagged across the grass, keeping to the shadowed areas as much as possible. I was rounding the Tabernacle when I felt a gentle breeze near my neck. I heard a whine like a large insect and what sounded like a single, expertly struck blow of a hammer on wood. As I rounded the Tabernacle, I looked back.

Pug-face wasn't on the ground anymore.

I heard the insect sound again, then the hammer sound, much closer, and accompanied by a spray of splintered wood across the side of my face. A gouge had appeared in the tree next to me.

Pug-face was shooting at me. My eyes darted around, looking for movement, but finding only shadows. As I took off again, I heard another whine and a distant ping. I turned and saw a stop sign half a block away, the dim light flashing on it as it wobbled back and forth.

I cut across the road and darted between two of the gingerbread houses and made a left, away from the Mustang. The last thing I wanted was for Pug-face to put two in my head while I was getting into the car, or for him to see what I was driving. Half a block later, I was thinking I'd lost him when a pair of intricately carved ducks on the house in front of me exploded into dust and a light came on inside the house.

I abandoned my evasive maneuvers and took off running, fast as I could. I could hear heavy footsteps getting louder and closer.

Picturing how angry that Pug-face would be attached to a dislocated elbow helped me run faster, but I could still hear him gaining
on me. I knew I had to slow him down before he got into sure-
thing firing range.

The air was thick with the scent of lilacs, but behind it I caught
a whiff of something definitely not floral. I looked up and recognized the big pink house with the tulip flag. In the darkness, I
could just see the wetness on the surface of the lawn.

There was caution tape across the gate and I pulled it down and
pushed the gate open, eliciting a loud squeak. I left the gate open
and vaulted over to a raised garden bed surrounded by stacked fence
rails, trying not to think about the smell or what would happen if I
fell. The rails wobbled and made a wet sucking sound as I made my
way along them toward the back of the house. A holly bush blocked
my way, but I forced my way through it, staying on the rails and
ignoring the cuts and scratches.

When I reached the backyard, I hopped over the fence and
onto the street beyond. As I started to run, I heard a sound like a
cross between a splash and a splat, and another one like a cross
between a yelp and a growl. It might have been my imagination,
but the smell seemed to grow suddenly stronger.

I smiled as I ran, but picturing that pug face even angrier made
me stop smiling.

The winding streets had me totally disoriented, but I found the
Mustang and took off, winding through the Campgrounds, worried that at any moment a bullet would shatter my windshield or
my skull.

Glimpses of the Tabernacle's spire through the trees taunted
me with how little ground I had covered. My speed crept up with
each wrong turn, as adorable little houses closed in menacingly
on all sides. I slammed on the brakes just short of plowing into a
small wooden house as the tiny lane I was on ended abruptly. An
older man got out of a wicker rocking chair on a porch less than
six feet from my window.

"Hey!" he yelled, reading glasses swinging from a chain around his neck. "Slow down!"

"Bob!" yelled a voice from inside the house. "Come inside!"

"What?" he said, turning to look back into the house. "Guy's driving like a maniac out here."

I backed up the car, and then turned hard to the left.

"Slow down!" the old guy yelled after me.

I didn't. I kept going, my tires singing as I pulled left again, and found myself behind the Wesley Hotel. I killed the lights and sat there, waiting and watching, letting my heart settle down.

After fifteen minutes, I slowly got out of the Mustang and went inside the hotel. The lobby had settled down, only a half dozen security types hanging around. They seemed to be legitimately ignoring me, as if they legitimately didn't care.

But I paused at the door and looked down at the floor, at the muddy footprints from the front door to the stairs. I was pretty sure I caught a faint whiff of poop.

Whoever had been trying to kill me was staying in the same hotel I was.

27

I slept half the night with one eye open, and the other half with both eyes open, wondering if some busted up meathead with crap on his shoes and a silencer on his gun was going to kill me in my sleep. A silencer. That was hard-core.

Teddy's shadowy friend seemed hard-core, too. I didn't know how the three of them fit together. I assumed they were together, but I didn't know that for sure. Pug-face could have been spying on them, just like I was. Hell, he could have had nothing to do with them, and just been pissed off at me for any number of things.

I thought about how whatever Teddy was up to would impact Nola, and at the thought of her, my stomach tightened. I didn't know what was going on between her and Teddy. Probably nothing. But I'd seen the way he looked at her, and the way she looked at him, too. I wondered if it would be any better if the guy wasn't such a douchebag.

When I finally drifted off to sleep, my thoughts turned to bees. Little ones flying this way and that. Huge containers of them swinging across the sky under helicopters that looked like bees themselves. Dead hives full of dead bees, or even worse, full of nothing at all but mystery and blackness and something sinister.

I woke to the sound of buzzing and swatted at the sound, but it was my phone, vibrating on the nightstand.

Moose.

"Doyle! Can't believe you left without saying good-bye." He actually sounded hurt, and I felt bad for a second, even though I hadn't left and that would have been ridiculous anyway.

"I didn't."

"You what?"

"I didn't leave. I'm still on the island."

"Really? Oh, cool. I thought Nola had said you were leaving yesterday."

I laughed convincingly. "No, apparently there was some kind of misunderstanding. I'm still here."

"So when are you leaving?"

"I'm not sure."

"Oh . . . okay. Well, in that case . . . are you available to help us today?"

"Um, yeah, I guess." It was nine-thirty. It occurred to me that while I'd been asleep, the one-fucked-up-armed man hadn't snuck in and shot me. "Why?" I asked. "What's going on?"

"We're short. Pete blew us off. And he's not answering his phone. Can you step in?"

I didn't really feel like it, and I'd agreed to keep an eye on Teddy, but Renfrew had said I didn't even need to be as involved as I had been. I decided to get a little less involved.

"Yeah, okay."

"Awesome. Thanks. I'm at the lab. I could pick you up at the farm in twenty minutes."

"I'm not at the farm."

"Oh, good." He laughed. "I thought I just woke you up."

"I'm at the Wesley."

"The hotel?"

"Yeah."

"Oh," he said, quiet and sad. I felt like I'd let him down. "You okay?" he asked.

"I'm okay. I'll be at the lab in fifteen."

It turned out to be more like thirty. Traffic was a mess in Vineyard Haven, a small convoy of black SUVs accompanied by a couple of cruisers and motorcycle cops turning left onto Main Street, toward Renfrew's house.

The day before, I'd been ready to tell Renfrew to forget it, and I was still on the fence. I didn't want to give back the money, but I also didn't want to go in there and say, yes, your punk-ass son is up to no good—not without having something more to back it up. I needed more information. Plus, when someone tries to kill me, I want to find out who and why. The more I thought about it, the more I was starting to regret telling Moose I would help him.

When I got to BeeWatch, Moose was checking the equipment in the back of his truck. He looked up and smiled, like he was glad to see me. "Thanks for helping out," he said as I walked over. "Better be careful, though. You're on your way to honorary person-who-gives-a-crap status."

"Yeah, well, just make sure it doesn't get out. So what's up with Pete?"

"I don't know. He still thinks we were keeping something from him. He'll get over it."

I nodded. "So what are we doing today?"

"We've got to move the units, switch out the hard drives again, and upload a software patch."

"Didn't we just switch out the hard drives?"

"There might be a software glitch. I hope there's a glitch."

"What do you mean?"

He stopped what he was doing, his eyes suddenly dark and

worried and serious. "No bees," he said quietly. "None. We're not picking up any. If it's not a glitch . . . I don't know."

We rode in silence for a while. Then Moose said, "So what's up with you and Nola?"

"What do you mean?" I preferred the silence.

He rolled his eyes. "Well, you're still on the island but you're not staying with her, for one."

I sighed. "I took some time off, so I could stay up here with her. She didn't want me to." He looked at me with his eyebrows raised. "She said the city wasn't the only thing she needed a break from."

"Ouch."

"It's been a little tough, back at home."

"How could it not be? You know she's not a city girl."

"This whole thing with the multiple chemical sensitivity doesn't help. She feels trapped in the apartment. She can't find a job she thinks is safe enough."

He gave me a hard squint. "You think she's making the MCS up?"

"No, of course not. Nothing like that . . ."

"But what?"

"Well, the whole thing is very vague, she'll tell you that herself. But she went for treatment and she hasn't had an event since then."

"Yeah, but that's where she met her friend Cheryl, who had the exact same treatment, then had another episode, and now she has to live out in the woods."

"Yeah, I know, but Nola's had some serious exposures. When we left Dunston, they used powerful chemicals for the decontamination. She didn't have any reaction. There have been other exposures, too."

"So what are you getting at?"

I shrugged, not wanting to say it. "I think on some level she suspects that she doesn't have MCS anymore, and it's freaking her out. Like it was such a big part of who she was, if she lets that go, she won't know who she is anymore."

"Wow." He nodded, thinking for a minute. "Don't they say it's extra hard for relationships that start out from some sort of crisis?"

"Some people say that." What Nola and I went through a back in Dunston was definitely a crisis.

Moose turned to me. "Nola's great."

"I know she's great. And I'm an asshole. I realize how improbable this thing is."

"I'm not saying that. You're both, I mean . . . it should work out."

"I hope it does work out. But you look at us and, if you're honest, you know the odds are against it."

He didn't counter that, and as we drove, I thought about how, really, the odds were against me and anybody. Especially if I couldn't make things work with Nola.

It was a gorgeous day, still a little nip in the air but a brilliant, warm sun that you could feel through your clothes. We'd been through the tasks at hand enough times now that we could do it without talking. It felt good to be moving.

At noon we went back to the BeeWatch headquarters for lunch and to drop off the switched-out hard drives. Benjy was pulling up the same time we did. Annalisa was with him.

Moose and Benjy started loading the hard drives out of the trucks and into the shed.

"This a new sideline for you?" Annalisa asked, walking up to me. She was wearing jeans and hiking boots, a crisp white shirt tucked in. The other times I'd seen her, she'd been either dolled up for work or dressed for running. She hadn't seemed like the type to wear jeans. I saw now that she was. She was pretty good at it.

"Beats police work," I replied. "How about you? Doing some field work?"

She smiled grimly. "Trying to find out what the hell is going on out here. I don't know for sure what's going on with Stoma and their GMO bees, but the native bees have disappeared completely. I'm helping Benjy analyze his data, but even just driving around this morning, I didn't see any bees at any of the bait stations. And there are more deadout hives. I'm analyzing samples, but I don't have any results yet." She sighed and lowered her voice. "I'm not saying I agree with bringing in the GMO bees, I don't, but if the native bees are decimated, at some point it might be a conversation you have to have. I can't even say anything remotely suggesting that possibility, because these guys think I'm some sort of stooge for Stoma, and I can understand that. Just because I work for them, doesn't mean they don't scare me, too."

"Scare you? You mean like, for the future?"

She laughed, but it was uneven and unconvincing. "No, I mean now. They've brought in all these security types. The way they look at me, I don't think they trust me any more than Moose does. And everybody seems tense and paranoid. I don't like it."

She stepped up closer, her face inches away. I could feel her body close to mine. "But I feel better knowing you're around. Maybe I'll see you at the Alehouse tonight."

I didn't know what to say to that. But as luck would have it, Moose emerged from the shed just then. Benjy came out behind him, his phone up against his ear.

"Okay," Moose said, loud and abrupt. He tossed me a burrito, hot from the microwave. In his other hand he was cradling another burrito and two bottles of water. "Let's go."

As we were getting into the truck, though, Moose seemed to notice that Benjy was still standing by the shed, one hand holding his phone up to his ear, the other hand covering his other ear.

He paused, waiting until Benjy put his phone down.

"Everything okay?" Moose asked.

Benjy nodded. "Yeah, my mom, though. I got to go up to Springfield tomorrow, take her to the doctor."

"Is she okay?"

"Yeah, she's fine. Probably just lonely, really. I'll be back day after tomorrow."

"Okay," Moose said, starting up the truck and giving him a thumbs-up. See you then."

The next monitoring station was at Polly Hill Arboretum, half a burrito away. When we had the stations positioned where we wanted, we leaned against a fieldstone wall and finished eating. The breeze felt great but then it died out, replaced by an unnatural stillness. Moose seemed to sense it, too, looking around like a dog with his ears back. The place was ablaze with tulips and azaleas, the air fragrant with perfume, but the silence was conspicuous. There were no bees.

The flowers looked almost desperate, all tarted up and no one around to take advantage of them. Some of the blossoms were already on their way out, the edges of their petals soft and brown and curling. The breeze picked back up, and the tulips dropped a flurry of yellow petals. Several of them transformed in moments to naked stalks, still waving in the breeze, like headless chickens running around, not knowing they are already dead.

We worked quietly the rest of the afternoon, Moose's dark depiction of "life without bees" hanging over us. The closest thing we saw was a small bright yellow jet arcing across the sky with a winking cartoon bee and the words BEE-PLUS on the tail. That didn't help, either.

As we drove back to the lab, I checked my phone. No calls, no e-mail, no messages, and especially none from Nola. She'd be out in the fields all day, I told myself. If she was going to call me, it would be later, after work.

I helped Moose unload the truck and said yes when he asked if I could help again the next day, since they'd be missing Benjy.

"Go out for a beer?" he asked, when we were done.

I looked at my watch. Four o'clock. "No, I have a stop to make."

He nodded, studying me. "And I guess you have plans for dinner."

I laughed and shook my head, thinking of Annalisa's suggestion of the Alehouse. "Nothing really. I'll call you later."

28

My original plan was to go home and clean up before anything else, but the traffic was so congested as I approached Main Street, I couldn't bear the thought of getting through it and then coming back.

It took ten minutes to traverse the mile and a half to Renfrew's compound. When I got there, I pulled onto the grass behind half a dozen black SUVs. As I got out of the car, a dozen Navy SEAL–types emerged from the SUVs, all wearing thin black sweaters and camo pants, looking at me through their shades. I held my hands halfway up as I crossed the street to let them know I'd prefer not to get shot.

"I'm working for Mr. Renfrew," I said.

They stared without saying anything.

As I walked up the driveway, a different kind of asshole walked down toward me. He was wearing a suit. But as he approached, he held up a badge with one hand while the other one hovered next to the gun on his hip. His fingers were visibly twitching.

"Right there," he said.

I stopped. There was a sniper on the roof, scoping me. For some reason I flipped him off.

"Can I get my ID?" I asked.

"Can if you like. Probably not the best idea to flip off the sniper right before you do, though."

"I'm with Philly P.D., but I'm doing a side job for Renfrew. He asked me to check in. Name's Doyle Carrick."

He put his ID away and held out his hand, wiggling his fingers.

I slowly reached into my jacket and pulled out my ID. He looked at it, looked at me, and then looked up at the sniper on the roof and nodded. I hoped that was a good thing.

"This way," he said, turning on his heel and walking back up the driveway. As I followed him, the sniper lowered his rifle. He looked about twenty, with spiky blond hair, or maybe a bad case of helmet head. I gave him a thumbs-up, and he shook his head and spat.

I followed my guide through the front door and into the living room. Percy and McCarter were sitting on the sofa in their new suits, watching TV. They looked at me with blank faces, then they turned back to the TV as we went out onto the patio. Renfrew was standing on the top step, looking out over a lawn that had been transformed. A large tent covered most of it, and the outdoor furniture where we had eaten our bisque had been replaced by a temporary wooden floor covered with rugs and several rows of seats surrounding a mahogany table encircled by ten plush leather chairs.

Security types in suits and earpieces were milling around, caterers darting back and forth between them.

Renfrew looked over at me, his eyes widening with mild surprise.

"Clowns or ponies?" I asked.

"What?"

"You're having a party, right?"

"I am and I'm quite busy, actually. What are you doing here?"

He looked over my shoulder and dismissed the guy who had led me there.

"Checking in."

"Oh. Okay, good. Go ahead."

"Well, I think you're right. Teddy is into something."

He looked at me, just for a second; then he turned back to watch whatever he was watching. "Like what?"

"I'm not sure. But he's skulking around, taking evasive actions to avoid being followed, having secret meetings."

Renfrew's head whipped around. "Meetings with whom?"

"I don't know. I didn't recognize him."

"But you saw him?"

"I caught a glimpse."

"I thought he took evasive actions and they were secret meetings."

I shrugged.

"Excellent!" He clapped his hands together. "I knew you were the right man for the job." He came over and put a hand on my shoulder, gently turning me around and walking me back toward the house. "That's great work, Carrick. Excellent. Percy and Mc-Carter are good men, loyal, but they couldn't keep up with him. So I can count on you to stay on the job?"

"Someone came at me with a gun while I was watching Teddy."

He stared at me, his eyes narrow. "Someone Teddy was meeting with?"

"He wasn't the guy Teddy was meeting, but I think he was with the guy Teddy was meeting."

"But you don't know."

"I don't."

"What happened to the man with the gun?"

I didn't want to go into detail. "I incapacitated him and escaped."

He nodded. "Good. Sounds like you did just what you were supposed to do. So, I can count on you to stay on the job?"

"Well . . . for the time being, but I—"

"At least until Saturday, right?"

"Sure, but I—"

"Excellent, excellent. That's what I like to hear." He led me back into the living room, shaking his head as he looked over at Percy and McCarter. "Well, you keep up the great work, and the updates. And I'll talk to you tomorrow, right? Just call the number I gave you, right?"

"Right."

Then the door was closed behind me. I stepped down onto the driveway, the sniper smiling at me. I flipped him off again.

As I walked back to my car, I heard the rhythmic thump of approaching rotors. Out over the water, a helicopter was coming straight at us. The security types casually repositioned themselves on the far sides of their vehicles. Back doors opened, and I could see them placing their hands on weapons, big ones. I quickened my pace, not quite accelerating out of my cool-guy gait in front of the guys but pushing it close.

As I got to the car, the helicopter banked sharply overhead. The Stoma Corporation logo was clearly visible as it swung broadside and roared away along the beach.

The agents moved away from their vehicles, trading comments and laughing a little. I got the sense they were disappointed things hadn't erupted into a firefight.

On my way back to the hotel, I took a detour through the Campgrounds, past the pink house with the septic problems. The lawn was a big wet crater, with muddy tracks going around to the back. As I drove by I could see a man-sized brown smudge on the back fence, where Pug-face had climbed over it. I felt bad for the homeowner—the lawn was going to need new turf—but I laughed out loud anyway, still picturing that angry pug face. I couldn't seem to picture it angry enough for having been flopping around in a cesspool with a dislocated elbow.

I was so distracted trying to picture one angry face, I almost drove straight into another one. Jimmy Frank was interviewing an elderly woman in seersucker pants, and he pointed at me with his pen. Then he used it to direct me to pull over.

I rolled down my window. "What seems to be the problem, Officer?"

He gave me a withering look, and continued reassuring the old lady that he would get to the bottom of it.

She walked away, and he shook his head and came over to the car, turning and leaning against the driver's side rear window.

"You know anything about this?" he asked without looking at me.

"About what?"

"Someone shot up the Campgrounds last night."

"Really? How do you mean?"

He sighed. "I mean, there's a bullet hole in the Tabernacle, one in a tree over there, a ding on that stop sign, and two ducks missing from Mrs. Farrell's gingerbread trim." He looked at me close. "You know anything about that?"

"When did it happen last night?"

He shrugged, like maybe I knew better than he did.

"I didn't hear anything," I said. "Did anybody else hear anything?"

He sighed, exasperated. "No, nobody heard a thing. A couple of people said they heard some banging noises, but they said it sounded more like a hammer on a nail than a gun."

"Could the hammer-on-nail sound have been the bullets hitting the Tabernacle, or the wood trim?"

He shook his head. "They're not going to hear the impact and not hear the gunshot."

"Well, unless the shooter was using a silencer."

He stared at me for a moment. "That could explain it, yeah."

"You got any ideas on who could have done it?"

He gave me a look to let me know he did, and I was one of them. Then he sighed and hooked a thumb over his shoulder. "Wesley Hotel is full of those Darkstar knuckleheads. Could be one of them's got PTSD, or maybe had a fight with his girlfriend. No offense. You don't have any other brilliant theories you would care to share, do you?"

I pointed at the mud patch in front of the big pink house. "What happened over there?"

"Well, I don't exactly know, but the homeowner's pretty upset about it. Having a hard enough time trying to get his septic system fixed, now his lawn's all torn to shit."

"Think it could be related?"

He eyed me again. "I'll look into it."

I nodded and smiled. "I bet it would take a lot of Irish Spring to get that much smell off you."

He thought some more.

"Well, I got to go," I said. "If you need me, I'm staying at the Wesley Hotel. With all the other knuckleheads."

29

I'd been hoping to get a call from Nola saying something like, "I'm so sorry. You are right about everything. How could I have been so misguided? I miss you so much. Let's go back to Philadelphia together and do everything the way you want to from now on." Something like that.

I didn't. And my bag was still in her cabin.

I needed some basic clothes. Luckily, I found a store called "Basics Clothing." I bought a pair of jeans, a couple of shirts, and a sweater.

I still didn't know what Nola had meant when said she needed a break. Fifteen minutes for coffee, or maybe we'll look back at this and laugh in the afterlife?

I have an almost pathologically well-developed sense of emotional self-defense, steel doors ready at a moment's notice to slam shut against that which can hurt me. I get over things fast, but sometimes too fast. Sometimes before they're even over. I felt like I was braced against those doors right now, trying to keep them open before they slammed shut on Nola and me, sending whatever it is we had tumbling into the past tense, into the dustbin of my emotional history.

It didn't help that I was about to see Annalisa. And I *was* about to see her. Even if there was nothing romantic between us, I liked her as a friend. And neither of us had enough friends on this island. But "friend" still wasn't the first thing that came to my mind when I thought of her.

Back at the hotel, I closed my eyes for ten minutes. Then I showered, changed into my new clothes, checked my phone one last time, and headed out. My head was buzzing, and as I stepped onto the porch, I welcomed the bracing breeze coming off the harbor. It didn't completely calm me, but it slowed my thoughts enough that I could pick them out individually—could separate the anxiety about Nola from the adolescent excitement about Annalisa from the ominous backdrop of paramilitary assholes and dying bees.

When I walked into the Alehouse, I spotted Annalisa right away, sitting at a booth. Her face looked as pensive and conflicted as mine had probably been on the walk over, but it lit up when she saw me. It had been a while since someone had seemed so happy to see me.

She stood up, as if to make sure I hadn't missed her, like that was possible. Everyone in the place turned to look at her.

Of course, it might not all have been appreciative. Pete the beekeeper was sitting at a table in the back, giving her the skunk eye.

When I approached, she stepped close, up on her toes, and put a kiss on my cheek. Her lips were soft.

We sat opposite each other and she leaned forward, her eyes sparkling. "It's good to see you," she said. "Outside of work."

"You, too," I said. "So how's things?"

"You mean apart from paramilitary goons turning the island into a militarized zone?" She leaned in closer. "Things at work are getting crazy. The tension is incredibly thick."

"From Sumner?"

She shook her head and shrugged. "From him, yes, but also from above, I think from Pearce himself. You know Sumner used to own Bee-Plus."

"Right. You mentioned that."

"Well, his assistant, Julie, she's a bit of a chatterbox. She says Sumner's in a tough spot. He got completely overextended and ran out of money. That's how Pearce came in and bought a majority stake. Sumner's seriously leveraged just to own the small piece of the company he still owns. Pearce is leaning on him hard to make this work, and Sumner's still, like, tinkering with the engineering, with the genetics, which is very late in the game. But he's put a lot of pressure on himself, too. If the Bee-Plus program fails, Sumner's ruined."

"Maybe that explains why he's such a dick."

She laughed at that. "He actually left this afternoon, which is nice, but I'm sure he'll be back soon."

"I think I saw him go. Bright yellow jet with the Bee-Plus logo?"

"That's him. Nothing if not subtle. Julie says he had that jet written into the deal, that he got to keep it." She cringed and laughed. "It's all very strange. Sad but exciting to be here in the middle of this, doing important science. Although I don't know if anyone will take it seriously if I ever release my findings."

"Because you're working for Stoma?"

She nodded. "No one trusts that they're not driving my results. And I don't even know if I'll have the resources to finish my work."

"Wait, I thought the upside of working with them was that you were well funded."

"Funding but no support. I used to have assistants. I had a wonderful assistant, Lynne, but she got transferred out when Stoma acquired us. She was great." Her eyes welled up. "She died a few months later, in a boating accident. She was a good friend." She took a deep breath and smiled. "Now it's just me. They've said

I can use Julie, if I need something specific, but she's next to use-less and very unpleasant. I got to know her a little on Samana Cay. She's a terrible bore, and a gossip. A good source of informa-tion, but I don't really trust her. She's got this faux hippie thing going, totally fake. She's actually very Stoma Corporation. And she's not very discreet." She shook her head and said, "Anyway," but then her eyes drifted over my shoulder.

I turned to follow her gaze and saw Teddy walking in, Elaine and Nola behind him. Elaine spotted me first. Almost immedi-ately, Nola turned and looked at me as well.

Our eyes met. Then she looked past me at Annalisa and I saw her stiffen. She looked away and sat with her back to me.

Teddy gave me a look as he pulled out his chair. He didn't smile, but I knew he was smiling inside. I wanted to kill him.

As we were staring at each other, a voice said loudly, "Now look at this asshole."

I was about to say, "Amen, brother," but then I noticed everyone was looking at the television above the bar, the bartender raising the remote to turn up the volume.

I recognized the guy on the television from pictures I'd seen. He was an older man, but big, towering over the same reporter who had interviewed Johnny Blue. He seemed even bigger than his size, filling the screen and, as the volume came up, filling the air with his booming Australian voice. Archibald Pearce the head of Stoma Corporation.

"These bees are already hard at work, pollinating the crops at Blue's berry farm, right on schedule, and making sweet, natural honey. Bee-Plus bees are absolutely environmentally safe," he said, holding up a printed Bee-Plus logo, "and they're a great advance in the fight against the terrible colony collapse disorder that has been plaguing other bees."

He was standing in front of a stack of hive boxes, the Stoma Corporation lab units visible in the background. In the distance, behind them, was the helicopter that had buzzed Renfrew's mansion that afternoon. Pearce smiled as a bee floated lazily around his head.

The reporter giggled nervously, the arm holding the microphone twitching as she resisted the urge to swat at the bee.

"And what makes your bees different?" she asked gently.

"Scientists think lack of genetic diversity is one of the causes of the colony collapse. Most people don't realize that the vast majority of American bees come from just six hives that came over with the colonists. They've been inbreeding for hundreds of years, and that has made them weak. What we've done is bring in some genes from other types of bees, bees that don't suffer from colony collapse disorder, to make European-style honeybees that aren't susceptible to colony collapse. But we didn't have time to do it the old-fashioned way, so we did it the modern way. I like to say, we made better bees without the birds and the bees, if you know what I mean." He grinned in a slightly bawdy, not leering old-man way.

"And what do you say to people who are concerned about the genetically engineered bees getting out, or mixing with regular bees?"

Pearce smiled indulgently. "Sierra, bees spread when a new queen comes along and the old queen takes part of the hive and swarms, or goes to start another hive somewhere else. Our queens have very tiny wings. They can't fly, so that can never happen."

Sierra Johnson brought the microphone back to her own lips and said, "Huh," before moving it back to Pearce.

"There are some very smart scientists out there working to stop the scourge of colony collapse. This is just a stopgap effort, filling in until they have succeeded."

She looked serious for a moment before changing back to her giggly face. Then she actually giggled as she turned to face the camera. "Well, there you have it, Jim. Better bees without the birds and the bees." She paused to laugh a little more. "Live from West Tisbury, I'm Sierra Johnson."

30

The room went quiet except for the news anchors tittering at Pearce's joke.

"It's not CCD," Annalisa mumbled.

"What's that?" I said.

"It's not CCD. It's not colony collapse disorder."

"What is it?"

"I don't know. It looks like mites, or something weakening the bees so the mites can get out of control."

"But wait, don't people think mites might have something to do with CCD?"

She shrugged. "It could be part of it, but colony collapse is a specific thing: the bees aren't just dead, they're gone, vanished. Mites have arguably done more to damage honeybees than CCD, and these are the worst mite infestations I've ever seen. But the bees haven't disappeared. It's irresponsible saying it's colony collapse when it isn't. There's enough misinformation out there already."

I was about to ask whether she'd told this to Moose and Benjy when I was distracted by a commotion at the table where Pete was sitting. He was drunk and upset. His friends were trying to calm him down, but his face was flushed and his eyes were angry.

"It's bullshit and it's not right," he said. "I can't just lie down and take it, whatever's causing it."

"But the island needs you," one of his friends was saying. "The farmers need you. Especially now. You're the only bees we got left."

Pete shook his head, a stubborn and childlike motion, but there was nothing childish about the anger and the anguish in his eyes. The emotion was raw and compelling, radiating off him like heat. The rest of the people in the dining room were just turning to look at him when we heard the *thump, thump, thump* of rotors. I knew without a doubt it was Pearce, and I think everybody else did, too. Most of them had been at the dock when the bees arrived. Some had probably seen the helicopter arrive that afternoon.

Heads looked up at the ceiling, tracking the noise as it grew louder and passed overhead.

In the midst of the commotion, Teddy took out his phone and put it to his ear. He smiled at first. Then his brow furrowed as he listened, a finger in his other ear. Recognition materialized on his face, and simultaneously a variation on fear.

"I don't need this crap," Pete said loudly, almost like he was reminding everyone that they had been paying attention to him before he was so rudely interrupted. It seemed to work, too, as everyone focused back on him, except Teddy and me.

Teddy tossed a couple of twenties on the table and headed for the door. Nola looked up at him, but he seemed oblivious.

I looked from Teddy to Annalisa, and realized she was already looking at me.

"I have to go," I told her. "I'll be back in a little while."

"What? Where are you going?"

I put two twenties on the table as I stood, realizing immediately it was way too much.

"I have to go take care of something. I'll tell you later."

Pete was getting louder as I made my way to the door.

"If that asshole wants his Frankenbees on this island, he can have it. I'm out of here." He brushed his hands against each other. "I'll take the bees I have left to the mainland. Find somewhere safe to keep them."

As I approached the door, Nola turned around and our eyes met. I broke her gaze and slipped out the door.

By the time I got outside, Teddy was at the end of the block, turning left. I jogged up to the intersection and stopped, peering around the corner. To the left was the Wesley Hotel, to the right, a long pier and the Oak Bluffs ferry terminal. But Teddy was walking briskly straight ahead, toward Oak Bluffs Harbor.

I hung back and watched him cross the road, ducking back as he looked all around him. I gave him a little space; then I hurried to catch up, but the only sign of him was the throaty sound of an outboard motor idling. By the time I figured out which boat he was on, it had taken off, racing across the lagoon.

I ran along the promenade, watching as the boat slipped out of the harbor. I watched for a moment as it disappeared onto the ocean, then I turned and walked back the way I had come.

By the time I got back to the Alehouse, Annalisa was gone. So was Nola. Jimmy Frank was there, though, sitting at a table in the corner. He waved me over to join him and before I could decline, he ordered me a beer.

As I stood there, I got two texts from Annalisa:

WHERE ARE YOU? followed by WENT HOME. I'LL CALL YOU IN THE MORNING.

I texted back, SORRY.

"They left around the same time," Jimmy Frank called out. "The ladies, I mean." He laughed. "But I don't think they were together."

* * *

We closed the place, sitting at that corner table.

I learned a lot about Jimmy, about his days on Boston P.D., the rise and fall of his marriage, and the fact that he could put away a lot of liquor. Actually, he didn't tell me about that so much as show me. Although the topic did come up. I brought it up.

Jimmy acknowledged it was a problem, that it was probably going to cost him a shot at being chief. He assured me it was just a phase, a stage in the whole divorce process. In fact, he elaborated, he had identified five stages of divorce: denial, being an asshole, being an angry asshole, wallowing, and acceptance. He was in the wallowing phase.

I didn't get through the night without revealing a bit about myself, either, and what had happened in Dunston. He looked at me with a little more respect after that, and a little more pity. "Lucky you came through that okay," he said, watching me.

I looked away.

"Nightmares?" he asked.

I shrugged. "Not much. Flashbacks, sometimes."

He ordered another round.

"You talk to the counselors?"

I gave him a look, and he laughed.

"Actually, I did," I told him. "It helped a bit, but mostly I feel like I just need to work through it. Unfortunately, I've had a couple of ill-timed pauses while mixing it up with bad guys."

"You think your flashbacks and stuff are affecting things with your girl?"

"Probably. She worries. And she's not crazy about me doing police work at all. Nola looks at police work the way I look at scrapple. I'm glad it's there, but I don't want to see how it happens. She's got her own stuff she's dealing with, too. Some of it from Dunston, some of it from before. She kind of has a chemical sensitivity syndrome, so she has to avoid exposure to a lot of chemicals. That's been limiting her options for work, et cetera."

"Kind of?"

"Well, it's tricky, I'm pretty sure she did have it. When she was younger she had a couple of bad episodes with lawn chemicals and new carpet, so they're pretty sure. And no one knows if it can be cured, but there's doctors who claim they can do it, and Nola went to one of them. She met one of her best friends there, Cheryl, but Cheryl went on to have another episode, and now she has to live like a hermit to stay away from all the stuff. It's got Nola scared out of her wits the same thing is going to happen to her."

"Jesus, I can understand that."

"Oh, absolutely. But the thing is, that was all before I knew her. Back in Dunston, Nola was hit with some intense chemical exposures, and she had no reaction. Since then, too. And she's had no reaction. I'm not saying she should start huffing Raid, but she doesn't even want to discuss the possibility that she could start loosening some of the limits on her life."

He blew out a long deep breath between his lips. "Sounds like she's dealing with a lot," he said. "You need to take it easy on her. Take it easy on yourself, too."

I shrugged.

"Nola seems like a great girl," he said. "My ex wasn't, at least not at the end, which was half of our marriage. She put me through hell almost every day, but I still miss her, or who she was supposed to be." He smiled sadly and leaned forward. "Relationships are hard, isn't that what they say? Well, let me tell you: ending them is no picnic either."

I was both relieved and disappointed that he let me drive home. I was in no shape for it, but I made it back to the hotel.

There was a small group smoking out on the porch, and as I climbed the steps and they stopped their conversation to stare at me, I realized any of them could have been working with the pug-faced guy with the silencer. I had enemies around, and I needed to be more careful. I looked back at them long enough to let them know I wasn't intimidated, but not so long as to provoke anything. I was in no state and in no mood. The only thing I was ready to fight were bed spins, and as it turned out even that was a mismatch.

31

The next morning I woke up with a pounding headache and a deep sense of regret that I had told Moose I would help him. The novel charm of physical labor outside in nature had largely worn off. A second cup of coffee helped, but I was still feeling better about having pursued a career in police work, and about working with a partner who could go longer than ten minutes without trying to start up a conversation.

One thing I continued to appreciate about the work, however, was the appetite it gave me, and I was seriously looking forward to a very hearty lunch when Annalisa called.

I felt weird answering it in front of Moose.

"Hi," I said, lowering my voice and immediately earning a suspicious look.

"Hi," she said. "Where are you?" Her voice sounded tight.

"I'm helping Moose, since Benjy's mom is sick."

"Doyle, I'm worried."

"I'm sure she'll be okay. Benjy seemed to think it was nothing."

Moose looked at me, eyebrow raised.

"No, I mean . . . yes, I'm worried about Benjy's mom, but . . . I need to see you."

"Do you want us to come over?"

"No," she said abruptly. "Can I meet you somewhere else?"

We met Annalisa at Felix Neck, a wildlife preserve on Sengekontacket Pond, near Oak Bluffs. She was in the small dirt parking lot, sitting in her car with the engine running. Her face looked nervous and drawn, but she smiled when she saw us. As I got out of the car, she ran up and hugged me. Moose raised an eyebrow, but it was a desperate hug, fearful and in need of reassurance. Moose's suspicious frown deepened into concern.

"Are you all right?" I asked when she finally let me go.

She nodded, but grabbed me by the elbow and guided me into the stand of trees, motioning with her head for Moose to follow.

When we had gone thirty yards, she stopped and leaned in close to me. Moose stepped up close to listen.

"So, last night, when you disappeared on me"—she cocked an annoyed eyebrow—"I got to thinking. Pearce kept talking about colony collapse disorder, and I kept thinking, no it's not. It's mites, Varroa mites. Yes, the Varroas might be involved in CCD, but this isn't CCD. The bees aren't disappearing, they're just dying. They're being killed by these mites.

"So, I went to the lab, and I ran a DNA analysis on some of the mite samples. I was there pretty late, and I'll tell you, it kind of creeped me out, you know? Being there all alone, at night." I thought to tell her she should have called me, but didn't want to in front of Moose. "Anyway, I ran the DNA analysis, then ran the sequence through the database. It came back inconsistent with what is in the database for Varroa destructor. In fact, it didn't match anything."

"What do you mean?" Moose asked.

She took a deep breath. "By then it was late, so to double-check,

I set up the DNA analysis to run again, overnight. When I got back this morning, Sumner was there with a bunch of security types. They said the lab had been vandalized."

"Vandalized how?"

She waved a hand and rolled her eyes. "They said someone had thrown a big rock at it. And there was graffiti—'Leave Our Island.' But the place was crawling with Sumner's men. Armed men. It was terrifying. At first they wouldn't let me inside, but then they did, just to get my things. The analysis was finished, and when I ran it through the database, it said Varroa mite."

"Had you done something wrong?" I asked.

"I didn't do anything wrong," she snapped. Then she took another deep breath. "I didn't do anything wrong. But when I double-checked the sample, I noticed that the seal on the cap had been completely removed. I don't do that. I break it and leave it in place."

"So what are you saying?"

She looked around and lowered her voice. "I'm saying someone switched the sample. Even before I checked the analysis, I could tell someone had been at my desk. I didn't have time to check anything out, because they rushed me out. They said they needed to complete their investigation, that I should take the day off and they would call me when I could get back in."

"So what do you think happened?" Moose asked.

"I think they were monitoring me. And something I did, maybe doing the DNA analysis on the mites, made them nervous. I think they staged the vandalism in order to hide their tracks, and to justify bringing in the soldiers."

"What did you mean earlier?" he asked. "When you said about the analysis not matching anything."

"Just that. It doesn't match anything in the database. It's a pretty big database, and I know Varroas are in it."

Moose's eyes were wide. "So what does this mean?"

Annalisa shook her head. "It means these mites could be something new."

32

Annalisa was afraid, and I was taking it seriously, but I didn't know what to do about it. I offered to follow her home, to make sure she was okay. But she shook her head and said she'd be fine. I reassured her it was a small island, and we were only a phone call away.

The next stop was the BeeWatch lab. I went first because it was too excruciating to drive behind Moose, but no matter how slowly I drove, he lagged behind. We were driving along County Road, through Oak Bluffs, when Annalisa texted to tell me she was safely home. When I glanced back at the rearview, another car had pulled in between Moose and me. Two blocks later, a second car pulled in, then a third. But the third one hadn't turned onto the road; it overtook Moose from behind.

I recognized the driver. It was Pug-face. He was following me.

I called Moose on speaker phone so the guy following wouldn't know I was on the phone.

"What's up?" Moose asked.

"Can you see me?"

"Yeah. There's a couple of cars between us. I thought you were going to wait for me, but yeah, I can see you. Why?"

"I have a tail. Someone following me. You see the green Dodge directly in front of you?"

He grunted. "Yeah, he cut me off."

"Right. Well, I'm pretty sure he's following me. Stay behind me. I'm going to make a few extra turns, see if he follows."

I did, and so did the tail, and so did Moose.

I was pretty sure I could lose the tail, but I didn't want to lose him. I wanted to find him.

We were driving up Kennebec Avenue, parallel to Circuit Avenue, where most of the shops were. There were no side streets between the two roads, but little pedestrian courtyards cut between the them every thirty yards. Driving past the sign for Back Door Donuts, the back entrance to the bakery, I got an idea.

"You still there?" I said.

Moose said, "Yeah. Why?"

"Keep following." I took Kennebec to the end, past the Flying Horses, then turned left and left again, looping back up Circuit.

"I need you to do me a favor. Pull over right where you are and wait for me."

"Um, okay." He sounded unsure, but in my rearview, I saw him pulling into one of the diagonal parking spaces fifty yards back. I pulled into one by the courtyard near the front entrance to the bakery. The green Dodge pulled into one roughly halfway between us.

I got out of the car at a leisurely pace, making sure Pug-face could see me. Then I went into the bakery and got a coffee and an apple fritter the size of my head. When the woman at the counter wasn't looking, I slipped through the door to the kitchen.

One of the bakers glanced up at me and said, "Hey—"

"Sorry," I said, holding up my coffee and fritter, as if that explained it. Then I ducked outside under the Back Door Donuts sign.

I cut left and hurried down Kennebec, looping around through one of the cut throughs the next one and back onto Circuit, near Moose's truck. I could see the Dodge parked up the street. I slurped my coffee down to a safe level then darted across the sidewalk and crouched next to Moose's truck.

He lowered the window. "What are you doing down there?"

"Don't look at me. Can you see the green Dodge?"

"Yeah. It's five cars up."

"What's he doing?"

"Not much by the looks of it."

I turned on my heel and sat down on the asphalt, my back against Moose's door. "Okay, so here's the thing," I said. "He's looking for me. I don't know exactly why. He tried to shoot me the other night."

"What?"

I looked up to see Moose looking down at me, his chin perched on the edge of the car door. "Don't look at me!" I snapped, and his head disappeared.

"What are you talking about?"

"The other night, I was following Teddy—"

"Why were you following Teddy?"

"It's a long story. I'll tell you later."

"Right," he said, judging me. "Wait, was this in the Camp-grounds?"

". . . Yes."

"Jesus, dude. You shot up half the gingerbread houses!"

I looked up and saw him looking down at me again. "Don't look at me! And no, I didn't. That guy in the green Dodge did. I didn't fire a shot. I don't even have my gun with me. Anyway, in a couple of seconds, he's going to realize I'm taking a long time in the bakery, and he's going to come looking for me."

"Okay . . ."

"I need to borrow your truck."

"What?"

"You can use my rental, but I'd recommend against it, since they've been following it and it's a little conspicuous. But I need your truck to follow this guy when he gives up and goes wherever it is he goes."

"What am I going to use? I still need to get around."

"It's a small island, and you've got lots of friends. I'm sure you can borrow a bike."

He sighed. "Okay. Your friend's headed into the bakery."

I moved to the side so Moose could get out. Then I slipped into the driver's seat, staying low. "Thanks. I'd say I owe you one, but I know our friendship isn't like that."

He gave me a sour look. Then he turned and walked briskly down the street, toward Mocha Mott's.

Even sitting low down in the seat, I felt vulnerable being so close to Pug-face's car. Moose had left his bag in the backseat, along with and his big, floppy, "farmer who's too cool to care how he looks" hat.

I let out a sad sigh and placed it on my head. Looking through his bag, I also found a pair of binoculars, several pairs of gloves, a couple of granola bars, and a first-aid kit. I thought about eating one of the granola bars, but then I remembered I had a big old apple fritter, so I started in on that. It was so good I almost didn't notice when Pug-face came out looking extra angry. He took five steps, pivoting in five different directions, but each time he paused and retraced them. Eventually he got back into his car. After a few minutes he pulled away. I waited a few seconds and went after him.

33

In my experience, people who are following other people, or trying to, tend not to think that they might be followed themselves. Especially not by the person they are supposed to be following. Even so, I gave the guy plenty of distance. And I kept the hat on, just in case.

Pug-face did his part by driving slowly and obliviously. We seemed to be randomly crisscrossing the island. Then I realized we were on the Doyle Carrick tour: we drove past the Offshore Alehouse, then swung by the Wesley on our way to the Black Dog. After that, we drove through Vineyard Haven and out to Teddy's farm. Pug-face pulled over in almost the exact spot where Percy and McCarter had stopped a few days earlier.

I turned up a driveway a hundred yards down and watched from there. I don't think surveillance was Pug-face's specialty, because after just a few minutes, he roared off, zipping past me doing sixty.

Well, that's no way to find me, I thought.

I gave him a nice cushion through West Tisbury and Chilmark and into Aquinnah before he turned right onto Pasture Road, curving around Menemsha Pond. The road began to twist and turn, and I lost him a couple of times but caught sight of him just as he turned onto Basin Road, curving around the pond once again. We were headed out to a dead end on a little spit of land across the lagoon pond from Menemsha Village, where I'd been so disappointed by my lobster roll.

I let more distance accumulate between us, but I knew I was running out of land and I didn't want to drive up on the guy. I turned onto a dirt road, thinking I would follow on foot through the brush on the opposite side of the road. Before I could, though, I saw Teddy Renfrew zip by in his vintage truck, headed the same way as Pug-face.

That stopped me. I still didn't know if Pug-face had been running interference for Teddy and his mystery pal, or if I had broken up his plan to kill them.

I was rooted by indecision, but I decided if there was a chance Pug-face was here to kill Teddy, I needed to stop him. I pictured my Glock in the trunk of the Impala, back on the mainland. I started up the truck, but before I could put it in gear, Pug-face drove by in his green Dodge, leaving. I paused again, wondering which way to go. I decided to check on Teddy, spinning up a little sand as I pulled out onto the road. After a quarter of a mile, the road widened out into a little parking area, eight spots on either side, maybe a half-dozen cars parked there. One of them was Teddy's truck.

I pulled into a spot directly across from it. At the far end of the parking area, the road continued on another fifty feet, curving down to the water. Teddy was down there on the little bit of beach that surrounded the pond, with a tall man wearing fatigue pants and a black sweater. It could have been his mystery pal. They were having an intense but hushed conversation. They were standing next to a small dock with a few tiny boats, including one that looked like a large aluminum raft. A small handmade sign read MENEMSHA BIKE FERRY.

I pulled out Moose's binoculars for a closer look. The guy

looked like a serious badass, more mercenary than thug. He had his hand on Teddy's shoulder, speaking intensely. Teddy was mostly nodding. I was reminded of a teacher talking to a child, or a coach talking to an athlete.

When the man turned, I could see the outline of the holster at his back. His boots had a built-in knife sheath; I could see the hilt poking out.

I lowered the binoculars, then raised them back up. I recognized those boots. This was the guy Teddy had been talking to in the Campgrounds, before Pug-face showed up. I lowered the binoculars again, wondering what to do next. When I raised them back up, Teddy and his friend were gone. I spotted the mystery man crossing the lagoon on the tiny bike ferry. Then I spotted Teddy in my side mirror, getting into his truck.

I ducked down low and watched him pull out, then got in the truck and went after him.

Teddy was a pain-in-the-ass-douchebag-spoiled-punk, rich kid, but he was involved in something way over his head. I needed to warn him. And then I needed to quit, before I got in over my head as well.

I ran out of Basin Road before I caught up with him, and I was worried that I had lost him. But Menemsha was almost at the western tip of the island, so I turned east and soon spotted him up ahead. He was moving at a decent clip, and I had to push it to catch up with him.

I flashed my lights at him and gave the horn a brief toot, but he didn't respond. On the next straightaway, I pulled alongside him, in the oncoming lane, and tapped the horn again.

He turned to look at me, annoyed, but not as much as I expected. I realized he didn't recognize me. I pulled off Moose's hat, and he rolled his eyes and shook his head.

"Teddy!" I yelled. "We need to talk. Pull over."

He nodded back at me with an utterly unbelievable expression of sincerity. Then he stood on his gas pedal and pulled ahead of me. We were approaching a bend, and suddenly a UPS truck, too. I tapped my brakes and pulled in behind Teddy, then had to push it again to catch up with him.

As we sped through Chilmark, I tried pulling alongside him again, but he tried to block me, flipping me off as he did.

We were speeding past the Chilmark Library, approaching a three-way intersection with a triangle in the middle, and Teddy wasn't even slowing down. At the last second, he jerked to the right, and almost plowed into a minivan when he did. It screeched and swerved into the other lane, causing more screeching and swerving. Suddenly, there was a knot of cars between us, and he was speeding away.

By the time things got straightened out, Teddy was a hundred yards away and I was still behind a minivan. Traffic had thickened up, and when I finally passed the minivan, Teddy was nowhere to be seen. I didn't know what else to do, so I just kept passing cars when I could. To my surprise, a couple of miles later I spotted him up ahead. I kept a little space between us and satisfied myself with keeping pace with him. We drove on like that for two or three miles, me following at a distance, him not making any effort to elude me. As we approached the airport, I could see cars backed up and a cluster of flashing lights.

Teddy's brake lights came on as he approached the mess. The two cars remaining between us both turned and went back the other way. I slowed down behind him.

There was no sign of an accident, but a cop was standing at the entrance to the airport, stopping traffic.

I was just pulling up behind Teddy's bumper when he coasted onto the side of the road. Instantly, the traffic cop was pointing and blowing his whistle as more cops climbed out of parked cruisers and feds began magically appearing out of unmarked black cars.

Teddy got out of the truck and lowered the tailgate, and for a moment I thought things were about to go violently bad. I pictured Teddy turning back with a weapon or a bomb, or even a banner or some paint. But instead he pulled out a dirt bike, bouncing it onto the ground.

I got out of the truck and watched as he swung a leg over the bike and paused to flip me off one last time. Then he started it up and took off, zigging and zagging between the trees as he disappeared into the woods across from the airport.

I stood there watching, wondering what that crazy asshole was up to.

"You know, I've been meaning to talk to you about the caliber of people you've been hanging out with."

It was Jimmy Frank, standing at my elbow. I nodded hello.

"What was that all about?" he asked, nodding in the direction of the distant sound of a dirt bike fading into the woods.

I shook my head. "I'm sure I don't know." I tilted my head toward the commotion in front of the airport. "What's this all about?"

"Motorcade," he said as two police motorcycles emerged from the airport and turned left, followed by a cruiser and a stretch limo.

I looked at him and raised an eyebrow as the limos kept coming. "Who are the bigwigs?"

He sighed and looked at me. Then he lowered his voice. "Well, lets see," he said as the limousines rolled out. "I believe that's Senator Wilson Deveaux, then Senator Jeffery Wilden, Senator George Burlholme. Maybe some others, but that's who's on my list."

"What are they here for?"

He looked at me sideways. "I was thinking of asking you the same thing."

"Me? What would I know about it?"

He shrugged. "You tell me."

The line of limousines was interrupted by another pair of motorcycles, then a string of massive black SUVs with diplomatic flags on the front fenders. I recognized the Kenyan flag, with its Masai warrior shield, and several others that were mostly just blocks of color.

As I watched, Jimmy stepped back. "I gotta go follow along," he said. "Part of the official 'make 'em feel important' escort."

He was deliberate about saying it, like he was telling me I should be listening to him.

I got back in my car and waited for the entire motorcade to pass, Jimmy Frank bringing up the rear. It took a few minutes for the knot of traffic in front of me to loosen. Then I followed along behind them.

34

As we made our way across the island, I had a pretty good idea where we were headed. Even before we turned toward Vineyard Haven, onto Main Street, past the stores and restaurants.

Way up ahead, I could see the motorcycles pulling over to the left, taking their places on either side of the grand entrance to the Renfrew house. The limousines turned up the driveway, and the security vehicles pulled over on either side of the street. By the time I pulled up behind Jimmy Frank's cruiser, it seemed like a re-enactment of the previous day, only four times as big. I half expected Archie Pearce's helicopter to come screaming over the water, but I guess with this much security, even Archie Pearce knew better than to pull any stunts.

Jimmy and I got out of our cars at the same time. He gave me a short nod and mumbled, "Fancy meeting you here." Then he ambled over to where the other local cops were standing, probably making snide comments about the feds and the private security types.

I strolled over to the driveway, near one of the motorcycle cops. "I just need a quick word with Mr. Renfrew," I said, holding up my badge.

He laughed. "Yeah, I don't think so, but you can try."

Before I could, though, the guy who had led me in on my last visit came striding down the driveway, shaking his head. "Sorry, sport," he said. "You're not getting anywhere close to him until after six o'clock, after all this wraps up. No chance."

I decided against leaving the message that I didn't want to work for Renfrew anymore and that his son the amateur screw-up was about to step up to the major leagues. Looking up at the roof, I saw the same sniper there, looking down at me. I waved to him, and this time he gave me the finger.

Whether he knew it or not, Teddy Renfrew was involved in something big and bad. I had tried to tell him, and I would try again. I had tried to tell his dad, and I would try to tell him again, too. I didn't know how close Nola had gotten to Teddy, but it was close enough that if he got hurt, she might get hurt. So I had to try to tell Nola, as well.

I wasn't looking forward to that, so I was kind of relieved when I got a text from Moose.

YOU STILL ALIVE?

YES. :)

I use smiley faces very sparingly, but I figured if not now, when, right?

IS MY TRUCK?

YES.

CAN I HAVE IT BACK?

Moose was back at Mocha Mott's getting lunch, but when I got there I could tell he was ready to go.

"Is my car okay?" he asked when I walked in.

"Without a scratch," I said as I handed him the keys.

He nodded as he pocketed the keys. "Not yours."

"What do you mean?"

"That guy came back and smashed one of your taillights."

"Are you serious?"

"He looked pissed." Moose sipped his coffee and leaned back in his chair, giving me an appraising look. "What's the story there? You said he shot at you before? What's up with that?"

I leaned forward and lowered my voice. "Teddy Renfrew is involved in something big and messed up. The other night he was having this secret meeting with some guy in the dark behind the Tabernacle. I followed him, and that guy, the guy who was following me today, he came up behind me and tried to take me out. I got away from him, he chased me, started taking shots at me."

"Why were you following Teddy?"

I didn't want to get into the whole thing. "It's a long story, but the other night, when I was staying in the cabin with Nola, Teddy was acting suspicious, and he went off for a secret meeting in the woods in the middle of the night."

"So you followed him?" Moose snorted and rolled his eyes. "Dude, you're unbelievable. How do you know he wasn't, like, meeting someone for sex, or buying a bag of weed or something?"

"Huh?" I said, because that hadn't occurred to me. "Well, you're right, that would have explained a lot. But he wasn't. They were just talking, and I saw them again at another secret meeting, only this time I got a good look at the guy."

"So you were following him."

"Yes. I was. And maybe that was totally messed up, but Moose, believe me, this guy he was meeting with, he was bad news. Seriously bad news. I know Teddy's gotten into some minor trouble before—spiking trees and graffiti and stuff—but this guy, he's on a different level."

"And how do you know this?"

"I just know."

He shook his head. "You're a piece of work."

I couldn't argue.

"Benjy's mom called."

"Is she okay?"

"Yeah, except she's pissed off that Benjy never showed up."

"Really?"

He nodded his head. "I called him but there was no answer, so I borrowed a bike and rode over to his place, but there was no sign of him." He fiddled with his cup. "Not like him to blow stuff off, but his mom's a bit of a pain, so maybe he just couldn't deal."

"Huh."

He shrugged and started to close his computer.

"Wait," I said, grabbing the top of it. "Can I look something up before you go?"

He rolled his eyes. "Dude, I have stuff I have to do."

"It'll only take a second."

He stood up. "Okay. I gotta take a leak anyway."

I opened a new tab in his browser and searched: "Senator Wilson Deveaux" "Jeffery Wilden" "George Burlholme."

That got me a million hits about the Senate, but several of the top ten referred to the Senate Foreign Relations Committee.

I added Kenya, and it narrowed down a fair amount, but it was the same mix of results. I added "Thompson Company" and came up with nothing.

Moose was walking back from the bathroom. On a hunch, I removed "Thompson Company" and added "Stoma Corporation" and the results dropped down to nine hundred hits, but almost all of them were about an initiative called Agricultural Solutions for Sustainable Peace, or ASSP. It seemed to be a controversial foreign-aid program exporting genetically modified corn to third-world countries.

"All right," Moose said as he walked up. "I'm out of here. I want to check the rest of the monitoring sites by tonight."

I nodded. "Okay. Maybe I can help you later."

"Where are you going now?"

"I have to go talk to Nola about Teddy."

35

It felt strange being back at Teddy's farm. I'd never felt like I belonged there, but now it felt like enemy territory. The place seemed strangely quiet, and I wondered if there was something going on, or if it was all inside my head.

The door to Nola's cabin opened, and she stepped onto the porch. Part of me wanted to run to her, to take her in my arms, to tell her I was sorry. Tell her that I loved her.

I couldn't tell if any part of her wanted to do the same thing. Neither of us did it.

My duffel bag was dangling from her right hand, swaying slightly. She moved her hand just a bit, and when the bag swung out away from her, she let it drop onto the porch.

"We need to talk," I said.

"Did you sleep with her?"

"What?" The question caught me off guard. "You mean Annalisa? No, of course not." I let a little laugh creep into my reply. I was relieved she didn't ask me if I'd thought about it.

She shook her head. "Anybody else, then?"

"No."

She sighed. "Then we can talk when I get home."

Deep inside, part of me was giddy that she was still planning on coming home. "Did you sleep with him?"

She looked indignant, then kind of repulsed. I hoped at the thought of the person I was referring to. "No," she said.

"Good," I said. I laughed again, just from nerves, but it seemed to thaw things out a little. She took a step forward, down off the porch. I took a step toward her as well.

"Doyle," she said. "I never . . . I just needed a break, okay? I needed some time to myself. That's all."

I nodded. "I understand."

"Just go on home, okay? And I'll be home soon. Then we can figure out where to go from here."

I started to nod, but then stopped abruptly.

"What is it?" she asked.

"You have to come away from here."

"What?"

"I know you need time, I get that, but it can't be here. You can't stay here."

"What are you taking about?"

"I can't explain all of it, because I don't know all of it, but Teddy is involved in something bad, something real bad. I don't know what it is, but I'm pretty sure it's about to blow up."

"I don't understand."

"Look, Teddy's done stupid stuff in the past, little stuff, but this is different."

"It wasn't stupid, it was important. He was making a stand for what he believed in."

"Well, this is different. He's been meeting with some hard-core bad guys. Secret meetings, off in the woods, in the middle of the night, that kind of stuff. And whatever it is, it's about to come to a head. I don't want you caught in the middle of it when it blows up."

"Have you been *following* him?"

Uh-oh. I guess I'd known that question was coming, but I hadn't really prepared for it.

"Have you been spying on Teddy?" she asked, because apparently I was taking too long to answer. "Have you been spying on *me?*"

"I wasn't spying on you," I snapped back. I took a deep breath. "Teddy's father said he was worried about him. About his safety. He asked me to keep an eye on him. It was a mistake. I should have said no and I didn't. I've been trying to get in touch with him to tell him I've quit. But the fact remains, Teddy is involved in something bad, and I don't want it to hurt you."

Nola growled and grabbed the strap of my duffel bag, flinging it at me.

"Get out of here, Doyle," she said. "And don't come back." This time when she turned around, she didn't look back. She stormed into the cabin and slammed the door.

The whole building shook, and in the back of my mind, I thought that tiny little cabin wouldn't hold up to a medium-sized huffing and puffing. But I didn't like picturing myself as the big bad wolf, so I picked up my bag and got into my car.

It felt sad and final, leaving that place, but I was angry enough and indignant enough not to dwell on it too hard. I needed to get out of there, and I needed to do it in a hurry. The car fishtailed a bit as I swerved around the big house, and I was just straightening out onto the driveway when Teddy showed up on his dirt bike. I braked hard and he swerved hard, pulling off the driveway and onto the grass. He ground out a wide circle, looping around me, then circling a second time before stopping next to my door.

"What are you doing here?" he asked.

"I was just leaving," I said.

"Good," he said. "Don't come back."

"Look, whatever it is you think you're involved in, I'm pretty sure you're wrong. The people you're involved with, they're seriously bad news."

He laughed. "You don't know shit about me or what I'm involved in. So here's my warning to you. You might think you know what's going on, but you have no idea, because you're an idiot, and an asshole, and a tool. So go on and get out of here before I call the real cops."

He gunned the bike's engine, and spun a half circle so his back wheel peppered the car with dirt and gravel. I thought about running him over.

Instead I hit the gas and pulled away, listening to the gravel pelting the paint job and thinking how much I was going to enjoy it when that douchebag inevitably went down.

The Mustang had been fun, but it was conspicuous, it was known, and it was damaged. And it was a rental.

Steve at the airport auto rental was happy to see me, but not for long.

"Can't stay away from here, huh?" he said, smiling as he came outside. "Leaving town, or you back for round three?"

"Round three," I replied. Then I lowered my voice. "I think I need something a little less flashy."

"Whoa," he said, walking around the back. "What happened here?"

I shrugged. "I don't know. I left it parked on the street. When I came back, boom."

He came around to the driver's side, and when he saw what Teddy had done to the paint, he let out a little shriek. "Jesus! What happened?"

"I think it incites envy," I told him. "The whole fancy sports car thing." I punched him in the arm. "But I sure am glad we got the extra insurance."

After filling out a lot more paperwork than before, I rolled off the lot in another Jeep.

36

When I called Moose, he told me he had finished checking the monitoring stations without me. He also said no one had seen Benjy, including his mom, who was freaking out and demanding we involve the police. I told Moose she might be right, and we arranged to meet Jimmy Frank at the Vineyard Haven police station.

Moose pulled up at the same time I did. "What happened to the midlife-crisis mobile? Did you wreck it?"

"Just traded it in for something less conspicuous," I said, but I knew he wasn't buying it. The ribbing would have continued if Jimmy hadn't arrived just then.

"Thanks for meeting with us," I said as he got out of his cruiser.

He waved me off. "Any excuse to get away from that damned security detail." He gave me a wink. "Very sensible vehicle you got there."

I changed the subject by introducing Moose, and Jimmy squinted at him. "October," he said. "A warning for riding a moped in an unsafe manner."

I was going to say I didn't know you could get a ticket for driving a moped too slow, but I kept it to myself.

"Dude, that was six months ago," Moose said. "You remember that?"

Jimmy laughed. "What good's a first warning if you don't know when it's a second one?" He tapped his temple. "Part of your permanent record."

He escorted us into a conference room, and we told him everything we knew about Benjy. Moose talked about his background, his work with the bees, and his whereabouts over the few days before he disappeared. I gave the chronology as I understood it of the last few days.

Jimmy took lots of notes, and when we were done he sat back and looked at Moose. "And that's everything?" Then he looked at me, letting me know that he seriously suspected I was leaving something out.

"He hasn't been on any social media," Moose added. "And he hasn't replied to any texts or e-mails."

Jimmy wrote that down, but he kept his eyes on me. "And that's everything?"

I nodded. "Everything that's relevant."

"I'll decide what's relevant."

I sat back, thinking. "I was born an only child . . ." I began.

"All right, smart-ass," he said. "You know what I mean."

"That's everything."

He nodded dubiously. "Right. Well, I have to tell you, it sounds like he flaked out and took off. Maybe he met a girl, or a guy. Maybe he had a fight with a girl or a guy you don't know about. But we'll file a report. You have a photo of him?"

Moose said, "On my phone."

Jimmy slid a business card across the table. "Send it to me."

Moose swiped through a few pictures on his phone and tapped at it for a moment, then looked up and nodded.

"Good," Jimmy said. "We'll send it around. Chances are pretty good he'll post something on Facebook, or he'll just show up with a new tattoo or something. But I'll send it out and we'll look into it."

When we got up to go, Jimmy asked if he could talk to me alone. I told Moose I'd meet him out front.

"So you think Benjy is really missing?" he asked.

"I don't know," I said. "I doubt it. His mom's worried, but it hasn't been that long. Why?"

"We're stretched pretty thin right now, all this bee stuff going on and no summer help yet. So it's not like we can spare people we don't need to, you know? Every day they're talking about pressure from up high, pressure to keep things under control, and the tension is getting thicker and thicker." He rubbed the back of his neck. "Anyway, we'll take a look around for Benjy, but I just wanted to tell you cop-to-cop that we have a lot on our plates right now."

As we left the police station, Moose asked how things had gone with Nola.

I told him. What I didn't tell him was that, when Nola said don't come back, I didn't know if she meant back to the farm or back to her.

"Yikes," he said, wincing. "So, what were you doing following Teddy?"

I shrugged. "What can I say, the guy sets off buzzers and bells for me, and when he starts doing suspicious things, I get suspicious."

He nodded absently, like he got it, even if he didn't approve. "So you were, like, douchebag profiling."

I laughed. "Yeah, pretty much. I guess so."

"Is that allowed?"

"I'm not trying to arrest him. I'm just trying to make sure people I care about don't get hurt by him."

He nodded. "So what are you doing now? Want to get something to eat?"

Before I could answer, Moose's phone buzzed. A moment later, so did mine. A text from Annalisa.

"I need to talk to you. 6:00. State beach—Jaws bridge. Moose, too."

Moose looked at his phone, and then at me, one eyebrow raised. "Meeting Annalisa at the beach?" He shrugged. "Okay."

The place might have been crawling with paramilitary types, including at least one who had probably tried to kill me, but as I carried my duffel up the steps, I couldn't help thinking the Wesley Hotel was starting to feel like home. Coming back downstairs after showering with a chair propped under the door, though, it occurred to me I should look for less-threatening lodging.

The place was quieter than it had been, and I figured most of the lodgers were probably at Renfrew's soiree, making sure nothing bad happened.

I looked around to make sure no one was watching before slipping into the Jeep as quickly as I could, trying to preserve whatever anonymity I'd gained by switching vehicles.

State Beach was a narrow strip of sand on the east side of the island that separated Sengekontacket Pond from the ocean. Jaws Bridge, made famous by the movie, was roughly in the middle, separating Oak Bluffs from Edgartown. Annalisa was standing on the bridge. She turned to watch as I made a quick U-turn and parked. Moose arrived from the other direction and pulled in behind me.

Annalisa walked up with a tight smile, and gestured to the beach. "Let's walk," she said, her voice almost wooden.

Moose gave me a questioning look and I shrugged in response as we fell in step behind her, between the shallow dunes and down onto the narrow beach. We walked in silence for twenty yards, the sun feeling lower the closer we got to the water. Finally, she turned and looked at us.

"Apart from Benjy, you two are the only people on the island I feel I can trust."

Moose's eyes widened, like he hadn't expected to be on that list.

"I didn't feel like we could talk in my office, or in any of our homes, really, and corresponding electronically didn't seem smart." She resumed walking, and after exchanging another glance, Moose and I walked along with her.

"I've been doing some digging," she said, "and I need to bounce some ideas off you two, okay?" She glanced back at us, but didn't wait for a reply. "I know you don't entirely trust me, Moose, because of my employer. And I'm somewhat suspicious myself. But while you and Benjy have been working on the census—which is good science, by the way—I've been working on the problem, too. One thing bugging me is that whatever has been going on here lately has looked like colony collapse in some ways, but it is very different in others." She sounded like she was still processing the information, saying it out loud to help herself think it through. "The mites are definitely involved and the hives aren't empty, so it's not classic CCD, not 'Mary Celeste syndrome.' This is a lot of dead bees, and a lot of mites. So, I'm thinking, the mites are acting different, maybe they are different. So, I ran an analysis, and it came back no match, right?"

She paused and looked at each of us, waiting until we both nodded.

"I thought maybe there was something new," she said. "But then I ran the analysis again, and it matched to normal Varroa."

"But you suspected it had been tampered with, right?" I said, keeping my voice down and looking around me, my paranoia feeding off Annalisa's.

Moose shook his head. "I totally wouldn't doubt it."

"So today, I ran another analysis," she said. "Only this time I did it in Sumner's lab. I got hold of his assistant's ID, while she was at lunch."

Moose's eyes went wide. "Really?"

She nodded. "The analysis came back just like the first one, not an exact match for anything else in the database."

Moose slowed a step. "So it is something new."

She nodded solemnly. "It looks like it, yes."

"Wait a second," I said. "You said it wasn't an 'exact match.' Was there some sort of partial match?"

"Well, that's just it." She took a deep breath. "Before I was just looking for a perfect match, a match for something we already know. But this time I asked the search algorithm to include partial matches." She crouched down on the sand. "And look what I found."

We crouched in a circle, and she pulled a manila envelope out of her jacket. The wind tried to grab it as she slipped out a piece of paper covered with a series of bars, maybe a dozen, each of them covered with little stripes of different colors. "Varroa Destructor" was printed across the top. "Here is a regular 'Varroa Destructor' genome." She handed it to me and pulled out another page, with the word "Sample" printed across the top. "Here is 'Varroa Martha's Vineyard,' for lack of a better name." It meant nothing to me until she lined them up. "See? Most of the DNA sequence is Varroa, but then there is a section that doesn't match at all." With her finger, she circled a portion of one of the bars. "This part is totally different, right?"

We both nodded like we understood. Maybe Moose did; I was taking her word for it. "But this sequence," she tapped the circle, "something about it looked familiar, or at least parts of it did. See these repetitive palindromic sequences? But I couldn't place it—at least, not until I looked at this." She handed Varroa Martha's Vineyard to Moose and pulled out a third paper with the header folded over. It looked totally different, but then she pointed at one section of one of the printouts and held it next to the mystery portion of the other printout.

"Son of a bitch," Moose whispered.

"Parts of that section match exactly, right?"

"What is it?" I asked.

She unfolded the top, revealing the header, and she read it aloud: "Stoma Corporation Proprietary Bee-Plus Engineered Honeybee."

37

Moose shot to his feet, kicking up two little clouds of sand that were quickly carried away by the wind. "What the fuck?"

"I'm with him," I said.

"I don't know," she said. "There's at least one explanation, but I'd love to hear of another one."

"Did it jump?" Moose asked. He looked scared.

She sighed. "It might have."

"Jump?" I asked. "What does that mean?"

"A transposon," Moose answered. "Once you start cutting and splicing genes, one of the many, many scary results is that it's not as stable anymore."

"So what does that mean?"

Annalisa let out a sigh. "It means the gene could jump from the species into which it was inserted and become part of the DNA of another species. Mites are parasites, living off the bees, including now the genetically modified bees. The spliced gene could become integrated into the genetic material of the mites."

"So what does that mean?" I asked.

Annalisa shook her head. "Who knows? I don't know what the

gene is for, or how it expresses." She took a couple of quick breaths, then slowed down with obvious effort. "I haven't been involved in the Bee-Plus project," she said quietly. "I'm a researcher, in a different division, a different subsidiary. I don't know that side of things. But I'm sure they've invested many millions of dollars in those bees."

Moose let out a low whistle. "If that splice has jumped, it'll cost them millions. Billions, if you count what they're hoping to earn from it. We need to tell someone."

"I know," Annalisa said quietly. Then she took a deep breath. "But we have to be damn sure. And even then . . . Stoma Corporation plays rough. They're known for it."

I looked at my watch. I needed to go see Renfrew.

Annalisa stood, then so did I.

Moose looked up at me. "Do you think this could have anything to do with the guy who was shooting at you last night?"

Annalisa's head whipped around. "Shooting at you? What are you talking about?"

I glared at Moose.

He put up his hands as he stood. "Sorry, I didn't know it was a secret."

"What happened?" Annalisa asked.

"It was nothing." I started walking.

"It was not nothing," Moose said, following along. "If someone was shooting at you, it was not nothing."

Annalisa put her hand on my arm. "Did you tell the police?"

"The police know about it."

"And what are they doing?"

"Well, they know there was a shooting. They just don't know it was directed at me."

"Wait," she said. "Was this in the Campgrounds?"

I glared at Moose, who was hurrying to catch up with us.

"Sorry," he said. "Seriously, though, it could be related. I mean, it's a pretty peaceful little island. They don't have a whole lot of shootings here. Seems like a bit of a coincidence all this stuff going on at once."

When we got to the car, Annalisa positioned herself in front of my car door, reached over, and pinched the skin on my ribs.

"Ouch!"

"Tell me what happened," she insisted. "All of it."

I told her about the incident at the Tabernacle, about Teddy and his shadowy friend, and then about Pug-face and his anger issues. When I got to the part about the muddy shoeprints at the Wesley Hotel, Annalisa practically shrieked, "And you stayed there?"

It did seem kind of foolhardy. I couldn't really change the subject, so I went on with the story, skipping ahead to the next day and Teddy's secret meeting in Menemsha. Then the motorcade out to Teddy's father's house.

"That reminds me," I said. "Do you guys know anything about something called ASSP, A-S-S-P?"

Moose looked up. "The aid program?"

Annalisa scowled at my changing the subject, but she nodded. "It's a Stoma program. A food aid program."

Moose shook his head. "It's bullshit is what it is, a way to get American taxpayers to subsidize Stoma's fucked-up GMO corn, and force developing nations to get on board with GMOs or watch their people starve." He looked at Annalisa. "No offense."

She waved him off. "No, you're right."

I was shocked. "He's right?"

She shrugged. "Mostly. I mean, really, there's no reason they can't send any old corn, instead of Stoma's GMO corn. Moose is right. Stoma contributes all this money, makes friends in Congress, then the friends make sure the aid legislation specifies Stoma corn. All these poor countries who don't want GMOs have to choose between the GMO corn or nothing at all. It's probably harmless but—"

"Are you serious?" Moose shrieked. "There's no research to back that up."

She shrugged. "Well, there's not enough, that's true, too. But regardless, it's a corrupt program. Helping the poor is definitely a secondary consideration at best."

"What does Thompson Company have to do with it?" I asked.

She shook her head. "Thompson Company? Nothing, I don't think. Thompson Company is small potatoes compared to Stoma. I mean, the Renfrews are rich and everything, but not like Archie Pearce."

Moose looked confused. "What do the Renfrews have to do with Thompson Company?"

I didn't realize he didn't know. "Teddy's family owns it."

"The Renfrews might be part of the one percent," Annalisa continued, "but Archibald Pearce is part of the one percent's one percent."

Moose was stunned. "The Renfrews own Thompson Company? They're just as horrible and corrupt as Stoma. They're more into the toxic chemicals than untested GMOs, although they do have some new lines of GMO corn they're pushing. Still, I don't think they're big league enough for something like ASSP."

"There seems to be some personal animosity between Renfrew and Pearce," I said.

Annalisa nodded. "I've heard that, too."

Moose laughed. "I don't like Renfrew's chances in that fight."

"Renfrew had a big to-do at his compound today," I said. "Lots of security, African diplomatic plates, and some senators: Wilden, Burlholme, and another one—"

Moose stopped. "Wilson Deveaux?"

"That's it."

"Son of a bitch."

"ASSP is up for reauthorization this month," Annalisa said quietly.

"Renfrew has totally leveraged himself, consolidating Thompson Company stock." They both looked at me. "Just what I heard,"

I said. "But it makes sense if he's trying to steal that program away from Stoma."

We stood there on the side of the road, long enough that the sun crept visibly lower, the shadows rising out of the ground, growing next to every little ripple of sand or bump in the road.

Moose turned to look at me again. "So do you think *that* could have anything to do with people shooting at you?"

I didn't want to talk about Renfrew hiring me, or me following Teddy. "I guess," I conceded. "But I don't know how."

Annalisa pointed a finger at me. "You are not going back to that hotel tonight. It's not safe."

I shrugged, but Moose shook his head. "She's right."

I laughed. "Well . . ."

"No," she said forcefully.

I laughed again. Nervously, I guess.

"It's not funny," she said, a quaver in her voice.

"I'll be fine," I said. Then I looked at my watch. "Look, I have to go take care of something, but I'll talk to you later, okay?"

"Where are you going?" Moose asked, the two of them looking at me, waiting for an answer.

"Nowhere," I said, stepping toward the Jeep. "I have to see somebody. I'll call you later, okay?"

Neither of them said anything, and I got the impression I was in trouble with them both. I waved as I drove away, but they just watched me go, their faces stern and worried.

38

Most of the security contingent was gone from Renfrew's house, replaced by a series of deep tire tracks in the grass. The sky was still light, but on the east side of West Chop it felt like night had already fallen.

Two black SUVs remained parked out front. One had a massive guy who looked to be of Viking descent sitting in the driver's seat. The other had two guys leaning against it, looking out on the water and smoking. I hoped they weren't getting combat pay.

The same guy who had led me in before came down the driveway, shaking his head. "You're relentless."

I considered relenting, just to confuse him. "Is he here?"

"Yeah, all right. Come on." He turned, and I followed him. He gave me a look over his shoulder. "He's enjoying his post-party glow."

A cool breeze was picking up. Renfrew was standing out on his front lawn amid the semi-disassembled jumble of tents and furniture and temporary flooring. He had what looked like a Manhattan in one hand, and he was looking out over the harbor. Archibald Pearce's yacht was still there but farther out, hazy in the distance, like a ghost ship. The *Mary Celeste*, I thought. Renfrew didn't seem all that perturbed by it.

"Carrick," he said without turning around. He gestured with his glass out at the harbor, the yacht in the distance. "Looks like I have him on the run, wouldn't you say?"

If anything, shrouded in mist, the boat looked even more sinister. "Did you have a nice party?" I asked.

He turned and gave me a smirk, his eyes slightly bloodshot, a faint blush on his cheeks. "I did indeed," he said, turning to look back at the yacht. "And thanks in part to you, I believe."

"How's that?"

"I'm pretty sure Teddy and his hippie trickster friends were planning to disrupt it. I don't know what he was going to pull to disrupt the motorcade, but you foiled it." He winked at me as he said it, but quickly turned back away.

"Well, I think you're right that his friends are up to something, but from what I saw, they weren't tricky hipsters, or whatever. They looked like serious trouble to me."

He smiled indulgently. "Well, they were no match for you, were they, Carrick?"

The lights on Pearce's yacht were just visible in the gathering darkness.

"I wouldn't be so sure they're finished trying whatever it is they have in mind."

"Well, if they try anything else, I'm sure you'll alert me to it and help me prevent it." He seemed almost giddy, and I thought I detected a slur in his voice.

"I'm alerting you to it now. But I won't be around to help prevent anything. I'm out."

"Really, Mr. Carrick?" He seemed genuinely surprised, his eyes staying on me for a good three seconds before turning back to look out over the water. "Easy money, an outmatched foe, a chance to keep an eye on your girlfriend as she gallivants around on our lovely island with my good-for nothing son I would have thought this was an ideal arrangement for you."

I could feel my mood souring. He flashed me a smug smile. "I'm surprised. I thought you'd be tougher than this." He shrugged. "Maybe your experiences in Dunston took more of a toll on you than I had realized."

I could feel the calm smile tightening on my face.

"Maybe that's got nothing to do with it," he said, waving his hands away. "Look, Carrick, obviously it's up to you. My offer is generous enough, so I'm not going to sweeten it. But this company is on the brink of something big. There could be a very lucrative place in it for a man like you."

"Not for a man like me."

"Suit yourself, Mr. Carrick."

I turned to go and he looked back at me, one eyebrow raised. "Last chance."

There wasn't anyone around to show me out. The security types were gone and the place seemed somehow vulnerable. I briefly thought how easy it would be to walk back up the driveway and kill Mr. Renfrew. I wondered how many people were out there who would want to.

I thought about the money I was giving up by not getting in deeper with him, and what I had taken already, what I had hoped to do with it. The vivid pictures I'd had of my future, Nola and me, our little house, they were fuzzy now, like Mungo's ghost ship out there in the mist.

I didn't know what Renfrew was up to, and I didn't want to know. He seemed pretty happy with the way things were going, but I had the strong sense they were not actually going the way he'd planned.

All I knew was that I couldn't put enough distance between me and him, between me and the fact that I had taken his money. Between me and whatever shit storm was about to break over him. I was glad to be rid of Darren Renfrew and his douchebag son. As the road curved and Renfrew's house disappeared behind the trees, I felt an odd sense of lightness, and I realized I was happy.

When my phone buzzed, I felt even better, because it was Nola.

"Hi," I said, trying hard not to sound surprised or happy or angry or pissy or relieved or anything else.

"Doyle, I need to see you. Can you come over?"

Everything seemed to be coming together. "I'll be there in ten minutes."

39

"I'm concerned about Teddy," she said when I arrived. I must have succeeded at keeping my face expressionless, because Nola didn't seem to pick up on what I was thinking. Or maybe she didn't care.

She'd been sitting on the front steps of the cabin when I drove up, looking scared and vulnerable, but at the same time strong and resolute. She stood as I walked up to her, but there was no tentative step forward, no, "How are you?"

"I think you were right, Doyle," she said. "I think Teddy's involved in something over his head. I want you to talk him out of it."

"I tried talking with him, Nola. After you told me you wanted me to leave. I knew it wouldn't do any good, and it didn't."

She looked up at me, almost defiant. "I want you to try again," she said. "For me."

The situation between us was tense, maybe even past tense, but "for me" still counted. I wondered what that meant about me and her, about us. I'd have to think about it. In the meantime, all I could do was sigh and say "okay," instead of "I told you so."

"I asked him about it after you left," she said. We were inside the cabin now, sitting on the bed. I'd been reluctant to sit on it, afraid of what it wouldn't mean, but she had sat down and patted the space next to her. And there was nowhere else to sit.

"He was already pretty worked up after talking to you," she said, her eyes flickering up at me.

I shrugged. I'd been pretty worked up, too.

"But when I asked him if he was up to something, he went off. He seemed manic, talking about making a statement, then saying it would be more than a statement. Saying he was going to strike a blow, and it would be just the beginning. Actually, he said 'we' are going to strike a blow."

"'We' meaning who?"

"I don't know. I asked him who he meant, and he said I'd see soon enough."

"Did he say anything else?"

"He said Stoma was planning on moving their GMO bees. Hiding them or something."

"Anything else?"

"He said a bunch of things about what to do if something 'happened to him.' Just logistical stuff to do with the farm, the chickens, that sort of thing."

"So, what do you want me to do?"

She stood up. "I want you to stop him before he does something incredibly stupid."

"What makes you think he's going to listen to me?"

"So don't talk to him. Just stop him."

I looked up at her. "I wouldn't even know where to look."

"I don't know what he's doing there, but he said he was going to the old Thompson Company place. It's a tiny place on Edgartown Road, just off Barnes. It's where the family business started, back when it was a farm supply company and not a chemical corporation."

"Okay."

"But you need to leave right now."

Her eyes looked into mine. *For me,* they said. *This is important to me.* And as much as it bothered me that what was important to her was Teddy, I knew I wasn't going to refuse her.

I nodded and as I turned to go she said, "Doyle," stepping up close enough that I could smell her—lemon verbena and lavender and whatever else it was, maybe her DNA. It felt like weeks since we'd been this close, and I almost staggered from the sudden sense of longing.

But I didn't. I kept my chin up and my lip stiff, even as she looked into my eyes, placed her hand softly on my cheek, and said, "Be careful."

I left in a hurry.

We hadn't made up, that much was clear. But we were back on the table, and that threw me. The way things had been going, I'd started to think that by Independence Day, I'd be, well, independent. I'd almost grown used to the idea. I needed to clear my head. I needed to think. My brain was stalling out, and I didn't want any other parts stepping up and making decisions that my brain might regret once it was back up and running.

Plus, I had to find Teddy. And stop him. I smiled at the thought that I didn't have to talk to him.

It was fully dark by the time my headlights splashed across the yellow "Thompson Farm Supply" sign, with its cartoon logo of a smiling farmer sitting on a tractor. It was at the entrance to a narrow driveway with small buildings and huts on either side, and even smaller roads crossing it. I eased down the middle, slowing at each crossing. The place seemed deserted, and I was approaching the fence at the back when I caught movement out of the corner of my eye.

I turned toward it, and saw Teddy Renfrew kneeling on the ground next to a corrugated steel shack, between a beat-up old pickup truck and a shiny black van. He jumped when my headlights passed over him, dropping a set of keys and what looked like a black plastic lid. The pickup said Thompson Farm Supply across the side. A big white plastic tank with a Thompson Chemical Company logo took up most of the bed. It had a large black spigot and a thick hose attached to it, half-unfurled, looping onto the ground at Teddy's feet, then curling up, into a smaller tank, like a five-gallon water container.

To his credit, Teddy quickly regained enough of his composure to roll his eyes and shake his head in that superior way that made me so want to hit him.

"Hey, whatcha doing?" I asked in an innocent, singsong voice as I got out of the Jeep.

"Carrick, go away," he said wearily. "Can't you take a hint? Nola doesn't want you here. No one wants you here." He laughed, a shrill, staccato burst. "Have a little self-respect and just go home."

His eyes were wide, and his skin was shiny. I wondered if he was on something, or if he was in the midst of an anxiety attack.

"Well, you might be right about Nola not wanting me here on the island, but she does want me here in this industrial park. She told me this is where you'd be."

That got his attention.

"She was afraid you were about to do something stupid." I laughed, loud. "What are the chances of that, right?"

Teddy's eyes smoldered, tight and small. Then they opened up and seemed to focus over my shoulder.

I opened my mouth to say something. I forget what, but I'm pretty sure it was hilarious and that it started with the letter "M," because that's the letter I got stuck on for what seemed like a long time as a shitload of electricity passed through my body.

I went totally rigid, which didn't interfere with the whole "Mmmmmmmmmmmmmmm," thing, then I teetered for a moment before slowly falling over onto the ground. Actually, when you fall like that, you start out slow, but by the time you hit you're going at a pretty decent clip. Luckily, the agony of being electrocuted kind of numbs you to the lesser pain of falling down. But I was pretty sure it was going to hurt later.

It wasn't until they cut the juice that I realized I'd been saying "Mmm" the whole time. When they killed the power, I moved onto "Oh."

I had a vague sense of someone stepping around me, and the sound of a car driving away. By the time I was able to stand up, I was alone. I staggered for a second, then stumbled over to the center lane as quickly as I could. I got there just in time to see the van's brake lights flare in the darkness, then twist to the right and disappear.

40

On my way back to the Jeep, I staggered and fell, but I managed to get the thing started and turned around without too much difficulty. I drove fast, a straight shot down the center of the lane, slamming on the brakes just before I turned onto the road.

I drove hard until I caught up with them, but once I did, I gave them plenty of distance.

They were driving annoyingly, conspicuously slow, and it took considerable effort to stay back as I followed them for several miles. For a while, I turned on the fog lights, hoping to look like a different vehicle. I considered whistling nonchalantly, but I didn't want to be too obvious.

We were approaching the telltale white picket fences of Edgartown when the van stopped at a stop sign up ahead and stayed there. I tapped the brakes, then harder, slowing almost to a stop.

I was torn between coasting toward them at half a mile an hour and pulling up like a normal driver and sitting directly behind them. I pictured a knife-in-the-boot paramilitary maniac throwing open the back door and spraying me with machine gun fire, hand grenades, and Chinese throwing stars. Next I pictured Teddy getting out and saying something snotty and hurtful about my relationship with Nola. I wasn't sure which was worse, so I added an embellishment to the second scenario in which I punched him in the face. Then I liked that one better.

I was starting to feel conspicuous *not* honking when they finally moved, turning onto Edgartown's Main Street. I coasted to a stop at the intersection, and had to wait while another car went by in front of me.

The street tightened in around us and the picket fences thickened as we drove into town. The van slowed even more, and I was glad to have the other car between us.

The street continued to constrict, down to a single lane as it turned one way. We were approaching the water, running out of land. The car between us turned off, and I realized there was only one block left before Main Street hit the waterfront and looped tightly around. I didn't want to get stuck right behind them.

I made a sharp left and sped up to the next intersection and waited, anxious that I'd lost them after following them for miles. Mercifully, the van appeared at the intersection a block to my right, moving in the same direction as I was. Once it cleared the intersection, I sped up to the next cross street and stopped. And I waited. And waited some more.

The road narrowed ahead of me, and a car pulled up behind me. I pulled over as far as I could, but there still wasn't room for him to pass.

The van had disappeared.

With a growl in my throat, I made the right turn. I stashed the Jeep in a small parking area halfway down the block and jogged the rest of the way.

I'd been so sure the van wouldn't be there, I almost walked

right out into the open. But I saw it just in time, pulled over on the side of the road, the engine running.

I ducked back and watched it, and after a few minutes, it rolled slowly forward sixty feet, stopping between a large seafood restaurant and a small building that backed onto the water. The smaller building had a sign in front that read MARTHA'S VINEYARD SHIPYARD, but it didn't seem to have any ships, or even much of a yard. It did have a set of what looked like railroad tracks running between the two buildings, out into the darkness and down into the water.

The back door to the van opened, and Teddy got out. The manic energy was replaced by a grim determination. Or numb determination—apart from the tension in his jaw, his face was blank. He reached back into the van and pulled out the tank he had been filling at the industrial park. He lifted it up, two hands, under his chin, elbows out. Then he turned and fast-walked around to the water side of the building, disappearing into the darkness.

For a long few seconds, nothing happened. I looked behind me, just for a moment, and when I did, the sky lit up. I could see myself silhouetted against the brick wall behind me, and for an instant, I was confused, immobile, wondering what the hell was happening. Then I was brought back to the moment by the sound of almost-screeching tires as the van sped away.

I didn't know if I should run to my car or run to see what was happening on the water. I wondered briefly if while I was distracted, Teddy had gotten into the van before it pulled away.

But he sprinted into view as I watched, skidding to a stop right where the van had been idling. He looked one way, then the other, then down at his feet, at the street beneath them. I would have felt sorry for him if it wasn't him.

The light in the sky was getting brighter, and it occurred to me I needed to be doing something. I took out my phone but before I could dial, I heard a siren rapidly getting louder.

Teddy was in a daze, but the siren snapped him out of it.

I called out to him. "Teddy!" I don't know why. Maybe I was going to tell him not to run, that he would only make it worse. But he took off before I could say anything else. Which was fine with me. I kind of liked the idea of it getting worse.

A police cruiser screeched as it swerved around the corner, the street exploding in flashing lights. As it sped past me, Jimmy Frank looked right at me and raised one eyebrow.

I waved.

Teddy had taken off running straight along the street, which meant the cruiser caught up with him after seventy feet instead of after thirty feet. It also meant that when the cruiser caught up with him, the cop inside it was that much more annoyed.

Jimmy rolled down the window as he slowed alongside Teddy. "Police," I heard him say. "Stop."

Teddy redoubled his efforts, leaning forward with his arms pumping hard, his hands flat like blades.

"Stop!" Jimmy said, his voice sounding more weary than anything else.

This time Teddy glanced over. But he didn't slow down.

Jimmy was still pacing him with the cruiser, and he reached out the window with his nightstick and gave Teddy a poke in the ribs, just enough get him off balance. Teddy took two more steps, almost in control, then a few more with his arms flailing. Then he seemed to come apart, limbs shooting out in all directions in a futile effort to regain his balance. He went over hard, his arms insufficient to stop what looked like a nasty face-plant.

I'll admit it—I laughed.

Jimmy got out of the car and looked back at me, shaking his head. He might have heard me.

The sirens had multiplied, and I looked back to see the fire trucks pulling up in front of the shipyard. The orange light illuminating the sky behind it was already dying back down.

Teddy was rolling on the ground, his hands over his face. Jimmy was standing over him. He gave me a look as I walked up, letting me know that we were going to have a talk.

Then Teddy groaned. Jimmy looked down at him and pulled out his handcuffs, saying, "You have the right to remain silent."

41

When Jimmy got him to his feet, I could see Teddy had a split lip, a red nose, and grit in his eyebrows. I let out a snort at the sight of him, earning glares from them both.

Jimmy led him past me to the car and when Teddy muttered, "Asshole," Jimmy looked at me and nodded, like the kid had a point. Then he palmed Teddy's skull and forced him down while he seated him in the back of the cruiser. He closed the door, and turned to face me.

"You think that was funny?" he said.

"Well . . . yeah. Parts of it were hilarious."

"Ha, ha. Okay, turn around."

"What for?" I protested.

"Just turn around, dumb-ass."

I turned around and felt a pair of sharp pinches on my back. "What the fuck?" I said, turning back to see Jimmy holding a pair of taser darts trailing wires.

He raised an eyebrow. "What's up with this?"

"You'll have to ask your prisoner over there. I was trying to talk him out of whatever stunt he just pulled when one of his friends tagged me from behind."

He grunted noncommittally. "And what stunt was that?"

We both looked over to where the firefighters were slowly rolling up their hoses.

"I don't know," I said. "Nola called me, concerned that he was about to do something stupid."

He snorted at that.

"I know, right? Anyway, she told me where to find him, at his dad's old Thompson Chemical Company place, on Edgartown Road. I tried to talk to him, and someone tased me from behind."

Jimmy let out a sigh and got into the car. "All right. We'll talk more about it later."

I turned and walked back down the street, past my Jeep and toward the shipyard, to see what had actually happened. I had just reached the shipyard when Jimmy pulled up next to me and got out of the cruiser.

"You know this is a crime scene under police control, right?" Teddy was fuming in the backseat.

I shrugged, but didn't stop walking. "I'm police."

He fell into step beside me. "Not here you're not."

"Come on, I'm just having a look-see."

He shook his head. "That kid might be right about you."

"Takes one to know one."

Behind the shipyard building was a small yard and a wooden dock, maybe forty feet long. Jimmy and I climbed the couple of steps up onto it and walked halfway out, to a blackened circle of charred wood with the crumpled ruins of what looked like a pile of crates, smoldering, smoking, and dripping with water. I felt a shiver go through me, and tensed my muscles against it. The air was heavy with the smell of smoke and wet ash, and behind it, almost as strong, harsh chemicals.

Jimmy tilted his head. "What the hell is that?"

"I can't say for sure. Looks like burned-out beehives."

Lying on the dock a couple of feet away was the white plastic container I'd seen Teddy filling back at the industrial park. I crouched down and touched my finger to the opening. Then I sniffed it, pulling my head back from the sharp chemical smell.

"Don't be touching every goddamned thing," Jimmy snapped.

"This is what he used," I said, looking up at him.

"What is it?" he asked. "Doesn't smell like gasoline or kerosene."

"Don't know. I saw him filling this from a bigger tank at the industrial park."

Jimmy nodded, and looked out over the water at a set of lights slowly approaching out of the darkness.

"What are you doing?" called a voice from the boat. It was Pete Westcamp. "You better not be messing with those bees! They're the last ones I got!"

Jimmy looked at me and winced.

"Goddamn it," Pete yelled, getting close enough that I could see him now. "You got no right taking those bees. I only left them there for a couple of hours. So you better bring 'em back this instant. I'm getting them off this goddamned island, taking them to Chappaquiddick, where maybe they'll be safe."

"Hey, Pete," Jimmy called out to him. The boat was coasting up to the dock. "These were your bees?"

Pete was craning his neck to see up over the dock. The boat hit the piling harder than it was supposed to. Pete staggered but he didn't fall. "What are you talking about?" he said, but his voice had lost its bluster, suddenly sounding old and confused. He didn't bother tying up the boat, and it kicked back out into the water as he clambered onto the dock. He charged forward, then stopped and fell to his knees just outside the charred circle. "Where's all my bees?" he asked, tears starting down his face. "What happened to my bees?"

42

It was midnight by the time they got Teddy booked, processed, and tucked into his cell. Martha's Vineyard had five or six police departments but only one jail, and it was by far the nicest one I'd ever seen. In the middle of scenic Edgartown, blending right in with white clapboard, black shutters, and a white picket fence.

Jimmy had emerged from the place five minutes earlier, carrying a couple of paper cups, and we were now drinking whiskey on the jail's front steps.

"You know, if I ever have to go to jail," I told him, "I think this is the one for me."

Jimmy snorted. "The way you're headed, you might get your wish." He got a laugh out of that one, but not a long one. We were tired.

"Did they set bail?"

He shook his head. "Bail commissioner's tied up until morning. Not really how it's supposed to work, but to be fair, this is a tricky one. He's not a typical flight risk, but he's got lots of money, he owns a boat, and now he's bragging about his connection to a shadowy cabal of eco-terrorists. Plus, I don't think they know what to make of the crime."

"So what do you think's going on?" I asked, nodding my head toward the jail building and the asshole inside it.

Jimmy shrugged. "He says he thought he was burning up the GMO bees. That much I believe, because just before I came out here, I told him they were Pete Westcamp's and he fell apart." Pete's honeybees were the last real ones on the island. And Teddy had just incinerated them. "Kid's in there crying worse than Pete did, talking about what people are going to think about him." He shook his head. "I still don't understand how someone could get so attached to some goddamned bugs. But anyway, I told him I don't care whose bees he thought he was burning up. He destroyed Westcamp's property. He committed a crime. Maybe he meant to commit a different crime, but he still committed a crime. I don't see how it changes things. And there's still going to be arson charges." He took a sip. "And I think he's full of shit about his secret eco-army. He says the Environmental Liberation Brigade is this big organization, but no one I asked has ever heard of it, not even Google. All I see is one asshole screwing up a stupid prank and getting in trouble for it on his own."

"He did have help, at least one guy, maybe two. And I'm pretty sure I know who, a big muscly hard-core mercenary type with a mean face and a knife tucked in his boot. I'm pretty sure that's who tased me. Teddy's been sneaking around to all these secret rendezvous. I'm pretty sure it's been with the same guy."

"So, what, you've been watching him?"

I shrugged. "I've been keeping an eye on him."

"That's what you've been doing for the old man?"

"Not anymore. Anyway, I was watching when his pal dropped him off. Then, when Teddy ran in there to do the deed, they took off. Left him there high and dry."

"So, what, you're saying they set him up?"

"How'd you get there so fast? And the fire department?"

He sighed. "Anonymous tip. I guess that would explain the phone calls."

"What's that?"

Jimmy shook his head. "Nothing really. Just that when we let him have his phone call, he couldn't get through to the number he was dialing. I could hear it from where I was sitting, 'This number is not in service,' with the little tone and everything. But he kept calling, same number, same result, over and over. Must have called it ten times. Got pretty worked up about it, too. Finally we told him he got one more try, he needed to call someone else." He sipped his whiskey and looked me in the eye. "He called your friend Nola Watkins."

"How'd that go?" I said, my voice flat.

Jimmy shrugged. "I think she told him to call his dad. He said he didn't want to. Then he asked her to call someone else for him." He snorted. "Gave her a bunch of instructions on how to take care of his chickens."

I drank some of my whiskey. Then drank some more. "So you believe someone else was involved."

He shrugged. "I don't see how it changes anything for Master Renfrew in there."

I shook my head. "Me neither. Lock him up and throw away the key, I say. Make an example out of him. And frankly, I wouldn't mind it if you found someplace a little less pleasant to keep him. But if there's other assholes working with him, they should be in there, too."

Jimmy drained his cup. "Well, you run into those friends of his, you let me know and I'll lock them up with him."

43

Renfrew had said he watched the sunrise from the front of his house every morning. The next morning before dawn, I was waiting for him.

I wasn't working for him anymore, but I felt an obligation to tell him about Teddy. Mostly, though, I wanted to see his face when I told him, see if he already knew.

Jimmy had wondered how someone could get so worked up over a bunch of insects, and I did, too. But knowing those were the last real honeybees on the island felt like a punch in the gut. If it was part of some bizarre family grudge on Renfrew's part, I wanted to know.

Annalisa was right about the Wesley, but by the time I left Jimmy, it was too late to go anywhere else. So I'd spent the night tossing and turning, thinking, worrying, and checking the chair wedged against the door. Not very restful, but at least it had been brief. When I left, I packed up my stuff and brought it with me. I didn't check out, though. If someone came looking for me, it was worth the nightly rate to keep them from figuring out I was staying somewhere else.

The sky had gone from deep blue when I got there to pale pink and then gray. It seemed now to be getting darker rather than lighter, and in the gloom I could see the lights on Archie Pearce's yacht.

The predawn cold and damp were working their way into my bones, and I was starting to think maybe Renfrew had been telling tales about his morning regimen when I heard the patio door slide open behind me, followed a few seconds later by the *shush, shush, shush* of footsteps in the wet grass.

Renfrew stepped around the chair next to me and eased himself into it without looking over. "A pleasant surprise, Mr. Carrick," he said, raising his coffee to take a sip. "Had you called ahead I would have poured you a cup."

I wished I'd called ahead. The coffee smelled incredible, and I couldn't tell if it was because it was cold and damp and five in the morning or if it was some special rich-guy coffee.

"Teddy's in jail," I told him.

He let out a soft grunt. "Teddy's an idiot."

"He incinerated Pete Westcamp's bees. Doused them with some kind of chemical and set them on fire."

Renfrew shook his head. "That doesn't sound like Teddy. Maybe if he had hugged them to death." He laughed. "Or if he had set light to me instead."

"Do you know anything about it?"

Renfrew let out a deep sigh. "I know Teddy has a track record of big, messy, stupid mistakes. And usually they end up biting me in the ass." He gave me a sour look. "I try to take precautions."

"I think he might have been set up."

"By whom?"

"By the people he thought he was working with. They left him stranded at the scene. And someone tipped off the police."

He looked thoughtful and maybe concerned for a moment. Then he held up his hand and pointed out at the water. The sun was just appearing over the horizon, a thin sliver of molten orange under a thickening blanket of clouds.

We watched for a moment. Then he slurped his coffee loudly and I wondered if he was doing it intentionally, just to spite me. "Doesn't look like you're in for much of a show this morning."

His phone buzzed and he sighed in annoyance, but looked puzzled when he read the display. "Sorry, I have to take this," he said distantly, putting the phone to his ear. "What is it?" His voice sounded like he wanted to snap but was withholding judgment. He listened for a few seconds, a deep furrow creasing his brow. Then he stood and turned away from me.

"Well, you must be wrong about that," he said, a hint of nervous laughter in his voice. Then his tone hardened. "That can't be. You heard what they said yesterday. They can't . . . What do you mean they can?"

Renfrew turned to look out over the water, his eye beginning to twitch. When I followed his gaze, I saw Pearce's yacht, the lights seeming suddenly brighter as the dark clouds swallowed up the rising sun. Together we watched as a small cluster of the lights rose away from the others. Pearce's helicopter was lifting off.

"This is bullshit, Stan," Renfrew said, his voice defiant but thin. "They made a goddamned commitment. They can't fuck us like that."

As the helicopter rose into the air, the sound of its rotors made its way across the water, that same deep *whump, whump, whump* I could feel in my chest.

Renfrew got to his feet, his eyes blazing. "*No!* No . . . Bullshit, Stan. You tell them—" His voice trailed off as he listened to what Stan was saying. The anger in his eyes was doused with fear. "No," he said quietly, almost pleadingly, one hand wrapped across his forehead.

The helicopter was flying straight at us. Without a word, Renfrew turned and walked back toward the house, away from me.

He looked over his shoulder, but he was oblivious to my presence. His eyes were on the helicopter, his feet quickening like he was scurrying to get inside before it reached us.

It was coming in fast, the rotors losing their low punch but growing louder and louder all the same. The breeze picked up as the helicopter banked low, right overhead, as if I could feel the wind from its rotors. Then it was gone.

As Renfrew went inside, I heard him saying, "Well . . . what am I going to do now?"

44

I was faced with the same question myself. Coffee was the first order, since that's just how it is. I stopped at a place called the Art Cliff Diner. They seemed to be doing a good breakfast trade, and the business smelled justified, but breakfast had to wait. Coffee was like that sometimes.

I took my coffee back to the Jeep and got out my phone.

I needed to call Nola, Moose, and Annalisa. Moose was the least urgent, but the only one where I knew where I stood. I was about to call Nola, but then a call came in from Annalisa.

"Doyle!" she said, scolding but relieved, her voice oddly hushed. "I was so worried about you. Are you okay? Why didn't you call?"

"Well, I—"

"Just tell me, are you okay?"

"I'm fine, but it was a long night—"

"Good," she said. "I'm glad you're okay. I can't really talk. I'm at work."

I looked at my watch. "It's quarter after six."

"I know. I came in early." Her voice sounded tight, and she

took a deep breath and let it out. "I need to talk to you. Can you meet me for lunch?"

"Sure. Are you okay?"

"How about noon. Do you know the Oceanview?"

"Okay, great, I'll—"

"I'll see you there." Then she was gone.

I sat there staring at the phone for a moment, wondering what was going on. She sounded stressed, but not frightened. I thought about going over to her lab, but I knew she wanted to talk far away from there.

I let a few more seconds tick by. Then I called Nola.

"Doyle?" she said tentatively.

"Yeah."

"I was worried about you."

"Sorry. I was going to call but we got finished pretty late last night. Plus, I figured you already knew what happened, since Teddy called you and all."

"Yes, I was surprised by his call as well . . . and to be hearing what happened from him, instead of from you."

"I was surprised by that, too."

"Look, we should talk. Things are crazy here right now. They were already crazy, but now I'm in charge until Teddy gets back."

"Why are you in charge?"

"Why wouldn't I be?"

"Well, you're the new girl, and . . ."

"Because, Doyle," she said, a little testy, "I'm the only one with a masters in horticulture and the only one who had run a farm of their own." She took a breath and let it out slowly. "I'm taking a break at noon for lunch. Can we meet then and talk in person?"

Part of me was cursing inside, but part of me was glad to be able to say no. "Actually, I can't, I have to meet someone. . . ."

"I see . . . Well, I guess we'll talk later."

I was relieved she didn't press me on my plans. "I can come over now," I offered, but she said no.

"So he told you what he did?" I asked.

"Yes, he told me. He thinks it's an important statement, and that it might give the native bees a chance to recover. I told him they're just going to bring more GMO bees in. But he wouldn't listen. He's so misguided, but he really does mean well."

She didn't know what had happened. Teddy had called her before he knew he'd killed Pete Westcamp's bees. "So, there's some parts of last night I might still need to tell you about."

"Okay . . ."

"After you asked me to stop him, I did find him at the industrial park, loading chemicals into a portable tank of some sort. I tried to talk him out of doing whatever he was planning, but he was his usual friendly self, and then one of his friends tased me from behind."

"Tased?"

"Shot me with a taser."

"You mean like a stun gun?"

"Kind of like, yeah."

"Oh, my God! Are you okay?"

"I recovered in time to follow them, and I caught up with them on their way to Edgartown. I got there in time to see Teddy get out of the van with the chemicals. Then he ran around behind the shipyard building. The sky lit up from the fire, and immediately, his friends took off and left him there, and the police showed up right away. Anonymous tip."

"A tip? Do you think he was set up?"

"Looks like it. Plus, well, he killed the wrong bees."

"What do you mean?"

"I mean those weren't the evil Stoma Corporation bees that he destroyed. They were Pete Westcamp's last remaining hives. Pete was getting them off the island, taking them to Chappaquiddick, where he hoped they'd be safe. Teddy killed the last regular honeybees on Martha's Vineyard."

* * *

Nola had been upset about the bees.

Moose was angry.

"What a fucking asshat!" he yelled when I told him what Teddy had done. I love Moose. "Stupid fucking idiot. Well, now we're truly screwed. Well and truly. Even if he'd killed the *right* bees, it would have given credibility to every bullshit stereotype Archie Pearce and his type say about anyone who protests when some mega corporation tries to make a few billion dollars off the destruction of something they don't own. But now, in addition, he's made those goddamned GMO bees all but necessary around here. People who were carrying pitchforks two days ago, ready to run Stoma off the island, they're going to be lining up for a chance to get GMO bees onto their farms." He finished with an unintelligible growl.

"Any word from Benjy?"

"No," he said, suddenly subdued. "Nothing."

"Nothing from the police either?"

"No. They seem to be busy with other things." He let out a long sigh, but my sense was he wished he'd taken a deeper breath before it so he could have sighed a little longer. "I don't know. I need to do another round of data checks, and see if there's any good news. But there won't be. Especially not now. Actually, I need to move two of the stations, but it's a two-man job. Any chance you could give me a hand for an hour?"

"Yeah, I can do that."

I regretted it as soon as I said yes, but I knew it would be good to do some physical work and not think about Nola or Teddy or any other Renfrews for that matter. I should have known that wouldn't last. We were driving from Felix Neck down to Trapp's pond when the subject of Teddy Renfrew came up again.

"So what do you suppose Teddy was thinking?" Moose wondered out loud.

"I don't know," I replied. "I don't know the guy that well. But

I've known a lot of other douchebags in my time, so I would imagine he was thinking about himself."

"What do you mean?"

"Whatever it was he thought he was doing, maybe he thought he was making the world a better place, but more likely, he thought he was making the world a better place for him. A place where he was regarded as a hero, a badass, or whatever. Where women like Nola would fall for his shit, or more of them would."

He laughed. "Seriously. I don't know what she sees in him."

My head snapped around so fast it hurt. "You think she sees something in him?"

He laughed again. But stopped when he saw my face. "No, not like that. I don't think so. I mean the ladies seem to think he's a good-looking guy, but I don't see it. And I don't think Nola does, really, either. But she does take him seriously as someone with something to say."

"And you don't?"

"We're on the same side of a lot of issues, and I did at first, but the more I've seen of him, I think he's a bit of a poseur. To be fair, he's built a pretty impressive farm operation. He brags about it a bit too much sometimes, but it's hard to make a living doing that."

"He's not."

"What do you mean?"

"According to his father, the farm's been losing money since day one. It's a hobby."

"Well, I didn't know about the Thompson connection, and I know his family's rich, but Teddy specifically told me he doesn't get any money from his dad."

I told him about the trust fund from his grandmother.

"Oh."

"Still take him seriously?"

"Serious pain in the ass."

I laughed. I love Moose.

* * *

He dropped me off at my car around eleven. My stomach was starting to grumble, but lunch wasn't too far off and I had a stop I needed to make.

As I drove to Edgartown, I called Jimmy Frank.

"Hey, Doyle. What's up?" He sounded tired, but he wasn't angry.

"Hey, Jimmy. Just checking in to see what new surprises have arisen in the last eight hours."

"Well, your pal Renfrew junior is still a guest of the citizens of this fine island."

"Really? No one bailed him out?"

"Apparently not. There were some delays with setting bail. His dad was going to send someone down, but by the time they had a number, twenty grand, Dad was incommunicado. Junior's kind of pissed about it."

"Huh." I didn't know what was going on with Renfrew, but he'd seemed more than a little preoccupied when I left him. "Any new information?"

"Just that he's even more annoying than I thought. Can't seem to make up his mind if he's a badass tough guy and we'll never break him, or a sniveling wuss who can't wait for Daddy to come and save him."

"Can I talk to him?"

"Probably. Why would you want to?"

I didn't want to tell Jimmy I wanted to find out who was responsible for killing those bees, and it wasn't just for Pete Westcamp, or anybody else. "Have you ever been tasered?"

Jimmy laughed. "Nope."

"Well, if you had, you'd want to find out who'd done it to you."

45

"What are you doing here?" Teddy asked through his cell door when he saw me, his busted lip curled in a swollen sneer. I wanted to say "gloating," but as much as that was true, I also wanted information.

"What are you doing here?" I countered. "Bail's been set, right?"

He rolled his eyes and looked at Jimmy, then away from both of us. "They're running late, that's all."

I nodded and he looked back at me, his head at an angle.

"So, did you mean to kill Pete Westcamp's bees?"

"I'm waiting for my lawyer."

I shrugged. "Okay with me. I just thought you wouldn't want people thinking that you'd gone over to the dark side."

"Of course I didn't mean to kill Pete's bees. Pete's my friend." I was pretty sure Pete Westcamp felt the same way I did toward Teddy, but I didn't say anything. "I already told them. That asshole Brecker set it up. They were supposed to be the Stoma Corporation bees."

"Brecker? Is that his name? That's the guy who drove away while you were killing the bees?"

He nodded.

"Is that the guy who tased me?"

"I don't know," he said, his busted lip widening in a sly smile. "It was dark." The smile widened. Then he winced and put his hand to his lip. It came away smeared with blood.

I wanted to say something else funny, see if I could make him laugh, but I focused on the matter at hand. "So that's the guy who set you up, who tricked you into killing your friend's bees, the last real honeybees on the island. The guy who stranded you and called the police on you?"

His cheeks were turning pink as I spoke. "Yes," he said, his voice a dry rasp.

I let it sit there for a second.

"So here's the thing," I said. "It doesn't bother me that you're in here. Frankly, I think you're an asshole, and it's nice not having to worry about running into you on the outside. Besides, setup or not, you fucked up big time. But I think this Brecker guy is an asshole of a different magnitude. It bothers me that he's not in here, too. It bothers me enough that I want to put him here even if it means you get out because of it. Plus, I have no idea what he's up to, but I doubt very much that putting you in jail and killing some bees is all of it. So why don't you tell me what you know about Brecker, and we'll see if we can stop him before he does whatever he's planning next."

It turned out, Teddy didn't know much. Maybe if he had known more he might have thought twice before being totally manipulated.

Brecker had approached him at a sustainable farming conference, knew his name, and said he recognized him from some earlier events, a G20 protest planning meeting, a couple of other places that he wouldn't have known about unless he'd been there. They bumped into each other at a few other places. Then Brecker told Teddy about a new group, the Environmental Liberation Brigade, and how they wanted Teddy to be a part of their leadership.

He reddened when he told me that, I think realizing how easily he'd been played.

"And when did that happen?" Jimmy asked. "When did you first meet him?"

"A few months ago. Maybe late January."

"So how did this plan come about?" I asked.

"Brecker had been saying for a while we were going to do something. They said they had information about where the GMO bees were going to be. A small window when all the hives would be at the same place at the same time."

"They?"

"Yeah, there were two of them. I mean, they always made it sound like there were others as well, other cells. But it was the three of us in our cell."

"Who was the other guy?"

"Eddie Sholes."

"Big guy with a kind of pushed-in nose?"

"Yeah, and a busted-up arm."

I laughed, and Jimmy looked at me questioningly. I shrugged and looked back at Teddy. "So where would we find these guys?"

"I don't know. All I knew was Brecker's phone number. And that stopped working the night I . . . the night I got arrested."

I turned to Jimmy. "You got a sketch artist on this island?"

"If your perpetrator is a golden-hued sunset or maybe a sand piper, sure. Otherwise, not so much. But I know a guy in New Bedford. Maybe I can get him on Skype with the ant bully here."

Annalisa was waiting at a table in the back corner when I walked into the restaurant. She seemed nervous but she smiled when she saw me.

Before I even sat down, the sound came up from the television mounted on the wall, and I turned to see Teddy Renfrew's mug shot.

"Details continue to emerge regarding last night's bizarre terror attack in Edgartown, on Martha's Vineyard," said Sierra Johnson, the same woman who had interviewed Archie Pearce and Johnny Blue. With all this craziness on the island, Sierra was becoming a star. Annalisa and I shared a look, and she shook her head as the report continued, cutting to a corporate headshot of Darren Renfrew. "Teddy Renfrew, son of Thompson Chemical Company owner and CEO Darren Renfrew, has been charged with arson, destruction of public property, and risking a catastrophe, among other charges, in a bizarre act of vandalism that may have killed the last remaining honeybees on the island of Martha's Vineyard."

Cut to security cam footage of Teddy on the dock, grainy but clearly recognizable, spraying the hive boxes, then lighting a match. The picture went white in the sudden glare from the fire. "Security footage from a nearby restaurant documented the crime, in which it now seems the younger Renfrew used an agricultural insecticide called Wipe-Out, manufactured by his father's company, to kill the bees. In a statement, Teddy Renfrew expressed sorrow at the death of the bees and claimed he had intended to destroy the hives of Stoma Corporation's controversial genetically engineered Bee-Plus bees, which now appear to be the only honeybees left on the island. Stoma Corporation and Thompson Company have been rivals since the early seventies. There is no comment from Thompson Company about the use of its chemical in the crime, or about speculation that the two Renfrews were working together. A Thompson Company spokesman said the company has launched an internal investigation and is cooperating fully with the authorities."

46

I continued to stare at the screen, even after the back-to-you-Jim banter and the sneak peak at the weekend weather.

"You okay?" Annalisa said.

I looked back to her and smiled. "I'm fine."

The waitress came and I ordered coffee and a cheeseburger. Annalisa ordered a salad. After watching the waitress walk away, she leaned forward again. "I've been doing some digging," she said, placing a manila folder on the table. "I used Julie's ID and accessed some of the Bee-Plus data to see if there was anything that might somehow suggest the gene splices were unstable. I found some very interesting data sheet anomalies."

"Is that safe?"

She looked at me and shrugged unconvincingly.

"What are data sheets?"

She opened the folder and spread out several sheets of paper, each covered with columns of numbers. "Sheets the lab techs fill out every day. How much nectar has been consumed, water, the weight of the hive, temperature, honey production—a whole range of data points. It's all entered into the computer, so we can analyze it and track it, look for trends or anomalies."

"Okay, and what did you find?"

She looked up at me for a second, her eyes fearful. "I didn't see anything in the data at first. And I still don't, really, not anything suggesting that the gene splice is unstable, but look at this." With her fingers she bracketed a series of numbers. "See these numbers?" It was a bunch of columns just like the others.

"Yes, but I don't know what they mean."

"They don't mean anything by themselves. But look at this." She pulled out another sheet, dated six weeks later, and with her fingers bracketed another set of data. "Do you notice anything?"

Before I could answer, she put the two sheets side by side, so the two data sets were right next to each other.

I looked up at her. "It's the same data."

"Exactly," she said quietly, sitting back in her seat. "Thirteen data points over seven days, identical in every aspect. Ninety-one data points. Six weeks apart."

"What are the chances—" I started to ask, but she shook her head.

"There are no chances."

"So it's faked?"

She stared at me for a second, silent, like she didn't want to say it out loud. Her eyes swept the room. Then she sat forward again. "Now look at this." With her finger, she indicated the column all the way to the right, each line showing the letters "LN."

"LN," she said, practically whispering. "Lynne Nathan. The lab assistant I told you about. My friend." She pointed to the date column on the later set of matching data points. "This is the week she died."

She stared at me, right in the eyes, her face deadpan but her eyes welling with tears.

"What does that mean?" I asked, whispering.

"I don't know." She gave me that stare again, like she was daring me to have a reaction. I didn't know what reaction to have.

"There's more." She put two more sheets in front of me, side by side, and simultaneously bracketed with her fingers a set of data on each page. "Identical data. Two months later, eight weeks apart. Every single data point matches."

"Seriously?"

"The data is clearly falsified. It's just a matter of happenstance that I saw it and noticed. The question is: what are they hiding?" Her finger drifted over to the initials column. "See the initials? CO, that's Claudia Osterman. I don't know her well, but I worked with her a few times on Samana Cay. This second data set, the fake one, those are the last entries in the records with her initials." She paused for a moment, chewing the inside of her cheek. "A few months ago, when I said I might be coming to Martha's Vineyard, she told me she was from Providence, not too far from here. This morning, when I saw this, I looked up her family and I called them. Her mother answered the phone, an older woman. Sounded very pleasant. But when I asked to speak to Claudia, she hung up immediately. Actually, she dropped the phone. Then she hung up."

"What do you think that means?"

Annalisa shrugged, biting her lip, like she didn't want to say it.

"Providence, huh?"

She nodded.

"Do you think I should go talk to them?"

"I don't know what to think. If Stoma is watching them, or watching you, it could be dangerous."

I laughed. "It's not like the island is so safe."

"I know, but if we are onto something here, and they realize where you're going . . ."

"If anybody notices, they'll probably just be glad I'm gone. It can't be much more than a few hours each way. I could be back for dinner."

"It's two hours, depending on how long you have to wait for the ferry."

"I wonder when the next ferry is."

She looked at her watch. "Next one leaves in thirty-five minutes." There was a gleam in her eye, and I got the feeling my going to Providence hadn't been purely my idea.

The waitress was walking by, and I motioned her over. "Can I have that cheeseburger to go?"

47

The clouds parted as the ferry churned its way out into the harbor. I tried to soak up some of the meager warmth from the sun, eating my cheeseburger on the deck despite the cold wind tearing at the foil wrapper. As I watched the island shrinking slowly away from me, I felt uneasy leaving Annalisa and Nola and Moose there, alone.

It didn't help that when I looked off to the east, I saw Archie Pearce's massive yacht, anchored like a pirate ship waiting to plunder the island. It helped even less that when I looked off to the west, I saw Renfrew's compound. I had no idea what state Renfrew was in, but my sense was that it wasn't good. I could practically feel the enmity between the two of them, and out on the deck, I felt a compulsion to stay down low, in case a shooting war broke out between them.

In Woods Hole, the bus took me to the parking lot. My car was there, just as I had left it. It felt strangely familiar and unfamiliar. It had only been a few days, but I was somehow surprised that it started right up and went where I told it.

Driving away from Woods Hole, I once again felt like I was

leaving things behind, anxious about what would be going on in my absence. And even though I'd only explored the tiniest bit of the island, I felt a strange sense of agoraphobia with an entire continent yawning in front of me.

I called Nola, told her I had to take care of something off island.

"Off island?" she said, her voice alarmed. "Where are you going?"

"It's nothing. I just have to look into something. Are you okay?"

"Well, yes, but . . . when are you coming back?"

"I'll be back in a few hours. Why?"

"Well . . . I don't know. It's just, I . . ." I thought she was going to say she missed me, and my foot eased off the gas pedal, in case I needed to turn the car around right there. "Things are getting weird on the island."

My foot resumed its pressure on the gas pedal. "How do you mean?"

"Well, a month ago, this place was an environmental Eden, and suddenly its about to become Stoma's Bee-Plus showroom."

I didn't say anything.

"It just feels like the beginning of the end of something. Something beautiful."

I wondered if she was in some way talking about us. "Right," I said softly.

She sniffed on the other end, and I wanted to put my arms around her, tell her it was going to be okay. But instead, I was driving away from her at eighty miles an hour.

"Call me when you get back, okay?"

"Okay. Just a few hours."

"Okay," she said, her voice cracking into a breathy whisper as the phone went dead.

I pressed down harder on the gas, anxious to get to where I was going, do what I needed to do, and get back to the people I cared about.

Swinging through New Bedford, I was struck by how urban it felt, jarring after the Island. Providence, which barely seemed to rise above ground level on the way up, now felt positively metropolitan.

The address for the Ostermans was a well-maintained stone house with a two-car parking area carved into the front lawn. I parked on the street, the only car on the block to do so, and rang the bell.

No answer. I tried two more times. The street felt deserted, and I looked at my watch. It was a quarter after three. I drove the car halfway down the block and turned around so I could watch the house.

Then I waited.

I was usually pretty good at waiting, turning off my brain, or at least the part of it that got impatient, and sitting tight until something happened.

This time, it wasn't so easy. My mind was spinning thinking about Nola and Annalisa, about Teddy and his father, about Stoma and Thompson Company, and about the bees. I generally didn't get too worked up about environmental issues. The notion of global warming was frightening and unsettling, but not in a concrete way. Not enough to make me stop driving my car, which I guess was part of why the world was so screwed.

Except it was starting to feel different. Maybe my time with Nola and being friends with Moose had changed me. Or seeing what had happened to Dunston. Maybe it was seeing Pete Westcamp breaking down, or all those dead bees.

Whatever it was, I couldn't stop thinking, and I felt myself getting angry. It was an amorphous anger at the world, and the more I stewed, the more that yacht of Archie Pearce's seemed to personify everything that was wrong in the world: rich beyond belief, ostentatious beyond any possibility of self-awareness, sitting there off the coast, pulling strings to make things happen. As much as I appreciated the hilarity of parking your behemoth yacht in the middle of your nemesis's thirty-million-dollar view, I couldn't get past the realization that Stoma was evil.

It was four-thirty and Providence P.D. had buzzed me twice when I saw two women coming up the block, a mother in her early sixties and a daughter in her mid-twenties. They maintained physical contact as they walked, the mother's arm interlinked with the daughter's.

I sat up in my seat for a better look. I'd Googled their images and was pretty sure this was them. When they reached the house I was watching, they headed up the front steps.

I waited until they were inside. Then I gave it another few minutes, so they wouldn't think I'd been watching the house.

The younger one opened the door. She was heavyset but solid, like an athlete. She had a smart face, smiling when she opened the door, but with a wariness in her eyes.

"Hello?" she said.

From the other room her mother called out, "Who is it?" but we both ignored her.

"Hi," I said, smiling back. "Is this the Osterman household?"

"Yes, what can I do for you?" she asked.

"Well, I was actually trying to find Claudia Osterman."

Her mother's voice got louder and closer. "Beth, close the door."

Beth's eyes narrowed and hardened. She looked like she wanted to take me apart. She looked like she could do it, too.

"What's this about?" she asked.

"Um, I just want to ask her some questions."

"About what?"

"Beth!" her mother's voice snapped. "Close the door."

Beth shook her head, turning to look back inside, her eyes momentarily flickering hatred and disgust with such intensity I took a step back. When her eyes returned to me, they were wet with anguish.

"She can't . . ." Her voice was swallowed up by a gulping sob. "We can't . . ."

Her mother appeared at her elbow, her face red and her eyes glaring. "Close the door!" she practically shrieked. Her eyes met mine, just for an instant. Then the door slammed shut. The house shook from the force of it.

I stepped back, realizing I'd been holding my breath. After a few seconds, I turned and went back to the car. But I didn't start the engine. Maybe I was stunned at the reaction I'd received, or maybe I was waiting for something else to happen. Sure enough, ten minutes later, the daughter came out of the house. She walked down the steps and paused on the sidewalk, then turned and walked toward me. We made eye contact as she approached, and as she walked past me, she said out of the corner of her mouth, "Follow me to the park."

I looked past her and saw a wall of green at the end of the next block.

I waited until she was almost at the corner. Then I drove past her, to the end of the block, then the block after that, parking on the corner near the entrance to the park.

She seemed like she was going to walk right past me. Then she abruptly turned her head and came over. As if I had called her.

She leaned toward the window.

"Who are you?" she asked.

I showed her my badge. "Doyle Carrick. I'm with the Philadelphia police, but I'm not here on official business."

"Then why are you here?"

"That's a good question. I was hoping to talk to Claudia."

"Claudia's dead."

I was stunned but not surprised. It was a lot of coincidence that the two women whose data had been faked were both dead, and I fought hard not to betray my alarm. ". . . I'm sorry to hear that. Can I ask how she died?"

"Go to the end of the block, make a right, then a left. Walk up the path into the other side of the park and I'll meet you."

With that she turned and walked into the park. I did as she

said, parking next to a grassy area across from the river. The sun had come out, and it was noticeably warmer than on the Island. I crossed the street, past a line of benches and some flowers along the sidewalk. Walking across a small grassy area toward the woods, something about the place tickled the back of my mind. I looked around me, trying figure out what it was, but as I entered the woods, I saw Beth standing among the trees.

48

She gave me an awkward wave, and I walked over to her. "Probably not the best place to meet someone I don't know," she said, "but I guess if they wanted to kill me, they'd just do it."

"Who's that?"

She stared at me for a second. "Let me see your badge."

I handed it to her and she studied it closely. Then she looked inside the wallet. I resisted the urge to snatch it back from her. She looked at a couple of credit cards, then handed the wallet back to me. "Sorry," she said. "I don't even know what I'm looking for. I just need to be sure, you know?" Her voice thickened for a second, but she cleared her throat and gave her head a good shake. "Sorry. You said you had questions. What do you want to know?" She turned and started walking.

I fell into step beside her. "What happened to Claudia?"

She let out a bitter laugh. "We don't know. I never got a good answer."

"What do you mean?"

"We're not supposed to talk to anyone about it. That was part of the deal. In fact, we're not even supposed to talk about the fact that we're not supposed to talk about it. But the fact is, I don't know what happened to her anyway."

"What deal?"

"Are you working for Stoma?"

"No."

She closed her eyes and nodded. "Claudia was working at Stoma. It was always kind of secret, but she was working on some sort of program on a deserted island in the Caribbean. She was making good money, but she wasn't allowed to talk about it."

I nodded. "So what happened?"

She sighed and looked away from me. "She never came back. They said there was an accident where she was working, that she was lost at sea."

"I'm sorry."

She nodded.

"They never recovered the body?" I asked.

She shrugged and wiped her nose. "They *said* they never recovered the body."

"What do you mean?"

She took a deep breath. "After they told us what happened, or, you know, what they said happened, they gave us this big box with all of Claudia's effects. And her Saint Christopher's medal was in it." She stopped and looked at me for emphasis. "She never took that medal off. Ever. Our grandmother gave it to her. She gave us each one. We swore we would never take them off, but also, I know Claudia got a lot of comfort from knowing that she was wearing that medal. I think the job was pretty intense, the people she worked with and the place she worked. Like I said, she made good money, but it was a hard job. Stressful and scary and lonely." She paused to collect herself. "Claudia would never have taken her medal off."

"So what do you think happened?"

"Something else. She died in some way that they didn't want us to see the body. Like maybe she was disfigured or . . . assaulted or something. I don't know. But I think they had her body, and they took the medal off it."

We walked quietly for a moment. "They told us in person," she said. "They sent three of them, to tell us to our faces that she was gone. It nearly killed my mom. My dad had just died a year earlier, so losing Claudia so soon, it hit her hard. Me, too."

"I'm sorry."

"Anyway, when they told us, they offered to make a cash settlement. They said part of it was insurance, but that they also wanted to express how sorry they were, to help ease our pain and suffering. They were really nice. The settlement was big, really big, and my mom had been in a tough spot financially. My dad wasn't the best financial planner, you know? But the deal included us agreeing that there were no more questions, and we weren't allowed to tell anyone what happened, or what we thought happened, or what they told us happened. We had to be silent. My mom said yes, because she was in such a bind, and neither of us were in any shape to be thinking critically. But later, just a couple of days later, we started thinking, and started wondering, and we had questions. And then they weren't so nice anymore. They made it clear, they would come back for the money. They also made it clear they would come back for more than that."

"What do you mean?"

"I mean they made it plain, they could go from nice to not nice, to really, really not nice, if we didn't keep quiet."

"So that's why we're in the woods?"

"Mostly so my mom doesn't see us, because she's terrified they're going to find out and come after us. Take the house away from us, or come after me. I honestly don't care about the money. I just want to know what happened to my sister."

"Are you scared?" I said quietly.

"Scared of Stoma?" She laughed bitterly. "Of course I am. You should be, too."

* * *

We each walked out of the park the way we had come in. I was in a daze, processing what she had told me. But as I cut across the grass, I realized what had struck me on the way in: bees. Not a lot of them, but enough. Half a dozen as I looked around me, floating, zipping, meandering. They wouldn't have been noteworthy in any way except that they were alive, and it made me realize how starkly absent they were on the island.

49

As I drove out of Providence, I called Annalisa. A line of dark clouds had formed low on the southern horizon. She was quiet when I told her about my conversation with Beth Osterman.

"Did you know Claudia well?" I asked her.

"Hardly at all," she said in a whisper. "But it's still sad. And scary. What does it mean?"

"I don't know."

"Did they kill her?"

"I don't know. Maybe. Beth said Claudia never took off her Saint Christopher medal. That says to me, whatever happened, they didn't want anyone seeing her body."

"We probably shouldn't talk about this on the phone. I have some news, too. Can you meet me at my place, when you get back?"

"Sure. I'll let you know when I get off the ferry."

Before I left the Impala in the parking lot, I opened the trunk and the safe and took out my Glock. I held it in my hand for a moment, enjoying the feel of it before putting it into its holster and wrapping it around my ankle.

I gave the Impala an apologetic shrug, feeling vaguely guilty leaving it behind once again. I don't think it expected anything more from me. I liked the car fine, but there was no pretense to anything more.

The line of dark gray clouds had followed me back to Woods Hole, creeping a little bit higher. By the time the shuttle dropped me off at the terminal, it was a solid gray wall taking up a quarter of the sky.

I waited outside the ferry terminal next to a large planter of pansies. A lone honeybee was going from bloom to bloom, doing the nectar and pollen thing. I watched with new fascination, wondering if it had any notion of what was going on in the world around it.

A few minutes before we boarded the boat, a car pulled up next to me. A misty-eyed middle-aged couple got out of the front and their twenty-something daughter got out of the back, holding a bouquet of flowers. The dad lifted a couple of small suitcases out of the trunk and the daughter tucked the flowers into a side pocket of one of the suitcases. They all hugged and stood together awkwardly until boarding was announced a couple of minutes later.

The parents drove away, and as we started moving forward I noticed that the bee had finished with the pansies and succumbed to the temptation of the bouquet, thorax-deep in some kind of lily. The flowers shook as we moved, and I expected the bee to fly away, but it hung in there as we ascended the gangway. I wondered if I should warn it that it might be headed to its death, or if somehow this bee was the island's last hope. When we got onto the boat, the girl made her way to the dining area and I lost sight of her and the bee.

Up on the deck, the wind was already picking up, so I headed back inside. As soon as I sat down, the sound of Archie Pearce's Outback Steakhouse accent caught my attention, and I turned to see his face on the television next to the snack bar.

"We're deeply saddened by the turn of events," he was saying.

"Our hearts go out to this disturbed young man, Teddy Renfrew, and to his father, Darren Renfrew, and the rest of the Renfrew family, and everyone at Thompson Chemical Company. Obviously we condemn any destruction of property, but while we were not directly harmed by this senseless act, we were its target, and we will be increasing security accordingly. But I want to make a pledge to the farmers on this island, who depend on honeybees for the pollination of their crops: while this act of vandalism has hastened the decimation of honeybees on the Island of Martha's Vineyard, we at Stoma Corporation are prepared to make our Bee-Plus bees available to any farmer who asks, at no charge. And to the farmers facing this plight across America, who are asking when Bee-Plus will be available to save their farms, the answer is: just as soon as possible."

I texted Moose: ARE YOU WATCHING THIS?

He called back less than a minute later. "Can't believe it," he said. "Leave it to Stoma Corporation to take advantage of a catastrophe and turn it into a PR coup."

I wasn't so sure it was a coincidence, but I kept that to myself.

"The island's going nuts," he said. "The farmers are in a panic, half of them desperate to get on Stoma's waiting list and the others trying to figure out any other way to take care of their crops. A couple days ago people were just worried about the early crops, but now they're freaking out about everything. And no mainland beekeeper in his right mind is going to bring his bees here now."

"No?"

"Are you kidding? Something just wiped out the island's entire honeybee population. A few weeks ago, we were keeping the mainland bees off the island so we didn't bring in the colony collapse disorder or whatever it is. Now whatever is happening here is a hundred times worse than anything out there. They don't want whatever happened to our bees happening to their bees."

We were both quiet for a moment.

"Have you talked to Nola?"

He sighed. "Yeah. She's freaked out. She's trying to run Teddy's farm for him while he's locked up. I mean, she knows what she's doing, she's a good farmer, but it's not her farm, and now she has to maintain the whole thing by herself, the chickens and everything, and she has less help than he did."

I called Nola as soon as I got off the phone with Moose, but she didn't answer. As I put away my phone, I saw helicopters coming in from the south, headed toward the island. There was no swooping or banking; they were headed in a straight line, rising just enough to maintain their altitude as they crossed over the land. They stayed low and immediately disappeared over the trees. The phone rang in my hand. Nola, calling me back.

"Sorry I missed you," she said breathlessly. "I was trying to get a few things done before dark."

As she spoke I could hear the sound of the helicopters growing on the phone.

"Helicopters?" I asked.

"That's the third time today," she said.

"I just saw them."

"They're headed to Katama. Stoma is setting up another staging area for Bee-Plus. Protesters are there already. Are you back on the island?"

"I'm on the ferry. Are you okay?"

"Things are getting weird here."

"Weird how?"

"The island feels like an armed camp. People are uneasy, and wherever you turn, there's some Darkstar goon with an ear piece and a strange bulge under his jacket. Stoma is pulling out the stops, security wise."

"Are you okay?"

"Yeah, I'm fine. It's just creepy."

"You should get out of there."

"Doyle, I can't just get out of here. I made a commitment and I need to take care of this place."

"You didn't make a commitment to do all of it yourself, Teddy should have made arrangements if he was going to go off and do something stupid. He should have planned for contingencies."

She sighed. "Well, he didn't. And it's not the chickens' fault, so they shouldn't suffer."

"Then I could come over," I said.

She sighed again, but this time with maybe a hint of a laugh in there. "Not yet, all right? I'm okay."

At least I made her laugh.

50

Jimmy answered on the first ring. "Hey, Doyle. Kind of in the middle of something."

The background noise sounded like the thing he was in the middle of was an all-out riot. "What's going on there?"

He laughed. "I got reassigned to the Eastern Front. Stoma's bringing in more of those bees, and they're setting up a staging area near Katama airport. Lots of knuckleheads from both sides."

"Any sign of Benjy?"

I heard the muffled sound of the phone coming away from his ear, his voice yelling, "Hey, get down from there!" Then he came back. "No, but he's probably okay."

I wasn't so sure. "I need to trade notes with you on some stuff. Can we touch base after your shift?"

He snorted. "Sure, whenever that is."

It was dark when I got off the ferry. Walking back to my rented Jeep, I immediately noticed the vibe, just like the lobby at the Wesley Hotel. It was like *Invasion of the Body Snatchers*, only instead of being transformed into aliens, half the population had been transformed into hard-faced, muscle-bound private soldiers. It was like a Darkstar corporate retreat.

It felt like prison yards I'd walked through, dead-eye stares blowing around like dandelion fluff in the air, like a piece of it could just land on you and all of a sudden you'd be in the middle of trouble. Not what you'd expect on the gentle streets of Vineyard Haven. A couple of the men looked at me as I opened my car door, and I looked back at them blankly. Just another asshole, just like them.

I texted Annalisa, told her I'd be there in a few minutes. She was waiting when I got there, watching through the tiny window in her front door. She came outside and locked the door behind her as soon as I pulled up.

I kept the engine running, because it seemed like we might be going somewhere. She got in the passenger side and fastened her safety belt.

"Can you drive me to the lab?" she asked. "And can you break into it with me?"

"What are you talking about? Why would you need to break into your own lab?"

"Not my lab. Sumner's."

"What are you talking about?"

"The fudged data on those data sheets is not just for external consumption. That's the data Sumner has been sending to Stoma. Whatever he's hiding from the world, he's hiding from Stoma, too. Without the original data, we're never going to know why, or why they seem to think it's worth killing someone over. But Sumner is a scientist, and that data is extremely valuable, so I know he won't have destroyed it. I'm pretty sure I know where it is on his secure server, but it's going to take a little while to get at it, too long to try to sneak it during the workday."

"We should go to the police," I said, feeling very mature and responsible saying it.

"Well, that crossed my mind, too. But we have two things here. One is the faked lab sheets, and yes, if we can prove Sumner has submitted them in some official way, then, yes, he could get into trouble. But it would take years and the result would probably be a small fine, if anything. And by then any damage will have been long since done."

I stayed quiet.

"The other thing is whatever happened to Claudia Osterman and Lynne Nathan," she said quietly. "But that's just a suspicion on our part, a suspicion of two murders with no bodies, that might have taken place on international waters, that have already been accepted as workplace accidents. Which they may have been."

I looked at her for a moment. This was the kind of reality check I was more used to giving than receiving.

She took a deep breath. "I'm already into this," she said, like it was taking a great effort to keep her voice steady. "If we stop now, without knowing what's going on, I'll spend the rest of my life worrying I'm going to end up like Lynne or Claudia."

"Okay," I said, "where are we going?"

As it turned out, we had a stop to make first.

"The gym," she said. "In Vineyard Haven."

"The gym?" I said. "Do you usually have to warm up before committing a felony?"

She gave me a look that was the opposite of laughter. "I have to pick something up."

She directed me to the Mansion House, a venerable grand dame of a hotel, right in the middle of Vineyard Haven.

"This is the gym?"

She nodded. "Gym/spa/hotel. Keep the engine running," she said as she got out of the car. "I'll be back in a minute."

I was double-parked in the middle of one of the busiest intersections on the island, preparing to commit one crime while acting as an accessory to another. It wasn't much more than the minute she promised, but sitting there so conspicuously, it felt excruciatingly long. As she got back in the car and I pulled into a knot of slow, congenial "Oh, no, I insist, after you" traffic, I crossed "getaway driver" off the mental list of occupations I might try if the whole police thing didn't work out.

"What was that all about?" I asked, compulsively checking my rearview as if we had just pulled off a bank job.

She held up a white plastic swipe card with a red Stoma logo on it. It looked almost identical to the one I'd seen around her neck. Except this one said Julie Padulla. Sumner's assistant.

I raised an eyebrow.

"She'll be swimming for another half hour, then forty minutes in the sauna and the whirlpool. The place is open till nine, and she closes it every Tuesday and Thursday. We just need to be sure I have this back in her locker before she's done."

"This is a side I didn't know you had."

She shrugged and looked out the window. "I didn't know it either."

51

Sumner's lab was on the back end of Johnny Blue's Farm, directly across the road from Annalisa's lab. A half-dozen protesters remained, but they looked tired and fed up. A few of them looked like they'd been drinking, their eyes heavy with beer and belligerence.

On the other side of the fence was a car that looked like a police car but wasn't. It looked more like mall security than Darkstar.

It seemed as though both sides had sent their "A" teams to Katama.

A couple of the protesters looked up at us wearily, but when we turned toward the gate across the street, they looked away.

I drove up the driveway and pulled in behind the lab unit, then killed the engine. The words "Leave Our Island" were spray-painted in red across the side, and the door was bent where it had been pried open.

"That's the vandalism?" I said.

She nodded and rolled her eyes. I wasn't buying it either.

"Okay, so how do you want to play this?" I asked.

"There didn't used to be guards," Annalisa replied with a tight, jittery shake of her head. "I'm allowed access to unit one. The server is in unit two. But once I'm inside the gate, I can use Julie's card to access unit two, where the server is. They're not going to let you in, though. Not with everything that's going on."

"Are there surveillance cameras?"

She nodded again. "Yes, but just at the front gate. To keep an eye on the protesters."

"Do they cover the entrance to this place?"

"They might."

I studied her face for a moment: nervous but resolute. "How are you going to get through the crowd?"

She shrugged, pretending she wasn't scared at the prospect. "I'll get through."

I stared at her for a moment, but she just shrugged again.

"Okay," I said. "Give me ten minutes to make my way around to the side. Then approach the gate. I'm thinking there should be enough commotion to cover the noise of me climbing the fence."

"Then what?"

"Go open your lab, but wait by the door. Keep an eye on the other unit. When I give the signal, you hightail it over there and we'll slip inside."

"Okay," her mouth said, the rest of her face silently signaling that it was not okay at all.

"You'll be fine," I said, my hand on her shoulder, but I was concerned about her getting through the small group of protesters.

Annalisa looked up at me, her eyes sparkling in the moonlight and a brave smile tugging at the corners of her mouth. She was an extremely beautiful woman, and I was struck by her strength, her bravery, her humor. And her proximity. She reached up and kissed my cheek, then whispered, "We'd better go."

I gave her shoulder a squeeze, and then jogged off toward the tree line. When I turned back she was standing in the moonlight, looking very alone. I gave her a wave, and she waved back. Then I plunged into the darkness.

The underbrush was thick, and the going was slow and loud, like sound effects from an old radio show. The smell of skunk was in the air, and I hoped the noise would scare them away before I got too close.

As my eyes adjusted to the darkness and I found my footing, the going got easier and quieter. I made a wide loop through the woods, crossing the road fifty yards up and doubling back on the other side until I came to a chain-link fence. I smiled. I'd done a lot of chain-link fence-climbing back in Dunston, and I had hoped I was done for a while. The smile faded as I thought about what had been behind those fences.

I paused and listened to the slight breeze, the ambient sound of insect life, and a quiet conversation not too far away.

On the other side of the fence, I could see the two lab units. One was just in front of me, back from the road and half obscured by shadows. The other was thirty yards past it. Twenty yards beyond that was the front gate.

The security cruiser was parked between the two units, the rear of it just visible. Two guards were leaning against the trunk, their backs to the gate. They looked as tired as the protesters.

I was starting to wonder what I would do if Annalisa got through the gate with no commotion. Then I heard her, voice raised. "Get your hands off me!"

The two guards were startled to attention, and they quickly hurried toward the gate, accompanied by a chorus of raised voices, mostly protesting their innocence. I took my cue, scrambling up and over the fence, dropping to the other side, and scurrying over behind the closest lab unit.

Clinging to the wall in the darkness, I could hear and feel a faint hum, like machinery running inside. I expected the outer wall to be cold in the night air, and metallic, but instead it was still warm from the day and it felt like wood. I caught a faint but distinct odor as well, homey but only vaguely familiar. A moment later, I saw the two guards accompanying Annalisa to the other trailer. They seemed apologetic, presumably for the reception she had gotten from the protesters. Annalisa was fumbling for her keys as she walked, squinting furtively into the darkness in my direction. I resisted the urge to wave to her.

They walked right up to the door with her, and they waited for her to open it. I felt on the ground and picked up a couple of small stones. The smaller one was the size of a quarter. I flipped it high into the air and cringed, waiting for the impact, but all I heard was a soft thud. One of the security types turned around to look.

His partner asked him something, and he shrugged. "I don't know," he said, turning slowly back around to watch Annalisa.

The next stone was bigger, maybe the size of a lemon. The difference in weight was substantial as I hefted it. As Annalisa opened the door, I flipped the rock up into the air.

This time it landed with a loud crack followed by the sound of it bouncing across the hood of the security car.

"What the fuck?" the first guard said as they both grabbed their sidearms and trotted back toward the gate.

I stepped into the moonlight, dropping the third rock onto the ground and waving frantically for Annalisa to run over as the chorus of voices rose up once again, this time even louder.

Annalisa was all business, hardly fumbling at all and barely looking at me as she swiped the card through the slot. She pulled me into the lab unit and pressed the door closed behind us with a soft click.

52

We stood with our backs against the door for a moment in what seemed like total darkness. Then I noticed a soft red glow coming from lights running along the base of the walls.

The smell was even stronger inside, but I still couldn't place it. Annalisa felt her way to a chair and a moment later a computer screen came to life, filling the room with harsh light.

She swiped the stolen card through a reader and navigated through a couple of different screens then started tapping at the keyboard, bringing columns of numbers sliding up the screen. Every few seconds she would stop, stare intently at the screen, and resume typing. A few times she lingered, tapping differently, and it wasn't until I noticed the paper sliding out onto the tray at my elbow that I realized she was printing. "There's no USB ports or disk drives," she said, reading my mind. "Security."

As she went about her business, I studied the lab, bathed now in the bluish light of the computer screen.

It was long, and narrower than I expected from the outside. There were no windows, just Formica countertops along each side and a couple of computer workstations with stools. The Formica curved up the wall six inches, like a backsplash. Every three or four feet, a pair of four-inch holes was cut into the wall. Above that, the wall was blank except for some shallow grooves, like horizontal paneling. Halfway down the counter was a rack of small glass test tubes. The Bee-Plus cartoon logo was sprinkled liberally around, on folders, binders, plastic bottles.

"What's the smell?" I asked.

She reached over to the wall, where there were two rows of switches marked INNER PARTITIONS and OUTER PARTITIONS. She flicked the switch at the end under INNER PARTITIONS and the paneled sections of the wall began to slide up into the ceiling, revealing metal mesh, like a heavy-duty window screen. The smell grew instantly stronger, a yeasty mixture of beeswax and honey. I recognized it from the hives we had opened my first day on the island. Squinting into the darkness, I could make out the faint movement of bees crawling on vertical wooden slats.

"Bees," Annalisa said, glancing over at me. "It's late. They're mostly asleep."

"What is this place?"

"This is Sumner's mobile clinical lab, so he can study the bees. The hives open up on the outside so the bees can go out and find nectar. They always come back at night. That's one of the things about honeybees." I turned to the nearest test-tube rack. There were four tubes, the first three marked HONEY, NECTAR, and API-TOXIN. The fourth one was marked APS9678. In the dim light, the liquid inside looked a pale amber.

"What's this stuff?" I asked, holding it up and swirling it around.

"I don't know," she said. "Put it down." She took it from my hand, but then looked at the rack and back at the tube in her hand. I could tell she was curious. Cocking an eyebrow, she lifted off the plastic stopper. She put her nose close to the mouth of the test tube, but she didn't need to—the smell seemed to fill the room, sweet but not like honey. More like bananas. The odor was accompanied almost immediately by a wall of noise, like a roiling, angry army of chainsaws.

Annalisa jumped to her feet, the liquid sloshing up the glass sides of the vial. I took a step back, too.

The metal screens were vibrating, and as I looked closer I saw that the few bees that had been crawling about had been suddenly transformed into a dense mat of tiny bodies, thousands of them, grinding against the screen, tiny limbs poking through it.

"What is that stuff?" I said, raising my voice over the roar.

"It smells like alarm pheromone, bees release it when they sting or are killed, or feel threatened. It incites the other bees to attack. But I've . . . I've never seen that kind of reaction."

As we looked down at the tube in her hand, a single droplet slid down the outside of it, just touching her finger. She moved her finger—too late—and jammed the cap back on. But whatever genie it was, it was out.

She put the tube back into the rack, her eyes wide in the dim light. She paused, staring at the wet spot on her finger. With her other hand, she reached out and flicked that same switch on the wall. Then she darted back to the middle of the room, as far from the sides as possible.

The wall panels slowly slid down, and I could see that the mesh screens were now glistening with moisture. Droplets were forming, dripping down to the bottom. I realized they weren't limbs poking through the screen, they were stingers. Venom was collecting in tiny puddles at the bottom of the screen.

"Those are stingers," I said. "That's venom."

She nodded.

"So are they all going to die now?"

"What do you mean?"

"Don't bees die after they sting?"

She shook her head. "Only when they sting soft flesh," she said absently. "And not all of them. A lot of them get away."

When the panels finally came down into place, Annalisa

looked up at me with wide eyes. "We have to get out of here," she said breathlessly. But then she looked down at her hand, the dim light reflecting off the moisture on her finger.

She went over to the small sink in the corner and started vigorously washing her hands. I noticed her shoulders were shaking.

I went over and put an arm around her, looking down at her hands as she frantically wrung them under the hot water.

"Hey," I said, as softly as I could. "You okay?"

She turned off the water. "This doesn't just wash off," she said.

I didn't say anything, and she turned to look up at me. "The alarm pheromone. I can rinse off most of it, and the rest will dissipate eventually, but meanwhile . . . I'm marked." Her eyes widened as she looked over my shoulder toward the muffled buzzing coming from behind the partitions. "I've never seen bees behave like that. Not even Africanized bees. Imagine if those screens hadn't been there."

I tried not to picture it, but I already had.

"It's nighttime, though, right? There shouldn't be any bees out there."

She shook her head. "No. But it woke these ones up, didn't it?"

I couldn't argue with that, or with any of it. This was her territory, not mine.

"We should get going," she said, reading my mind. The bees were quieting down, just enough to let me worry about the armed guards outside.

"How about hand sanitizer, or something like that?" I said. "Could that break it down?"

She looked up at me and smiled, momentarily distracted by the cuteness of my scientific ignorance. Then she shook her head. "You can't break it down, Doyle. The best you can do is try to mask it or cover it up, with something else, like . . ." Her eyes went unfocused, staring into space as she tried to think.

"Julie!" she said, yanking open a drawer under one of the workstations, rooting around in it with her unaffected hand. She pulled out a bandana, a hacky sack ball, a bag full of hair scrunchies, and a miniature Rubik's cube before exclaiming a triumphant, "Aha!" and plucking out a small bottle with a white label. "Julie Patchouli," she said by way of explanation, as she unscrewed the cap and dabbed a tiny drop onto her finger.

As she rubbed it over her hand, the enclosed space filled with the scent of earnest hippies.

"That's powerful stuff," I said, my eyes watering.

She smiled. "Here's hoping. I actually don't mind the smell, except that it reminds me of Julie, who's annoying." The relief on her face faded as once again she seemed to read my mind.

"We need to get going," she said.

I nodded. "Yes, we do."

She sat at the computer and with one hand started closing windows. When she finished shutting it down, she looked up at me. "Now what?"

"I'll look out and see where the guards are. When I say the word, you get over to that other unit, open and close the door, and then ask them to let you out. While you're going through the gate, I'll go over the fence. Meet you back at your car, okay?"

She gave me a brave nod. Then she put her non-hippie hand behind my neck and pulled me down for a wet, lingering kiss that left my toes tingling.

I knew I should tell her not to do that, but I didn't want to.

"Okay," I said hoarsely. "You ready?"

She grabbed a couple of paper towels and wrapped them around her finger, then nodded. She stuffed the printouts in her bag, turned off the computer, and the lab went dark except for the faint red floor lights.

I took a few seconds to let my eyes adjust to the darkness, then I peeked out the door. The cool night air coming through the gap smelled clean and fresh.

The guards were once again leaning against their car, but this time on the front of it, facing away from us and toward the gate.

In the dim light coming through the door, I nodded and Annalisa nodded back. She stepped forward, and I opened the door just enough for her to squeeze through. As she slowly descended the steps, I let the door ease back almost closed.

I could hear her footsteps as she scurried over to the other unit. The guards didn't seem to notice.

When she reached the shadows by the entrance to the lab unit, I let out a breath I hadn't known I'd been holding. She seemed to be doing the same, clinging to the wall, collecting herself. She opened the door to the other lab unit, making a big, loud production of it, shaking her keys, letting the door slam.

I pulled back from the doorway, watching through the crack as the guards turned toward the noise Annalisa was making. One of them got up, his hand resting on his holster, until Annalisa emerged from the shadows.

"All done?" he asked, friendly, probably happy to see a beautiful face in the middle of a boring assignment.

"Done for now," she said cheerily. "Thanks for your help."

"Our pleasure," said the other guard, coming closer.

They both gestured for her to go first. Then they fell in behind her, checking out her butt as they walked toward the gate. She seemed to be giving it a little extra swing.

I slipped out the door and crept around the side of the unit, not clinging so close now that I knew there were a hundred thousand angry bees inside. I couldn't hear them, but I could sense them, their power, just inches away.

I scrambled up the fence and swung myself over the top. I would have been in a hurry to get out of there anyway, but those bees helped provide a little extra motivation.

53

Pulling up in front of the Mansion House, I felt like a criminal returning to the scene of a crime. We had embraced briefly back at her lab, then got in the car and hightailed it over here as fast as we could. Annalisa sat for a moment, Julie Patchouli's ID card in one hand, her patchouli on the other. She tucked the ID into her shirt pocket and slipped out of the car without a word.

As soon as she left, I slumped down in my seat, the need to appear strong having left with Annalisa. She startled me when she opened the car door just a few seconds later.

"She's gone," she said as she got in, the car filling with the faint but distinct smell of patchouli.

"What?"

"We're too late. We missed her. She's gone."

"Did you leave the card anyway?"

"What do you mean?"

"I mean did you leave the card there? She could have dropped it while she was getting dressed, right?"

She stared at me for a moment, thinking. Then she turned away. "I can't go back in there now—they're locking up. I'll have to try to return the card tomorrow." Her hands trembled as she fastened her seat belt.

"She could have lost it anywhere," I told her. "It'll be okay."

She turned to look at me. "If she reports her card missing, they'll check the activity on it. They'll see someone used it. It won't take them long to figure out I was there and put it together."

"Does she wear it around her neck or carry it in her wallet?"

"She keeps it on a lanyard," she said, holding up the card so I could see the orange tether dangling from it. "But she doesn't wear it. She keeps it in her handbag."

"Look, she's not going to know it's gone until morning. Probably not until she gets to the lab. We can go back right now and leave it at the gym. She'll notice it's gone in the morning, call the gym, and they'll say, yes, here it is. She's not going to tell anyone, risk getting in trouble, right? She'll keep it to herself, so no one will know."

"They're already closed. I can't get back in there." She thought for a moment. "What about her house? We're about to drive right past it."

"What do you mean?"

"She lives on this street. Her house is coming up on the left." She pointed and I followed her gaze to a small bungalow with a dark green SUV in the driveway. I took my foot off the gas but didn't touch the brake. "Is that her car?"

"Yes. We could leave it next to her driver's side door. As if she'd dropped it."

Two women were standing next to the driveway, one of them holding a small dog on a leash. "Is that her standing there?" I asked.

Annalisa gasped and slid down in her seat. "That's her," she said in a hoarse whisper.

As my foot dropped back onto the gas pedal, the dog started barking at me and the two women looked over. I kept driving, eyes front, feeling them watching me. Annalisa waited a couple of hundred yards before popping back up and looking out the rear window. "What are we going to do?"

"It's okay," I told her. "We'll go back to the gym in the morn-ing. What time do they open?"

"Six, I think."

"What time does Julie get to the lab?"

"Usually nine. Sometimes eight-thirty."

"Okay, so we go back early, get there at six, go in, and drop the card. It will be fine."

She looked doubtful but hopeful. "Do you think?"

I was maybe sixty-percent confident. "Absolutely," I said.

Annalisa laid the papers out, covering the entire dining room table. Immediately, she began studying them with great intensity, staring at them, rearranging them, scribbling notes in her notebook.

I left her to it and went onto her back deck to call Nola. The phone rang for a while but she picked up before voice mail could.

"Hello, Doyle," she said, sounding very sleepy.

"Hi," I said quietly. "You in bed?"

"I am," she replied with a yawn. "It's been a long day."

"Yes it has. You doing okay?"

"Just tired."

"Is Teddy out of jail yet?" I asked.

"No." She sighed. "Not as far as I know. Any word from Benjy?"

"No. Moose and I filed a report, but Jimmy thinks he probably just flaked off somewhere."

"Probably so. Where have you been staying?"

"At the Wesley."

She let out a soft laugh. "I heard it was full of paramilitary thugs."

She sounded like she was falling asleep on the phone. I couldn't tell if she was accusing me of being one of them. "I know," I said. "It got very strange, so I moved out."

"Where are you staying tonight?"

"I don't know."

"It's late." She yawned again. "Where are you now?"

I paused. "I'm at Annalisa's. I'm helping her . . ."

"Tell her I said goodnight."

Then she was gone. For a moment, I thought maybe she had fallen asleep on the phone, but then the line went dead. She'd hung up on me.

54

I took a couple of deep breaths to settle myself down. Between the first one and the second one, a cloud of skunk drifted through. Not quite eye-wateringly close, but well within face-wrinkling range.

I called Jimmy, but he didn't answer, probably up to his ears in chanting protesters. Moose didn't answer, either. He was probably one of the chanting protesters.

By the time I went back inside, the day had caught up with Annalisa. Her shoulders sagged, and as I watched, she started to yawn. Once, then twice, then again and again. Tears formed at the corners of her eyes.

I was about to ask her if she needed to take a break when she sat back and rubbed her eyes. "I'm done."

"Did you find anything?"

"Maybe," she said, standing and stretching, then bending over and palming the floor. I don't think it was for my benefit, but I benefited nonetheless. She came out of it a little quicker than I expected, but I managed to get my eyes back in place. "I'll have to get back to it in the morning."

She came up close and put a soft kiss on my cheek, letting it linger just a little longer than a peck. She pulled slowly away and paused, inches away from me, looking me in the eye. She didn't give it anything more than that, but she seemed to be saying the offer still stood.

Then she yawned, and the moment was gone.

Fifteen minutes later, I was sprawled out on the sofa, listening to her gently snoring upstairs in bed.

I'm not the best sleeper, especially not on a sofa, especially not with a million thoughts spinning through my brain, but I must have been pretty tired, because shortly after I looked at the clock and saw that it was almost two, I fell asleep.

Some time after two, I awoke to a creaking sound and saw a figure at the bottom of the stairs. I was still wondering if and how strenuously I was going to tell Annalisa this was not a good idea, when I realized the figure was going up the stairs, not coming down. And that it was twice Annalisa's size. And covered in black, including a black balaclava over its face.

Instantly, I was awake and taking in the scene.

My gun was close-by on the floor, but I didn't want to risk fumbling for it in the dark, so I flipped over the back of the sofa and sprang at the intruder. I had the advantage of surprise, but it turned out he had the advantages of size, speed, and weaponry. And apparently hearing.

I was halfway there when he spun around. I sensed more than saw his leg coming at my face. I was saved from his kick by my own lack of momentum, but I landed hard on the stairs at his feet. Almost immediately, a bullet cut through the air right above my head.

The room was captured in a dull orange flash from the muzzle of his gun. The guy was massive. Between that and the gun, it already wasn't a fair fight. So I felt okay about sending my fist and everything behind it up into his groinal area. The punch landed solid and hard. He seemed like the kind of guy who had a pretty thorough workout regimen, but he was going to have to skip the Kegels for a while. He made a soft whimpering noise that sounded like it wanted to be louder, but he immediately started firing again. Each shot lit up the room, and I kept moving, so he wouldn't get a fix on me—I flattened myself against the banister, then the wall, then vaulted off the stair completely. With each flash, my silhouette appeared on a different expanse of wall, in a different pose. I could feel a part of my brain seizing up, and another part forcing through it.

The muzzle flashes were giving him a fix on me, but they also gave me a fix on him. As I landed on the floor, he fired again and I grabbed at the gun, my fingers squeezing the hot steel barrel. I yanked it hard, flipping him over my head and onto what my memory and my ears told me was a small accent table with a vase full of daffodils.

By the time I realized I still had the gun in my hand, he had recovered and kicked it away. I stepped to the side. When the lights came on, he was swinging a knife upward in a brutal arc that started right about where my navel had been. For an instant I pictured myself split up the middle and spilling out onto the floor.

Annalisa screamed from the top of the stairs. "Doyle!"

"Stay back," I yelled, aiming a kick at the knife in his hand. But he was much too fast. The tip of my shoelace flew up into the air, and then he was closing on me, the knife zipping back and forth, me retreating, trying to weave around it. When I felt the banister against my back, he came in fast, his arm a blur. I twisted and slid to the side as he brought the knife down hard and the blade sank deep into the wooden railing. For an instant, he paused, trying to yank it free, and I kicked him in the kidney, hard enough that he let go. It worked so well I did it twice more.

I spotted his gun, ten feet away, but before I could make a move for it, he turned and sprang. His hands were aimed at my throat. I got one hand under his chin while the other one raked his face. I hooked my fingers and clawed at him, trying to grab his mask and rip it off, at least see who I was fighting. Instead, my finger sank into something soft and wet.

Having already committed to the low road, I pushed my finger in, and at the same time lashed out with a savage kick that landed just south of his genitals.

He howled, stumbling backward and clutching his masked face. As he turned and lurched unevenly toward the door, I dove for the gun, grabbing it as I slid across the floor. But before I could level it at him, another figure appeared in the doorway from the kitchen, similarly masked and clad in black. He was shorter and heavier, and he was carrying an assault rifle.

For an instant, he just stood there, his masked face looking somehow confused as he watched his colleague crash through the window next to the front door and onto the front lawn. I kept my eyes on the guy with the gun, and when he turned to me, I said, "Drop it."

He didn't.

Instead he swung it in my direction, a move that cost him a few ounces of shoulder as I squeezed off a shot.

Blood sprayed the doorframe behind him, and he returned a few rounds as he stumbled backward into the kitchen. A blossom of fluff appeared from the back of the sofa.

Outside, a car started up and sped away. I assumed it was the first guy tagging out and leaving the new guy to get home on his own. I dove behind the now-perforated sofa, for visual cover if nothing else. When I peeked over it, I saw the guy in the kitchen standing by the back door, his rifle hanging down as he looked at his bloody shoulder.

Sometimes the cop voice can be enough to shake someone into compliance. I didn't think it was going to work with this guy, but figured the hole in his shoulder might help. The alternatives were staying in hiding or picking him off. I jumped to my feet, the gun two-handed in front of me.

"Freeze!" I thundered, loud and deep.

He squeezed off a few rounds, simply out of shock. I fired twice, and as I dropped back down behind the sofa, I heard the sliding door shatter and dissolve, followed by the sound of feet crunching on broken glass.

Once again, I flipped myself over the sofa. Sprinting after him, I remembered too late that the floor was covered with shards of glass and my feet weren't covered at all. Luckily the same momentum that made it impossible to stop was enough to carry me over it. I landed on the deck outside and almost bumped into a couple of bullets traveling in the opposite direction, zipping past my ears. I saw a muzzle flash in the darkness, and I realized I was silhouetted against the light from the doorway. Stepping to the side, I aimed at the spot where I'd last seen the muzzle, but I didn't know what was through those woods and I couldn't risk collateral damage. I considered going after him, but I didn't want to leave Annalisa alone and I doubted I'd find him anyway.

As the sound of him tromping through the brush faded away, I heard a weird, strangled cry. A moment later my eyes watered and I gagged, but I smiled.

He'd been skunked.

55

Annalisa was a bit of a mess, which was just as well, because if she wasn't, I would have been. As it was, I had to tell her everything was okay.

"They know," she said. "They must. Why else would they send men after me? What am I going to do?"

"They could have been coming for me."

"What do you mean?"

"I've made some friends here over the last week." I did a quick mental count of who I'd pissed off over the course of the week, and it occurred to me that maybe I needed to work on my people skills. "It's entirely possible that they came after me, and as far as they're concerned your only infraction is a questionable taste in friends."

She looked doubtful but she let out a brief snorting laugh. That was a good sign. Then she turned to look at the papers laid out on the dinner table. "Did they see that?"

The first guy hadn't, I was pretty sure of that. The lights had been out; then he'd been busy trying to kill me. The other guy, I couldn't be sure. There was a moment, when he was standing in the entry to the kitchen, that he could have seen them. "I don't think so."

She let out a small sigh. "So what are we going to do?"

"Tomorrow morning at six we bring the ID back to the gym. Then you call out sick to work and we figure out someplace safe to go."

She stared at me for a moment. Then she nodded. "We should call the police, right?"

"I'll call Jimmy."

He answered on the third ring. "It's two-thirty in the goddamned morning."

"It's Doyle."

"I know who it is. It's two-thirty in the goddamned morning. You know the kind of day I've had? How little sleep I'm on?"

"Two masked gunmen just broke into Annalisa's house."

"Jesus, is she okay?"

"We're okay. The assailants are a little banged up."

"You want me to call it in for you?"

As he said it, I heard a car pull up out outside. Through the missing front window, I saw two uniforms getting out of a cruiser. "Never mind. They're here already. Get some sleep and I'll call you later."

Annalisa was looking out the window. "The neighbors must have called it in," I said. "We need to get those papers out of sight."

She started picking them up, carefully arranging them in order, then sliding them into her shoulder bag at the same moment the knock came at the door. I slid my Glock into it's ankle holster.

"I'll handle this," I said, although I hadn't decided how. "Just tell them you were upstairs for the whole thing." Then I opened the door.

The two cops were young and big, and they looked very tired. "Thanks for coming out, guys," I said. "Come on in."

"We got reports of gunshots," said the bigger of the two, "some kind of disturbance." His eyes swept the place, lingering on the blood on the kitchen door jamb.

I held up my badge. "I'm with Philly P.D. Yeah, we had a couple of armed intruders."

They nodded at the mess, but raised their eyebrows because that's probably not the usual call on the island.

"I see," said the one that talked, taking out a pad.

He took our names, then asked for the story. I told it to him, mostly. We had no idea who they were, I told him, but I knew there were a lot of security types on the island. Maybe they were drunk or high, I said, or maybe they came to the wrong house. "They got away, but one of them left a couple of ounces of shoulder behind, and the other one might have a permanent squint."

"So, the first guy had a gun and a knife, and you got them both away from him?" he asked when I was done. They both looked dubious.

"I guess so, yeah. I took the gun, the knife got stuck in the banister, then we grappled hand to hand. I poked him in the eye and he left."

"And that's when the other guy showed up with an assault rifle?"

"Right. By then I had the first guy's gun, and I shot him."

"And then he ran away?"

I nodded. "Through the woods. And I'm pretty sure he got skunked."

They interviewed Annalisa, but she just said she woke up to the gunshots, by the time she came to the stairs it was over.

"And you were on the sofa?" he asked me.

I nodded.

"So you two are . . . ?"

"Friends," Annalisa said.

I told the story a few more times, the sky a little bit lighter each time. They bagged the intruder's gun, and I was glad I hadn't used the Glock, because they would have bagged that, too. When they were done with the interview, they told us not to leave the island without notifying them, then said they were going to have to declare the place a crime scene. Did we have a place to stay?

I said yes, drawing a questioning look from Annalisa.

It was almost six.

56

"Where are we staying?" Annalisa asked as soon as we got into the car.

"I don't know, but I didn't want them to find us a place, because then they'd know where we were. We should probably get you off island." I figured they would probably have the ferries watched. Maybe I could hire a boat.

She shook her head. "They know who I am," she said. "If I don't stay here and figure out what's going on, they'll stay after me."

I couldn't argue. "Let's just get rid of this ID, then we'll figure it out."

The truth was, I needed to think. I thought about protective custody, but I didn't know if I trusted it. Jimmy had talked a lot about pressure from high up. And I suspected that pressure might have something to do with why Teddy was still in jail.

As we drove in silence, the deserted streets and early morning fog magnified the surrealism of the situation. It intensified further when we saw flashing red lights slicing through the mist up ahead.

Annalisa squinted, trying to see what was going on. "I know

another route," she said, glancing down at her watch, nervous. "You can make this right and go around it."

"Hold on," I said quietly, slowing down but still driving forward.

"The street looks closed . . ." she said, her voice trailing off.

As we got closer to the lights, the fog thinned. The street was not closed, but it was partially blocked by a pair of fire trucks, an ambulance, and two police cars, one from Tisbury and one from Edgartown. As I coasted toward them, I saw a cop waving us around. Jimmy Frank, looking the way I felt.

I lowered the passenger's side window, but as we slowed to a stop, Annalisa let out sharp gasp.

Jimmy came over to the car. "So much for sleep," he said to me, then turned to Annalisa. "Are you okay, ma'am?"

But she was looking over his shoulder, at Julie Patchouli's house, half of it turned to a blackened, smoking ruin. The front tires of her SUV were melted. Black water was running down the driveway, looking like death as it curled into the gutter and down the road in search of a storm drain.

Annalisa turned to look at me, her eyes wide and her lips trembling. Then she looked back out the window.

Jimmy looked at Annalisa's face as she stared out the window. Then he looked at me with one eyebrow raised.

"What happened?" I asked.

"House fire. Accident by the looks of it, but it's early. Girl was killed." He paused to study Annalisa's face. "You know anything about it?"

"I knew her," Annalisa said softly.

"They *worked* together," I said, my face underlining my words.

"Are you okay?" he asked her again, gently.

She nodded and he put his hand on her shoulder.

"We need a place to stay," I said.

He nodded. "My place is tiny, but . . ."

"I'd like to get Nola somewhere safe, too. Until things settle down. What about one of your caretaker places?" I'd already had the "How about you leave this crazy island" conversation with Nola in my head. It hadn't ended well.

He thought for a moment, then he nodded. "Yeah, I have a place." He looked at me, adding, "And these folks are totally organic or whatever, with the chemical thing. Should be fine. Meet me back here in an hour."

57

Nola hadn't answered her phone. Not unusual when she was working, but it still made my foot a little heavier on the accelerator. I expected early morning to be bustling on the farm, but the place was deserted. As I parked in front of Nola's cabin, pockets of mist hung in the air around us. I got out of the car and stepped onto the tiny porch, my concerns coalescing into a knot in the pit of my stomach. Annalisa hung back. She looked down at my hand, then up at my face. I realized I was holding the Glock.

I was just about to knock on the door when I heard the slap of the screen door on the big house and the unsettling sound of a shotgun being racked.

I turned and saw Nola at the top of the steps. "Doyle?" she said, lowering the gun, but only a little.

I've never been one of those guys who gets off on the whole "guns and girls" thing. I'm not actually all that big on the whole "guns" thing, although I've learned to appreciate them in the right situation. But seeing Nola standing up there on the porch, her hip cocked and holding that shotgun, it was just hot. Even still, I would have felt better about it if she'd lowered the gun all the way. And if she hadn't just come out of Teddy's house.

"Hi, Nola."

She raised an eyebrow and looked over at Annalisa, then back at me. There was a hardness to her face that I'd never seen before. I'd seen plenty of tough, but never hard. I felt a wave of sadness about it, and a rush of guilt, knowing I had something to do with it.

She looked me in the eye for a moment. Then she turned and said, "Come on in."

As soon as we got inside, her demeanor softened, almost liquefied. Her shoulders slumped and she leaned the shotgun next to the back door, delicately, like she was afraid it was going to bite her. The kitchen was black-and-white tile, white enameled fixtures, and white painted cabinets.

I looked at Annalisa and gave her a smile. I think she tried to smile back, but she missed it by a wide margin.

I cleared my throat. Things were in a precarious state and I didn't want to make them any worse, but I had a question. "So, have you been staying in here?" I tried to say it nonchalantly. I might not have nailed it.

"Yes, that's right, Doyle," she snapped. "I'm just waiting for my man to get out of jail." She laughed, bitterly, then shook her head. "Teddy. That weasel gets to make one call from jail and he calls me, tells me I have to maintain the farm, take care of the chickens. As far as I know, he's still in jail and I'm stuck here, barely able to fend off the rabbits, and suddenly it's like I'm in a war zone. There's carloads of goddamned mercenaries driving around, and people coming in from off island to join the protesters."

She buried her face in her hands, and I couldn't tell if she was crying. I put my hand on her knee, wondering if she was going to slap it, or push it off. When she didn't, I moved closer and put an arm around her shoulder, and she slumped against me.

"You're not the only ones I've had to point that thing at," she said, her voice muffled against my shoulder.

"Did someone come for you?" I asked.

She pulled back and shook her head. "They were just drunk and lost. But I was scared."

She rested her head on my shoulder again, but before I could put my arm around her, she jerked away from me.

"Wait," she said. "Did someone come after you?"

Annalisa and I shared a look, then I looked back at Nola and nodded.

I told her about Annalisa's concerns about the bees, about what happened at Annalisa's and then about Julie Patchouli. Her eyes were pinned to me the whole time, except for a flickering glance at Annalisa when I mentioned that I'd been sleeping on the sofa.

When I was done, I told her I wanted to get her off the island. I figured it was worth a shot, but she cut me off, shaking her head. "I took a job, I have responsibilities. I have animals I need to take care of."

"Where are Gwen and Elaine?" I asked.

"They left right after Teddy got arrested. Elaine said she wasn't going to work for him for free. When things started getting crazy, Gwen left, too. She said I was nuts to stay. She was probably right."

I opened my mouth to agree, but she cut me off. "I'm not them."

"Jimmy has a place we can stay," I told her. "I think it would be safer."

"What kind of place?"

I knew what she meant. "A house. Jimmy says they're very . . . organic or whatever. He says they're hard-core." I didn't ever want to disregard her concerns about chemical sensitivity, my suspicions regarding her current status notwithstanding, but even still, I was struggling not to remind her that we all suffered from bullet sensitivity syndrome.

She bit her lip. "I don't care about the crops, so much, but I need to feed and water the chickens."

"They'll be fine."

"They won't."

"Then we can come back."

It took fifteen minutes to pack up all of Nola's stuff. She gave the chickens some extra food and water, and we were ready to go.

Nola grabbed the shotgun as we slipped out the back door. As we approached the Jeep, she looked at Annalisa and called, "Shotgun."

58

As we drove, Annalisa's phone buzzed, and a moment later I heard a gasp from the backseat.

"What is it?" I asked, looking at Annalisa in the rearview.

"I just got a company e-mail from Stoma, 'Stoma Corporation would like to welcome Thompson Company as the newest member of the Stoma Corporate family.' It also says all Stoma operations on the island are being consolidated at the Katama site."

"They bought them?" I was shocked.

Nola looked at me. "When I tried to call Teddy's dad, the number he gave me forwarded to Stoma Corporation."

Annalisa leaned forward. "You mean his personal number?"

"It was supposed to be."

Suddenly, Teddy still being in jail made sense. "Renfrew is rich, but Jimmy told me he'd heard everything was in the company's name, trying to game the system, avoid taxes and stuff. If he's lost the company, it's entirely possible that he's lost his phone, and a lot more than that."

* * *

Jimmy was standing by his cruiser and when he saw us, he nodded and got in, then drove off. As I fell in behind him, Nola and Annalisa quietly looked out the window at the burnt remains of Julie's house.

He led us along a winding road up the side of a hill in the thick woods. Ten minutes later we were following him up a driveway to a sleek but modest A-frame looking out over a steep slope.

"You know where you are?" Jimmy asked.

The road had been windy but the route was simple. I nodded.

He took a key out from under a plant pot and opened the door. The house consisted of a spacious common area with a living and dining area under a vaulted ceiling, and two bedrooms and a bathroom on either side.

Jimmy told us the lay of the place, then stood with his hands on his hips. "I need to get back," he said. "I'll check in later. But you'll be fine. No one will find you here."

He reached out and gave Annalisa's arm a reassuring squeeze. "I'll see you soon, okay?"

She smiled and nodded.

As he stepped toward the door, he caught my eye. "Can I have a word with you, Doyle?"

I followed him outside and closed the door behind us.

"Looks like the Padulla woman was doing her nails," he said, as we stepped outside. It took me a moment to realize he was talking about Julie Patchouli. "Knocked the bottle over and the stuff caught fire. She didn't get out in time."

"Think that's what really happened?"

"Looks suspicious as hell to me, but I'm suspicious by nature. What do you know about it?"

"There's serious shit going on."

He laughed. "You think? Even apart from all the shooting you seem to be attracting, Katama's like a war zone between all the corporate security Rambo wannabes and the crazy-ass protesters coming in from off island. Serious shit? Tell me something I don't know." He laughed again, then cut it short for effect. "Seriously. Tell me something I don't know."

"This thing with the bees. There's something fishy going on."

"I already know that. Big fishy, too, involving all sorts of big fish. What's this got to do with Annalisa?"

"She's been poking around," I said, lowering my voice for some reason. "Trying to figure out what's going on."

His eyes narrowed.

"Last night Annalisa logged onto their computers using Julie Padulla's user ID. A couple of hours later, we get our midnight visitors." I hooked my thumb back the way we'd come. "This morning that happens."

"Jesus."

"What about Teddy?"

"What about him? He brought his stuff down on himself."

"What about him still being in jail?"

He shrugged. "Bail was set and he didn't post it."

"Is that part of the pressure you're talking about? Is someone keeping him there on purpose, keeping him out of the way?"

"I don't know. Maybe."

"You think I could get in there to talk to him again?"

"Why?"

"See if a couple of days inside has given him any fresh insights."

He thought about that, then said, "Yeah. I'll call them on my way in, tell them you're coming. Just say you're a friend of the family, okay?"

I nodded. "So who do you think it is, applying all this pressure, anyway?"

He looked at me as he opened the car door. "Stoma, I assume."

We paused, thinking about that.

"You think they're safe up here?"

"No one's going to find them up here."

"I want to go out and do some leg work. Try to figure out what's going on."

He thought about that. "Just make sure no one follows you back."

I nodded and turned to go back inside.

"Hey, Carrick," he called out. "One last question."

I stopped half inside my car.

"So what were you doing over there last night, anyway? At Annalisa's house."

"Why you asking?"

"I'm just asking."

I saw a look in his eyes I hadn't seen before and I smiled. "I was just sleeping on the sofa, in case something like this happened."

By the time I got back inside, Annalisa was standing with her thumbnail wedged between her front teeth, staring at the papers spread out over the dinner table.

Nola tilted her head and beckoned me over to the sofa. When I sat next to her, she looked at me with a sad little smile. "It feels like I haven't seen you in a long time."

I smiled back at her, rested my hand on her thigh.

"I'm trying to get a picture of all this stuff that's going on," she said. "I think there's some things I don't know about. So I need you to tell me, what the hell is going on here?"

I took a deep breath and gave her the full version, almost. I felt bad laying it all on her.

"Jesus," she said breathlessly when I got up to the part where she was pointing a shotgun at me.

"I don't know how, but I have a strong feeling whatever Teddy was up to is somehow related."

Annalisa had stopped working and was listening. Her eyes were wet, and I realized she'd been reliving the traumatic events. Nola turned to look at her.

"Are you okay?" Nola asked.

Annalisa nodded, sniffing back tears. I wanted to comfort her, but I couldn't, not in front of Nola. I was relieved when Nola did.

They disappeared into the bedroom, and I could hear the soft sound of women reassuring each other. I tried Moose again, but there was still no answer.

A few minutes later Nola came back into the living room and sat down across from me, studying me again. "Sounds like she's been through a lot."

I nodded.

"How about you? How are you doing?" she asked.

"You know me," I said. "I'm fine."

She raised an eyebrow.

"I'm fine," I repeated.

A moment later Annalisa came out. "Sorry about that," she said, flashing an awkward smile and gesturing toward the papers on the table. "I should get back to work."

Within seconds she was immersed, staring intently at the numbers on the table.

"What is she looking for?" Nola asked quietly.

I told her about the gene sequence that showed up in the mites, and the possibility that the genetic material was unstable and had jumped from the bees to the mites. "She's looking for evidence of that, but she's also trying to find the data that was replaced, thinking if they went to that much trouble to hide it, it must tell us something."

"Oh." She looked over at Annalisa with new respect.

"So here's the thing," I said. "While Annalisa's going at this from the scientific angle, I have some other things I should check on. I asked Jimmy and he thinks you're safe here. Are you two going to be okay?"

I wasn't entirely comfortable leaving Nola and Annalisa alone, for their safety in case the bad guys figured out Annalisa was there, and for mine in case the two of them got to talking about me. But I needed to figure out what was going on.

"I think so, yeah. Are you going to be okay out there?"

I smiled. "Of course."

I walked over to the dining area, where Annalisa was standing over the table, deep in thought.

"I'm going out for a little bit," I said.

She looked up, distracted. "Oh," she said. "Okay," as in, "Now go away and let me get back to my work."

Nola followed me to the door, but no farther. I stepped out, then turned to face her. Against my better judgment, I leaned toward her, but she stepped back and smiled, letting me know that wasn't going to happen. Not yet.

I smiled as well, despite myself.

She looked me in the eye. "Be careful," she said quietly.

"You, too."

59

The windows were dark at Darren Renfrew's house, but the sense that there was no one home came from something deeper than that. I knocked on the door and rang the bell but there was no answer. I gave it a good two minutes, trying three times with the bell and three times with the knocking.

As I was walking back down the driveway a voice called out, "You looking for Renfrew?"

I turned and didn't see anyone at first. Then I looked up and saw that same sniper up on the roof. Scoping me.

"Yeah," I called up to him. "Is he home?"

"He might be. He doesn't live here anymore."

"Seriously?"

He lowered the gun a bit. "I know. Crazy, right?"

"You work for him, right?"

He took a sip of coffee from a thermos lid. "Used to. I work for the company, and it's not his company anymore. Same thing with the house. Owned by the company. They kicked him out, changed the locks, told me to shoot him if he came back." He laughed and shook his head. "I mean, don't get me wrong: the guy is a class-A asshole, but seems a little harsh."

"You know where he's living?"

"No idea." He took another sip of coffee. "I imagine a guy like that, he's probably got houses in other places. Then again, I wouldn't have thought he'd do something like put the house in the company's name. But there you go." He put down the coffee and raised his gun again. "Anyway, you should get going. Technically, I should have shot you by now."

The guy at the jail was friendly and polite and I thought once more that the place was too nice for Teddy Renfrew.

Then they let me in to see him, and I thought maybe he'd had enough. His cell was a concrete and cinder block box with a cot and a toilet. He was sitting on the floor with his back against the wall and his head on his knees. When he looked up, his face was pale, the rings under his eyes were dark, and his nose was running.

"What do you want?" he said when he saw me.

"You're still here," I said.

"No shit."

I felt a little better about it. "Why do you think that is?"

He gave me a sneer, but I guess he couldn't think of anything snotty to say.

"You know about the bees, right? Stoma has brought theirs in all over the island."

He looked away from me.

"You know they bought Thompson Company, right?" I lowered my voice. "Teddy, there's something going on out here. Stoma is up to something big. I'm trying to stop it."

Nothing.

"You know anything about Benjy?"

He looked around. "What about him?"

"He's disappeared. I was wondering if you knew anything about it."

He rolled his eyes. "I heard he went to visit his mom."

"He never got there."

Just for a second, the fear behind his eyes spilled out, then he looked away again.

"If you know anything that can help me, now is the time."

He kept his eyes down and let his middle finger do the talking.

I drove through Katama on my way back, to see if I could find Moose. Jimmy had told me where it was, but before I got within a quarter mile of the place, I had to pull over. Traffic was completely stopped. Up ahead, I could see plenty of black SUVs and a perimeter of hard-core Darkstar types, all shades, earpieces, and biceps.

Lined up in front of them were the protesters. Some seemed peaceful, a lot more didn't, and there were plenty of signs and placards, like SAVE THE BEES and HELL NO, GMO. I found Moose helping a guy hold up a sign that said FRANKEN-FUCK YOU, TOO.

"Doyle," he shouted over the sound of the crowd. "What are you doing here?"

"I need to talk to you," I shouted back.

He seemed disappointed to be giving up his great spot, but he followed me to the fringe of the crowd.

"What's up?" he said in a normal voice.

"Have you heard anything from Benjy?"

He shook his head, his eyes suddenly sad.

I put my head close to his. "Things have gotten violent. One of Annalisa's coworkers is dead, and two gunmen broke into Annalisa's house last night."

He jerked his head back. "Oh my God, are you serious? Is she okay?"

"She's fine. But we're all a little scared. She and Nola are hiding out in a house in the woods."

His face was deadly serious, then he let out a barking laugh. "Annalisa and Nola are in a hideout together? No wonder you're scared."

I smiled. "I know. I need to get back there. I'm thinking maybe you should come with me. For safety's sake."

He shook his head. "No man, I'm good. I need to make my voice heard, right here with my peeps."

"Okay. Be safe."

"You, too." He gave me a quick hug, then turned and headed back, joining in with the unintelligible chants of the crowd as he disappeared into it.

60

When I got back, Nola met me at the door, but I got the feeling it was more out of boredom that anything else.

"Did you find out anything?" she asked. I shook my head.

Annalisa was still at the dining room table, studying the pages and typing on her computer.

"Anything new here?" I asked.

Nola shook her head, but Annalisa looked up and said, "Maybe."

We both walked over to her and she pulled two sheets of paper from the top of one of the piles, each one covered with columns of numbers, and each with a large red circle around a chunk of those numbers.

"I found the original data," she announced.

"That's great!" I said. "What does it say?"

She looked up at us. "I'm working on that." Then she was reabsorbed into her work.

Nola brought me a coffee. I sat on the sofa and took a scalding gulp, then another one. I figured I should let it cool for a minute, so I put it down on the coffee table and rested my eyes. Just for a moment.

I awoke with a start, wondering how long I'd been asleep. The light coming in from the window was still overcast and gray. My body felt achy and stiff. My coffee was cold. I sat up and drank it anyway.

Nola and Annalisa were sitting at the table, talking quietly. Nola leaned back in her chair so she could see me.

"You're up," she said.

I nodded, drinking more coffee. "What did I miss?"

Annalisa got up. "I hit a wall," she said quietly, walking into the living room and dropping into an armchair. "I have the missing data, but I don't have enough other data to know what to make of it. There are similar trends during the two events, steep elevations in certain markers, building to some kind of event and then dropping steeply back to the baseline. The events are consistent with each other, but I don't know what they are, and I don't have enough data to figure it out."

"So does this mean that whatever happened when Claudia Osterman died is the same thing that happened when the other girl died?" Nola asked.

"Lynne. And probably, yes. And in both instances they faked the data and covered it up." She pinched the bridge of her nose. "I didn't find anything that might tell us one way or the other if the splice is unstable. I should have just stayed there and run the searches on the computer. I panicked."

"It was probably encrypted anyway, right?" Nola said. "If it's that sensitive?"

Annalisa smiled. "With a little time, I'm sure I could get past whatever they have in place."

I shrugged. "We still have Julie's card."

Annalisa's eyes went wide at the thought.

"You can't go back," Nola told her firmly. Then she looked at me like I was some kind of animal for suggesting it.

Annalisa shook her head, her eyes fearful. "No, I can't. I don't know if the card even works anymore, but after what happened to Julie, I can't risk being seen by them. I don't know what I'll do for the rest of my life, but right now, I need to be invisible."

"Of course *you're* not going back," I said, rolling my eyes. "I am."

Annalisa shook her head. "Doyle, you don't have the skills to get through the encryption. And I don't even know what it would look like so I can't tell you. What would you do when you got there?"

"I'll take the whole goddamned server and bring it back here."

Nola was still shaking her head when the expression on Annalisa's face told her she was taking the idea seriously. Unfortunately, by the time Nola bought in, Annalisa was shaking her head, too.

"It's too dangerous," she said. "We should just go to the authorities."

"I don't know what authorities I trust, other than Jimmy Frank," I said. "And right now, I don't think he trusts any, either. Sorry, but to me that says we need to figure this out on our own."

Nola shook her head. "No," she said. Simple and final.

"We need to know what's going on, right?" I said. "They're hiding something big, something big enough to kill people over—"

"Exactly," Nola cut in. "And you're not going to be next."

"The place has probably been cleaned out already," I said. "But if it hasn't been, if the server is still there, it won't be for long. That e-mail said operations are being moved to Katama, so I need to go now and check it out."

"It will be crawling with security," Annalisa said.

"I don't know, the Katama site is crawling with security, and mobbed with protesters. They might have all hands on deck there. If I can't get in and out safely, I'll turn around and come back."

"And then what?"

"And then we'll figure out something else."

61

I drove past the place doing sixty, head straight, eyes barely glancing over. Five minutes later I came back the other way doing twenty-five and took a good long look.

My plan had been to create some sort of diversion, but there didn't seem to be anyone there to divert. The gate was closed and locked, but the place looked deserted. No guards, no protesters. No one.

I parked across the street behind Annalisa's lab and walked the same route through the woods as the night before, crossing the road and doubling back. Another layer of clouds had moved in, lower and darker, but I still felt exposed in the daylight. The twigs breaking underfoot seemed louder than before, and without the cover of darkness, it felt silly trying to sneak in at all.

The fence appeared up ahead, and through it the lab units. I listened silently for five minutes, but it was quiet. Even the wildlife seemed to have gone, and I felt the hairs on the back of my neck stirring as vague dark scenarios played out in the back of my mind.

Finally I pulled myself up onto the fence, trying to keep the clanging of the chain-link against the poles to a minimum. The tools in my front pocket dug into my leg as I climbed over the top.

When I dropped down to the other side, I pulled the Glock out of my ankle holster and paused, listening. Then I stepped quickly and quietly to the nearest trailer.

I laid my hand on the painted wood exterior. I couldn't feel the vibrations I'd felt before, and I wondered if the bees were gone. That would explain the lack of guards. I was troubled by the implications but relieved as well.

Stepping up to the door, I swiped the card through the reader. I was surprised and vaguely disappointed by the green blink and the muted click as the lock released. I took a deep breath. Then I went inside.

It took a few seconds for my eyes to adjust to the darkness. The place was just as we'd left it: a dull red glow splashed here and there, everywhere else awash in shadows. I could smell a hint of patchouli. I put my gun on top of the server cabinet and slid the server out, released the clips on either side. The server easily lifted up and out, but the cords in the back had very little slack. I reached around and released the power cable, gaining a few more inches but no more.

The rest of the cords were tightly bundled and fastened to the side of the rack with a plastic tie. I reached around with my wire cutters to snip the plastic, squinting hard to see in the darkness.

Then suddenly I could see just fine.

Light was pouring in from the open door, framing a large silhouette. As the door closed, I saw a gun rising in my direction. Then the lab returned to darkness. I jammed the wire cutters against the entire bundle of cables and squeezed as hard as I could. The server came free and I heaved it at the figure stepping through the curtain. He put up his hands, but the server caught him on the bridge of his nose with a wet, meaty *thunk*. His head snapped back, and the gun went off. A small circle of light appeared in the ceiling. Below it, a larger one appeared on the floor.

That's when the buzzing started: deep and throaty, sounding far off and close at the same time. In the light from the hole in the roof, I recognized Pug-face, bloody and angry.

He tried to bring up his gun again, but the server somehow snagged onto his sleeve. I didn't have time to go for my own gun, so I closed on him, grabbing his wrist, trapping the server between our bodies. I caught a whiff of something nasty coming off him, and for a moment I thought he still smelled of the sewage I had lured him through. But that wasn't it. It was skunk.

I laughed—not taunting or victorious or even maniacal—just a laugh because I thought it was funny. But as I did he got his gun hand loose and chopped it down on my collar bone, causing me to step back and giving him enough space to take another shot. The server came down on his foot, making the shot go wild.

Another hole appeared, this one in the back wall, and I was relieved it wasn't in me or the panels separating us from all those bees, now sounding louder and angrier.

I tensed to lunge for the gun on the server cabinet, but Pug-face was swinging his gun at me once again. I crashed into him and grabbed his wrist. He tried to throw me but I dragged him with me. Together, we slammed into the opposite wall.

I felt something dig into my back and the drone of the bees grew louder still, accompanied now by a mechanical hum as the wall panels started to slide up into the ceiling. Grappling, we fell sideways against one of the workstations. I heard glass breaking and something splashed my arm, my sleeve. The sound of the bees rose from a buzz to a scream. I spun away, sending Pug-face sprawling across the counter, his shirt soaking up phero-mone and whatever else we'd spilled, his face inches from the mesh.

Even in the dim light, I could see the screen bristling with tiny daggers, already wet with venom as the bees frantically tried to inject their poison into something, someone, anything.

The smell of skunk was still strong coming off Pug-face, but over it I could detect the sweet, dangerous smell of the alarm pheromone.

Pug-face seemed mesmerized by the sight of the screen, maybe not realizing what it was. Maybe I was mesmerized, too, because I should have grabbed my gun and shot him. Then he seemed to understand, and his eyes went wide, their whites vivid even in the dim light. He spun, frantically trying to get away, trying to point that damned gun at me again.

I grabbed his wrist with two hands, leaving his other hand free to land three quick punches to my abdomen that altered the arrangement of my internal organs. But it gave me the leverage I needed to push his gun hand up against the mesh screen, against the thousands of bees frantically trying to sting.

He let out a growl, low at first but increasing in pitch as I held his hand in place and hundreds of stingers plunged into his skin. He stopped punching me and pried my hands off his. Then he gave me a savage shove and pulled his hand away from the screen, tugging it, like it was stuck on with Velcro. He got it free, but it was already useless. The gun fell away, hitting the counter and tumbling into the shadows.

He went for my gun, still on the server cabinet, but when I sprung at him he turned to fend me off. I tried to picture him standing in Annalisa's kitchen, the blood spurting out of his shoulder, and I drove my fist as hard as I could into that exact same place.

He howled like a coyote. I punched him again in the same place, then once more. When he moved his other hand to protect his shoulder, I punched him in the throat, cutting off his howl with a sharp gurgling sound. I could still see his eyes in the darkness. No longer round and scared, they were angry and hot. Maybe I should have been studying his hands instead, because one of his fists came out of the darkness, connecting with the side of my head and creating a shower of sparks behind my eyes.

He punched me again and I wrapped my arms around him, trying to pin his arms to his sides, trying to find that divot in his arm, but he shook me off with a roar, sending me crashing against the far wall. As I slid to the floor, I heard another mechanical hum and the lab grew brighter as daylight filtered through the bees massed on the mesh screen.

The outer panels were opening.

Pug-face was looking down at me now, pointing my gun at me. It wasn't his gun hand, but this close I was pretty sure he wouldn't miss. His smile said he was pretty sure, too.

62

I was expecting a bang and that would be it, but instead he screamed, "Ow," and slapped the hand with the gun against his neck, rubbing it and then flinging something away from him. "Fuck!" he yelled, frantically brushing at the large wet spot on the front of his shirt. His hands were wet as well.

We both looked up at the bullet hole in the ceiling. A bee crawled in as we watched, joining two more that were already buzzing in the narrow cone of daylight. One of them seemed to find him, darting at him and weaving around his flailing gun hand.

He kept trying to line up his shot, but had to stop to swat at the bee, now two bees, darting and diving at him. I searched the shadows, trying to find his gun, but I gave up, cowering in the corner instead, watching him fight it out with the bees and hoping none of them would notice me. More bees had made their way in, and his swatting had grown more frantic. He yelped again and clamped a hand on the back of his thigh. Another bee landed on his cheek. He plucked it off and squished it, throwing it onto the floor, stomping on it, his face momentarily triumphant. There were more of them, now, half a dozen circling him, darting in and then retreating, feinting and thrusting. One landed on his shoulder, another in his thinning hair.

He backed up against the plastic strips. Then he turned and plunged through them. I saw his blurred figure staggering through the doorway, silhouetted once more against the daylight. There was a moment that felt like silence, but I realized it wasn't, because as the door closed behind him, the sound of the bees lessened even more and the room lightened considerably as the bees crowding against the mesh quickly dispersed.

I wondered where they had gone. Then from outside I heard a hoarse, horrible, agonized scream.

There were only a couple of bees still with me in the unit, but with Pug-face gone, they turned their attention to me.

I tried to swat them, listening to Pug-face's screams punctuated by gagging and coughing.

One of the bees got me right where the pheromone had splashed my forearm. It paid the ultimate price, but I paid, too, a searing pain shooting up my arm, making me feel momentarily faint. Suddenly, I was that much more determined to fend off the other one. I connected once with the back of my hand, bouncing it off the plastic curtain, but it came back at me almost instantaneously, recovering before it even hit the floor. I whipped off my shirt, waving it in front of me, doused with pheromone. When the bee came at me again, it connected with the shirt.

Maybe I trapped it, or maybe it was content to unload its payload into the pheromone-soaked folds of cloth, but I wrapped it up and crushed it underfoot. For a moment, I was alone, catching my breath and listening to Pug-face's screams faltering outside. I looked down and saw dampness on my arm and my stomach.

The alarm pheromone. That's what they were after. That's what was driving them. Glancing up at the holes in the ceiling, I knew it was only a matter of time before they came after me, too.

I went to the small sink in the corner and soaped and rinsed my arm and stomach, then again, then once more. When I was confident I had removed as much of the pheromone as possible, I dried off with paper towels from the dispenser. As Pug-face's screams faded into a muffled moan, I jerked open the drawer Annalisa had gone to before and found Julie's patchouli. I pried off the plastic spout and poured half the bottle onto my arm and smeared it around. Then poured the rest onto my stomach. The air filled with the aroma of it. I'd never liked the smell, and at this dosage it was nauseating.

I took a deep breath anyway. Then I picked up the server and went outside.

Pug-face was on the ground twenty feet away, covered in a thick layer of bees. Thousands more were zipping through the air above him, as if waiting for a spot to open up so they could stab him as well. The sky had grown dark, and the air felt heavy with the threat of rain.

Pug-face's car was forty feet past his body, the driver's side door ajar, the engine running.

My Glock was at the bottom of the steps to the lab.

I paused, ready to dive back inside and come up with another plan.

But the bees seemed content to concentrate on Pug-face. I stooped to pick up the gun, paused again, then started walking a slow, wide arc around his body, no sudden movements, toward the car. When I was halfway there, I looked back at the hive boxes mounted on the outside of the lab unit, encased in some sort of white plastic. Bees were still coming out of them. Pug-face stirred, moaning and twitching his hand, eliciting an angry rise in pitch and volume from the bees that covered him. The pile seemed to constrict around him, and even through the bees I could see him shudder.

I stopped for a moment, thinking I should do something. But I knew I'd be lucky to save myself.

He had tried to kill me several times, I told myself. I kept walking, slowly and deliberately, through air thick with patchouli and angry bees, resisting the urge to swat or run or scream in horror.

When I reached the car, I slid in behind the wheel and pulled the door closed. Letting out a long breath, I noticed a bee crawling on my arm. I lowered the window and flicked it out. Then I closed the window and drove through the open gate.

63

The smell of patchouli was smothering, but it took a strong and deliberate act of will to open the door knowing I was just across the road from that mass of bees. I had parked so the driver's side door of Pug-face's car was two feet away from the Jeep's, just enough space to slide from one to the other. I craned my head to look up through the windshield, searching for any sign of bees. When I was satisfied there were none, I threw open the door and jumped into my car.

Safely inside, I took two slow breaths. A smattering of fat raindrops landed on the windshield with a suddenness that made me jump.

As I drove out. I looked through the gate across the road at Pug-face's lifeless body, still black with bees. My arm had a welt the size of a plum, and I thought about how he'd gone down. I fought off a shiver and gave the car a little more gas.

Things were still uncertain with Nola, and being around her and Annalisa together was bound to be awkward. But pulling up in front of the A-frame, I looked forward to being comforted by two women who cared about me, who would praise me for having returned victorious with the spoils of war against overwhelming odds, and who would soothe the pain of experiences too awful to mention.

Unfortunately, no one was there.

I put the server on the floor next to the dining room table and went into the living room. No one. For some reason, I didn't want to yell. I checked each room, letting my gun lead the way.

The place was empty.

I took out my phone, but before I could call, the phone vibrated in my hand with a text from Nola.

DOYLE, IT'S NOLA. WE ARE AT GAY HEAD CLIFFS. WE NEED YOU. COME QUICK.

I called her, but the line went straight to voice mail. I texted, "What's going on?" but got nothing back. I called Annalisa, and her phone vibrated on the table. I called Jimmy Frank, but his line went straight to voice mail, too. Same thing with Moose. I left them both messages and thought about calling 911, but I didn't know if it was an emergency, and I didn't know who would be on the other end of that call.

The shotgun was gone, and I didn't know if that was good news or bad.

The cliffs were in Aquinnah, at the western tip of the island, five miles away. The clouds seemed to be scraping the treetops and as I got back in the car, the rain started up again.

It bothered me that I didn't know what I was driving into. It bothered me that I couldn't contact Nola, and that she'd sent that text, then not replied, with everything that was going on. That didn't seem like Nola. It made me suspect even more strongly that she was under some sort of duress.

The rain was getting heavier and the sky darker. I could barely see the lighthouse as it finally rose over the treetops on my right. Then the light pulsed and swept around. I pushed the car a little faster. Then I was there.

In front of me, the road curved into a wide loop with a large grassy area in the middle. At the far end of it were the gift shops and snack bar, and the path to the observation area. During the summer season it would be packed, the loop necessary to keep the tourists' cars moving in an orderly line. In the off-season it was desolate, especially in the rain. Everything was closed and no one was around. I was driving through the last intersection before the loop when the rain started coming down harder. Something about the lighthouse caught my eye, but I couldn't tell what.

In my rearview, lightning flashed in the black clouds, and beneath them, a flatbed tow truck was driving up slowly behind me. On the side street to the right was a black SUV with tinted windows, a wisp of exhaust drifting away from it. To the left was another one.

I tapped the brakes hard, and I heard a strange popping sound. A subtle vibration ran through the car. At first I thought it was a mechanical problem. Then I saw a small pothole in the rain-soaked road ten feet in front of me, a curl of smoke rising from it. My eyes returned to the lighthouse, this time finding what had drawn them earlier. A sniper. But this was no precision tool; from the hole in the asphalt, it looked more like a fifty-cal. I stomped on the gas, rocketing forward as the back windshield exploded. In the rearview, I could see one of the SUVs from the side streets speeding up behind me. The other one was coming up the other side of the loop, on a course that would meet me head on.

I was approaching the far end of the loop—wondering if I should try to cut across the grass, thread the needle and get past both cars—when the car shook violently and seemed to rise up off the road. The hood buckled, and for an instant I thought I'd hit something. Then I saw the hole in the hood and realized something had hit me.

Luckily, the airbag hadn't deployed, but the car was dead, drifting forward at a couple of miles per hour. The car behind me was closing fast, and the other one was screaming around the curve toward me. I threw open the car door and spilled out onto the road just as another round punched through the car, shattering the rear passenger window and the front driver's side window, shredding the headrest in between. Tiny cubes of glass showered down on me, mixing with the heavy rain that soaked me almost instantly.

I rolled to my feet, the glass cutting into my hands and knees, and I started running. The angle away from the two cars took me toward the steps leading past the gift shops and snack stand, toward the observation area. It also left me totally exposed to the sniper. I tried to vary my stride, resisting the urge to run flat out. The rain was coming down even heavier now, the wind picking up, but I still felt the breeze when a sniper round zipped past my face. To my left, a patch of grass turned into a jet of mud, squirting up into the air. I took two more strides, then dove for the steps as another round slammed into the metal trash can. At the top of the steps was a wide path that led through the little shops to a restaurant before curving up to the observation area.

Looking back as I ran, I saw the car behind me bouncing up the grass next to the steps. The sky had continued to darken, gloomy day turning to dark night. As I ran up the path, lightning flashed all around me. Headlights captured me from the left, casting my shadow across the wall to my right. I skidded to a halt, torn by indecision, maybe by something else. As I blinked and shook my head, I was skewered by a second pair of headlights as the second car bounced up the steps behind me.

An arm came out the passenger's side window, a hand holding a gun. As I jumped out of the way, a pair of bullets slammed into my shadow on the wall in front of me. I stumbled sideways, my feet slipping in the rain but staying under me as I scrambled along the path, toward the lookout area on top of the cliff. I was running out of path, running out of options, the prospects of panic and death solidifying in the back of my mind.

Away from the shelter of the building, the wind took on a new magnitude. The rain was blowing sideways, pelting my skin where it hit. The observation area was completely exposed, a twenty- by sixty-foot rectangle of broken macadam and gravel surrounded by a simple rail fence. In the center was a stone pylon, five feet tall, with coin-operated binoculars on top.

The second car was still barreling toward me, two men following on foot, presumably from the car that had come up the steps. On one side I was hemmed in by the cliff, and on the other by an expanse of thick, low brush. I had decided to take my chances with the brush and was turning in that direction when I felt a hot breath on my neck and one of the fence rails snapped in two and fell out of its mounting.

Somehow, I had briefly forgotten about the sniper on the lighthouse. The light was visible now in the darkness, sweeping across everything, taunting me, showing me all the places I was vulnerable to it. I dove behind the rock pylon, huddling behind it as the rain came down. It protected me from the sniper, but left me completely exposed to my pursuers.

I was bleeding from a dozen small cuts from the broken glass, little rivulets of blood diluting in the rain into a pink sheen. The car coming up the path had clipped one of the fence posts, slowing it down the slightest bit, giving me another few moments of life.

I tried to will myself a way out, to conjure the mental energy to think of something to do and the physical energy to do it. But I knew I was going to die, and at that moment, it didn't seem so bad. I reminded myself that the bad guys would get away with whatever they were doing, that people would get hurt. I told myself I couldn't live with that. Then I remembered I wouldn't have to. I reached for my gun, thinking I could go down shooting, maybe take a couple with me.

Then, through the downpour, I caught a whiff of the patchouli coming off me and my mind flashed on Pug-face, lying there dead, covered with bees, helpless and exposed to the world. I pictured myself bleeding out in the rain, a hole in my head, some asshole nudging my body with the wet toe of his shoe.

Then I thought about Nola, the feel of her body in my arms, her lips on mine. Maybe I just needed to catch my breath, or to let my mind clear, but when I thought about never feeling those lips again, I sprung to my feet and started running.

Toward the cliff.

64

I didn't zig or zag. It was past the time for that. I ran flat out, pumping my legs and trying not to think about the bullets whizzing past me.

Another rail in the fence splintered and collapsed, and I angled toward it; face-planting a hurdle would be bad enough at the best of times, I was determined not to do it while being chased by bad guys with guns. I crossed the fence without breaking stride, out onto a swath of low, dense brush. The cliff was getting close, and I didn't know what I expected to happen next. I pumped my legs and lifted my feet high so I didn't trip. Another volley of bullets zipped past me, unpleasantly reminiscent of the bees that had gotten Pug-face. I hoped I hadn't already been shot, that I wasn't a dead man running, unaware that the fight was already over.

The cliff was coming up faster than I expected. In a flash of lightning, I saw myself outlined on the ground. It caused me to slow a step, and that may have saved my life. I was about to push off, to try to get as much distance from the cliff as possible, but I remembered I wasn't trying to clear the cliff. I wasn't trying to jump out to the water. My only hope lay in staying close, dropping and sliding down the cliff as much as possible.

The way the cliff had eroded, there was an overhang at the top. I pulled up short and let myself drop, still falling six feet before I touched the cliff face. The angle was steep but when I hit the side of the cliff, it took the wind out of me. The surface was slick with a mixture of clay and water, and there was nothing to grab onto. I felt like I was going down a very steep water slide, with chunks of rock sticking out like jagged speed bumps, slowing me down and giving me contusions. I found myself funneled down a small channel in the cliff face, accompanied by a torrent of clay-colored water.

The bottom came up fast, and I hit it with a bone-jarring thud. My feet sank into the wet sandy clay at the bottom. I took a moment to get my bearings; then I crawled out from under all the water coming down. The beach was narrow and strewn with boulders that extended out into the water. I was about to dash down the beach when one of my pursuers came sliding down the cliff twenty feet away from me. I sank back against the cliff, into the sandy clay. I wiped it all over my face, narrowing my eyes to slits, and waited in the dark.

He trotted back and forth, searching for me, his assault rifle at the ready.

Suddenly he seemed to sense I was there, taking a few cautious steps in my direction. My eyes were all but closed, and I decided that if he came any nearer, or if he raised his gun, I would have to try to take him down before he could kill me. If I could get his gun, maybe I could take out the others.

But then a gruff voice barked out, "Where is he?"

The guy in front of me turned to face an older guy just walking up. "Don't know," the first one said. Three more walked up, each carrying an assault rifle.

I should have gone when I could, I told myself.

The older guy split the others up and sent two down the beach and two up the beach.

Then it was just him and me. He stood there with his back to me. I had the feeling he was trying to lure me out, and I was planning a move, wondering if I could close the distance between us without making any noise. He seemed the kind of grizzled vet who could silently disembowel you using a library card.

I was tensing to make my move when he spun to face me, marched to a spot ten feet away, unzipped his fly, and let out a deep sigh, along with a stream of urine. He was just a little too far away for me to take advantage, so I closed my eyes, waited for him to finish, and then waited a little longer, just in case.

When I opened my eyes, he was thirty feet away and headed up the beach. Beyond him, I could see two of the others, still moving away from me. I could only assume the others were a similar distance in the other direction. Before long, they'd all turn and head back, and then I'd be screwed. The rain was still coming down at a decent clip, rinsing the clay from my skin. I was running out of time.

The mud made a sucking sound as I pulled away from the cliff. I froze, but no one else seemed to have heard it. Then I dashed across the sand, headed straight for a boulder in the surf. When my feet hit the water, I gasped out loud from the cold. A couple of feet deeper I let out a similar sound, slightly higher pitched. Then I dove in and swam.

The boulder was thirty feet out, and I didn't stop until I'd reached it. The waves weren't as big as I'd feared, but they were waves, and I was getting weaker from the cold. Each successive wave threatened to smack me against the stone, but I didn't dare leave it. When I peeked back over it, I saw a trail of clay-colored water in the darkness, an incriminating line pointing to my location, but it soon dissipated enough to be barely visible, the current pulling it to the west. Everybody was still headed away from me, so I swam with the current to the next boulder, then the one after that.

I hop-scotched my way down the beach, watching the gunmen as they slowed, then stopped, then turned around and headed back. We were headed in opposite directions, just about even with each other, when I came to the last big boulder. I clung to it and watched as they headed back down the beach.

The numbness was working its way up my limbs, and the relief as I watched them go was quickly outweighed by a distant but growing sense of panic as the occasional waves splashing over my head came with greater frequency. I was starting to feel heavy. I knew I needed to get moving, get my blood pumping, or I was going to wash up on a beach somewhere and ruin someone's vacation.

After pushing off the rock as hard as I could, I kicked my legs and started swimming, trying to put a little more distance between me and my pursuers. That's when I heard it. At first I thought it was my heart. But it wasn't my heart. It was a helicopter coming around the cliff, its searchlight slicing through the darkness.

I could feel my limbs weakening when I needed them stronger. A wave closed over my head, and it occurred to me that drowning wasn't the worst way to go. If I went down, at least it wouldn't be these guys who found me. I smiled at the thought that, even if just for a few days, they'd think I'd gotten away.

Then I thought about Nola once again. I pictured Jimmy Frank bringing her in to identify my body. I'd seen my share of floaters. Drowning might not be the worst way to die, but it might be the worst way to be found. I couldn't do that to Nola.

I closed my eyes and pictured her, safe and warm, just a few miles away. I could feel her arms wrapping around me, the heat from her body, the softness of her kiss. I could be with her in less than an hour, less than a half hour, if I could survive the next fifteen minutes.

Then it occurred to me that if these guys were here trying to kill me, others at that moment might be trying to kill Nola and Annalisa.

The helicopter was hovering in front of the cliffs, scouring them with its searchlight. I kicked toward the shore, and had just reached the point where the swells were starting to break when the helicopter stopped circling the waters in front of the cliff and started drifting west, toward me. As it approached, the searchlight swept back and forth, from twenty feet into the grasses and scrubby underbrush that lined the beach, then out to sea, where the light faded to nothing hundreds of feet away.

My arms and legs were numb and practically useless. The sound of the helicopter was getting louder as I pulled myself up the wet sand, unable to stand even in the shallow water. The noise grew as the wet sand sucked at my hands and knees, like it didn't want to let me go.

I felt massively heavy as I crawled up the beach, until finally, the sand firmed up beneath me and the waves could no longer reach me. It felt strange being on land, a feeling I thought I'd never experience again. I looked down the beach, amazed at how far I'd come. But it wasn't far enough. The searchlight was slicing across the beach barely a hundred yards away. Straight ahead, a clump of bushes rose from the beach grasses, and I headed for it. The dry sand gave way underneath me, and I stumbled and fell, my limbs treading land as I tried to scramble away.

Finally, my hands reached the edge of the brush. I grabbed a branch, thorns digging into my skin, and pulled myself in, tucking myself as far as I could under the prickly leaves. I prayed that the men looking for me didn't have thermal vision; telling myself that if they did, I'd have already been dead.

The searchlight swept over me, a hundred shafts of light piercing the low canopy of the brush. I kept my head down and my legs tucked in tight, and I tried not to move.

When the searchlight moved on, I opened my eyes the tiniest bit and I smiled.

In the light from the helicopter, I could see the bushes surrounding me were beach plums, half a dozen at least, happily growing on their own, covered in white blossoms, wild at the beach.

65

I waited until the helicopter was eighty yards up the beach before I crawled out from under the bushes. I sniffed one of the
beach plum blossoms before I left, but all I could smell was
patchouli.

I crawled the first fifty feet, but by then the helicopter was far
enough away that I could move in the darkness undetected. They
weren't going to give up that quickly. Speed was more important
than anything else.

After a hundred yards of tough terrain, I came to a thick stand
of sea grass, six feet tall, looking very out of place. I whacked at
it with my arms, and came up against a massive fieldstone wall, at
least eight feet high. But it was only five feet wide. Sliding around
it, I realized it was a fireplace, surrounded by a slate patio.

I turned slowly and almost sobbed when I saw the clean modern lines of the glass house where Jimmy was Tesla-sitting.

The key was in the back porch light, right where Jimmy Frank
had found it before. I slipped into the kitchen and closed the door

behind me, slumping against it just for a moment, listening to the sand and pebbles falling off me and onto the tile floor.

I got a beer from the refrigerator and drank half of it in a gulp. I thought about going upstairs and seeing if I could find some dry, sand-free clothes, but I was in a hurry. Instead I went through the door on the opposite end of the kitchen, and into the garage.

Except for the crunch of the wheels on the gravel and sand, the occasional scrape of a branch on the side, the Tesla was silent as I coasted down the driveway. When I got to the road, I paused for a moment. The helicopter was headed back up toward the cliffs. I waited for it to pass; then I took a deep breath and turned on the headlights. Leaving them off would make me less visible, but if they saw me driving without lights, they'd know it was me. Instead, I drove at a reasonable speed, ten miles above the speed limit, headlights on. Not a care in the world.

I made my way back to State Road, then pulled over and waited, looking in the rearview to see if I was being followed. I took out my gun and my phone. I knew the phone would be ruined, and it was, completely dead, water dripping out of it. A couple of cars went by, but nothing suspicious looking. I pulled out behind them and drove off.

66

Jimmy Frank was sitting on the porch drinking a beer when I drove up. His face flashed alarm because he didn't recognize the car. He smiled when he saw it was me, then he did recognize the car, and he stopped smiling.

"Son of a bitch," he said, knocking over his beer as he got to his feet. "Tell me you didn't steal the Constantines' car. Those rich sons of bitches are the best gig I have and you break in and steal their car?"

"Sorry," I said as I got out. "I'll bring it back."

"Jesus Christ," he said, looking me up and down. "What the fuck?"

Nola and Annalisa came out the front door, and Nola ran up to me.

"Where were you?" she asked, wrapping her arms around me, squeezing me tight, then stepping back, brushing the sand off her. "You're a mess. What happened?"

Images came back to me: bullets flying past me, sliding down the cliff, cowering next to a rock, waves breaking over my head. It seemed unreal and long ago, but it provoked a wave of emotion that broke over me. I pulled her to me again, and held her tight, not letting go, partly so she wouldn't see the emotion in my eyes, and partly because I didn't want to, ever.

"Baby, what happened?" she said quietly. "Are you okay?"

"I'm okay," I said, my face in her hair.

I opened my eyes and saw Annalisa smiling wistfully. Jimmy stepped up next to her as I pulled back and looked down at Nola, wiped the tears from her cheeks.

"You look terrible," she said.

"I'm okay," I said.

"You're not okay. Look at you. Where were you?"

"Let's get you inside," Jimmy said, guiding me up the steps with a hand on my back.

"I got a text," I said. "From Nola's phone. It told me to meet you at the lighthouse, at Gay Head."

She screwed up her face. "I never sent that." She took out her phone and tapped the screen; then she showed me the last text between us—"Be careful"—from when Teddy almost started a riot at the ferry dock.

"Easy enough to fake a text like that," Jimmy said.

"So what happened?" Nola asked. "At the lighthouse?"

Out of the corner of my eye I saw the server set up on the dining room table, a monitor and keyboard plugged into it. "Have you learned anything?" I asked, pointing at it.

"A little," Annalisa replied.

Nola sniffed the air. "Is that patchouli?"

Annalisa's eyes widened. "Patchouli? What happened?"

"Really," Nola said with a crooked smile. "Were you at a rave?"

Annalisa came right up to me. "What happened?" she said urgently. "Are you okay?"

I laughed, because it was kind of a ridiculous question, but I knew what she meant. I held up my arm. The welt had shrunk to the size of quarter. "I got stung once."

Nola stopped between us. "What's going on? What are you two talking about?"

I spotted the sofa and started moving toward it, but Jimmy headed me off with a chair from the dining area.

"Sorry, pal," he said, pushing me down onto it, "but you're a mess."

"What happened?" Nola demanded, stepping in front of me.

I took a deep breath and told the part about Pug-face and the bees. I skipped over most of the details, but Nola was still horrified. By the time I got to the part where I came back to the A-frame and she and Annalisa were gone, she was kneeling on the floor beside me, wrapping my hand in hers.

"We were picking watercress for lunch," she said quietly.

"What?" I asked.

"For salad," Annalisa added. "Nola found some growing wild."

I told them about the text, and by the time I was finished with the trip to the lighthouse and my dip in the ocean, Nola was squeezing my hand tightly.

"So what the hell is going on?" Jimmy asked, his voice gravelly and low.

I leaned forward and lowered my voice. "We know the Osterman girl died suspiciously, and another lab tech, Lynne Nathan. We know Julie Padulla died suspiciously as well. We know two guys with guns broke into Annalisa's house. We know the lab sheets were faked. We also know that the bee mites on this island, the little pests that are part of what's wiping out the bees, they seem to have absorbed the genetic material from the genetically engineered bees."

"Yeah, but what does it all mean?" Jimmy asked. Nola's face was asking the same question.

"If the gene splice has jumped from the bees to the bee mites, the splice is unstable," said Annalisa. "If that's the case, they might have to start all over, from the beginning, or close to it."

"And that would cost them a lot of money," Jimmy said.

"Could that explain why the lab sheets are faked?" Nola asked. "To hide something like that?"

Annalisa shook her head. "That's what I thought, but I can't find any evidence of genetic instability. I just completed an analysis of the real data, though. Some of the anomalies seem unrelated, but the rest of the numbers suggest that the hive was swarming, which is what bees do when a colony splits off. That's nothing terrible on its own."

"But these bees aren't supposed to swarm, are they?" Nola asked. "Isn't that what Pearce said when they asked him about the bees spreading?"

"He did." She shrugged. "And from what I gathered, when the bees swarmed, it was totally unexpected. Not only were they surprised the bees could swarm, but they seemed to do it surprisingly quickly, unexpectedly. In a way it's a big deal, but it's not the kind of thing you murder people over."

The room was quiet when I said, "They're aggressive." Everybody looked at me. "I know the guy I was fighting with at the lab was covered with the pheromone, but he wasn't just stung to death, he was annihilated . . . I didn't want to lay it on too thick, but it was one of the most horrific things I've ever seen."

"You're right," Annalisa said. "Even their reaction when I was there. I've never seen anything like that."

"Do bees get more aggressive when they swarm?" Jimmy asked.

Annalisa shook her head. "Just the opposite. When a hive swarms, the old queen takes a portion of the colony and they split off, to go start a new hive. Before they go, they gorge themselves on honey, and that makes them docile. Sometimes they're so bloated they're physically unable to sting."

"Wait," I said, "so the old queen leaves the hive?"

Annalisa nodded.

"So does that mean there's a new queen in the old hive?"

She nodded again. "Usually, yeah."

"And the queen lays all the eggs. So it's like, a new generation, right?" I thought for a second. "Could the aggressiveness be a recessive trait? Something that doesn't show up in the first generation?"

Annalisa didn't react at first. After a few seconds, she said, "Hmm. Actually, it could."

"So maybe when they faked the data, they weren't just hiding the fact that the hive was swarming, they were hiding what came after it. The aggressiveness."

"That would make sense," she said.

"But they couldn't hope to release those bees, knowing they're going to turn aggressive," Nola said. "Not because it's morally reprehensible, but because they'd never get away with it."

"Sumner might think he could," Annalisa said. "They're licensing the bees, not selling them. If Bee-Plus technicians are working them, I'm sure they are getting rid of any new queens. And with the flightless queens, any that got by shouldn't be able to fly away. I think Sumner is still working on a fix," Annalisa said quietly. "He sent the faked data to Stoma, but he was still working on the Bee-Plus bees. Maybe he's hoping to fix it before a wider release."

"That's a hell of a risk he's willing to take," Nola said.

"And that might be something worth killing to hide," Jimmy added.

"Unless it really wasn't murder," I said. "Or at least not first degree. Maybe it was a cover-up to hide the cause of an accidental death." They all looked over at me, and I paused, hoping someone else would finish the thought so I wouldn't have to. No one did. "I wonder if the cause of death for Claudia and Lynne was a bee attack. That would explain why they had to dispose of the bodies."

Annalisa gasped and put her hand over her mouth. "Poor Lynne."

Jimmy put his arm around her, and she leaned against him.

Nola put her hand on my knee. "Let's get you cleaned up."

67

Nola ran a bath and helped me out of my clothes, revealing the scratches and cuts and bruises from the glass and thorns and cliffs. Dried blood streaked my limbs. As steam rose from the tub, Nola cupped my cheek, her eyes teary.

"I'm okay," I said with a smile.

She responded with a kiss, a strong, hungry, desperate kiss. The kind of kiss that makes you take a step back to steady yourself. The kind of kiss that sends a shiver through your body, that makes certain parts of your body try to convince the other parts that maybe they're not as tired as they seem.

Nola noticed the effect she'd had on me with a raised eyebrow and a very soft touch. Suddenly, a bath wasn't the first thing on my mind. I put my hands on her ribs and kissed her back, my hands sliding up, squeezing and caressing, eliciting a soft sound from deep in her throat. She broke away, her face flushed, and pointed at the tub.

I submerged myself completely, washing my hair, then I lay back and closed my eyes as Nola washed the rest of me. She lingered on the dirtiest parts. When she was done, my body was clean and my thoughts were most certainly not.

She wrapped me in a towel, running her hands all over me. "Jimmy said we could have the bedroom," she said, leading me to it. The bath had soothed and relaxed me, and I was more than half asleep. But not completely asleep. Part of me was wide awake.

I flopped onto the bed and she straddled me.

"I think Jimmy has the hots for Annalisa," she said, looking down at me. "Then again, I thought you did, too."

"I have the hots for you," I mumbled.

"So I see," she said, reaching down and making me groan.

I let her do the driving, and she seemed to know where she was going. It was gentle and sweet, in part because I wasn't capable of anything else, in part because that was what we needed. When we were done, she rolled off me and we held each other tight.

"I missed you," she said, running her fingers lightly across my chest.

I reached over and brushed the hair away from her face. "I missed you, too," I said, realizing as I said it how intensely it was true.

She leaned over for a long, slow kiss. Then I fell asleep.

The sun was up when I awoke. Everyone was downstairs, sitting around the dining room table. Moose was there, too. He came over and wrapped me in an awkward hug.

"They told me what happened," he said, not letting go.

"Okay," I said, arms at my sides, hugged into place. "Could use some oxygen."

After a couple more seconds he let go and stood back. "You doing okay?"

"Yeah, I'm okay. Any word from Benjy?"

"Nothing."

Nola came over with a cup of coffee, and I sat at the table.

She pulled a chair up next to mine and held my hand, running her fingers through mine.

They had gotten Moose up to speed and now they were all talking it out, trying to figure out what was going on. I took a gulp of coffee, trying to follow along and hoping the caffeine would help.

"This morning, Annalisa decrypted a few e-mails from the server," Nola explained. "There are repeated references to a 'new site' at 'TFS,' whatever that is, and talk about moving the next phase up. Something is supposed to be coming to a head in the next couple of days."

"So, 'TFS,'" Jimmy said, turning to me. "I thought maybe they were referring to Katama somehow, but that doesn't make sense. Any ideas?"

I looked at Moose, and he shook his head. I did, too.

Moose and Annalisa took over the conversation, talking about gene vectors, transposons, and genomic sequences. Something about the whole thing had been bothering me, though, and as the caffeine did its thing, it came to me.

"The Bee-Plus bees were brought in because the bees on the island started dying, right?" I said. "Wouldn't that mean the mites were acting up before the Bee-Plus bees even got here? And wouldn't that mean it couldn't have jumped from the bees to the mites?"

Moose and Annalisa were quiet for a moment, Nola and Jimmy looking back and forth between them.

Moose looked down and said, "Shit."

Nola looked at him "What?"

"He's right," Moose replied. Then he looked up Annalisa.

She nodded. "Unless they brought the Bee-Plus bees before they had permission."

"Do you have any samples of the mites from before last week?" I asked. "And is there any way to test them?"

Annalisa was shaking her head, but Moose said, "Benjy has some." She turned to look at him. "In his shack. He has samples going back to the end of last summer. You have access to a thermal cycler, right?"

"What's that?" I asked.

"A machine that does polymerase chain reactions," she said. "It amplifies a DNA sample so you can sequence it. There's one at my lab, if it's still there. And a gel electrophoresis unit, too. But I don't dare go back. And it would take hours to run the test," Annalisa said.

"How big are they?" Moose asked.

She stared at him for a moment, thinking. "They're not that big. What are you thinking, bring them back here?"

He shrugged. "Or somewhere else, but yeah."

She looked frightened at the thought, but she nodded her head. "That might actually work."

68

Jimmy drove to the lab. We slowed down at the front entrance to Johnny Blue's farm. The gate was seriously banged up and spattered with garbage. We kept going, curving around to the left, and slowed to a stop in the middle of the road. To the left was the back entrance to Johnny Blue's property. The two Stoma lab units were gone. So was Pug-face's body, but I could still picture it.

I tapped Jimmy on the arm and pointed. "The labs are gone."

He nodded and we pulled into the other driveway. We both let out a breath when we saw Annalisa's lab still there.

As we got out of the car, I looked around carefully for any sign of bees.

Annalisa had sat us down and coached us on what to do if we saw them: no loud noises, no sudden moves, no hesitating, just get back to the car. Even covered with bees, just get back into the car.

Jimmy was reading my face. "Bad way to go, huh?"

I nodded. "Worst I've seen so far."

"Guess we better be careful, then."

"Careful and fast. If they already moved the two units across the road, they'll be coming back for this one soon enough."

We approached the lab with our guns out. I swiped Annalisa's ID through the slot, pushed open the door, and we stepped inside.

Annalisa had shown us pictures of the two units online, and they were right there when we walked in. I grabbed one and Jimmy grabbed the other and we carried them out to Jimmy's truck. We went back and took the mini fridge from under the bench, which held all the reagents, and a small two-drawer cabinet full of tubes, pipettes, and other supplies. As we brought them outside, we could hear a helicopter approaching and we quickly placed everything in the back of the truck and got out of there before it showed up.

We dropped off the equipment back at the safe house, and Annalisa immediately started setting it up. Nola gave me a kiss and a squeeze, then started helping her.

I traded Jimmy in for Moose before heading out to Benjy's shack to get the mite samples. As we drove away, I felt better knowing Jimmy was there with Nola and Annalisa. No offense, Moose.

Benjy's shack was an actual shack, a tiny wooden structure on the edge of a small industrial site in Tisbury. Inside it was a desktop computer on a plywood workstation, with a chair in front of it. Next to that were a plastic porch chair and what looked like a trash-picked coffee table, both strewn with papers and printouts. Moose opened a metal cabinet in the corner, and started poking around one of the shelves. It was crowded with tiny glass jars labeled with white stickers.

While he was rummaging around, I stood in the middle of the floor, trying to keep out of the way. There were papers lying everywhere, but next to the computer, right on top, were two dated the day before Benjy disappeared. One was a printout of a half page of numbers. Across the bottom were large handwritten characters from a red felt-tipped pen: "225 Hz," circled and underlined.

The paper next to it was a printed map of the island. There were pencil lines all over it, but a half-dozen were traced in red felt tip, all converging at a point on the edge of the forest, just west of the airport.

"Bingo," Moose said, pulling out one glass jar, then another, then two more. "August and October of last year, April and May of this year."

"What are these?" I asked.

Moose glanced at them. Then he did a double take. "I don't know," he said. "It looks wrong."

"What do you mean?"

He took them out of my hand, studying them more closely. "The numbers are wrong." He looked from the papers to the computer. "So, are we camping out at that house now? Is that, like, our control center?"

"Yeah. I don't think Jimmy's too happy about it."

Moose thought for a second. Then he handed me back the papers and started pulling plugs out of the back of the computer. "Give me a hand with this."

"Whoa, whoa, whoa," Jimmy said as we walked in with Benjy's computer. He was sitting with Annalisa at the dining room table, now covered with the server and the lab equipment. "What is this, the goddamned control center?"

Annalisa looked up at him, a wry and almost intimate look on her face. He seemed to sense it, looking back at her and slumping his shoulders. "Okay," he said. "All right, whatever." He slid some of the beakers out of the way to make room.

"What did you find?" Annalisa asked.

We put everything on the table, and Moose started unpacking the box. "We got the mite samples we need," he said, sliding the glass jars toward her. "We also found some information that could be important, but I'm going to have to get on Benjy's computer and check it out."

Moose got to work on the computer, and Annalisa started pulverizing the mites with the back of a fork, mixing them with different solutions. At one point she was using the salad spinner as centrifuge. Nola and I got out of their way, but Jimmy stayed right where he was, sitting close by Annalisa's side. I looked back as we walked out of the room, and a tiny wistful pang passed through me, but I put my arm around Nola and she pulled me in tight.

Nola and I found enough canned ingredients in the cupboard to make a passable chili, and we worked quietly but comfortably together in the kitchen. By the time the chili was ready, Annalisa had finished preparing the samples and she and Jimmy were sitting close together, staring at the thermal cycler.

Moose pushed himself away from the computer. "I'm onto something here," he said, rubbing his face. He paused and looked with a sudden intensity at the chili I'd set next to him, then shoveled in a few quick spoonfuls.

"Okay," he said around the third spoonful. "So, we've been tracking the bees on the island since Benjy started this project last year, counting the number of bees with these LIDAR units, then mapping out where the colonies are. The LIDAR picks up all the movement around them—a massive amount of data. Then we filter it. We're looking for honeybees, so we filter the data for two hundred hertz, the frequency of honeybee wings. You filter the data, you look at which direction the honeybees are flying, and you plot the line. You do it from a few different locations, and where the lines intersect, is where there's a hive. Then we would go visit it and add it to our census map."

Jimmy's forehead looked like there was an aneurysm behind it. I wondered if that was how I looked when Moose first explained it to me.

"So a few weeks ago," Moose said, "the number of bees flying around starts dropping, then the bees stopped showing up altogether." He sat back and took a deep breath. "Apparently, a few days ago, Benjy started filtering for different frequency signatures. And at two hundred and twenty-five hertz, he got hits. Lots of them. When I plug those numbers in, I get the same result."

"Could the calibration have been off?" Annalisa asked. "Could it have actually been two hundred, and just registering as two-twenty-five?"

"It's possible. And I'm going to check the LIDAR units to make sure. But it's also true that maybe what he was getting hits from weren't regular honeybees."

"You mean Bee-Plus bees?" Nola asked.

"Or maybe more accurately Bee-Plus-plus, right?" he said with a bitter laugh. "Because if they're swarming, that means another generation is involved. Stoma said the queens are supposed to be flightless, to prevent that from happening, but they could be wrong. Imagine that: a genetic modification not doing what it's supposed to, right?" he said sarcastically. "Makes you wonder what else they're wrong about. Or lying about. Either way, if these aren't regular bees, it wouldn't be a total shock that they had a different signature."

The table fell quiet as that sunk in.

"So what do we do now?" I asked.

"We need to check the LIDAR units, that's for sure," Moose said as he picked up the map we'd found at Benjy's. "But first we need to go check and see if this info is right, because if it is," he said, poking it with his finger, "there should be a feral hive right here."

69

The lines on Benjy's map converged on a small wooded area fifty yards inside the state forest. Nola looked worried when we left. I kept it light, asked her if she wanted us to bring her some honey, but I was worried, too.

Moose had the coordinates on his phone, and we parked on the side of the road and sat there for a moment.

As he opened the door, I said, "Shouldn't we have beekeeper suits or whatever?"

"Yeah," he said with a grim smile. "We should."

Then he got out.

I did, too, thinking that if he'd seen what I'd seen, he wouldn't be so glib. Annalisa had assured me that the alarm pheromone would have long since worn off, and maybe the patchouli had, too, but I swore I could still smell them both, and it was giving me the heebie jeebies.

The forest was buzzing with flies and gnats as we walked as quietly as we could into the woods. The buzzing grew louder, making my hair stand up. When I looked at Moose, I could tell he heard it, too.

That's when I caught the smell. At first so faint that, if I hadn't known what it was, I wouldn't have even noticed. Then Moose smelled it, too, a furrow creasing his brow.

His face was screwed up at the stench, and he was opening his mouth to speak when I pointed out a deer lying at the base of a large pine tree twenty yards away, its stomach grotesquely bloated.

Moose saw it and looked back at me. I held up a finger, for him to wait, but when I walked over to it, he followed. The smell was intense. Maggots squirmed around the animal's eyes, nose, and mouth. It was peppered with dead bees and stingers.

Moose was trying to keep cool, but his eyes were wide with fear. I hoped my own efforts to fake it were more successful.

He took out his phone and checked the GPS. Then he jerked his thumb over his shoulder. Still looking at his phone, he turned to lead the way, then tripped and went sprawling. I reached out to grab him but missed, and he tumbled over a fallen tree and down into a slight gully.

Almost immediately, a scream tore through the forest, loud and high and chilling. I jumped over the downed tree after him, and when I landed, I saw Moose, on his hands and knees, his face inches away from what was left of Benjy's.

It was bad. Worse than the deer. Benjy was slumped against an old tree trunk. His flesh was bloated, but it was also swollen beyond that, misshapen and covered with stingers. His beard was a tangle of dead bees.

The scream shut off, and I thought he was done, but he was just catching his breath. When he resumed it was less high-pitched surprise and more ragged horror and anguish. I grabbed him by the collar and pulled him to the other side of the gully, stumbling backward until we fell onto the roots of another tree several yards away.

I held him until he stopped screaming, trying to calm him down. But when he finally stopped, through the sound of his sobs and my soothing whispers, I heard another sound.

Looking up, I saw a branch hanging low under the weight of a large papery hive with thousands of bees pouring out, filling the air above us. When Moose looked up and saw them, he started screaming again.

I pulled him to his feet, but he didn't need any more coaxing. He took off like a jack rabbit through the woods. I trusted he was going in the right direction, because I was following him. The old joke went through my head about how you don't have to run faster than the bear, just faster than your friend. I felt an unreasonable resentment against Moose, now fifteen feet ahead of me.

I had just spied his truck, maybe sixty feet away, when the first bee got me in the back of the neck. I swatted it and crushed it and threw it to the side. I slowed a step when I did, but the pain inspired my legs, and I made it to the truck at the same time as Moose.

A couple of bees followed us into the truck. The first one was no match for my frantic freak-out jujitsu. But the second one was—penetrating my defenses while I was dispatching its cousin. It stung me on the shoulder.

Between the fact that Moose had outrun me and the fact that we weren't driving away at a high rate of speed, I was almost annoyed with him. But when I killed the second bee and turned to ask him if perhaps we could leave, I saw that his face was a silent mask of anguish, and I remembered he had just come face-to-face with a dead friend.

I patted him on the shoulder and tried not to panic as the cloud of bees outside the car thickened. Moose's sobs entered the audible range, and we sat there for a few more awkward seconds. Then he opened his eyes and saw the bees crawling on the windshield. "Oh, shit," he said. He fumbled for the keys, and we were off.

70

When we walked through the front door, Nola took one look at Moose and wrapped him in a hug. I could have used a hug myself, but when you're supposed to be a tough guy, sometimes you have to wait. Annalisa looked at me, concerned, but she stayed where she was. Jimmy came over and slapped my shoulder.

"You okay?" he said. "You look a little freaked out."

I guess that would have to do.

"We found Benjy," I said.

"He's dead," Moose blurted out.

"We also found a big hive of angry bees."

"A feral hive?" Annalisa asked. "Of Bee-Plus? Then the queens aren't flightless."

"Wait," I said. "I thought the old queen and the old bees left the hive to the new queen and the new bees. So the bees that left should be the less aggressive ones, right?"

She bit her knuckle, thinking. "That is true, usually. Although it's possible for a single hive to send out multiple swarms, even over the course of a couple of days. All but one of those are going to be the next generation. It's rare, but with these bees, who knows?"

Moose got himself together enough to pull away from Nola and shake his head. "I don't know if they're the Bee-Plus bees, the next generation, or what. They're very aggressive." He started losing it again. "They killed Benjy."

"I think he followed the same data we did and went looking for them," I said, now pretty much just talking to Jimmy. "I guess he found them."

"So are these bees all over the island now?" Jimmy asked, anger mixing with the alarm in his voice. He looked down at Annalisa, then over at me. "We're not going to make any friends, and I don't know if it will do any good, but if these bees are killing people, it's time to kick this thing upstairs."

Jimmy drove with his arm locked and his jaw set, the muscles in his temple visibly throbbing.

"This is going to get me in all sorts of shit with people who already don't like me," he said, "so I need to know that you're not going to get cute. I need to know you're going to tell what you know, and play it straight. Don't give them any reasons to blow us off. Are you ready for that?"

I did a quick mental calculation of all I had done, what I could bend the truth about, and which parts of it could get me in trouble. "Yeah, okay. What's this guy like?"

"Chief Wilks is a tool," he said. "The worst kind of simpering kiss-up political animal. Everything he does is calculated, every decision based on how it impacts his career objectives. And frankly, I hope it works out for him. I hope he gets whatever job is next on his ladder of success, so at least he'll be out of my hair."

Wilks's office was in the same building as Jimmy's, across from the ferry terminal in Vineyard Haven. Wilks sighed when he saw Jimmy, and he frowned when he saw me.

"Hello, Jimmy," he said with a big, insincere smile. "Thought I told you to go home and get some sleep."

"There's some shit going on we need to talk about."

Wilks winced at the expletive, and I almost did, too. Not in front of the children, I thought.

"Who's your friend?" Wilks asked, looking at me.

"Doyle Carrick. He's with Philly P.D. He's involved in some of this, so I brought him along."

I didn't like the way he said I was involved in it. Sounded guilty.

Wilks put down his pen. "You were involved in that home invasion, right?"

I nodded.

"This is about the bees," Jimmy said, lowering his voice.

Wilks grimaced and closed his eyes. "What have I told you about the bees?" he snapped.

"But this—"

"What have I told you about the bees?"

"There's a body."

"What?"

"In the woods. One of the bee researchers, Benjy Hazelton, stung to death by the bees, from a hive there." He put a slip of paper on the desk. "Here are the GPS coordinates."

Wilks gave me the same smile he'd given Jimmy when we walked in. "I'm sorry. Could you please excuse us for a few moments?"

As soon as I was out in the hallway, Wilks started in on Jimmy. I could hear the whole thing.

"This is exactly what I didn't want to hear about, Sergeant Frank. This is big, these people are big. And sometimes, you got to let the big kids play and stay out of the way so you don't get hurt. Have you not been listening to me? I thought I'd made myself very clear."

"A body, Wilks. Are you listening to *me*?"

"And how did this body die?"

"Looks like it was stung to death."

"Well, that sounds like an awful way to go, but hardly a police matter. Sounds like you need to call animal control, and the medical examiner."

"I guess I'll do that, then."

"Good. And now you better get home and rest up. You know I need you back in Katama first thing."

Jimmy flashed me a look as he stormed out of the office. He was too angry to speak. He might have been too angry to drive, too, but at least we were getting where we were going in a hurry.

"Sorry," I told him. "If it's any consolation, my lieutenant's an asshole, too."

Jimmy took out his phone and dialed as he drove. Sitting in the passenger seat, I had my foot jammed on the imaginary brake pedal. I wondered if this was how Nola felt when I was driving "impatiently."

"Hi, Letitia," he said, cradling the phone between his jaw and his shoulder while he pulled out the piece of paper I'd given him. The car veered perilously close to the edge of the road as we bounced up the winding hill. "I need to report a body. . . . It's just west of the state forest. I got GPS coordinates for you . . . appears to be natural causes . . . No, I'm not a doctor, but apparently Wilks is, and he assures me this is not a police matter and I should just report it to you. Looks like he was attacked by bees. . . . That's right, and you need to tell whoever is going out there they should be prepared for very aggressive bees, make sure the same thing doesn't happen to them. You ready?"

He read her the numbers, holding his phone in one hand and the paper in the other. I resisted the urge to grab the wheel, knowing I did much worse on a regular basis. We pulled up to the house, and he killed the engine but didn't move to get out.

"Wilks isn't just an asshole," he said, eyes front, like he was thinking it through. "He's sleazy and stupid, a political animal whose every instinct is geared toward ladder-climbing instead of crime-solving. I wouldn't expect anything better from him, but there was something else going on back there." He paused and looked at me. "He was scared."

71

When we walked in, Annalisa was staring intently at the computer. She didn't even look up at first, but when she did, she hurried over to us. "Are you okay?"

I was about to answer when I realized she was talking to Jimmy. He gave her a smile and nodded. "My boss is a first-class asshole is all."

Nola came down the steps and gave me a wry smile, like maybe she had heard that line somewhere else before.

Annalisa put her hand on Jimmy's arm. Her eyes met mine for a fraction of a second, then locked on his. "Did you learn anything new?"

"Just that the political pressure around this thing is intense. How about you?"

She looked around the room and nodded.

"What did you find?" I asked.

She took a deep breath. "I'm still digging through the data, but the fragment analysis is done. The mites from last summer are typical varroa destructor, but the samples from March have the same anomaly, the same marker, as the new ones, two months before the Bee-Plus bees were supposedly introduced."

"So does that mean they brought in the Bee-Plus bees before they said?" I asked.

"Actually, I don't think so," Annalisa said. "I may have been looking at this wrong. Those matching gene sequences may have been incidental, the vector or bridge material they used to get the splice to stick. The sequence between them doesn't match anything, as far as I can tell."

"So what does that mean?" Nola asked.

Annalisa took a deep breath. "I think it means the mites have a totally different splice, just using the same technique. They have been genetically engineered as well."

"For what?" Nola asked.

I had already been wondering, and it came to me just as she asked. I laughed. I couldn't help it. "How do you create demand if you've got a supply of bees that are immune to mites?"

Nola got there before I finished, her face twisting into the same combination of loathing and admiration that I was feeling. "Bastards," she whispered.

"What?" Annalisa asked.

"What's the best way to sell bees that are juiced up to resist the mites that may or may not be wiping out all the regular bees?" I asked. "Juice up the mites as well, so you *know* they're wiping out the regular bees."

Annalisa was quiet for a second, stunned. "They did this on purpose."

Nola looked scared and angry. "There's bees dying all around the planet, and these bastards see it as a niche, a new market." I moved closer and put my arm around her. "They didn't do all this so they could corner the bee market on the tiny island of Martha's Vineyard. They're going to try to take it global."

"But what about the aggression?" Moose asked. "They can't just put these bees out there knowing they're killing people."

"I wouldn't put it past Sumner," Annalisa said. "It sounds insane, but he's working on a newer iteration of the Bee-Plus bees, a 'two-point-oh' or whatever. He's probably trying to fix the aggression and the swarming. It doesn't seem to be ready yet, and it doesn't seem like he's shared it with Stoma. But with the kind of pressure he's under from Pearce, I wouldn't put it past him to release them even when he knows they're not ready. And the Bee-Plus licensing agreements are even more ironclad than the GMO seed licenses. Maybe he thinks that since only the Bee-Plus workers will be handling the bees, they'll be able to keep them under control."

"That's ridiculous," Moose said. "They're already getting out, and this is just a few hives on the island."

"I know," Annalisa said. "You're absolutely right."

Nola looked up at me. "What are we going to do?"

"If Stoma doesn't know," Annalisa said quietly. "Maybe we could tell them."

Moose made a strange snorting, hiccupping sound. "Tell Stoma? Really? Sumner might not have told them everything, but a company like Stoma, they've got to know."

Annalisa looked at the server and bit her lip. "There's something else," she said. "I've been poking around on that server. There are mentions of an advance team working on the special exemption on the mainland, but there's something else, too. It's heavily encrypted, but there is something big going down, and it is happening tomorrow. I could get through the encryption, but it will take a while."

"I've got to remind you," Jimmy said, pointing at the computer. "That computer is stolen, so anything you get off of there is going to be inadmissible in a court of law. That could be the difference between whoever is responsible spending a long time in jail and getting off scot-free."

"A court of law?" Nola laughed, rolling her eyes. "Are you kidding me? I'm sorry, people as rich as Archie Pearce don't go to jail."

"Sumner's not rich," Annalisa said. "He acts like it, and he used to be, but he's not. He's in hock up to his eyeballs so he could retain a share of the company. If he gets away with this, maybe he'll be rich again." She shook her head. "Anyway, something big is happening tomorrow. It's like, their end date." She looked around at us. "I think they're planning on taking the bees off island tomorrow."

"They can't," Jimmy said, shaking his head. "They're not allowed to. The provisional approval that let them bring Bee-Plus bees onto the island isn't even up for review for another month."

"People!" Nola clapped her hands loudly, like a school teacher trying to get a class's attention. "They. Don't. Care. About any of that stuff. None of it. They're not going to jail. They don't care about 'provisional approvals.' They are going to do exactly what they want to do, and then later, when their genetically modified Frankenbees have killed off all the regular bees—and a whole bunch of people—they'll say, 'Oops, sorry. My bad.' And not a goddamned thing is going to happen to them. Maybe they'll pay a big fine and see a two-percent dip on their quarterly profits, but you know what? It won't even be that."

I turned to Jimmy Frank. "She's got a point. So what do we do?"

"I still think we need to go through proper channels."

Just as he said it, his phone buzzed. He looked at it, then looked at us, then he answered it.

"Hey . . . What's that? Pretty sure, yeah. Hold on." He pulled out the paper with the GPS coordinates. "Yep. That's them. So what do you mean, are you guys sure? I'm not saying they're idiots, I'm asking if they're sure. . . . No, I wasn't talking about a dead deer." He looked at me.

"The body was in a gully ten feet from the deer," I whispered.

"Let me talk to Chuck," he said. "Hey, Chuck, Jimmy Frank here. I'm told the body was in a gully ten feet away from that deer. . . . You saw the gully, huh? . . . No, I'm not saying you don't know how to do your job, I'm just making sure is all. Did you see any bees? . . . It's a simple goddamned question, Chuck, did you see any bees? Yeah, well you, too." He thumbed off the phone. "Asshole." He shook his head. "There was no sign of a body when they got there. Except for the deer."

"We need to tell the authorities," Annalisa said. "And I don't mean animal control or the local medical examiner."

Nola snorted. "The authorities know, and they immediately tipped off Stoma, and that's why Benjy's body is gone. And don't think for a moment you're ever going to see it again." Her bottom lip was trembling. "Benjy's gone. He's wherever they put Claudia Osterman and your friend Lynne."

"She's right," Jimmy said. "Wilks wasn't talking about pressure from the town board of selectmen. He's talking serious, heavy-duty pressure from way up high, the feds, you name it."

The room was silent, then Benjy's computer chimed loudly. Moose went over to it. "I ran an analysis of data from some of the other monitoring stations," he said, tapping a few keys. The screen showed a jumble of bee lines, including the familiar spokes indicating a colony laid over a satellite image of the island. He put his finger over the spot where the lines converged, then he looked around the room. "Johnny Blue's berry farm."

72

The sign at the front of Blue's farm was a mess, parts of it splintered, parts burned, half of it covered with eggs. The gate was propped closed but it was easy to see that at some point someone had busted it in.

Jimmy and I shared a look. Then he gently pushed the gate open. It creaked loudly, the hinges a couple of swings away from falling off completely.

There was a long driveway ahead of us, stretching to a house a hundred yards away. The driveway was lined by a dense wall of tall conifers. Beyond them, around the house and behind it, were fields of blueberries. The GPS coordinates put the feral hive in the woods to the left, about halfway to the house.

We were going to knock on the door, warn Johnny Blue, and have a look in the woods. But before we could get there, Blue emerged from the trees near where the bees were supposed to be. He was carrying a shotgun.

Tyrique and Dawson stepped out after him.

"Oh shit," said Tyrique with a grin, pointing me out to Dawson. "It's this motherfucker."

"You're trespassing," said Johnny. He sounded drunk.

Jimmy held up his badge. "Police."

"You got a warrant?" As he said it I noticed a bee flying around his head. He waved at it lazily.

Jimmy sighed. "Looks like someone's been messing with your gate. I got probable cause. But really, I'm only here to give you some information."

Johnny smirked. "And what's that?"

I saw a couple of more bees flying around.

"There's something gone wrong with Stoma's bees."

Johnny laughed and shook his head. "What is it with you hippies and all this bullshit about the bees?"

I laughed out loud, because calling us hippies was ridiculous. Then I wondered if he could smell the patchouli.

"First you're all worried about the bees," he said. "Then you're all worried about the new bees. Then you're worried that there aren't any more old bees. I still don't know what the big deal is about any of them, but there seems to be plenty of them around here, doing a great job. Busy little fucking bees." He brought up the shotgun. "So I think maybe you'd better just get the fuck off my property." He swatted at another bee, but missed.

"Johnny," I said. "Those aren't regular bees. Those are the Stoma bees."

He laughed. "No, they aren't. Stoma keeps their bees locked up tight and under control. These are regular local bees like the ones you assholes said were all wiped out. But even if they were, so what? Bees is bees. They're pollinating the shit out of my crops, doing whatever they're supposed to be doing. Soon, they'll be doing it on the mainland, and those farmers will be as happy as I am. The rest of it's bullshit. Now get the fuck off my property."

"Johnny—" I said.

"Bullshit!" he thundered, firing the shotgun into the air. Tyrique and Dawson jumped, then shared a look that said, "We got to find a new gig."

As the echo of the shot faded, I heard another sound, one that made my hair stand up, a low buzz in the background. Not far from where Johnny and his guys were standing, I could see bees flying around, emerging from the trees, then zipping back in. They weren't meandering; they were moving with great purpose.

"Bees to the left," I muttered to Jimmy.

"I see them," he replied.

"Johnny, don't do that," I said. I kept my voice soft and held out my hands, palms out. "Those bees aren't normal bees. Loud noises set them off, and if you keep shooting that gun, they're going to—"

He pointed the gun in the air and squeezed off another blast. More bees started darting out through the trees.

"You don't tell me what to do with my mother—ouch!"

He slapped his neck, his face turning dark red with anger before his eyes went round with the pain.

Tyrique looked down, suppressing laughter, until Dawson yelped and slapped one hand with the other, fast and hard. He looked triumphant, holding up the bee and crushing it between his fingers. But the tide had already turned. I turned to Jimmy, but he was already backing up slowly.

The trees seemed to be shooting bees at them, little brown darts flying past Blue and his men, then curving around and snapping back, circling and darting in. Blue yelped, a high-pitch squeal against the grunts and muttered obscenities of his men.

"Blue!" I yelled, back-stepping toward the car. "Run for it! The house or the car, either one, but you can't stay out here." One of the bees arced past me, and I pulled back but didn't swat at it.

Blue was still swatting and dancing. He'd probably been stung a half-dozen times. Tyrique and Dawson must have been listening because they turned and started running. Then Blue let out a ragged yell and raised the shotgun again. For a moment I thought he was going to take out his bodyguards for running away, or turn the gun on Jimmy and me, but instead he fired into the trees, blasting a hole two feet wide in the dense conifers.

For an instant, there was a quiet stillness. Dawson stopped and looked back, absent-mindedly waving his hand at a bee that had followed him. Even the bees seemed taken aback by the shotgun blast.

Then there was a sound like a chainsaw and a column of bees gushed through the hole in the trees like a fire hose on full-bore. It hit Johnny Blue and it stuck—a thick, roiling mass that enveloped him from head to toe. The shotgun fell out of his hand, and he dropped to his knees. Tyrique and Dawson took off, fast.

Jimmy and I jumped into the car, and as Jimmy started it up, Johnny Blue pitched forward onto the ground. We drove up and I reached for my door handle, but Jimmy grabbed my wrist, shaking his head.

"It's too late," he said. "Nothing we can do for him." He looked ahead at the bodyguards. "But those guys could probably use a lift."

Before I could acknowledge he was right, we were rocketing forward in a spray of gravel, bees bouncing off the windshield. "You ready to get stung?" I asked Jimmy when we pulled ahead of Tyrique. Jimmy kept the car rolling as I reached behind me and opened the back door.

Tyrique dove onto the backseat, four or five bees coming in with him. I swatted at them with a rolled-up copy of the *Vineyard Gazette* Jimmy had left on the floor of the car. The last one landed on Tyrique's bald head and I swatted it hard, with a loud smack. Tyrique looked up at me, eyes smoldering out of a face pebbled with welts.

Then Jimmy slammed on the brakes and Dawson dove in from the other side, blindsiding Tyrique and bringing in another handful of bees.

I handed the newspaper to Tyrique and the backseat became a flurry of newspaper whacks and thrashing limbs until the bees were dead and the two men lay on top of each other, breathing heavily but without any signs of an allergic reaction.

Dawson raised his head. "What the fuck was that?"

"I told that crazy little fuck this was some bad shit," Tyrique said. "I told him from the get-go, shit wasn't going to end well. They put up that much money, they ain't going to be asking for a little bit in return."

"Who's they?" Jimmy asked.

Tyrique looked almost surprised, like he'd forgotten we were there. Then he seemed to decide he didn't care. "Stoma," he said, trying to pluck one of the stingers out of his neck. I wanted to tell him to scratch it, not squeeze it, but I didn't think he'd be receptive to my advice. "That dude Sumner, creepy-ass motherfucker."

"What was the deal?" Jimmy asked.

Tyrique and Dawson looked at each other.

Dawson shrugged. "Not like Blue's going to mind at this point."

Tyrique nodded slowly. "Blue didn't have the money to buy that farm. I don't know where he even got the idea to do it, crazy little motherfucker. That dude from Stoma fronted him the money for it, but said he had to do what they say for the first few months, bringing in them bees. Blue started freaking out when shit got intense, all these protesters and shit. Sumner told him to sit tight, that they was moving things up."

"Moving what up?"

"They said they were moving something to the mainland ahead of schedule."

Annalisa's suspicions had been right. "The bees?"

He shook his head. "I don't know. But they said it was happening tomorrow."

"You heard them say that?"

"Sumner talked shit right in front of us, like we deaf or something." He shook his head. "Blue thought he was home free. I knew he was too much a dumb-ass to be long for this world, but I didn't think he was going to go out like that."

"You hear anything else about Stoma or bees or anything like that?"

He shook his head, finally getting the stinger out of his neck, flicking it away. "Nah, man, just that."

Jimmy offered to take them to the hospital, but they just wanted to get to their own car, parked behind the house. They looked out the windows for a solid minute, checking for bees. Then they got out of Jimmy's car and very quickly got into a pimped-out Jeep Grand Cherokee. We followed them back down the driveway, but when we stopped next to Johnny Blue's body, still covered with bees, they kept going.

"Jesus Christ," Jimmy said, fighting a visible shudder.

Tyrique and Dawson didn't even slow down when they hit the road, squealing their tires as they turned onto the street and disappeared.

Jimmy turned to me, looking scared—and unnerved by the fact that he was. I don't think it was a familiar sensation for him. "So what do we do now?"

73

The question was still hanging in the air when we got back to the house.

"Johnny Blue, Benjy, Julie the lab tech, plus Claudia Osterman and Lynne Nathan," I said as we pulled up. "Kind of feels like we should tell someone."

Jimmy laughed grimly. "I agree," he said as we pulled into the driveway. "But from what Wilks was saying, and from what happened to Benjy's body, there's no one left to tell."

As we stood there talking, the front door opened and Nola walked out. When I looked over at her, she said, "I need to feed the chickens."

"What?"

"The chickens, back at the farm. I need to feed them."

"No." I shook my head. "It's too crazy out there."

"I believe you," she said. "But they need to eat. And I have to feed them. If we leave now we can be back before dark."

"Johnny Blue is dead. We just saw him being stung to death."

She stepped back, closed her eyes for a second. "Doyle," she said quietly. "I have to go."

I let out a deep sigh and turned to Jimmy. "We'll be back in fifteen minutes. We'll figure out what's next then."

The streets seemed deserted. Everyone was either lying low or in Katama, protesting for one side or another. I couldn't shake the feeling as we drove that unseen gears were grinding away, that things were happening out of sight, things I should be stopping. I drove even faster than usual, and Nola didn't complain. The farm looked exactly as it had when we'd left. It hadn't been a full day, but somehow I expected it to be overgrown with weeds and out of control.

As I waited for Nola, a bee circled me. I could feel myself tensing, but it wasn't threatening, just looking for a flower. After a couple of seconds it made its way over to a pot of geraniums on the back porch.

It looked like just a regular bee, but I knew it probably wasn't, and I felt sorry for it. I thought about the butterflies back in Dunston, the things that had been done to them. This bee probably thought it was a normal bee, unaware that its genes had been scrambled to produce such a terrible result. It occurred to me that the people weren't the only victims here.

When Nola was finished, we got back in the car, relieved to be getting away from the farm.

We were just at the end of the driveway when her phone rang.

She looked at me as she answered it, her face suspicious.

"Oh, hi, Jimmy," she said. Then, "Sure," and she handed the phone to me.

"There's developments," he said. "Apparently the special exemption is being granted. They're going to let Stoma take their bees to the mainland. Archie Pearce is coming to the island himself to make the announcement."

"Are you serious?"

"That's what they're saying on the radio. He's holding a press event at the Katama site. Probably timing it to get that nice sunset light for the TV cameras."

I laughed in disbelief. "That's insanity. It's already crazy there. He'll cause a riot."

"I know it. They just called me in. So what do we do?"

"We could arrest them."

He laughed. "We've got nothing on Pearce, not that we'd ever get close enough to arrest him, or have enough manpower, or the political support."

"What about Sumner?"

"Probably the same thing. Besides, we don't even know where he is." He let out a sigh. "Where are you?"

"Just left Teddy's farm. Heading back to the house."

"Okay. I have to go. I'll feel better knowing someone is here with Annalisa."

When I got off the phone, Nola had tears in her eyes.

"You heard?" I asked her.

She nodded.

I reached over to squeeze her hand.

As a cop, you know sometimes the bad guys get away with it. It hurts, but you get used to it. This one hurt more than most. Maybe because the stakes were so big, or because the victims were so small. Or maybe it was because the reason they were getting away with it was because they always got away with it. Because they were bigger than the apparatus that was in place to stop them.

I heard the now-familiar sound of helicopters and looked up to see the Stoma Corp logo, flying toward Katama. I wanted to stop my car and shake my fist at their arrogance, how they rearranged the world to suit their liking. From altering life so it fit their plans to risking a catastrophe so they could stage a publicity event in the middle of a war zone.

Even the way they dismantled Renfrew, taking his home, ruining his family, absorbing the Thompson Chemical Company, which had been in the Renfrew family for a hundred years. He was probably as bad as Pearce, just not as smart or as rich. But the way they destroyed him on every level was evil.

A cop sped past us in the same direction as the helicopter, blue lights flashing in his grill. Jimmy Frank was headed there, too, along with probably every other cop on the island. And every protester, too. I wondered if the whole island would tip over, as everyone rushed to Katama, just so Archie Pearce could gloat.

That's when it hit me.

"What?" Nola asked, wondering why I'd taken my foot off the accelerator.

I plunged it back down.

"TFS," I said. "Thompson Farm Supply. That's the old name of Thompson Chemical Company's place here on the island, Renfrew's chemical unit in Vineyard Haven. Stoma owns it now. I bet that's where they're doing whatever they're doing, while everybody's on the other side of the island, in Katama, looking at Archie Pearce's dog-and-pony show."

"So what are we going to do?"

I pressed the gas a little harder. "We're going to try to stop them."

The newly repaired gate was unlocked when we arrived. The old sign was still visible behind the new one: Thompson Farm Supply, with the happy farmer on the cartoon tractor.

Nola tried to call Jimmy to tell him what we were doing, but she couldn't get through. He probably had his hands full in Katama.

I pulled up and stopped a few feet in front of the gate. The grass was high on either side of the driveway. I had no idea what I was going to find in there—bullets or bees or nothing at all—but I wasn't about to bring Nola. She could be pretty stubborn, but this time I was going to hold my ground. Luckily, I didn't have to.

"I can't go in there," she said.

"What?"

She put her hand on my arm. "I've been thinking, and maybe you're right, maybe I'm not sensitive like I was, but . . . It's a chemical facility. Jesus—"

"Wait out here," I said, resting my hand on hers. "I mean, it could get very dangerous in there and I'd rather you wait outside, but I think you would be fine. There's something I need to tell you."

She paused with her hand on the door handle.

"Remember when we were leaving the apartment, before we came up here, when I had to get your bags because the guy was spraying the hallway?"

She was looking at me intently, probably wondering where this was going. "Yes."

"That was Roskov, the landlord. He said he was spraying for bugs. But he also said he had been doing it every month, for years. I wanted to make sure you knew that."

She stared at me, processing that information. "Okay," she said. "Well, let's talk about that some more later."

I nodded. "Now, go hide in those trees. Try Jimmy again. If I'm not back in a half hour, get out of here. Just stay clear of the roads until you're a couple of miles away."

She looked in my eyes for a second, then grabbed my face and crushed hers against it. Then she grabbed the shotgun and got out.

74

Nola opened the gate, gave me a brave smile, then ran across the grass and disappeared into the trees.

I coasted slowly down the driveway and pulled in between two metal shacks. I took out my Glock, double-checking the clip as I got out of the car. The chemical truck Teddy had filled his tank from was still there, in the middle of the cluster of buildings. I crept around to the back of the nearest structure.

The sun hadn't set, but the shadows were getting long. The weeds and bushes were growing close to the buildings, but there was enough space to slip between the branches and the metal walls. I had squeezed around three of the shacks when I heard the sound of metal sliding across metal and footsteps in the gravel. I poked my head around the corner and saw Sumner standing at the back of a pickup truck with two stacks of metal boxes in the back. He was holding a clipboard and looking at his watch. Then he looked up at me and smiled.

"Carrick. There you are." He smiled. "I've been looking for you."

"I've been looking for you, too," I said, stepping out with the Glock in front of me.

"Really?" He laughed. "Are you here to arrest me?"

"Maybe. Why, what are you doing?"

I tried to keep my eyes on him while at the same time scanning the area for company. I knew it was highly unlikely he was here alone, but I didn't know where his friends were.

He smiled condescendingly. "Nothing you need to concern yourself with." I heard a crunch of gravel behind me, but before I could turn around, I felt a sharp poke in the back. Like the barrel of a gun. "Now, please hold that gun by the barrel and hand it over your shoulder to the nice gentleman behind you."

I turned to look and saw Teddy's friend Brecker, his stony face almost dashing with the dramatic addition of a black eye patch. He was the masked man I'd fought at Annalisa's. I'd always wondered how the movie bad guys got their eye patches. Now I knew.

"You think this is funny?" Brecker said, cocking the brow over his good eye. He had an UZI tucked under his arm, and I didn't think that was the least bit funny, especially not when he swung it hard against the side of my head.

Suddenly, I was on my knees, with blood streaming down the side of my head. I tried to say, "Hilarious," but it came out more like "Urk."

Fortunately, no one was paying any attention to me anyway.

Brecker had his hands in the air, his good eye staring like a laser. When I followed his gaze, I saw Darren Renfrew standing off to the side, looking like hell but holding a massive revolver. Apparently, the situation had changed while I'd been distracted. I actually did think this was funny, but I kept that fact to myself.

The ringing in my ears cleared enough that I realized Renfrew was speaking. "You people think you can just do whatever you want, ruin people's lives. You've got another thing coming." The corners of his mouth were flecked with spit. "You can go to hell. My great grandfather built this company, and I'm not going to let you take it from me, take everything I've worked so hard for."

Sumner held up his hands. "Sorry, Renfrew, but your beef is with Pearce." He smiled, a kindly sympathetic smile. "I understand where you're coming from. That bastard bought me out, too. I had to sell my soul to save the company I'd spent my whole life building. And now I'm under his thumb, just as much as you are."

Renfrew faltered, the gun sagging in his hands.

"He's on the island, you know," Sumner said. "Right now, at Katama, making a big announcement about my Bee-Plus project, taking the glory while I'm doing all the work."

Sumner flashed a look at Brecker, a slight nod of his head. I could feel Brecker tensing to move, and as he grabbed the UZI and swung it toward Renfrew, I drove my shoulder into him, slamming him against the metal wall behind us. He fired wildly into the air. Renfrew screamed, spinning in our direction and squeezing off shots. I let my momentum carry me behind the building. I shook my head to clear it, realized I still had my gun, and turned back around the corner of the building.

But everyone was gone.

One of the metal cases lay on the ground where the pickup truck had been, its lid half off. The box was filled with coarse brown powder, but when I looked closer, in the fading light, I could see the powder moving.

It was mites. Sumner was moving the mites.

I nudged the lid back into place with my foot, then stepped back. I know the mites didn't normally feed on humans, but I had no idea what to expect with these things.

I could hear someone running headlong through the brush to my right. To my left, the pickup truck was speeding away. I ran after the truck, reaching the main driveway just in time to see a burst of machine gun fire from the pickup tearing into the front grill of the Jeep. I took careful aim and squeezed off one shot, but it pinged off the metal frame of the truck's rear window. Then the truck was through the gate and out on the street.

I took two steps after them. Then I pivoted and ran the other way, back toward the chemical truck, wondering if I could hot-wire it. I saw something shiny behind the front tire and when I dropped to my knees, I saw it was the keys Teddy had dropped when I surprised him as he was filling his chemical tank. There was one long key, a Chevrolet logo on it. I jumped into the truck, jammed the key into the ignition, and started it up.

The radio was already turned on, and when I started it up, the truck was instantly filled with the sound of Archie Pearce and a background of angry protesters trying to shout him down. The sun was setting, and I could picture him in the perfect-for-television golden light. He sounded like a sweet old man, explaining how the special exemption would allow Stoma to bring the benefits of Bee-Plus to the rest of the country, bringing down food prices and ultimately saving a third of our food supply.

I stomped on the gas pedal and sprayed gravel as I took off after them. The truck shimmied violently, and when I turned onto the driveway it tipped up as the liquid in the tank sloshed against the sides.

I barely straightened it out before I reached the gate, and when I slammed on the brakes, the whole truck rocked back and forth.

"Nola!" I called through the open window.

She emerged from the trees carrying the shotgun, and I wondered if I was having a bad influence on her. She hurried over, but stopped halfway.

"Come on," I said. "They're getting away."

"You're kidding me, right?" she said, a look of horror on her face, pointing at the back of the truck. "Not in that."

I looked back at the chemical tank. "Oh," I said, "Right. They killed the Jeep. They're moving the mites. I have to go after them. Remember what I said, stay clear of the road—"

She looked me in the eye, set her jaw, and got in. I tried to give her a reassuring smile but she gave me a fast, fierce kiss, then she sat back with her eyes closed and said, "Drive."

We shot out of the driveway, the truck tipping again as we turned onto the street. Nola's fingers dug into the upholstery. I wanted to hold her hand, but I didn't dare take a hand off the wheel.

The truck was old and it drove that way, but it had a lot of horses and I quickly got it up to eighty barreling down Edgartown Road. I caught up enough that I could see the pickup ahead of us. I didn't know where we were headed, but I had a feeling the chase wasn't going to remain on land. There were two airports on the island, and we were headed away from both of them, toward Vineyard Haven. Toward the ocean.

I saw brake lights flash up ahead, swerving, and I realized we were heading toward a traffic roundabout.

"Hold on," I said, and Nola opened her eyes, wide, then closed them again.

The tires screeched and we went up on two wheels. I had to jerk the wheel hard and the chemicals in the back sloshed hard. I struggled to keep the truck upright, compensating one way, then the other. I just got it straightened out when it stalled. Ahead of us, the taillights were receding into the gathering dark. I frantically turned the key, and on the third try it started up again.

Up ahead, the brake lights flared again, then disappeared to the left. Toward the water.

"Crap," I said loudly as I gunned the engine.

Nola looked over at me. "What is it?" She was visibly terrified, and it broke my heart to see her this way.

"They're headed out onto the lagoon pond," I said. "If they get past the drawbridge and out into Vineyard Haven Harbor, they're gone. It's over. What are we going to do?"

"I don't know," I said, thinking hard. "I either go after them here and try to stop them before they get out on the water, or try to head them off at the bridge." I tipped my head toward the tank on the back of the truck. "Hit them with this stuff when they go under the bridge."

We were quickly approaching the place where they had turned off.

Nola took a deep breath. "I'll do it."

"Do what?"

"You stop them here. I'll get to the drawbridge. Just in case." She closed her eyes and took another deep breath. "Just tell me what I need to do."

I was stunned that she would consider it. Part of me knew I shouldn't let her, but part of me knew I had to. Instead of trying to talk her out of it, I said, "Are you sure?"

She gave a jittery nod.

I paused, hating myself. "Okay, there's a thick hose on the back, with a spigot. Just open up the spigot on the back of the tank, point the hose, and try to get as much of it on them as you can. Try not to get it on you and breathe it in."

She nodded as we skidded up to the driveway where the truck had turned. I could see their taillights glowing in the darkness.

"Call Jimmy, and tell him what's happening," I said. I gave her a desperate kiss, and for an instant we looked into each other's eyes. She smiled.

"I love you," I said. Then I opened the door and jumped out.

75

I hit the ground running and headed toward the taillights, listening to the sound of the truck pulling away behind me. Down a short driveway was a small house surrounded by a fence, and beyond it, a gravelly beach and a floating dock with a handful of boats tied to it.

The only movement I could see was out on the water, an old fisherman standing upright in his boat, coasting slowly up to the end of the dock, preparing to throw his line. I had just stepped onto the dock when one of the other boats started, revved, and took off. Brecker was standing at the wheel, looking like a pirate with his black eye patch. I ran down the dock as the boat swerved back and forth, Brecker struggling to get it under control with the throttle all the way up. He was headed straight for the old guy's boat, swerving out of the way at the last second, but sending up a swell of water that almost flipped the other boat.

The old guy went into the water, but he came up immediately, his mouth spraying equal parts salty water and saltier language. He turned his head to keep the invective focused on the boat that had pitched him over, until I jumped off the end of the dock, over his head, and landed awkwardly in his boat. He was quiet for a moment, looking at me. Then I pushed the throttle up, turned the wheel hard, and took off, sending a plume of water up behind me as I shot out into the lagoon. I couldn't hear anything over the roar of the engine, but I'm sure he had something to say about it.

The lights of the bridge weren't far enough away for Nola to get there in time. I could see Brecker's boat in the dim light, headed straight for the bridge. To my surprise I seemed to be gaining on him.

I glanced up at the bridge, but there was no sign of Nola. I tried not to think about how scared and conflicted she would be. Or what would happen if I was wrong, and she still had chemical sensitivity. Or if it was gone and this much chemical exposure would bring it back. I also tried not to think about what would happen if we failed.

Instead, I focused on the boat in front of me.

I was closing on Brecker, but not enough to catch up with him before we got out of the lagoon. I had a quarter tank of gas. On the open sea, he could simply outrun me. I needed to slow him down.

I steadied the boat as much as I could. Then I braced my hands against the wind screen, and squeezed off a shot. I saw a spark in the darkness as the bullet struck metal on the boat. The lights rocked back and forth and the boat veered off course. I had slowed him down, but I had also gotten his attention. I could see his face in the darkness, turning my way. I hit the deck and got as low as I could, covering my head with my hands as a volley of bullets tore through the boat. Immediately, the vessel started filling with water and the smell of gasoline. I heard Brecker's boat clang off a channel marker, and I popped up to see it veering back toward the right. By the time he corrected his course, I was on him.

The two boats hit, rocking violently, and I jumped from mine onto his. It was slightly bigger than the boat I'd been on, but much of the room was taken up by the metal boxes. I tried not to think about the thousands of tiny parasites inside them. Instead, I focused on the guy with the eye patch, snarling at me and swinging an UZI in my direction. I dove for him, but he got off two shots before I got past the gun. The second one creased my arm. It stung like hell, but reminded me we were playing for keeps. My chances of saving the world were much lower if I was dead. I drove him backward, hard against the windshield. He grimaced in pain as the edge dug into his back. Then he got a hand onto my throat and squeezed. The gun was trapped between us, and I grabbed the barrel and pushed it until it was almost pointing up under his nose.

We were totally off course now, tracing a wide circle in the lagoon. The boat I'd been on was doing the same, in the opposite direction, the two vessels performing a graceful duet.

I looked up at the bridge and saw the truck, right where it was supposed to be, and Nola, looking out over the water, watching us fight.

Brecker spun out from in front of me, and we both crashed into the metal boxes, knocking them over. The entire stack came open, the dark masses of mites spreading out like a living shadow.

I landed on top of Brecker, pinning him against the jumble of boxes. He screamed, his one eye wide in horror. Both of mine might have been, as well. Suddenly, he was an animal, clawing and kicking, almost whimpering. He threw me off of him, seemingly oblivious to the fact that I'd come up with the gun.

But as I pointed it at him, the boat clanged off another channel marker, lurching and tossing me into the water.

I went under when I hit, but came up in time to see Brecker frantically brushing mites off of him with one hand, grabbing the controls with the other. The boat straightened out, heading right for the bridge.

The salt water stung the bleeding furrow in my arm, and for the first time since I'd been on the island, I thought about sharks.

The second boat was slowing down, but its wide circle was taking it right toward me. I put the UZI over my shoulder and swam out to intercept it, hoping I wouldn't be cut to ribbons by the propeller. The rope was trailing in the water, and I grabbed it tight and pulled it in quickly, jerking the boat into an even tighter circle as I climbed aboard. I got it straightened out and pointed it at the lights of Brecker's boat, but the smell of gasoline was intense and I could feel the water rising up to my calf. I was low in the water and riding sluggish.

Brecker was almost at the bridge, and Nola was no longer standing there watching.

As the boat passed under, I saw Nola at the back of the truck, one hand grabbing the hose and the other one fumbling with the spigot. Then the hose jumped, issuing forth a torrent of Thompson Chemical Company's worst. She held the nozzle with both hands, her arms fully extended. She averted her face, her eyes tightly closed and her cheeks puffed out with held breath. The stuff splashed onto the bridge, cascading down through the metal structure and showering onto Brecker and the mites. Like a heavy rain, it coated the entire boat in poison.

Even from where I was, I could smell it. Brecker screamed, jerking about and clawing at his eyes, but his boat didn't stop.

Mine did. The motor shuddered and coughed and died, the boat filling more quickly with water as Brecker and his boat, framed by the bridge, faded into the darkness of the harbor at night.

I had no idea what was left in the UZI, but I lined up the sights with my best guess of where Brecker had been, and I squeezed the trigger until it was empty.

In the darkness, I saw a tiny blue flash, just for a moment. Then the night lit up with orange as a dirty ball of flame rose into the sky. I might have seen Brecker thrashing around, on fire. Then there was an even bigger explosion as the gas tank went up, sending flaming debris twenty yards in every direction.

The current pulled my sinking boat under the bridge and into the harbor. I saw Nola looking down at me, the streetlights illuminating her hair from behind like a halo. As the boat sank underneath me, all I could do was look back up at her, overwhelmed by love and the hope that I hadn't just killed her.

76

I was climbing onto the tiny beach on the far side of the bridge when Nola grabbed me by my shirt and pulled me out of the water. Her face was shining bright with a combination of terror and exhilaration.

"Oh, my God, you've been shot," she said, looking at the blood oozing out of my arm.

"I'm okay," I told her, brushing the hair away from her face. "Are you okay?"

"I don't know," she said, laughing and crying at the same time. I put my arms around her and squeezed her tight, wondering if I was contaminating her with chemical-laden water. But she held me even tighter.

The wreckage of Brecker's boat was flickering out, slowly spinning in the harbor.

I looked around us, but we were alone. "Did you reach Jimmy?"

She shook her head. "I left a message, said it was important. I didn't want to say anything more than that." Her voice was muffled against my chest. "So is that it? The mites are dead, right?"

I didn't know for sure about the mites. The bees were still

around, and so was Sumner. So was Pearce. I didn't know what to say. But before I was forced to admit it, I heard a low whistle that turned into a roar as a streak of yellow flashed across the sky— Jordan Sumner's jet, low enough that I could see its winking bee logo skimming the treetops.

"Son of a bitch," I said.

"What is it?"

"Sumner's jet," I told her. "Let's go."

"Where?" she asked, falling in behind me.

"The airport."

The truck handled better without the load of chemicals, but I more than made up for it by driving even faster. We kept the windows down, trying to rid the cab of the chemical smell coming off us. Nola called Jimmy again as we drove, and left another message and a text saying he should come to the airport as soon as possible. She was almost hyperventilating, but she insisted she was okay, and she began to calm down, taking slow, deep breaths.

Then we were there.

The access gate was open, and I killed the headlights and turned in, taking it slower in the darkness. Once past the fence, I could see Sumner's yellow jet sitting across the end of the runway. Ahead of us, a black pickup truck was speeding toward it, looking like it had come through the same gate we had.

I turned to Nola. "You okay?" I'd been asking her that a lot, putting her in harm's way a lot. I wondered if I would ever stop.

She nodded. "I'm okay."

We both jumped as her phone buzzed.

It was Jimmy Frank, so I answered. "It's Doyle," I said.

"We just got done here. I'm on my way to the airport. What's going on?"

"They tried to get the mites off the island, but we stopped them."

"Was that in the harbor?"

"Yeah."

"I got reports."

"Sumner's jet is here. I think he's trying to take the bees."

"I'm five minutes away."

"You bringing any friends?"

He paused for an instant. "No."

"Get here quick. They're at the west end of the runway."

I put the phone down, and Nola said, "Is he bringing help?"

I shook my head. "Just him."

I drove out onto the grass, flanking the runaway, giving the jet plenty of distance. When we were positioned so the jet was between us and the black truck, I stopped and turned to Nola.

"I need you to take the truck up another fifty yards or so, then double back onto the runway. You're going to block their exit. You don't have to get right up close, just as close as you feel safe. Then park across the runway. Use the parking brake. Lock the doors. Take the keys. Then run the other way, through the airport building. Find a restroom and wash as much of that stuff off you as possible, okay?"

She nodded, her eyes shiny and wide. "What are you going to do?"

I laughed. "I'm going to crash their party. Slow them down until Jimmy gets here." I didn't know what I expected to happen after that.

I gave her a kiss, and slipped out the door.

The truck rolled away, its taillights bright in the darkness. I hoped that between the lights from the airport and the lights from the plane, no one would notice.

Creeping up on the jet, I saw Sumner and one other guy loading boxes out of the back of the pickup and stacking them onto a hand truck. They were moving gingerly, and when I looked closely, I saw the same kind of white plastic hive boxes from Sumner's lab, each bound with bungee cords, and not very securely. I'd be moving gingerly, too.

Sumner and his pal were wearing Tyvek suits, but they looked flimsy and they were open at the throat, with no hoods.

The pilot's red face poked out the front hatch. "Jesus Christ, Sumner," I heard him exclaim over the sound of the jet's idling engine. "Are you fucking kidding me? This is bullshit."

Sumner shook his head, smiling at his helper, like, "Can you believe this guy?" But the helper was stony-faced. Maybe wondering what happened to the last guy who had his job.

The helper had a sidearm. Sumner didn't seem to. I couldn't see anyone else.

"Five minutes," the pilot said, watching them anxiously. "I swear to God, then I'm leaving."

Sumner ignored him, lifting another box from the back of the truck.

In the distance, I heard helicopters, and in my mind I pictured Jimmy Frank and the cavalry coming to back me up. But I knew that's not what it was.

I stepped out from behind the tail of the plane, holding my gun and my badge out in front, hoping nobody had the visual acuity to see the word "Philadelphia."

"Hold it right there," I said, using my cop voice.

Sumner looked over, surprised but not alarmed. His helper stacked the box he was holding on top of the others. Then he pulled his sidearm and pointed it at me. Beyond them, on the other side of the plane, I saw the Thompson Farm Supply truck rolling out of the darkness, right up next to the front of the plane. The dome light came on, and I saw a flash of Nola's shirt. A second later I caught a glimpse of her silhouette as she ran toward the airport buildings.

"You're under arrest," I said, ignoring the guy with the gun.

Sumner shook his head, wearily. "Go away, Carrick. This doesn't concern you."

The helicopter rotors were getting louder. I could see lights coming in low over the treetops. Sumner didn't seem to notice them, or at least not to mind.

"Put the box down," I said. "And put your hands in the air."

Sumner turned to his new sidekick and said, "If he tries to stop us, shoot him."

The sidekick smiled like this was the first good news he'd heard all day. Sumner looked back at me, as if he had proven the point he was trying to make.

I looked around, hoping to see some sign of Jimmy, feeling the situation getting out of control.

The helicopter was right above us now, and descending. My heart fell as I saw the Stoma logo. But when Sumner looked up, he didn't seem any happier about it than I was, squinting into the light, his face twisted in fear.

The helicopter touched down, and I expected a dozen Darkstar tactical troops, but instead it was a single aging billionaire.

77

Archibald Pearce teetered slightly as he crouched under the rotors; but he straightened as he walked up and stood tall a few feet away, ignoring me, my gun, and my out-of-state badge.

"There you are, Jordan," he said. "I've been looking for you." He grinned, and it was scary. "That's such a fancy jet. Makes me think I'm paying you too much."

Sumner smiled but no one was buying it. "I'm just preparing for the special exemption."

"I see," Pearce said, nodding his head genially. He took out a cigar, bit off the tip of it and spat it onto the ground. "That's good. I thought perhaps you were absconding with my bees."

"*Our* bees, Pearce, not yours."

"Yes, yes, of course," he said, lighting the cigar, puffing up a cloud of smoke. "Interesting specimens these bees, aye? So much promise. I'm glad we were able to rescue them from the ruins of your company. Glad we were able to rescue you, as well, old friend. Good thing we're able to trust each other, aye? So important in a partnership, don't you think?"

"Certainly is."

"To show you how much I trust you," Pearce said, putting the cigar into his mouth and reaching inside his jacket, "I am going to give you this. I think you missed it when you cleared out your lab." He pulled out a handkerchief and unfolded it to reveal a vial of amber liquid, identical to the one in Sumner's lab that was filled with alarm pheromone. "I don't even know what it is," he said loudly, fiddling with it a bit. "But I am sure if it had any noteworthy properties you would have told me already."

Sumner paled. "I have every intention of telling you about it," he said. "I can tell you about it right now, it's—"

"Sh, sh, sh," Pearce said gently, barely audible above the sound of the jet engine. He held up his hand. "No worries, mate. All about trust, right? You can tell me about it all in good time, okay?"

Sumner smiled and relaxed, relief flooding his face.

"But here," Pearce said, smiling back at him. "Since you're still working on it, you should probably take it with you for now."

He tossed the vial straight to Sumner, whose eyes went round in terror as they tracked it through the air. He released the case he was holding, just in time to catch the vial. His focus was so intense that when he caught it, he smiled, just for a second, before he noticed the dampness on his hand, the wet spots on his chest. The cap missing from the vial.

I stepped toward Sumner, but I knew he was a dead man.

"Careful," Pearce called out. "The top might be loose."

The box split open as it hit the ground. Sumner looked down at it as the swarm gushed out and swirled around him in a tight cone, a cyclone of bees. A thin tendril peeled off to wrap around the henchman with the hand truck.

The pilot pulled in his head and closed the hatch. The sound of the jet engine rose in pitch and volume, but it couldn't mask Sumner's screams. The bees covered his head, burrowing under his suit. The sidekick stumbled, knocking over the stack of boxes. As he turned and ran, they all came open, releasing their contents to form an even more massive cloud. As the bees swirled into the air, already agitated, the vial fell from Sumner's bee-covered hand, shattering between his feet. The cloud collapsed into a solid mass, coalescing around him, obliterating him from sight.

I stepped back and turned my gun onto Pearce, who continued to ignore me. I looked back at Sumner, telling myself that if the bees came our way, I could outrun Pearce.

As Sumner's screams became more muffled, the whine of the jet engine continued to ascend. The plane rolled forward, pushing against the truck now, denting the door, slowly nudging it aside. The engine was screaming now, and the bees in the air succumbed to its pull, zipping into the intake.

Sumner had remained standing much longer than Pug-face or Johnny Blue. His back seemed to be resting on the front of the wing. Then I realized the pull of the jet was holding him upright.

As the noise of the engine grew louder still, clumps of bees began to detach from the pile and shoot into the engine, sucked into the jet like it was a giant vacuum.

The passenger's side window of the truck shattered, and the plane surged forward, pushing the truck almost out of the way.

By then most of the bees were gone, transformed into a smoky black spray shooting out the back of the engine. Sumner was visible but unrecognizable, his face a horrific mask, swollen shut against itself and twisted in agony. His arms raised, beseechingly, as he swayed back and forth like a nightmare version of those twenty-foot-tall air dancers in front of cell phone stores or used car lots.

He bent backward toward the intake, up on his toes. For a moment, I thought the engine was going to suck him in after the bees, then it sputtered and the sound dropped a few octaves. Flames flickered from the back, then it coughed black smoke and died altogether.

Sumner's arms fell to his sides. He stood motionless for a moment. Then his knees buckled, and he slid to the tarmac.

As the sound of the engine fell away, I could hear more helicopters. A trio of them was coming in low over the trees. Part of me again hoped it was Jimmy Frank, coming with the cavalry. The other parts of me made fun of that part, teasing that part and calling it names.

I turned to Archie Pearce and for the first time he looked at me. "You're under arrest," I said.

Pearce took the cigar out of his mouth and laughed. "No, I'm not. You have no jurisdiction here, Detective Carrick. And you have no proof of anything. You have no evidence of any wrongdoing on my part." He paused, his eyes twinkling. "But more important, I'm just not. And you know that."

The helicopters were hovering over us now. The pilot of the jet slipped out of the the cockpit door and ran off into the darkness.

Flashing police lights appeared next to the airport buildings, a single cruiser swinging around in our direction. Jimmy Frank.

I heard a strange zipping noise, and simultaneously eight black-clad tactical agents descended on cables from two of the helicopters. They hit the ground with a slight flex of the knees, and suddenly eight assault weapons were pointed at my midsection.

They didn't tell me to drop my weapon, so I didn't, but holding it while they ignored it made me feel even more stupid. Pearce walked over to the jumbled pile of bee boxes and turned to the nearest agent. "Give me your knife," he said. It was a big knife.

"You guys Darkstar?" I asked the guy closest to me.

His voice was muffled by his helmet and visor, but I'm pretty sure he said, "Darkstar's for pussies."

The third helicopter landed twenty yards away. In the light from the jet I could see that this one wasn't black. It was green.

Pearce puffed the cigar furiously, blowing the smoke over the hive. Then he poked the knife into the side of the beehive and twisted, prying it open. He slid out one of the frames, then another, puffing smoke at it all the while. The third frame he pulled out had a single bee. "The queen," he said triumphantly, to no one in particular. Then he slid the frame back into the box and repeated the process with the next box.

Jimmy screeched to a halt. As he got out of his cruiser, three of the assault weapons swiveled in his direction.

I called over to Pearce. "Now you're in trouble."

Jimmy looked at me, and I shrugged.

"What'd I miss?" he asked.

I gestured at Pearce, standing and brushing off his pant legs, his head in a cloud of cigar smoke. "I told him he was under arrest."

"How'd he take it?"

"First stage is denial."

The door to the green helicopter slid open, and a chest full of medals with gray hair and impeccable posture stepped out and walked toward us. "I'm Major General Vincent Van Cleef, U.S. Army," he said. "What's going on here?"

"He's under arrest," I said, pointing at Pearce. "And I'm pretty sure he is not going to come quietly."

"Hello, Vincent," Pearce said as he returned the knife to the agent who had loaned it to him.

Vincent nodded to him, and then turned to me. "On what grounds?"

I looked at Jimmy and raised an eyebrow.

"Fraud, theft, conspiracy to murder, racketeering. Violating the harbor's anchorage rules. For starters."

Pearce laughed and handed the cigar to the agent, as well. "Get those," he said, pointing at the bee boxes. Then he walked back toward his helicopter, patting Van Cleef on the shoulder as he did.

Vincent nodded and cleared his throat. "Well, I'm afraid I am going to have to assume jurisdiction here."

The agent with the cigar spoke into his wrist. A moment later a massive black canvas cargo bag descended on another black cable. The agent started gingerly loading the boxes into the sack.

"You know, these guys risked a catastrophe," I said, loud enough for Pearce to hear. "Put millions of lives and a third of our food supply at risk, submitted falsified reporting documents."

Van Cleef stared at me impassively. Pearce put one foot on the step to the helicopter; then he turned and gave me a little salute. I still had a gun in my hand, and I thought about using it, figuring I might be able to get off one shot before they cut me down. Then Pearce disappeared inside the helicopter.

The agents must have read my mind, or at least my face, because when I looked away I saw that three of them had my head in their sights.

"There's at least five dead bodies, Van Cleef," I called out as the rotors started up on Pearce's helicopter. "Those bees are how most of them died." The agent packing the bee boxes stopped and looked over at me. "You can't just let him go," I said.

He smiled at me, sadly and almost fondly, like I was a child who had observed for the first time that life is unfair. He gave his shoulders a slight hitch, probably the closest thing to a helpless shrug a man like him could muster.

"National Security," he said, as if that explained it all. Then he turned on his heel and walked back to his helicopter.

Pearce's copter rose into the air, and a moment later, so did Van Cleef's. Once the bee boxes were all in the cargo bag, it disappeared into the air. The tactical agents each grabbed their lines and tugged, almost in unison, rising into the air as a group.

Jimmy and I watched as they rose and the helicopters holding them banked away into the night sky.

"What just happened?" he asked as the sound of the helicopters faded away to nothing and the lights disappeared over the treetops.

"Same thing that always happens."

78

In the flashing red light of the approaching fire truck, I saw Nola running toward me across the tarmac, and in that moment I knew she was all that really mattered. She almost stumbled when she saw Sumner's body from the corner of her eye, but she didn't slow down, not a step. She kept coming until she wrapped her arms around my neck, holding me like she was never going to let me go. I hoped she never would.

"Is that Sumner?" she asked, her eyes darting toward his disfigured body, then away as she buried her face against my shoulder. She was wearing an extra large Martha's Vineyard T-shirt with the tags still on it. Her hair was damp and she smelled of cheap soap.

"It was," I said, stroking her hair.

She pulled away from me, suddenly panicked. "What about the bees? Where are they?"

"They're dead," I said. "Sucked into the jet engine." She looked over at the burned-out engine, at the front of the jet pressed up against the truck. "Or most of them are."

She looked up at me. "What do you mean?"

"Archibald Pearce was here," Jimmy said. "He showed up with some ninja SEAL Delta Force Texas Ranger types and the blessing of the U.S. government."

She looked up at me, and I nodded.

"He did that to Sumner," I said. "Then he left with the queens."

"Are you serious?"

Jimmy nodded. Then so did I.

She thought about it for a second, then said, "I'm glad you're okay," burying her face against my shoulder, holding me almost as tight as I was holding her.

Eventually, she pulled away. "What about Sumner?" She gestured at the crumpled body without looking at it. "We should tell the authorities what happened."

I looked around at the jet, flames licking out of the engine, then at the smashed truck and the approaching fire units. "I'm pretty sure they already know."

79

A bee hovered in front of my face and I froze, resisting the urge to swat it away. It meandered over to the tomatoes and then settled on some cucumbers. It was late July, and the garden was exploding. I knew Nola had a knack, but I hadn't fully appreciated it until the salads started appearing every night, all produced in our own little garden.

The bees still made me jumpy, but I was getting over it. Seeing how hard they worked, I had to admire them.

The events on Martha's Vineyard caused enough of an uproar that the special exemption was rescinded, and the pilot program on the island cancelled. All the Bee-Plus bees were removed from the island and returned to isolation at Stoma's facility on Samana Cay. More than a dozen feral hives were found on the island and destroyed.

We had stopped the bee-pocalypse. Hooray.

It was a victory in a lot of ways. But not in every way.

Sumner took the blame, posthumously, for everything that happened. Stoma said he had falsified documents and misled them, which was true. Archibald Pearce and Stoma Corporation effectively distanced themselves from the entire thing. They were victims just like everyone else, if not more so, defrauded of millions of dollars by a dishonest business partner who preyed on their desire to help America's farmers and save the world's food supply. Luckily, they were able to salvage enough of Sumner's research that they could continue their efforts to do something about the terrible scourge of colony collapse disorder. By something, of course, they didn't mean stopping it, they meant cashing in on it. *Stoma Corporation: Technology to feed the world today, and tomorrow.*

The unintended aggression of the bees was a footnote to the story, part of what Sumner had been irresponsibly trying to hide until he could fix it. But while Sumner did try to hide it from Stoma, Pearce knew. And if playing dumb and letting Sumner try to work things out was the price of cornering the pollination services of a third of the world's agricultural sector, Pearce was willing to go along, as long as things remained under control. But where Sumner only saw a setback, Pearce recognized an opportunity, as well. And his high-placed friends in Washington were only too happy to fund research into a new class of bio-weapons.

BeeWatch got funding to hire a few more people to make sure the Bee-Plus mites were eradicated before the beekeepers brought their bees back. Moose stayed on the island to help them, and to keep us posted on other developments. Chief Wilks stepped down to spend more time with his family, and Jimmy stepped in as acting chief. According to Moose, the conventional wisdom was that the job was Jimmy's to lose, and most people thought that's what would happen. But Moose said Jimmy was doing good, drinking less, taking care of himself. A new girlfriend will do that to you.

I was happy when I heard he and Annalisa were an item, but I'd felt a pang of something else, too. Jimmy was a lucky guy.

Darren Renfrew wasn't quite as lucky. He tried to take on the big guys, gambling everything on a political maneuver to take Stoma's place in the ASSP program. He'd gone into hock to buy the political favors to do it, then leveraged himself even further, consolidating as much Thompson Company stock as he could get his hands on to maximize his profits when the windfall came. When the bid failed, the stock tanked. He lost everything.

Hell, I even thought about giving him his money back. But then I thought about not giving it back, and decided that was the way to go.

After all, he still had family he could stay with. Teddy got out of jail after a few more days, with probation and community service. I liked the idea of Renfrew sleeping in one of Teddy's cabins, his feet sticking out of the bed. Who knows, maybe they could bond over the experience. If they didn't kill each other first.

Things on the island weren't all that had changed. Nola had changed, too. We drove to see her specialists in South Carolina almost as soon as we got back.

We told them about her exposure to massive amounts of pesticides. "That's not very smart," the doctor said. "You shouldn't do that even if you don't suffer from chemical sensitivity."

I told him we were quite aware of that fact. I didn't tell him she had done it to save the world, including his sorry ass, that despite her history of chemical sensitivity she had exposed herself to a torrent of chemicals that very well could have condemned her to a life of sickness and isolation. But I did tell him it was the single bravest act I had ever witnessed.

Nola shushed me. She can be quite modest.

They ran a battery of tests over the course of several days, and at the end of it, they said she seemed fine. Still a good idea to be careful around chemicals, and no one would say the word "cured," because maybe she wasn't. But she was better.

We moved anyway, but not because we had to.

"No, Doyle, I don't want to live in a place that's regularly doused with poison," Nola had said, "but I also don't want to live in the kind of dump where the landlord feels he needs to."

Hard to argue with that.

I told her about the money I had put away, enough for a down payment on our dream house. She gave me a big wet kiss, then cupped my face in her hands and said, "I love you, Doyle Carrick. But maybe we should rent for a while first." Then, as she led me into the bedroom, she added, "Besides, I could learn to enjoy city living."

She took that job at Greensgrow Farms after all—farming in the city, a ten-minute walk from our new house. Her new boss had friends who were renovating a place, and they had gutted it but not finished it. They liked the idea of a nontoxic house, so we signed a lease and helped them finish the place, virtually chemical-free.

Nola said it was the first time since she left Dunston that she felt at home. A week after we moved in, her friend Cheryl came to visit. The one with the severe chemical sensitivities.

The two of them cried for the first half hour. But after that she seemed really nice.

I flipped the burgers and walked to the edge of the garden to wait, pausing as another bee buzzed past, drawn by the row of big yellow squash blossoms. It hopped from one to the other. Then apparently it had enough, because it flew in a straight line—a beeline—to the roof across the street. Don Shump, the neighborhood beekeeper, was over there tending his rooftop hives. No veil, no gloves, just him and his bees.

Nola had talked about getting some hives. I cupped her face and told her I loved her. "Maybe some day," I said. "But not just yet."

It was ten after five, which meant Nola would soon be home. I liked to watch her walking home. I like to watch her most of the time, but something about watching her walking up the street—tired after a full day of work but with a spring in her step because she is happy—makes me love her a little bit more each time. I looked over the edge of the roof, and there she was, right on schedule, wearing shorts and a T-shirt, her arms and legs strong and browned by the sun.

She gave me a big wave and that smile. And I thought, yeah, Jimmy Frank is a lucky guy. But I'm luckier.